CHASE MARTIN

A Breath of Power

The Players

Kinglands:

King Hurvir de'Tro - King of Viguran, Sophie's husband, and the father of Devro

Queen Sophie Margia - Queen of Viguran and Hurvir's fourth wife

Prince Ultiir de'Tro - lord of Goldfield, Hurvir's younger brother, and heir to the throne

Rila de'Tro - Queen Mother, mother of Hurvir and Ultiir, married to the late King Ferrick

King's Council - Lords Urses de'Marisco, Gofrei Geary, Tedbalt Masson, Alan Hirons, Serle Verrier, Dovi Lyons, and Henk Zazí

King's Guards - Sir Lovis and Sir Lird

Queen's Council - Lady Abre, Countess Filra, Lady Betal, Baroness Mara, Lady Fica, Lady Rila

Sir Achen - chief knight of Sophie's guard

Eastlands:

Maller of Forecreak - doma of Forecreak

Duke Adyn Gallient - Duke of the Eastlands

Lady Annue Gallient - the Duke's elder sister and first wife of King Hurvir

Lands of Asara:

Duke David Rely - Duke of the Lands of Asara
Yvanne Rely - youngest daughter of David
Sir Pollard - youngest son of David and knight of Whitehall
Helge - local doma of Whitehall
Knights of Whitehall - Sirs Loc, Groel, Rye, and Rickart

Gereduss:

Prince Devro de'Tro - bastard son of Hurvir
Sir Raimund - knight of Viguran, a member of Devro's guard, and born in the North
Sir Mar - knight of Viguran and member of Devro's guard
Tundavik Vandes - once a duke in Viguran but now lives in Attrima, the capital of Baragio

Rowan:

King Bartel Thomas - King of Rowan
Prince Bertin Thomas - Prince of Rowan and heir to the throne
Bertin's Guards - Sirs Gerg, Robalt, Wilclef, and Gordo

Elves:

King Blaenda - an elven leader, part of the Circle of Elders
Sharet - elvish mage
Kuslu - leader of the elves in Telemaw
Elvish Guards - Ryfor, Kelltar, Ioelena

Prologue

"Anything over there?" Utra called out to Vosi, who said nothing in return. He didn't want to get separated, but Vosi was stubborn and would run off to look in hidey-holes and scare whoever he could find. Usually travelers. Never elves.

Utra sighed and tightened his grip around his dagger; the spear on his back hit his legs as he walked through the mess of twisted tree roots, thickets of thorns, and water. The swamps around Lemaium grew brighter as autumn set in, the leaves changing to reds and yellows. He usually went north to sell cattails or chickens to those who starved in the snow-laden areas near the mountains when winter arrived. But this year he was hunting for the person who killed a girl and boy who were stupid and got themselves killed. He just hoped it was over quickly.

I told them that was a bad idea, but no one ever listens to ole Utra, he thought with a roll of his eyes. Amie and Arte had been found in a shallow grave. Whoever dug it didn't realize that the dead float in swamps. Amie's parents had been hysterical, and now the whole of Lemaium was out trying to catch a killer.

Utra didn't like thinking about their bodies. He had been

hunting with them earlier that day when Amie saw some magical … something. She wanted to go closer, to touch it, but Utra had told her not to. *But she went back anyway, didn't she?* Amie's throat was crushed. The marks of a metal hand had bored themselves into her skin. Arte had been cut open. Utra didn't know which was worse. At least he would've been able to kill the attacker. Arte and Amie were younger, less experienced. He was alive to fight the mites and push them back south of the Ters-Veck. He knew how to use the spear on his back. If the killer was still in the woods, Utra would win.

But first he had to find Vosi.

The thickets and roots clawed at his ankles as he made his way through brown-colored water, kicking away bugs that tried to latch onto his trouser leg. He certainly wasn't going to die from a bug. The sun was above them, but the thick canopy of trees made it seem later, like a thick, gray fog was settling in. He used a knife to cut away vines that hung in his way. *If Vosi had gone this way, surely he would've cut them.* Utra stopped and took in his surroundings. The problem being, it was all trees and low water for as far as he could see. He had the best eyes in Lemaium; that's what he told himself. He could spot a worm a mile away like a hawk. But not Vosi.

The trees made him feel small as they towered over him. This wasn't an area he usually explored. He stayed mostly to the main paths unless Arte talked him into venturing deeper into the woods. That's what got the boy killed, and Utra wasn't going to end up like that. Except he was alone. And a killer was still out there. A murderer.

A splash.

Utra whipped his head around, not quite sure where the

noise came from. Birds chirped like nothing was wrong. Insects buzzed about his face. He sank lower into the wet soil from standing still. He had to get moving. Eventually it would be nightfall, and he didn't want to be lost.

The rustling of leaves made his hair stand on end. A shiver went over his entire body as he slowly turned around to where he cut the vines. The splotches of sunlight did little to help. That's when something jumped from the brush and Utra screamed while swinging his knife, not able to grab the shortsword on his hip.

He tasted mud after he fell into the water and dirt. His face covered. Then he heard laughing. Utra wiped his eyes clean and saw Vosi. The young boy was doubling over with tears in his eyes as he laughed and laughed. "I … got … you," he said with a lack of breath.

Utra stood and felt his face burning from embarrassment. Luckily, Vosi was the only other person in this part of the swamp. "Now I'm a mess," he pushed Vosi playfully. The boy was only a child, maybe thirteen, younger than Amie and Arte. He didn't want to hurt him. "If we run into a murderer, you think they're going to be threatened by me now?"

"Threatened by you?" Vosi started laughing again.

"Let's go," Utra said. "We need to get back before dark." They started toward … nowhere. Utra didn't know where he was. The trees and dirt and roots and water all looked the same. *No need to scare the boy,* Utra thought, as Vosi followed him with confidence. *I'll figure it out in no time.*

"Where'd you go anyhow?" Utra asked to pass the time as he headed north, or what he thought was north.

"I just went around some trees," Vosi shrugged, "not far. Just wanted to scare you."

Utra rolled his eyes. "Funny."

"You heard my pa's theories, right?" The boy asked. His father was one of the leaders of Lemaium, and one to cause the most panic. Utra ignored him, so he shook his head no at Vosi. "He says it was a ghost. Like the ones they have in the North. Some ancient specter that's come back to seek revenge."

"Why would a ghost want revenge against Arte and Amie?" Utra asked, feeling like his eyes couldn't stop rolling.

"Not just them," Vosi's voice dropped. "All of us. The ghost is some Ritae queen who was killed hundreds of years ago when Viguran united. She wants all the Veck'kop dead. She wants to kill all of us."

"Enough," Utra said. "Ghosts aren't real, and your father doesn't always know what he's talking about. Now," he gazed at the canopy of leaves, at the thick tree trunks, at the bugs hopping around the water, "I think we're lost."

Any mention of ghosts from Vosi was gone. His face scrunched up and his head twisted and turned. "No, we're not," but as he kept looking around, spinning in circles, he said, "maybe we are. How could you let this happen?"

"Me?" Utra didn't want to argue with a child, but the stress of it all caused him to say, "it's your fault. You went running off, and I had to find you. Had you peeked through the bushes like I told you, this wouldn't be happening."

Now it was Vosi's turn to say, "Me? I —" But then he stopped as he whipped his head around. "Hear that?"

The boy ran toward some noise he heard. Utra heard nothing. *Just like with Amie.* His eyes got wide, and he ran after Vosi. "Wait!" He shouted. But the boy was following a trail.

"They're calling to me," he said.

Vosi crawled under a fallen branch and flung off bugs that attached to him. Utra climbed over the log, and his worst nightmare was realized. The glowing orb. It floated in the same place, but the surrounding trees had twisted and made shadows of demons. Branches clawed toward the orb, leaves and birds and bugs were blown in with the breeze. Never to be seen again.

"Don't go near that," Utra said. Vosi kept getting closer, the black boy bathed in pale light. "No," Utra screamed, but his foot got tangled on a vine, and he splashed into the water. When he looked up, Vosi was gone. Vanished.

Footsteps and twigs snapping and splashing water meant people were coming near. *Hopefully the villagers. They can help me,* he thought as he stood and brushed the mud off. On the other side of the orb he saw who was coming, and it wasn't people. The tall, skinny creatures wore armor that looked like scales, with jagged, thin blades, and pointed ears. "Stay away!" Utra found his sword and was ready to fight them off. It seemed like a dozen elves were moving toward him.

This is how Arte and Amie died. The elves murdered them and left their bodies for us to find. It's a war. Utra's eyes focused on the orb. Vosi went in. *He's safe. He has to be.* And even if Vosi was dead, it seemed much less painful than having a bunch of elves stab and slice you. Utra did little thinking. He ran as fast as his feet could carry him, water splashing all around. His eyes burned as the orb shone brighter and brighter the closer he got. He reached out his fingers, and the light pulled him in.

He was in nothing. Only white light on all sides, but he felt like he was falling. And all he heard was *"Abhai senn"* repeated over and over until his ears were ringing. So Utra fell, and fell, and fell, and fell …

Bertin

A knight dressed in white crashed to the ground below with a thud, his horse kicking up grass as he ran from the handlers. The gold champion bowed. Making sure to show off his gleaming armor that reflected the sun into the crowds' eyes. The man balanced on his mare, but as he dismounted, he got caught in the stirrup, following his adversary to the ground below. The crowd roared with laughter, shaking the wooden stands. Mud left over from yesterday's brief shower smothered both men. Dakens had already raced over to check on the white knight and tend to his wounds. A young squire was helping the gold knight to his feet. A group of boys came out and cleared the jousting field of broken shields and thrown lances, trying to scrape away the hoofprints, and officials called for the next riders.

"Don't you find this a bit boring?" Devro whispered from atop the box overlooking the field and the crowd below.

Yellow banners flapped in the breeze. The king's stallion imprinted on them. Bertin caught the sight of a pretty girl across the way. She wore a lovely purple dress, very short, and barely holding in her breasts. His favorite thing about summer. Unfortunately, it was ending soon. He prayed Samosay would never bring autumn and the cold and that women wouldn't have to wrap themselves in layers of fur.

Devro continued on, running his fingers through his blond hair. "Surely there are more exciting things to do."

"Like what?" Bertin said as he waved to the pretty girl, who seemed to turn red. *Hopefully, I can find her later,* he thought. "You've been here over five years; surely you've come to love the sport? A sport fit for kings."

"If I wanted to see men fight on horseback, I would travel with the Northern clans."

Bertin huffed, the small crown on his head shaking. "Those barbarians don't ride the same. They are rough, untrained. I hear they even make love to their horses." He had to push the thought out of his mind as his face twisted. "The riders in Rowan are civilized. My father told me how before the flames, the winner of the joust would drown in women's desire." He imagined himself on a horse, fighting against the rebels during the Brutahki Flames, when the entire kingdom shattered. He wasn't trained all that well, but against rowdy peasants, he could surely do anything.

"I would rather watch a melee," Devro took a moment, then shook his head, "or maybe fire throwing, even sword swallowing."

Bertin sighed as he looked to Sir Wilclef, the head of his guard, behind him. The gruff man shrugged at Devro's suggestion. "Let's go find some sword swallowers." Bertin said and stood, straightening his golden crown. In Rowan, as well as other cities like Coastburg, Dunniage, any other place in the kingdom really, the people would stand and bow. Not in Gereduss. Not in a city full of the Gorthair people. "See that." Of course Devro had seen it, they weren't particularly fond of him either. "No respect for the rulers who civilized them." Men with shaggy brown beards and hair held faces of contempt as they glared at Bertin and Devro and the knights and guards accompanying them. The woman across the stands kept her head down. *At least I could fuck a woman if I wanted. These pockmarked men have nothing but hatred in their hearts.*

"I've been told some in Viguran are like that, though not as bad," Devro said. "These people here would rather spit on the food offered by the king than feed their starving children." His young cousin rolled his eyes.

Bertin pulled Devro down the steps away from the box. Not wanting to act afraid, but not wanting the contempt to turn violent. "And these men would happily kill both of us and send our heads to our fathers."

"We would never let that happen, my prince." Sir Robalt said, one of his knights who guarded the bottom the steps. "You have nothing to fear."

"I do not fear Gorthair." Bertin lied. He trusted his men to guard him, but he trusted the city of Gereduss to be able to defeat a handful of knights if they so pleased.

"At least my father would see me again." Devro laughed as they turned a bend by a rock face.

The tourney grounds of Gereduss were a spectacular sight to behold. Bertin hated that. The grounds in Rowan were old, falling apart, and never as busy. A rainbow cast by flags in the air rippled above the stalls and carts. Red, yellow, green. Smoke rose with the smell of baked bread, charred salmon, and salted meats. Dozens of ships awaited in the harbor for the unloading of their wines and delicacies from the West and cold drinks from the North. Animals from Kruhesh; black and white horses, blue birds, striped cats larger than cows; kicked and screamed at their handlers and those who gathered to gawk at them. Fire shot into the air from a troupe of performers known as the Dragon's Pride. Some believed they used magic in their craft, but no one investigated in fear of being right and causing the pride to be extinguished, and the onlookers didn't care either way.

They stopped at a melee ring. The official either did not realize who they were, or knew full well and ignored them. He stood in their way, blocking the fight. It wasn't until Gordo, another of Bertin's guards, showed him the dirk he wore at his side that the official moved. The two fighters were larger than bears, and just as hairy. Northerners. Bertin's face contorted as he looked the men up and down. One had strange markings on his palms, swirling snakes it looked like, probably some clan insignia; the other had so very few teeth it was a surprise he could still eat, the ones he did have were rotted brown. The men shouted indistinct, rough words at one another as their fists flew. Left hook, parry, uppercut, parry. They danced together for another five minutes, onlookers shouting so loud for the men to beat each other to death and throwing coin for bets. Bertin could barely hear himself think.

He was looking for another girl, as he would probably never see the first one again. Preferably a Bruthaki and not a Gorthair. He didn't need a bastard running around with the people who hated him and his family. He looked at Devro. His young cousin was a bastard. Banished to Rowan seven years ago by his father, the king of Viguran. At least if Bertin had a bastard, he wouldn't know, so no problems in the future with sending him away or disowning him. He saw a pretty girl and was about to smile at her when the toothless bear fell to the wet ground. Mud splashed on Bertin and Devro's shoes. Shoes made from the finest leather cobbled in River's Meadow and fetching a high price.

The official quickly named the marked Northerner the winner. He was about to call for the next fighters when Bertin cleared his throat. "Are you forgetting something?" He pointed to his boots, and the official saw the transgression.

"Your Highness." He said once he saw the crown, the crowd grumbling.

"Do you travel to other tourneys?" Bertin asked, and the man shook his head. "What is your name?"

"Raif, my Prince of Rowan." He bowed his head.

"Do you wish to continue your travels?" Bertin crossed his arms, and the skinny official nodded. "Then I believe there is something I ask."

"Let me assure you," Raif cleared his throat, "this will be paid in full. The northern beast will give all his gold to make this right."

"It's fi—" Devro said, but Bertin cut him off.

"We also demand compensation from the winner. He is the one who caused the other to splash our feet."

Raif fell to his knees. "Yes, yes, of course. I will make him pay. I will meet you right after the next match with pouches of coin."

Bertin nodded and patted Devro's back. The entire crowd had been silent. The pretty girl had left. *Spent so much time with this damn Raif, I let another slip away.* His cousin was bouncing on his feet. "You need new ones anyhow. Those are fit for no prince, maybe a farmer or vagrant."

"I have gold enough." Devro said.

Bertin waved away his argument before he could say more.

"No such thing." He pulled a gold coin from his pocket. A horse reared on the front; the back was printed with the words *House Thomas*. "You think any of these people would turn down gold? They say there is no coin in Gereduss anymore, but they would kill for it. Finally able to pay for some shipments of grain and chickens. Why should I turn down gold? Because I'm a prince? That isn't my fault. I never asked to be born into this life." He bit the gold to show anyone watching that it was the closest they would come to ever seeing the real thing and put it back in his pocket. "Besides, it has my family's name on it."

Devro rolled his eyes but chuckled before turning to the fighting ring. "Competing to take the title against the great Rufun of Moon Bay is Sir Mar of Ruwy." The crowd was growing larger now, more active, excited at the names. Bets flew in and Bertin's ears wanted to fall off. Sir Mar was one of Devro's knights. The other, Sir Raimund, was behind Bertin's guards somewhere, probably shaking his head as well. *Now this is the man I should spend time with,* he thought, as he saw a horde of women cheering and waving their favors toward the knight. "May the Four guide your hands." Raif stepped to the side, and the men were off.

Rufun, a man whose muscles definitely stretched his clothes, stalked near the fence, men and women trying to touch him. Mar didn't seem to move. He swayed, never leaving too much weight on one foot. Rufun charged, but Mar jumped, turning on his left foot and bringing a fist down on Rufun's swollen neck. The fighter from Moon Bay fell into the mud below; the white of his eyes the only thing unscathed. He charged again like a bull, but Mar jumped and kicked at Rufun's knee. The man fell again. Bertin kept his boots away from the fence.

Behind them, Raimund pushed his way through. The knight, supposedly from Viguran, was a pale, black-haired, tall man, clad in steel with a sword at his side. Bertin wasn't sure if Devro's father was too simple-minded to be king or didn't care, but Raimund was obviously a Northerner. His accent wasn't perfect, and his intimate knowledge of Heller customs and language was a big giveaway. His father would never let an outsider become a knight of Rowan. But Bertin knew King Hurvir of Viguran paled in comparison to any king of Rowan.

Devro didn't turn but asked the knight, "Did you know he'd be here?" Sir Raimund found himself next to Devro, leaning on the fence, watching Mar and Rufun swing at one another.

"Yestermorn Madam Arabell spoke to me about his new-found obsession. I didn't want to believe her." Raimund sighed.

"You mean the woman who runs the whorehouse near the docks?" Bertin interrupted. "I've always liked her."

Raimund acknowledged the prince. "Yes, that's the one, Your Grace." He cleared his throat. "Apparently, he can't even finish if the whores don't call him their champion." The trio chuckled. Mar dodged another blow before landing an uppercut. "I haven't seen him in any fighting pit for years."

"He fought? When?" Devro asked. Bertin leaned in to hear the answer. He had known Mar ever since he had arrived in Gereduss with Devro, but didn't know much about the knight.

"Long ago." Raimund swatted away the question like a bug.

Devro pointed to Raimund's sword, Valkyr. "You think Mar will need protection?"

"Not at all." Raimund tapped on the fence. "But these festivals aren't always safe. Don't you remember Lord Geary telling you about the stampede that took place in Bardekan? Hundreds dead. Like fucking bulls let loose."

"The mites are very similar to bulls," Bertin said and smirked as he imagined all the dead Rainvealandians south of the bay. "Does that surprise anyone? But you think a lone sword could stop the whole of Gereduss?" He looked at his guards with their swords and daggers, circling their prince, keeping them away from a short-sighted Gorthair freedom fighter. *I'm not sure any amount of weapons would be enough.*

"It could help." Devro shrugged.

Bertin turned to the fight, where grunts and slamming fists were drowned out only by the ever-growing crowd. "Continue to put in coin, folks," Raif cried, pretending the Gorthair had money. "Silver and bronze and all else. Any coin from the Kormat to the Kash. Longest fight I've had today."

Before anyone could throw coins, Rufun landed a right hook on Mar's face. The knight fell to the brown mud for the first time. Rufun dropped to the ground and let his bear-like fists melee poor Mar's face. The crowd shuttered while the official pressed for more money. Mar wasn't moving, his face becoming more red than brown. Sir Gerg pulled Bertin aside as Raimund and the royal guards jumped the fence, yanking the mass of muscle from atop Sir Mar.

The official ran over to Raimund. "My good sir, you are disrupting my match. Sir Mar could have gotten to his feet."

"The match was over. The giant is the winner." Raimund rested his hand on his sword.

Bertin made a click with his mouth to get Raif's attention.

The official's eyes widened when he noticed who Raimund was with. "Of course, Sir, Your Highness. If you say the match is over, then Rufun has won again. A glorious victory he had." The crowd was booing at Mar being allowed to leave with his life, and Raif turned to calm them.

"I think paying for Sir Mar's face is in order." Bertin called. Raif stiffened, but continued with the crowd. "I will have my coin now or send men to collect."

Raif rummaged through a locked chest guarded by a large-headed man. He threw three pouches of stallions to Gordo, who pocketed the gold, silver and bronze. Rufun the Great called out, "What of my match? My money?" He started for Raif, his guard not stepping in to help.

"Time we leave." Wilclef said.

Raimund was dragging Mar away as Raif was pelted with rocks, and Rufun cracked his knuckles. Robalt handed Mar a handkerchief for the blood.

"Drunk already?" Raimund asked when Mar gave a sigh.

"First thing in the morning. Need to be drunk to fight." Mar mustered a laugh. "Will the girls still flock to me like Rowai sheep?" He waved at his broken nose, swollen cheeks, and blackened eyes.

"They're whores, Mar. They'll fuck a fish if you pay them." Raimund said.

"Madam Arabell always said my face was the best part about me. Of course, she hasn't fucked me even though I offer her all my holdings in Ruwy." Bertin let out a laugh. "What's funny?" Mar asked. "Ruwy is beautiful in the winter when everything's dead; it doesn't smell like shit, and my family stays indoors."

"Why are you out here?" Devro wiped the mud from his

boots.

"*Were*. I'm finished. Rufun, that dumb oaf, is the champion. Hope you didn't bet on me." Mar spat blood.

"You?" Raimund slapped Mar's back, who let out a groan. "Never."

Mar swiveled a quick fist. "Fuck off," he said with a smile. He wiped his mouth, which had begun to drool with blood. "I really am a mess."

Raimund patted his back and watched the muddy ground. "It's time you came back to the cliff. You've drunk and whored around enough to last a lifetime."

Mar pushed Raimund's hand away. "Madam Arabell's is close enough. I was thinking I'll go there, get my mind off losing."

"Perhaps I'll join." Bertin said. "You can come too, Devro. I hear Madam Arabell's is better than the one near King Artin's statue." Wilclef and Gordo were whispering with a lean boy who was out of breath. "What is it?" He left Raimund and Devro to worry about Mar.

"A message, my prince," Wilclef said. "From His Grace, your father. He wants you back in the capital. Says it's urgent."

Bertin rolled his eyes at the thought of no brothel, but said, "Well, if he says it, then it must be true." He held great respect for his father. The man who doused the flames and brought the kingdom back together, even though his idea of urgency wasn't always the same as Bertin's. "I'll tell my cousin." The guards bowed their heads.

Devro was telling Mar, "I don't think the brothel is for me. Make sure you're back so Raimund doesn't have to search the whole of the city for you again."

"You know," Bertin strutted from behind, "I've heard stories of men who have died in the act in Rowan brothels. The man and the woman are having a nice time, then, before you know it, he's stuck inside her dead. Must be traumatic for the whore." He bounced his head. "At least they were paid."

"Shall we go back to the cliff or find more games to bet on?" Devro asked his cousin.

"You do what you want. My father wants me back in the capital. Apparently it's important."

"Hopefully not war," Devro said. "That would bring an end to the festivities." *Father would never fight another war, would he?*

Raimund shook his head. "Not war. The Gorthair may not care about the world beyond their cliffs, but the word would spread. I hope you have a safe journey back."

"By sea or the marches?" Devro asked, almost like he wanted to go with Bertin. He hadn't been to the capital in years. *It isn't much, cousin.*

"By road, young prince." Gordo came forward. "News of a storm near Edincassone has come with the ships in the harbor, better be safe."

"And you trust the Gorthair won't ambush us in the marches?" Bertin gulped. He didn't want to bleed out in the middle of some rocky hills surrounded by his enemies. *That's not a fitting end for a prince like me.*

Gerg fingered his sword hilt. "They'd be making a foolish mistake. An easy trip to see the Four and the Many."

"Be safe." Devro said, his eyes shaky. Mar grumbled some words before he coughed up blood.

"And with that, I'm off." Bertin embraced Devro, not wanting to let go of his cousin and face whatever lay to the east. Then he shook Raimund's and an aching Mar's arm. "I hope to see you again in time for Meret's Feast." He strode away with his entourage of guardsmen and knights, people pointing to the crown atop his short brown hair. Glares never ending. He didn't know if he should worry more about the marches or whatever his father deemed urgent.

Ultiir

Feet aching, Ultiir looked over the petitioners who had traveled to the capital, hearing their complaints and passing judgment. "I declare in the name of King Hurvir de'Tro that you are sentenced to hang." He told an old man, who should've known better than to rape the young girl, who had pleaded just moments ago. "Take him outside," he said, and the guards obeyed as the old man kicked and cried as he was dragged down the long corridor to the grand oak doors. "You will be given a bag of copper," he said to the girl, "hopefully that relieves the trouble."

"Thank you, my king," she said, and Ultiir felt like the largest man in the world. *She thinks me king. If only that were true*, he thought.

The day was over. Earlier, the throne room had people along the walls, between the swirling marble columns and stained windows. Now, it was empty. Those who watched the judgment had already filed out from boredom, probably. The central colonnade and gray stone floor caused the small girl's footsteps to echo like a giant.

The throne was behind him, the large chair made of the same marble as the palace. A single red velvet cushion looked like a bloodstain. His brother, the king, had decided to be late for court today, like every day. The lords had scratched their heads, debated taxes, shouted about the approaching harvest, and argued over the lack of new slaves before leaving for their manses in the city. Then, mostly commoners filled the room until Ultiir was finished. Now, it was only the six councilors and guards.

As heir to the throne, Ultiir was to administer the king's justice according to the laws of this kingdom. It never bothered him like it did the others in the King's Council when his brother was late or never showed. And he knew the reason. Hurvir's beautiful wife was still young and fertile, and Hurvir needed an heir. Not some banished bastard.

Lord Urses de'Marisco, the chief informant, let out a sigh of relief. His cheeks red, his face younger than he actually was. "Productive." He gathered his parchments and letters. A page helped him get organized. "If only His Grace were here. I'm sure the old man would've been thrown in a fire."

Lord Tedbalt Masson, gray hairs poking from his ears and nose, said, "We cannot expect the king to attend every day of the royal court. That is far too much to ask." Another lord, Alan Hirons, the stubborn chief commander, chuckled but quickly stopped.

"Surely, he will meet us in the council chamber." Lord Gofrei Geary, the dark-skinned lord of Montlahead, said. "His wife is beautiful, but I doubt he can fuck all day."

As if on cue, the throne room door opened. A herald came in, but Hurvir quieted him. Ultiir and the other lords bowed. "I was worried you would never give up power, brother." Hurvir said with a booming laugh, his muscles shaking under his velvet tunic. "I fear you enjoy passing judgment too much."

"Not at all." Ultiir stepped away from the throne. "There's

a reason it's your job." *But the kingdom would fall apart without me,* he thought.

"Your Majesty," Lord de'Marisco said, "shall we finish our discussions elsewhere."

"Worried the guards will hear me joking with my brother?" Hurvir walked to the back of the throne room, to a small door and hall that led to the council chamber and the councilors' studies.

"I told you he'd be here." Lord Geary said to no one before following.

Lord Hirons sifted through letters detailing foreign affairs, Lord Geary stared out the turret window at the end of the chamber, and Lord Dovi Lyons played with coins. Lord Masson pulled at his white daken robes while Lord Serle Verrier brushed dirt off his blue and red ambassador robes. The lord of the Insurgent Redington, Hank Zazí, the bald weasel, filled their cups with wine from Baragio. Lord de'Marisco was whispering to himself. *Always whispering.*

His brother sat at the head of the long birch table. Carved from the trees of the Ritaewood, with the faces of the Four on each leg, the table had sat in this palace for hundreds of years. Not one blemish. Until his brother decided war with the South was a good idea. He pounded the table, and it had cracked. Whispers of the gods' judgment were quick. Hurvir ignored all. His brother was over a decade older than him, but still had all the muscles of his youth. Not like Ultiir's lean arms. His brother's hair had completely turned white. Like snow sitting atop a mountain. Ultiir still with blond hair. *I wonder if Sophie looks at me as the better version of Hurvir.* He laughed silently to himself.

"First," Hurvir began, "I would like to apologize for not

being at court, but I was busy and my brother does a fine job in my stead. My wife's needs are more important than my own." Everyone around told him it was no worry, save for Ultiir, who rolled his eyes when no one was looking. "Shall we start? Or, if you like, we can move on with the day?"

No one said anything. All the important news was either already said or would be said when his brother stalked back to his naked wife waiting in bed. No one had cared about Hurvir's opinion on any matter since he had gone and got thousands killed. He imagined a naked Sophie. The queen with her smooth skin, round breasts, wide hips. *Perfect.* How Hurvir got so lucky he never knew. It would seem the gods favored him if it weren't for all his curses.

"Your Majesty, I have some important information that may interest you." Lord Hirons spoke up. "I have heard rumors that independence seekers in the Flewthlands have spoken with Lord Blume. I worry the duke may try to follow his father's footsteps of revolt. Losing that duchy would bring great harm to your kingdom."

Hurvir waved that away. "I stopped both the Esol Rebellion and his father's rebellion. He owes everything he has to me. The Duke of the Flewthlands will not separate. And I will crush them again if they do."

"They have also sought the support of the queen of Maertan and king of Rowan."

"Queen Maide would do right to remember her place in this world." Hurvir tapped the table. "And my cousin in Rowan knows not to go against me. His kingdom was broken, and I'm supposed to fear the Rowai again? At least I know how to put down rebellion. I was the one who led the war against the Rainvealandians, not him. They were too busy falling apart every which way."

The room stayed silent except for a bird chirping at the window.

"I'm sure you are right, Your Grace," Alan said. "King Bartel would never go against Viguran." The chief commander twiddled his thumbs.

Hurvir seemed lost in his thoughts. "How great history would have remembered me had I taken Rowan when King Anton died. Instead, I let that bitch wife ruin her country." His eyes focused back on the room. "Write to Lord Blume. Tell him to remember my strength. To remember Ritaeum." Lord Hirons gave a sharp nod. The king turned to Lord Geary. "How has the city been? I haven't been off the palace grounds since those farmers stormed the warehouses at the docks."

"The guard have been able to retrieve all stolen grain, and the perpetrators have been dealt with. The High Doma has already ordered Gods' Gift to be cleaned for your feast in the coming weeks. All vagrants and beggars will be pushed to the Rat's Nest in no time. No more stepping in shit on your way to the domaton." Gofrei acted deferential, but his tone was that of annoyance as he fingered through letters and parchments.

"My feast." Hurvir leaned in his velvet chair. "How large will the gathering be? The queen has told me nothing."

Lord Verrier straightened his black doublet. "Emissaries from all of Adedor have sent word of their coming. Lords and dukes and barons from the North. Some Western nobles, even a man from Eotros who calls himself the Prince of the East. Unfortunately, it seems the only monarch gracing Vigur will be your wife's father, King Anvrin."

"He just wants to keep me satisfied with our alliance. Doesn't want me to cast out his daughter like I have my other wives. He knows that if Sophie has a boy, we will be a step closer to uniting the second empire."

Talk of the second empire while you let this one starve? Ultiir thought. He knew how important a male heir was for Hurvir. The only child he had was a bastard who lived in Rowan. Ultiir imagined himself as the father of Sophie's son. King Anvrin would gift him all the gold in the world. He got lost thinking of Sophie. Her spotless face, her lips the color of ocean coral. How sweet her kisses must be. He remembered what she had worn on her wedding night. How the tight-fitted dress hugged her body, showing off more than some whores. *But she's no whore. She's a queen. And she's wasted on Hurvir.*

"And what of my mother?" Hurvir asked the table, and Ultiir remembered where he was.

"You know mother hasn't left Goldfield in years, Your Grace." Ultiir kept up the pleasantries. "It would take Vigura himself to come down from the heavens for her to travel upriver."

"I think our mother's stubbornness would best Vigura's miracles."

Lord Hirons combed through pages until he found a small map. "Perhaps, if Your Grace allows it, we can speak of your feast another time. It is still weeks away." Hurvir nodded. "I wanted to speak about Redington." Ultiir eyed the chief commander, Lord Hirons, while Lord Zazí's ears perked. "The city seems to be falling apart. The debt they accumulated during the Riorské occupation is far too much. Entire buildings decay and murderers run amok as the city governors try to cobble together any coin they can find."

"I heard," Lord Lyons said, "that vagrants recently plundered the city chamber. It seems to be turning into Gereduss with every passing day. All the more reason to clean the Gods' Gift." Dovi still played with coins. "The treasury is near empty, if not already."

"How anyone could let this happen is beyond me." Henk said. "If I were the lord in charge, those animals would be dealt with like the vermin they are."

"What would you have me do?" Hurvir asked.

"Gain a valuable ally and help pay their debts." Lord Lyons said.

Lord Zazí said, "Take the city."

Ultiir rubbed his head. The sun was high in the sky and was burning his face through the window. His stomach hungered. "Taking the city seems a drastic step. The whole of Adedor would begrudge us for it."

"We made quick work of the mites," his brother said. "No army can defeat us." Ultiir wished he could scream at his brother. Tell him how lucky they were that the Rainvealandians didn't wipe out the entire kingdom. How blind he was. Lord de'Marisco was chewing his lip, Tedbalt shaking his head. *At least I'm not alone in my thoughts.*

But Lord Henk Zazí, the dimwit from the city of the Reds, was filling Hurvir's goblet just as much as his ear. "You would go down in history as a great uniter. Reclaiming Redington for the crown and showing all the kingdoms of the world how strong you are. Take back a port city before Pyre Blume makes us concede more. A port open to slaves. You should've heard the complaints of the cripples and old men who the lords have to rely on, Your Majesty, an utter catastrophe if all the slaves were to up and die."

"I think that is enough, my lord." Ultiir rose to his feet. "This is a matter for another time." Henk bowed away, but Hurvir was nodding.

"Feeling the wind on my face would be a great deal of fun. Swinging a sword." Hurvir laughed. "I should've taken the city when my men freed it from the mites."

"Your feast." Ultiir said.

Hurvir seemed to snap back. Birds sang outside the windows; an insect buzzed around Hurvir's head. "Of course. Nothing can happen until my feast is over and done. We don't want the nobles to rescind their letters of acceptance."

"Then it is decided." The council stood and bowed as Hurvir stood. Dele, a page who waited outside, ushered the king from the chamber, guards following. Lords Hirons and Zazí followed the king, probably to whisper about Redington or military campaigns. Sir Lovis stood outside now, the chief of Ultiir's household guard. The rest of the lords stayed behind to catch up on work. Or so they said.

"Was Lord Hirons trying to get us pulled into another war?" Ultiir asked the table.

"I'm sure he just wanted to make conversation, my lord." Dovi said. "It was Henk who wanted us to die for a city he hasn't set foot in for years."

"The insufferable cunt." Gofrei said as he rubbed his baggy eyes. "I say we tie him to a stallion, give him a sword of flames, and push him to the city. If he wants it he can have it."

"Perhaps," Urses' breathy voice whispered, "it is good for His Grace to be distracted by the thought of war with Redington. It will keep him busy while we plan the feast." Urses de'Marisco let an ominous note hang.

"I did find a man today, in the city, whose name I can't recall, but he said he would gladly set fire to the docks. The city guard should be busy with sand and water while dinner is served." Gofrei said.

"You're sure that man will keep quiet?" Lord Masson asked.

"I borrowed enough money from our dear friend Dovi here." Gofrei motioned to the chief collector. "And I burrowed more for the assassin to push are arsonist into his fire as it rages."

"And I found a group in Keeland who sells any and all mixes of potions and poultices you can imagine." Urses said. "They sell deadly mixtures as well. They wish to meet me in the mountains first thing next week. I will tell the king I have gone to meet an old friend. I think, my lords, that will suffice."

Lord Masson chimed in, "Some of these bandits tell stories for gold, as anyone else would. Most of their elixirs are nothing more than water mixed with salt."

"We can try it on you if you're worried." Lord de'Marisco smirked.

"No need. Bring me the poison, and I will test it on a lily." Tedbalt turned to Ultiir. "But we should be worried if it doesn't work. What if all it does is give the king a stomach bug?"

"Perhaps he'll shit himself to death." Gofrei laughed. "I feel that's a more dignified way to go, don't you think?"

Lord Verrier coughed, his dark skin soaking the sunlight from the windows. "Are we forgetting your nephew in Rowan, my lord?" He asked Ultiir. "The Bastard Law still exists. Viguran had to go through the Bastard Wars. It would be a silly thing not to deal with our problem to the west before we dealt with the problem in this very palace."

Lord Geary waved a hand. "Hire some Gorthair and be done with it. They still yearn for the days of the Bruthaki Flames and want for nothing more than to see dead royalty."

"We must be going now, my lords." Tedbalt said. "As to not raise suspicion."

"I must say this will probably be the last time I see you before the feast." Gofrei said. "Her Grace, the queen, wishes for me to treat with her parents in Udello, guide them here. As if they don't know the way to a riverboat and up the Montla-Ritae."

"We'll need to discuss what's to happen to her as well." Lord Verrier said. "We've avoided the subject far too long."

"I will take care of that." Ultiir said, a slight eye roll from Dovi Lyons followed.

The room emptied except for Urses and Ultiir. The rose-cheeked man smirked as he cleared the table of his things. "I've never known someone to be so cavalier about the murder of their own brother and nephew."

"I'm not doing it for myself. I am doing it for Viguran. Too long have the people starved, frozen in the winter, had failed harvests. The gods will forgive me." He hoped. The best way for him not to care about his family was to pretend they weren't. He barely knew his bastard of a nephew, and his brother was much older than him. It was easier as long as he didn't step foot in Goldfield and see his mother.

Urses' hand rested on the door handle. "Are you worried about what's to come?"

Ultiir didn't hesitate to say, "Never."

Raimund

I'll have that there sword." The old man pointed his crooked finger at the sword at Raimund's side, Valkyr. "I think that a fair trade." The old man's hands were charred from the red oven behind him. Rows of fresh bread filled his small stand, which didn't even have a cover. The smell intoxicated Raimund.

The knight couldn't help but laugh. In Viguran; his kingdom of birth, Gerot-Staller; and everywhere else he'd been, coins were used. The stallions in Rowan and the scales in Viguran. Not here. Not when a tourney wasn't taking place and foreigners from all across the continent came to the city for glory. "I only want a piece of bread." He couldn't help but smile at the old man. *He tried.* Raimund rubbed the red stone on his sword's hilt.

"I know where you come from." The crooked finger pointed to the black cliffs above the city. The castle was built atop to watch over Gereduss to the east and the vast ocean to the west. "I've seen you come down the steps. You have many and more swords for me to have one. Prepare myself to defend our people if needed."

"How about," Raimund set his hand on the wooden counter, the smells of fire and baking bread filling his nose, "you bring up half your daily bread to the palace, and I give you a few swords."

The old man crunched his back. "A bit too old for that, I am." He rubbed his balding head, sweat from the fire making it glisten in the rising sun. "You know I used to live in the castle, a little over a decade ago I did, when the kingdom broke." Raimund knew all too well that the castle had once been overrun with commoners. The lord killed. His home opened for those who had nothing. Until Devro came in and took it for himself.

The castle loomed over the city perched on its cliff, its towers clawing into the orange and pink sky. The old man continued, "It was a pleasant home for me and my family before the crown took it back. Are you enjoying it?" Raimund nodded even though the old man was looking at the cliff. "Surely I can find someone, perhaps my youngest grandson, Adale, who will carry the bread for me." He ripped off a piece of the round, dark bread. "Have it." He motioned to a man in ragged clothing, with a long shaggy beard and a gaunt face. "Give the rest to that man if you wish." Raimund nodded his thanks and went to the vagrant. He stank of piss and mead.

"For your trouble." He gave the rest of the bread to him. The vagrant clasped his hands together and said a few prayers of thanks.

Strange place, but every year I get more and more used to it. He crunched the bread as he walked around the market square. Peddlers from across the Gorthair Marches came to Gereduss once a month to sell their wares, and this time it was just after the tourney had left. All the excitement drained from the city. Now, a relaxing market took its place. The sun hadn't fully come up from beyond the horizon, so it wasn't as busy as it would soon get. A large shade tree grew in the center, providing relief in the late summer heat. A few vagrants slept under it. Some children were playing in a puddle, their parents laughing at the splashes.

Sir Mar was talking to a whore who peddled her wares the same as the rest. The bags under Mar's eyes were wide. They drooped as he kept himself from sleep. His hair hadn't been combed in days, and his beard was a patchy map on his face. Yet, the girl still smiled at him.

They were laughing at a joke Mar told when Raimund came up from behind. "Will she take bread as payment?"

"His humor is all I need." The girl said.

Mar's bruised face turned red. "I'll give more than jokes as payment."

Raimund grabbed the knight's arm. "Not today." He said to the woman. "My friend here just spent two days at a brothel near the docks. He needs time to rest."

"Not true." Mar started.

Raimund said, "But it is." The girl smiled before turning to another man to talk business. Raimund gave Mar a bit of bread. "Don't you think you should be back at the castle? Devro's been wondering where you are."

"That doesn't work on me. He isn't a small child anymore." Mar said as he huffed onto a stone bench.

Some men were bartering or trading labor by the well near the great shade tree. Raimund imagined all the men who had nothing to do today or any day. "What if you went to train some men to fight?" he asked Mar. "The Gorthair are always preparing for the Bruthaki to attack again; they would love to have you."

Mar laughed his eyes open. "How will the king of Viguran

feel if I am training the enemies of his cousin? Devro and Bertin would both denounce me." He cocked his head. "Though, Hurvir would go mad if he found out, and it's always fun to see him angry."

Raimund laid a hand on his friend's back. "Before you decide, you need rest. Climb the stairs, get a litter if you need it, but go to the castle and sleep. Fucking whores at night and drinking the day away won't anger Hurvir."

"And what do you have planned today?"

"Just to enjoy the city. It's market time." Sir Mar patted Raimund's knee as he stood from the bench and went off toward the castle. Whether or not he got there, Raimund would find out later, but he yelled out, "And make sure you bathe. You smell worse than the fisheries in the summer sun."

There were more markets popping up around Gereduss as the morning went on. Vendors along the street, tents under the statue of King Artin, whose head was a slightly different color than the rest of his body from being knocked off a decade ago. He walked the long road, what they called the 'street of oppression', from the statue to the chancellery, the temple of the Gorthair close by with its smashed windows and missing gems and stones from when all of Rowan went up in flames. The grounds near the chancellery were also set up as a market. It was a new building. Built with stone and granite instead of the brick used in the rest of the city.

He traded a few rings he found in his room for cheese and crackers. The diamond necklace got him barrels of wine to be carried up the steps of the castle. People watched him from the shadows of the brick buildings as he went about. Feeling their daggers or cracking knuckles. *They don't know who I am. No one in all of Rowan knows who I am.* But they acted like it. Like they knew he was a knight protecting the Prince of Viguran, who knew the Prince of Rowan, the son of the man who reconquered them. He shook his head. *I'm only seeing things.*

The tourney grounds were empty. The rings for fighting, arenas for jousting, stands to buy cheeses and wine from all across Adedor had vanished as if overnight. Just patches of dead grass and the occasional tree lingered. His black hair covered his eyes as the wind blew over the desolate place. Nothing would move in. Not until the next tourney. The cliff guided him home. If he got lost within the cramped houses and shops that lined the maze of streets, he just had to look down an empty alley to the castle hugging those black cliffs.

He heard a scream. A woman. It came from behind, and he turned with his hand on his hilt and fingers on the jewel. There was another. *The same woman, and laughter this time.* He stalked down the streets. Some people were poking their heads out of their doors and windows. Ladies froze as they hung clothes to dry, men stopping their carts and searching. Even the dogs barked. Raimund couldn't hear anything from the city when he was in the castle, but a woman's scream didn't seem normal. The people of Gereduss didn't scream. They went to their neighbors for help. Bread, jewels for travel, protection against thieves. In only a few short weeks, the entirety of the city, those who wished to partake, would meet in the chancellery and discuss plans for the future. They called it *la durnid.* They never screamed.

As he made his way down the cobbled streets, another scream pierced the air, causing his body to jolt. *Found you.* He turned to an alley, and three men were ripping the clothes off a lady, laughing and pushing her down. "Help." She cried when she saw Raimund. The men turned to him. One was bald, the other had a chiseled chin, the last with a long beard to his stomach. They all eyed Valkyr at the same time. Daggers sheathed at two of their belts, the bald one with a sword.

"We don' wan no trouble." The bearded man said. "Not with you." He whipped out his dagger and twirled it in his hands. "Lila here owes us a few gold pieces."

"So go bout your day." The bald man said; fingering his sword hilt.

"Why don't you ask politely instead of beating the poor girl?" Raimund kept his hands up, not wanting to fight and make a scene. He could feel eyes on his back. People wanting to watch. A few with clubs. *Hopefully, those aren't for me.*

"We've given her months," the bald man answered, "but we were promised by Meret's third day this month that we would get it." He held out his palms. "Do ya see any gold in our hands? Do you, David?" he asked the chiseled man, who shook his head with a grin.

"Let the girl alone." An old man called from behind. "Lila's a sweet girl; I've known her all my life. We can figure this out without violence." A wooden club hung at his side.

"Little Olli, is that you?" A woman from behind yelled. The man with the long beard stiffened. "Don't make me bring your name up at *la durnid*. Ya wouldn't want to be sent into the marches for beating this here poor girl."

The three men spoke to one another quietly. Raimund heard, "We'll try again some other time." He massaged the hilt. The bald man grabbed Lila by the arm and threw her over toward Raimund. She bunched up her torn clothes and ran to the woman behind him. "Why don' you get going." Olli said. "No more trouble from us."

The crowd behind dispersed, some grumbling they didn't get to use their weapons. The old man and the woman helped Lila away, dabbing at the blood on her face. Raimund turned to leave, wondering how long Lila had until they tried to beat her again.

His head jerked forward, his neck popping, and his eyes blurring. He stumbled into a wall. Barely could he see his fingers in front of his face. He had been punched in the back of his head, and the three moved closer, surrounding him. "Ya messed with our money." The man named David said. "No ones messes with us."

Raimund unsheathed his sword, but he was already knocked to the ground, daggers drawn, and the bald man had his sword. Valkyr dropped a few feet away, the metal echoing in the alley. They kicked at his ribs, his chest, his legs, his groin. He cried curses as he protected his head. He could feel his fingers itching for power. They wanted to burn, but his sword wasn't in his hand, the stone on the hilt not near him. He could feel the energy whipping at his hands. Wanting to go in. *Too dangerous.* He thought before David punched at his head. Raimund could taste blood.

He kicked at Olli and heard the man fall over as his knee buckled. He rolled to the side, causing the punches to hit the street below. Valkyr was within reach. He stretched his fingers as far as he could, and the bald man brought his sword up. "Shoulda left us alone."

Raimund touched Valkyr. The stone glowed bright red. His fingers turned a light red, like he had waved them over candlelight.

A stream of fire erupted from his other hand. There was a

quick scream as the bald man dropped his sword and burned to death. Olli was crawling to his feet and limping away as fast as he could. David was already running.

Raimund stood, wiping away blood, panting. His body ached. But he was much more alive than the smoking body beneath him. It had been so long since Raimund had to kill anyone. *So much for a peaceful life.* The sides of the buildings had charred, embers floating in the sky. In the street was the old man with the wooden club. Mouth agape. *Please tell me I don't have to kill you too.*

The old man pointed down the alley, past where Olli was limping into a run. "You best get. Wouldn't want anyone else to see what you caused." Raimund nodded his thanks and left as quickly as he could. He could hear people gather again and gasp at the body as he turned the corner. The castle rose above the houses. Calling him. He sheathed Valkyr and watched as his fingers went back to normal. A small stream of smoke rose from behind. The castle wasn't only home. It was safety.

The daken rubbed ointment on him; Raimund squirmed but had no choice but to allow it.

The young Prince Devro, only fourteen and always hot-headed, shook his head. "We should go down there and find the men who did this." He pounded a fist on the table. Probably not as loud as he had hoped. "You said one's name was Olli. The other David. Surely we can track him down."

"Thank you." Raimund said to Gilroy, the daken, as he cleaned up his supplies. He looked at his chest and stomach. *Much better than before.* His gashes were stitched closed and the blood wiped away. His body still hurt, but whatever ointment was used seemed to have relaxed him. "It doesn't matter. I'm still alive. The girl is still alive. There's nothing to be done."

Mar, who stumbled in a few minutes ago, said to Devro, "Besides, I doubt the Gorthair would look kindly on a few knights of Rowan and Viguran searching through their streets and bashing in heads. Do you want a riot? For the castle to burn?"

Devro's shoulders dropped. "You're right."

A knight of Rowan opened the door. "There is a rider here for you, Devro." The prince followed out the door, his head low. The daken soon followed, leaving Mar and Raimund alone in his bedchamber. He slipped a coat over his bruises and opened the curtains to let in the sun. Waves crashed below. Mar sat on Raimund's bed, a brow raised. "What?" Raimund asked.

Mar had a knowing look, and Raimund knew what the knight was about to say. "I heard some rumblings among the guards. Apparently, there was a body found in an alleyway, completely burned and blackened like a cooked chicken. You wouldn't happen to know why?"

Raimund looked over the expanse of the sea below. Dolphins, small gray dots as they jumped out of the water, boats gliding across like cutting through butter. "No one saw."

"They never do, do they?" Mar looked at the paintings on the walls showing the conquest of King Artin over the Gorthair people, ripped and shredded by the common folk years ago. "You need to be more careful. Just because the Gorthair claim to love everyone doesn't mean éithrio are included."

Raimund paused, knowing the éithrio—mages like him— were never to be trusted. "This hasn't happened in years.

It's more dangerous for us to be here because of Devro and Bertin's visits, not because of me." Mar only nodded before the door banged open. The prince was out of breath and swung around a piece of parchment.

"It's from the King's Council, my uncle, my father." His smile was brighter than the noon sun. "I've been invited, as have my protectors, back to Vigur to celebrate my father's feast." Mar and Raimund made eye contact. "We're to go to Udello and meet with Gofrei, who will escort us the rest of the way." Mar gave a quick smile. Raimund looked back over the ocean. If this palace was safety, Vigur certainly wasn't.

Sophie

it for a queen. She thought as Renna and Amalla helped her step into a laced, ocean and sky blue dress. "Does this one work, Your Grace?" Amalla, the youngest of the two handmaids, with her black skin like onyx, asked with a bow.

"It's perfectly fine, Amalla. See if Lord Durcy's wife has those brown shoes she wore to Samosay's Feast." Amalla left the room with another bow while Renna finished Sophie's face, white powder fluffing into the air, getting caught in the sun's rays. They sat in a room off to the side of her bedchamber. Her bed veiled, columns and arches holding the curtain. New stone pillars and gray stone walls covered the elven marble that one could see in the past. *The marble was probably beautiful. Shame what they did.*

"Amalla told me that your parents are coming to the feast." Renna said as she brushed Sophie's mahogany hair. "How wonderful for you."

"It will be nice to see them. They don't visit as much as I would hope." The queen said, remembering when she would play in the palace in Udello while her father held court. Ducking under the legs of lords and admiring the ladies' dresses. Her mother would swat her for disturbing the nobles. Eventually they sent her away to the old, but handsome king in Viguran to be wed. And just like a dutiful daughter, she followed through with no complaints. Renna applied makeup to Sophie's cheek, usually done to hide the redness. "When was the last time you saw your parents?"

"Years before I entered your service. They left Zhepatev to wander east and left me with my sister. Eventually I went west and found Viguran."

"I always wanted to go to Eotros." Sophie imagined the huge eastern continent was full of new wonders and new foods and languages she'd never heard. "My father told me it was unlike anything he saw on Adedor. 'A fog of mystery surrounds that place', he told me."

"I don't know about mystery." Renna said. "Why was your father in Eotros?"

"To treat with your king in Masa Naq. I was left in Aele with my uncles. My parents were gone a whole month, which is a long time when you're young and have nothing to do. They danced some strange dance and heard instruments they'd never seen before. Ate spiced food from Saamrakaa; millet porridge, which my father said was surprisingly delightful; and heard stories of travelers in the east. Perhaps your parents were among those."

"My king sits the throne of Viguran," Renna said in a show of loyalty that Sophie didn't need. "Though I'm sure I can teach you a strange dance."

"My parents told me of boats that sail over grasslands, racing with the winds."

"I'm not sure of that." The Masani girl said. "But I've never been over the *Kii La'ar*, the mountains in Masa Naq."

"That's a long way away anyhow. Do you miss your

parents?" Renna nodded and went back to work.

They sat in silence, save for Sophie's hair being pulled and yanked by the brush, until Amalla came back with brown, flat shoes. She lifted the large train, and Amalla slipped the shoes on while Renna fastened a yellow armlet to her, then a brown leather belt. Stepping toward the mirror, she grabbed her silver diadem, with the light bouncing off the large sapphire, and fastened it to her hair. Renna carefully placed the yellow veil over her head. She was ready.

"Where are you going today that you dressed in your house colors?" Amalla puzzled.

"Just to hear some gossip," *and to see a certain king's brother.* Something her handmaids need not know. Guards stood outside her door, bowing as she exited her chamber. Slaves too, but they were cleaning the dirt off the floor and dead bugs from the wall. That was something she still hadn't gotten used to. There were no slaves in Terrop, servants yes, but not ones with chains around their ankles if they misbehaved. The worst her mother ever did to a servant was send her to a working mine in the Asara and the occasional whipping, but nothing as heinous as what was done to these slaves.

Sir Achen followed closely behind her, his metal boots thumping atop the parquet. Lords and ladies littered the halls throughout the palace. The feast was still weeks away, but some had to come early, make alliances or trading compacts or gossip. Sophie kept her eyes down. Looks and whispers followed her as close as Sir Achen. He drew closer, putting a gloved hand on her back. "Your Grace, there is nothing to fear. You are not among the common folk of Vigur, but lords and ladies of grand houses and ruling dynasties."

"Should I not fear them?"

Rubbing her head, they went through a small door used only by slaves. Sir Achen let out a small sigh. "I want to remind you I hate going this way, my queen."

"And I quite enjoy it." The slaves bowed their heads at the sight of Sophie's diadem. "All my life I was ushered down grand staircases to the applause and gasps of many a fat lord and pale lady. I would rather sneak about and keep some of my sanity."

Achen gave a nod. *Surely he understands me by now. I spend enough time with eyes on me.* "You're not the only one who enjoys sneaking in back corridors." Her knight said.

She played with the rings on her fingers, especially the one given to her by her grandmother. "I've yet to be assassinated," she said, knowing Achen would let no harm come to her.

At that moment, glass shattered. Her household guard was in front of her with a knife, while a scream bounced up the stairs. A small enslaved girl cowered, a bottle of wine broken at her feet, the red liquid spilling down the stone steps. Achen took a breath and sheathed his dagger. The slave got to work cleaning, scraping broken glass into her hands, pricking her dark skin, the blood getting lost in wine. Sophie and her knight carefully passed her. "If the masters hear of this," Sir Achen said, "she won't carry another bottle again."

"Good thing they won't find out."

The knight didn't speak again. He stood outside the door with palace guards as she entered a small solar where five other ladies were present, her ladies-in-waiting, sipping on wine and eating goat cheese. When they saw her, they stood and curtsied. "My queen." They all said as Sophie sat trying to keep the wrinkles out of her dress. Quickly, the gossip began again. The 'Queen's Council' is what they called it, where the whispers of sex and scandal spread as quick as ivy. It reminded Sophie of her friend group in Aele when she was just a child.

"I hear the Lady Daisa has rejected her marriage proposal, spurning the Lord of the Seeded Field," Lady Abre Volles said, her violet hair wrapping around her cheeks. "Never has such a match been denied in the Flewthlands."

"I can tell you," Countess Filra whispered, "I hear Daisa is with babe, fathered by a close cousin."

The ladies gasped. Sophie smiled but paid them no mind. Marriages of lesser lords and ladies did not concern her; she wondered what Ultiir would tell her today. *I have seen him eyeing me more of late, and eyeing that crown.* The king's brother was always ambitious. Somehow he convinced Hurvir to raise him to chief consultant even though Ultiir had only ever managed his home of Goldfield with his mother by his side. The looks he would give Sophie were full of lust and hunger. She would merely smile. He had treasonous thoughts, and she tried to pay them no mind.

"Your Grace?" Lady Rila said. Sophie leaned in. "We were talking about marriage. Some of us did not have the pleasure of being here when you married His Grace, the king. We were wondering if you would tell us what it was like?"

The queen cleared her throat and drank some wine. "Of course." She chewed off a piece of white cheese so she could think. "I was in Vallnioc when my father agreed to the betrothal. The snow had just melted away, and I was riding my horse through the dead flower gardens when my doma came to fetch me. It was magical being whisked away to Vigur on a ship. The city was a marvel. In truth, I should have made a pilgrimage years before. Though learning your dialect scared me, it proved easy. Before I knew it, it was the day. My mother was ecstatic. She chose a beautiful golden gown for the ceremony, and Hurvir was so handsome in his red." *And old, and grumpy.* "The high doma said some prayers and we were wed." The ladies seemed to want more, but Sophie had nothing else to say. Later that night, just as her parents had commanded her to, she and Hurvir consummated the marriage. Of course, Hurvir could barely do that from all the drinking, and Sophie heard rumors of the curse that afflicted his seed. "It was the greatest day of my life." She drank more wine to swallow the lie.

The ladies fawned and told of their own weddings. Lady Betal's marriage aboard a ship, Baroness Mara's in the mountains, Countess Filra's in the domaton. *All sound better than my own.* Sir Achen knocked on the door before stepping in. "My queen, the Lord of Goldfield has requested an audience."

Sophie stood. "Thank you, my ladies."

They all stood and bowed. "My queen."

As she left, she heard Lady Ficca say, "the king's brother," to laughing ladies, but Sophie kept her eyes straight and her head high. The ladies wouldn't know she heard their giggles.

"Where does he wish to meet, my good sir?" She said after the door was closed.

"The river." Her knight led the way.

Having avoided the rest of the court folk, she made it outside. They kept their distance from the slave fields, where some of the food for the palace was grown and harvested. Instead, walking through the gardens. Elegant plants of every color known to man lined the cobble walkway. Oranges and lemons were being plucked by the cooks. Apples and strawberries drew the eye in the midst of green. Even a rowan tree grew in the garden, a symbol of peace between Viguran and Rowan. Stone pines lined the path to the river.

"Will you wait?" Sophie said to her guard.

"And risk a slave drowning you?" He shook his head. "I do not want the whole of Terrop wishing for my head on a pike. I'll come to the river with you."

"Good thing it wasn't a question."

Sir Achen puffed, but Sophie ignored him. She made sure her veil was resting properly; her dress free of scuffs and dust.

Ultiir stood along the shore of the Ritae. *The river of death.* The place Vigura led the first man to a peaceful, eternal slumber. He wore his gold cloak befitting the chief consultant, his blond hair pushed back, the river breeze grazing it. His tunic was woven with golden strands that made shapes of wheat and grass. Prince of Goldfield. The ancestral home of the de'Tro family, and the title given to the heir apparent. His smile wiped away any seriousness that was on his face. Sophie breathed. *If Hurvir finds me ...* She let the thought die, touching her cheek that was swollen last month after Hurvir found out she had dinner with a lesser lord near her dowager lands of Eiselton. *He just wanted to trade,* she thought bitterly.

"My queen." Ultiir bowed. After she curtsied, he grabbed her hands and kissed both. "I assume you never expected I would invite you for a walk along the shore."

She wiped the kiss from her hands when he looked to the sky. Sophie took in the smells of autumn. The lingering scent of rain and mud, the smell of the crisp air blowing from the mountains. To the north of the river, small villages dotted the valleys between Valor's Cliffs. Behind, the city bustled, but the world was quiet by the River Ritae. "It's a beautiful day. I'm grateful you thought to invite me out." The sun felt good as the breeze from the water washed over her, the river reflecting the blue of the sky. "I wish to enjoy time outdoors before the dreariness of winter blows from the Asara."

"Perhaps a vacation to Ealna is in order?" Ultiir crunched some red and yellow leaves beneath his boot before picking up a flat, smooth rock and rubbing the edges.

"Too muggy." She said while a fisherman waved to the Prince of Viguran. "I miss my home. Udello is lovely in the spring; perhaps I will go there for Swallow's Feast."

"We could go together. I have yet to see Udello. The furthest I've sailed the Ters-Veck is Awara." Ultiir gave a pleasant smile. "I would love to see your home."

Sophie hated when Hurvir went to Udello, always making a drunken fool of himself; she didn't want to see how Ultiir acted. "Lord Gofrei was adamant he be the one sent to Udello to bring my parents to the city. Perhaps you could go with him." Ultiir rubbed his chin and smiled. Pulling on her belt, she looked at the mountains in the distance. Eventually, the peaks wouldn't be the only thing covered in snow and death. "Are you excited for your brother's feast?"

Ultiir pulled away. He bounced the rock across the water. "Excited to waste thousands of coins on one man while thousands of people starve?"

So that's how he feels, she thought as she went over in her head if her true feelings would be safe with Ultiir, or if trusting him was foolish. But Ultiir always looked upset when he would see bruises on her. The only one outside her handmaids who seemed to care. "I'm not terribly excited either. Hundreds of lords of who knows where and their lady wives all clamoring to speak with me and ask me when a son will be put inside my belly." Ultiir opened his mouth to speak, then closed it. *He wants a son.* "Why have you never married? If Hurvir and you do not have legitimate sons, the de'Tro name will die."

Ultiir's face turned red. "I've yet to find the right woman."

"There must be hundreds of women calling for your hand in marriage. Who wouldn't want to be the wife to the Lord of Goldfield?"

The prince took Sophie by the hand. "It seems the best women are taken."

Sophie knew she was blushing, but her parents sent her to wed Hurvir, not his brother, not an heir who might never be king. Pulling her hand away, she said, "I heard Lady Rista of Clear Port came to Goldfield looking for a husband. What happened to her?"

"She's older than my brother."

"And I'm younger than you while being married to your brother. I believe your mother was around fifty when you were born. Is age such a problem?"

"I was a gift to my parents from the Four. My mother calls me her miracle child." Ultiir brushed his hair from his eyes. The river seemed to flow upstream. The breeze from the mountains made her hair stand. They walked on the short grass toward the wall that separated them from the city. The spires and peaks of the old elvish town peered over the stone. "What if my brother had never been born? What if I were king? Would you still have come to Vigur?"

"I think my parents would've sent me anywhere with an eligible suitor." *Maertan would've been nice, perhaps even Plajul. Away from all the happenings of the world, too bad my parents need me here. Need me to strengthen our line.* "Yes. I would still have come here. Married the king." It would've been better for her to have been born a commoner than have to deal with this king and prince. At least her parents would ask her to fetch water instead of placating royals.

Ultiir brushed his hand across Sophie's once swollen cheek. "If you were my queen, I would treat you like one."

They grew closer. Their lips guided themselves to one another. Sophie stepped back. "We are always being watched." Sir Achen swayed in the gardens. "The court doesn't need a scandal on its hands, and your brother doesn't need to execute you for treason."

"He doesn't have another heir. He would never kill me."

"The bastard. My son-by-law."

"A bastard." Ultiir sighed. "My brother's poisoned seed has caused many problems for Viguran. All his dead wives and their parents mad at the failed alliances, now a bastard who could start a war like Barnet the Bastard or Urses the Slayer. Who knows how many whores he gave a child to? If I were king, this all would have been avoided. My seed is strong; I know it. My queen would've borne numerous children, male children, all ready to take over when I die. Now, Hurvir grows old, and he doesn't care. The fate of our kingdom decided by his cursed loins." His blue eyes bore into hers. "I could give you a child. Something to be proud of. Make your father and mother and all of Terrop happy at this alliance, more than that failed marriage with the Rowai."

Her eyes darted every way. *This is treason. But my parents would be glad for a grandchild.* "No one can hear of this."

His fingers intertwined with hers, she didn't pull away, praying to the Four that Sir Achen wasn't watching. "No one will know. I will be king. You, my queen. We will raise an heir and help the people of our kingdom avoid further war and bloodshed."

"You? King?"

"The council is planning something." His face was only an inch away. "You mustn't tell anyone, not your handmaids nor your knights, not your parents, or even the gods." Sophie nodded, but hoped he didn't want her to play a part; she didn't think her parents would be happy if she committed murder. "The king's feast will be his last. That is all you can know. I am Lord of Goldfield, next in line to the throne. You will help strengthen my claim when some lords start to question if the bastard should be king."

Her breathing quickened, but she knew Ultiir wouldn't like her silence. "I don't know …" Sophie began.

"You are one of the most popular queens in the history of this kingdom. You feed the hungry, help the poor, house the vagrants. I would say you're more popular than the queen mother is; the people adore you; the ladies envy you. I need you by my side."

She nodded again to bring the conversation to an end. She didn't want to hear how much this man wished to be with her. Already she had to deal with his brother's mood swings and outbursts; she didn't need another. "I must be going before anyone sees us."

Ultiir didn't seem to care. He pulled her tight and kissed her right on the lips. His own were dry. "Tell no one."

Tundavik

T undavik made sure all the lids were on tight, all the barrels fastened so not to roll as the ship cut through the water below

"Seems to be ready to dock," Potter, a young man with enough fat to show off his family's wealth, said. Tundavik nodded as he made sure his crate didn't fall overboard. "Ye ever been to this city?"

"No," Tundavik said.

"Me neither. Always wanted to see." Potter leaned on the railing. "Ye ever been this side of the Vlylahl Sea?"

Tundavik sat on the deck and slipped his boots on. His feet ached from the weeks of work while at sea. The ship lurched. When they first set out to sea, Tundavik couldn't keep himself from vomiting; now he was used to it. "I came here a lot." Tundavik looked to the rocky shores. "A long time ago."

"I'm sure it's just like you 'member it." Potter whistled a song about a some man climbing a mountain as his head faced the cliffs.

"Did the captain say where you'll be heading after you drop me off?"

"Zadova," Potter whispered as if it were a secret. "Never been there either. Haven't been much places, have I?"

Tundavik shivered at the thought. "Winter's going to settle in soon. It wouldn't surprise me if the northern mountains already have snow. You going to stay up there until spring?"

"I hope not. My family in Verva will miss me plenty. Sure you don't wanna come?"

"I just want to sell my fish and go back home." *But not my western home.*

"Get ready to dock." The helmsman yelled. The deckhands went to work, Tundavik and Potter staying out of the way.

The great black cliffs of Gereduss towered over the ship as they sailed into the harbor, almost hidden by the rocks. Large ships not unlike this one lined the docks. Workers scurrying atop them. Sun beating down. The sails were raised, and the anchor dropped. "Make it quick." The helmsman shouted. Some deckhands left the ship. Others stayed. Tundavik was the only one not continuing north. He grabbed his crate of fish and tried not to fall off the gangplank. Potter called out from behind. "Maybe we'll see one another some other time."

Tundavik waved goodbye as a cat stalked from the shadows toward his fish. "Don't freeze out there."

He kicked the cat away. The only other living thing on the docks beside the deckhands. The streets were empty. It was as if midnight had called. It wasn't even noon. The fish sloshed around in the wooden crate as Tundavik made his way past the warehouses and docks. Looking back at the ships sitting in the harbor, he saw men aboard with plain faces. Where is everyone? *Some plague? Has a monster swooped down and gobbled up half the town?* Reaching the markets, he set the crate down. A few vagrants walked by, a couple of fishermen, even a child who was going through the stalls looking for food. A wooden sign cracked against a post, and

Tundavik saw one stall open. The cat came back and stole a fish before Tundavik could catch it. He hiked the crate up to the stall.

"*Ailtè.*" A woman with one eyebrow said. "Ya looking to buy some undergarments?" She motioned to her wares, white garments, hastily sewn together. "I'll take some fish if ya want em."

"I was looking to sell these." He looked again at the empty stalls. "But no one seems to be in town. And, sorry to say, undergarments don't seem like a fair trade."

"Well, today you won't be getting any fair trade 'cept my wares. So decide or be gone with ya."

The child from before came over with his hands out. He was a mess of dirt and grime, wheezing as he walked. "*Podyn?*"

Tundavik's eyebrows rose. The woman rolled her eyes. "Fish. He wants ta fish."

"No." He clutched his crate harder. "I'm sorry, not without coin. I didn't sail all this way from the West to hand out fish for free."

The one eyebrow on the woman's head lowered. Wrinkles appearing. "Ya would withhold food from this here sickly boy? What kinda monster are ya?"

"Monster?"

The woman bent down to the child. "If I had food with me, I would give ya some. I know a nice man near the oppressor's statue; he gives out bread on days like this."

The boy smiled and ran off, as fast as his wheezing would allow. Tundavik didn't want to look at the lady to face his shame, and when he did, all he saw was a scowl. "Where ya from?"

"Attrima." Tundavik's answer was met with a *tsk tsk.* "I don't understand. Usually when I visit Coastburg or Dunniage, their docks are as busy as Vigura's Feast. What's happened here?"

"Nothing's happened. Ya arrived on the day of *la durnid.*" The woman spat at his feet. "Coastburg?" Her head was shaking. "I can't even stand the sight of ya, refusing that poor boy food. Get away from me stall unless you want something." He shook his head. "Then find another buyer."

Tundavik's mouth was opened in disbelief as he continued down the stretch of market stalls. *Thousands of people. Nowhere to be seen.* He turned and saw the ship he was on getting ready to depart. If he went back, he would end up in Zadova, not the best place to be when winter comes. A few more women were walking the street. They smiled and touched themselves as they passed, hoping for some business, no doubt. He could hear moans to his left, where a sign showed a woman with her legs spread open. *If I wanted a woman I would've stayed in Baragio.*

A dark-headed man came stumbling out of the brothel with tired eyes and a swollen lip. He held his head and his stomach. "Fun night?" Tundavik called out.

The man looked up but waved him away. Tundavik chuckled and saw a statue in the distance. *If the man with the bread is there, maybe he'll buy some fish.* The man from the brothel came closer, now his eyes fixated on Tundavik. *Is he that upset at my jape?* He didn't want to drop his crate, but that was the only way to get the dagger in his shoe. *One step closer.*

"Do I know you?" He didn't sound like he came from Rowan; his accent was eerily similar to Tundavik's.

His shoulders relaxed. "Excuse me?"

"You look familiar." The man hiccuped as he massaged his bruised face. "Do you come to the market a lot? The whorehouse?" His hands rested on his hips. "I don't think we've fucked before, but I don't remember most nights."

"No, we haven't." Tundavik looked the man up and down. *Do I know him?* He couldn't find a matching face in his memory.

The man's eyes widened. "Lord Tundavik Vandes?"

It was like an arrow pierced his stomach. He set the fish down so he wouldn't drop them. "How do you know that name?"

"Because I know you," the man's swollen face contorted into a smile. "You don't remember me. I mean, why would you? We only talked for a day or so. It was a crazy time." He straightened his posture and pushed back his hair. "I am Sir Mar. We spoke before you went to Panscar and I went to Awara."

"During the war with the Rainvealandians," Tundavik thought back to the war, before his campaign along the Bezir. A short, young man had been making jokes all night, mostly about the mites and his prowess.

Mar stepped closer. "Yes." Now it was his turn to look Tundavik up and down. "It's been so long. I didn't even know you were in Gereduss."

"I'm only trying to sell my fish. I sailed here from Attrima."

"Attrima? So that's where you went after the mess that happened." Mar's smile faded. "You know, no one really knows why you left."

"That's the way I want it."

"There are rumors. Rainvealandians, the king."

"All rumors."

The knight gave a nod and bent over, stumbling for a moment on the cobbled road, and picked up the crate of fish. "You won't find many people out today. Come with me. I'm sure the prince would love to buy these."

"The prince?" Tundavik didn't have time to object as Mar strolled down the street with his fish. They walked in silence for a few minutes as they went north, through both narrow streets and a large field where tourney games were usually held. "And where is everyone? I think it would be difficult to empty a city of thousands."

"It's that time again." Mar must've seen the confused look on the old lord's face. "Every few weeks, and especially after a tourney, the Gorthair gather in their chancellery to discuss their feelings or something to that effect. I never go."

"Why not? Don't you live here?"

Mar laughed. "I'm sure you remember when Rowan burned?" Tundavik nodded, remembering hearing the news of revolt and killings and the kingdom almost crumbling. "Well, they don't like people like me all that much, or the people I serve. And I don't feel like getting thrown in a river like a certain dead queen."

"I just wanted to sell some fish. Maybe make enough stallions to hire a boat to Viguran."

"Coins?" Mar laughed. "No coins in the Gorthair Marches. You'll have to barter, take whatever you find down to Coastburg then hire a ship from there." Tundavik scratched his head. The domaton rose in the distance, chisels and hammers sounding like instruments. Either it was being rebuilt or stripped of its valuables. *I guess the flames really did change Gereduss, and I thought Coastburg got it the worst.* "Did I hear you right?" Mar asked. "A ship to Viguran?"

They turned to the west toward the black cliffs and the palace atop them, hundreds of stairs slithering up the hill. "You heard right." His old home called to him. Not since he left has he wanted to go back. *So why now?* He didn't question it; it was as if no matter what he did, his body ached to go home. "I wish to see it before I die."

Mar almost dropped the crate because of his laughs. "You're not that old. Unless the gods have cursed you."

"I just want to see it." He shrugged, to himself as much as to Mar. "Attrima is so much different from Ritaeum."

"I bet." Mar climbed the first step to the cliff. "I've never been to Baragio; the only thing I know is the wine. Maybe we can trade places."

Tundavik was already tired after a few steps. *How am I supposed to make it to the top?* "How has life treated you? The Savior of Vikry, once a renowned knight of Viguran, living with some prince atop a cliff."

"Well, you know knights can't refuse orders." Mar took a deep breath. "Maybe the Gorthair people were right about that no-king thing."

Tundavik looked back at the city. The cliffs along the shore and the large, rocky hills that made up the marches, stretching inland as far as he could see, with the city growing in the center of it all. The domaton being worked on. A crowd by the statue. The empty market. An ornate bell tower that rang out on the hour. "Maybe they were."

The palace seemed so far, as did the city behind them. A few guards stood along the cliffside. Mar chatted whenever they came upon one, asking about their day and telling them about some fight during the tourney. The guards wore surcoats over their chainmail. An owl. In the owl's talons, a bushel of wheat. As they continued, Tundavik had the sinking feeling that he didn't want to know which prince lived with Sir Mar. He felt the dagger pushing against his foot. *Revenge? Come to Rowan and kill a prince before fleeing back to Attrima? Would I forgive myself?* He didn't want to think anymore. He took deep breaths, some because of the thousand steps, to rid his mind of thoughts. Sir Mar smiled as they reached the top.

The castle hugged the edge of the black cliffs. There was no wall, only bricks with towering spires and large central buildings ten stories high with sloping roofs for the rain and snow. There were guards with owl surcoats along the path. Guards with horse surcoats manned a tower above the steps, watching with bows at their side. Mar nodded and said pleasantries to a few. Tundavik followed to a central courtyard, bricks littered the grass, masons and bricklayers hard at work on the eastern wing.

"What happened here?" Tundavik asked, stepping over small shards of glass.

"When the flames broke out," Mar began, "the people took the castle over. They looted it and some even moved in. We had to take it back when we came seven years ago. The city was not happy, but we had more swords and arrows. Kicked all the vagrants out. It's been in a constant state of rebuilding since. These things take a while."

Mar continued to talk to guards as they entered through a stone door carved with snaking wisps. The halls were lit by torches, shadows dancing off the walls. The floor beneath was black like the cliffs, muffling footsteps as they wandered. "Not as fancy as the elvish palaces, but nicer than your ducal place in Ritaeum." The knight laughed.

Tundavik could barely remember his home before the

blood splashed the walls like paint. "Dreary though."

"That's the Gorthair for you, dreary people."

They made their way up more stairs, Tundavik's heart wanting to burst from his chest. He couldn't tell if it was from the long climb or nerves about the person who could be inside. A single door was waiting. They had to be on the third or fourth floor; he had lost count focusing on his breathing.

Mar opened the door. "Greetings. I'm sure you missed me."

"Where have you been?" A tall, pale man said, sounding like he was hiding an accent. "And who's this?"

"An old acquaintance who just happened to be in Gereduss, Tundavik Vandes."

The man's face puzzled. "Who?"

Tundavik's boot buzzed as a child came in from the stone balcony. "Tundavik Vandes? As in the Duke of the Woodlands?" The child was blond, his face a younger version of his father's. Tundavik couldn't see all the hate of the king in his son, though. He played through the consequences of taking his knife out and stabbing the child's throat. *They would only kill me. Not much worse than that.* The kid came closer. Tundavik's fingers itched to grab the dagger. "I've heard a lot about you."

Tundavik's hand stopped moving. The boy's voice broke as he said that. *Just a child.* He held out his arm, and the Prince of Viguran shook it.

Bertin

The last thrust and release left him tired and falling. The whore below him kissed his neck as his seed spilled out between her thighs. Bertin rolled to her side. Playing with her hair, he saw her tired eyes, the shadows under them growing larger. "I really needed that." He stood and found his trousers, making sure any coin was still in pouches and pockets. "They'd never believe me if I told them Gorthair women are as beautiful as any other."

Her lustful eyes looked over his body. Her smooth voice said, "You're right; most men in Rowan wouldn't agree. Don't tell them I come from the marches." As he slipped his tunic on, tying his belt, the whore rubbed her hands on his neck, nibbling his ears. "Come back to bed. It's very rare I get to meet a prince."

Bertin pushed her hands away. He didn't need any woman at the moment, especially one he paid. "You only want one thing, and I thank you for pleasuring me, but I don't need some hired whore in my service. I'm sure dockworkers and travelers carry more than enough coin."

"You're wrong. I only have eyes for you."

"You know," the prince said with a sly smile, "the reason the whorehouses are better in Gereduss is because they don't take coin. You have to find better ways to pay. More inventive. It almost seems lazy giving you stallions so you can pretend to enjoy my fucking." He pushed the whore away and went to the door. "I don't remember your name, nor care enough to learn it, but I wish you well in your endeavors." The whore's mouth was agape as he walked into the corridor. It smelled of piss, and his nose burned as the scent of ale wafted up the steps. It was dim due to the lack of windows and the large buildings on either side casting an engulfing shadow.

Sir Gerg was chatting with some girl when Bertin found him near the exit. The knight straightened and gave a curt nod. "Wilclef says you've spent too much time here, Your Grace."

"It was a long journey."

The rest of his guardsmen were waiting outside on their horses. They had arrived a day ago. No doubt his father was expecting him, but Bertin wanted to make a stop, so they went to the whorehouse at the west gate. No one, save the whores knew the prince was here. They didn't announce when any member of the royal family arrived or departed the city anymore. His father told him stories of the time before the river caught fire, before the nobility ran away. Men and women and their children, rich or poor, starving or fat, would fill the streets and watch the procession of guards accompanying the king or prince or princess. Even noble cousins would be given a warm welcome. "They loved us all," his father would tell him. "I never imagined a day that would change."

Now, Bertin didn't even wear his crown once the gates of Rowan opened. His guards were close, with their hands resting atop the hilts of their swords. The streets were lively, but cold. No one cared for him except to get out of the way of his black mare, Brissa. They traveled down the western road toward the center of the capital, cutting a straight path through the dense city. The dome of the Royal Chancellery unmistakable over the thousands of five-story houses. The western road was where the city's undesirables lived. Gorthairs from the marches, Rainvealandians from the South, Deleri from the West, and Hellers from the North all huddled together in their filth while the Brutahki built their streets and shops.

Bertin pulled the reins as a team of pigs crossed the street, eating and shitting as they went. "I hate the western road, if you didn't know."

Wilclef, his head guard, smiled. "Doesn't everyone? No Brutahki would complain if this whole side of town was burned to ash."

"If only we were so lucky." Bertin quieted as suspicious eyes fell on him. People in the street began to whisper and point. *I stayed hidden longer than last.* Wilclef made a hand gesture, and his guard drew closer. Now, instead of some rich nobleman, Bertin was the prince. Just a little over twenty years ago, his grandmother, the Queen Amalia, was murdered on the Bruthak Ridge in the center of the city, her lifeless body flung into the river. Bertin knew these people would do it again if they felt the need, especially those on the western road.

Lucky for Bertin, Wilclef was as good a guard as any. He had fought for his father when the flames died down, fighting anyone who dared oppose the true king. Wilclef was the hero of Queen's Valley, taking the village back with only his sword and shield, defeating the large garrison of traitors. Bertin could see Wilclef's eyes darting everywhere. At every corner and dark alley, every window and crack, every person, no matter their look.

Bertin's mare pushed through a herd of pigs that were eating the never-ending trash. More people stepped out onto the road. "The prince." An old man said. "Come to ask for more gold." A woman with a strong accent said. "I hope he falls in pigshit." Another laughed. Bertin smiled to himself. *The jealousy of these people.* "We kill him now, the king won't know who did it." An ugly, three toothed, Northerner said. Bertin threw up his hood and ignored the rest of the comments. He couldn't show them he was brave, for that could make them angrier, and he couldn't show them he was scared, for that could make them do something bold and stupid.

Wilclef went farther ahead of Bertin's guard, checking the streets and corners. He tilted his head left, and the entourage turned down a narrow alley, barely the size of Bertin's mare. Rats scurried as the horses trotted through, and the people jumped to any door for safety. Bertin held a rose-scented cloth to his nose, and even that didn't mask the smell. "Please tell me if my bedchamber smells like this." He told Gordo, who laughed through a plugged nose.

The smell began to fade into a distant memory as they reached the center of the capital. Men wearing ceremonial blue robes and masks held staffs holding perfume. Helping to drown out the stench of the common people. The palace was not as large as Vigur's, but it was astonishingly beautiful. *The most beautiful place in the world. And it's mine,* Bertin thought as the gates opened. The palace was elven-mined marble, from the steps to the palisades to the roof. Purple-stained stone recessed into the white, a new feature made by man. The columns adorned with the adventures of the elves. From finding this river, to building their trading palace, to the eventual war with the humans. New stories, human stories, were etched along the windows and doorways, beginning with King Artin and continuing to the death of Queen Amalia. Bertin wondered what stories would be etched about him. Maybe he would finally solve the issues with the Gorthair, or deal with the crowd of people that always gathered at gates with hate in their eyes. He could go down as one of the most famous kings.

"Daydreaming again?" A woman's voice said once they were safely inside the gate.

Bertin hadn't realized his sister and her handmaiden, Mari, were standing near Brissa. "Of course. What else is there to do?" He said as servants helped him down from the mare and led her away. Bertin and Aveline embraced. "Back so soon? I thought you would've stayed in Bardekan until the festivals were over?"

Aveline's face twisted, and her eyes rolled. "I was *summoned.* I've been here for a few weeks. You know Father doesn't like me going there. And apparently there is some baron's son that wants my hand in marriage."

"I guess father hasn't learned you don't want that."

"When has he learned anything?" They walked together with their many guards, ignoring the jeering from outside the palace walls. The stairs were slick from last night's rain, but a purple cloth had been rolled out to keep them from slipping.

"And where's Baldewin?" Bertin asked, looking for his little brother.

"He and Blis sailed to Decaro on some fishing trip. I can only imagine how Baldewin likes it."

"Crying out for his mother at the smallest nibble of a minnow." They laughed together. "Have you met your future husband?"

Aveline shook her head with a laugh as the palace doors, rotted and worn, creaked open. "He would be so lucky." She eyed Mari for a moment. "He's a Northerner. Lives somewhere in North Ferga. You'd think that father would at least find his only daughter a prince to marry, but no, I'm stuck with a man who probably has two acres to his name."

The halls got quieter as their guard fell behind, chatting about their respective journeys. The paintings of kings and queens watched over them. Bertin saw the portrait of King Wycleaf, the first Thomas king, and his second wife, Eliza. They both had half-closed eyes, like they couldn't care to be the most powerful rulers in Adedor. Bertin turned to his sister. "I'm sure there's a nice Rainvealandian prince out there. The king of Attamek has a few sons."

"You know father would never allow that. Something about a war …" They smiled because they knew. Their father had fought the mites, the Rainvealandian vermin, and protected the capital from an invasion. "It was a scandal that I even learned the dreadful language. I think he would jump off the same rocks as mother if I found a mite for a husband."

They wandered down the chambers together, servants and courtiers and knights all bowing as they went. Saying, "Your Grace." *Much better than the western road. This is how the whole city should be.* The door to the throne room was modest, stripped bare of its decorative gold and lapis lazuli when it was overrun all those years ago. "So, North Ferga?" Bertin scratched his head. "It's going to be winter soon."

"The Northerner will warm me, I hope." Aveline smirked, and Mari laughed.

"I can't believe Father would let you marry a Heller. I don't think any prince or princess has married anyone other than a Brutahki."

Bertin noticed Aveline slightly roll her eyes. "Alliances are more important than purity, and he spent most of the flames up north. I guess he grew fond of it."

Bertin watched the door as if it were going to snatch him away itself. "What do you think he wants with me?"

"Why don't you find out?"

"It must be important." Bertin's face turned red. "He pulled me away from the tourney in Gereduss."

"How *dare* he." Aveline pushed Bertin playfully. She then embraced him. "I waited to see you, but I have to leave. The river is far, and I want to be there before the first snow falls."

"I understand." Sometimes he couldn't believe how much she looked like his mother. Mahogany hair and deep brown eyes. "Be safe. The Hellers can be savage."

"I hope all is well with father." She wiped away a tear as she left Bertin alone at the door. He watched as Mari embraced Aveline, sniffling. *She must've already cried. Strange that Aveline's favorite handmaid is staying here.* He waved once more to his sister.

Bertin pushed the dirt off his dark yellow riding clothes, turned the iron handle, and pushed the door open. His father, wisps of gray in his brown hair showing his age, paced in front of the purple cushioned throne. Windows high above streamed in sunlight. Tapestries of blue and red hung on columns. If you looked close enough, you could see the holes where the inlaid gemstones once were. Taken by the barbaric commoners when they sacked the palace.

"Don't you want to sit?" Bertin asked as he swiped a cracker from a tray near the door. Servants along the wall bowed.

His father's eyes lit and a smile showed his new wrinkles. "My son." They embraced, Bertin's arms feeling like they might bruise. "I've awaited your arrival."

"The journey through the marches added some time, but it was worth it. Showed the Gorthair that I'm not afraid of them."

"Good, good. Leave us." The servants scurried away. King Bartel finally sat, his golden crown falling lopsided. "After what they did, they should always fear the Thomas family."

Bertin remembered the glares and jeers he received. The contempt shown to him by the city and Gorthair leaders. "They feared me," he said. "I had my hand on my sword, ready to strike. I didn't even need Wilclef to protect me."

His father belted out a laugh. "I feel like I never see you anymore. First, you ride off with some girl to Edincassone and then find your cousin in Gereduss." The king rubbed his chest. "How many times must you go to that city?"

"Devro and his guards are great to be around. I get to watch the waves and fight in tourneys. What's not to like about that place?"

"Did you win any fights?"

"Of course, even took on a fighter from Moon Bay, Rufun. It was difficult, but I managed just fine. All those classes you made me take when I was younger seemed to have paid off." Bertin laughed until he noticed his father didn't. The king's eyes dropped. "Rufun wasn't actually that big, and I didn't get hurt."

"It's not about being hurt." His father's breath was heavy and loud. "Believe me when I tell you, I am glad you do not have to live in exile in a foreign place. Hearing the news that my mother was brutally murdered and that my sister was captured. It was hell. But you must stop these playful things. You are going to be king. You must act like one."

"I *do* act like a king. Everywhere I go the people know who I am. I sit in on meetings when I'm here and know the goings-ons of Adedor."

The king forced himself to stand, rested a hard hand on Bertin's shoulder, and said, "There is still so much you have to learn. Alliances are always changing. The Gorthair could rise at any minute. The mites your sister is so fascinated with could cross the bay and march for the capital once more. You need a wife, sons, further our line."

"But I'm not the one being sent to North Ferga to find a wife. You sent Aveline instead."

"I've tried waiting. I wished for you to find your own wife on your own time, as I did your mother." Bartel said. "But I may have given you too much freedom. You smell of a brothel."

"Aren't young men supposed to bed instead of wed?"

"And have bastards run amok? My cousin, Hurvir, bedded ladies of the night, and look what happened. His wives' neglected. His only son not a lawful heir." Bartel rubbed his temples. "His only surviving brother without wife and children as well. My uncle didn't become king of Viguran for his line to end only with his sons. He went to start a dynasty."

"And you think your dynasty will end with me and Baldewin?" Bertin asked. "Just don't send me to the North. I know you enjoyed your time there, as much as you could, but I hate the cold. You know how I feel about our winter rains. Decaro with Baldewin could be fun though. I hear the island is beautiful except for the wind."

"And what's in Decaro? A wife? Training? Baldewin is there to learn to fish in the deep waters, not to father children or solve a crisis."

A crisis. Bertin thought with a confused face. *What in the warm embrace of Mother Meret does he have in mind?*

His father continued with deep breaths. "You must know how to keep the people happy, just ask my mother's watery grave what happens when you don't. You need to respond to their issues, no matter how small. Protect them and this kingdom from its enemies. I pieced Rowan back together after it was fractured. Could you do the same?"

"You know I could. You and Blis, and everyone else taught me everything I need to know," Bertin said.

Bertin's father locked eyes with him. Bertin could see the sadness and loss beneath them. His family's death, the war that made everyone in the kingdom turn on one another. All the death and destruction that was brought and how Bartel stopped it with even more blood. "I need you to learn more. I think it will only help if I send you away."

Not another threat. "I enjoy the scents of Attrima. Maybe Meera would be better. The vineyards are supposed to be marvelous. I'll even go to Maertan and brave the snow whipping across the steppe."

"No. There have been troubling reports coming from the West. The desert being attacked and overrun. The king of Telemaw is strong, descended from the house that united the many factions. He will show you the way to deal with problems. Deal with revolts and war." Bartel walked over to an old map that hung on the wall. It ripped and a corner had burned, but Bertin looked over all of Adedor with his father. The king's finger found a patch of nothing southwest of the Kash Mountains. Bertin refused to believe it. He kept his eyes away. *If I don't acknowledge him, then it won't happen. I'll just sneak back to the brothel on the western way. Forget my worries.* "I've already sent word to King Hasíb of Telemaw. He awaits your arrival in Vaandet."

Bertin couldn't protest. Nothing he could say would stop this. His father was stubborn and wanted him to learn to be more of a king in some foreign place. To command and conquer. Bertin would have to travel to a poor and dirty kingdom in the middle of a desert.

Ultiir

They carried him on a golden sedan through the old cobbled streets of the Noble Lands, built by elves, with their marble houses and sun-soaking balconies. Now, lords and ladies of the court settled there. Even the occasional whore of the King's Brothel could be found in a manse if she had enough patrons. The elves had been pushed out a thousand years ago when humans went to war for the Ters-Veck and its tributaries.

Ultiir imagined what it must've been like when the Veck'kop, so used to mud huts and grass roofs, stumbled upon this place. *No wonder they killed for it. Keeping all this to yourself.* He knew when the litter reached the Gods' Gift. The buildings turned to wood or painted stone; the streets were big enough for carriages and horses, and the domaton appeared with its four pointed corners.

The slaves let Ultiir out on the steps of the domaton. He told his guards to watch them and wait near Meret's Well. The domaton towered over the shops and houses around it, seven or eight stories tall. Much smaller than the elven palace he called home. Four statues topped the points of the star. Mother Meret's welcoming face looked down on all who entered from the south. He made his way up the steps with the chief of his household guard, Lovis, and another knight, Sir Lird.

Two slaves of the domaton bowed as the curved iron and wood doors parted. Lovis and Lird, both clad in copper-toned armor, waited outside by the door. Inside, the antechamber was lit by more slaves with torches. "Please remove your clothes." Ultiir partook in the normal routine. He stripped down and found a green robe with a gold star stitched to the front. A lower doma washed his hair with water from the Montla before saying, "The Four and the Many bless you as you enter their domain. May they help you find peace."

It was not peace Ultiir wished to find. He had a king to kill.

The grand hall beyond was lit by a thousand torches. His bare footsteps echoed as he made his way under the great curved ceilings made of stone, a hole in the center with a single beam of light shining where the high doma would give his teachings. Ultiir passed through the light and mingling people and lower doma. Behind the great room was a row of small chambers. The walls painted with scenes from the Book of the Four. Under a painting of Vigura raising a man from the River Montla was where the high doma would be.

Ultiir entered. The room was a mess of parchments and scrolls, a bed in the corner littered with copies of the Book of Swallow. Albon sat at a desk, his blue robe turning brown. "Ultiir." He put down whatever letter he had been reading. "Come to do penance?"

"In due time."

Albon's ears perked up. "Finally going to be like that sister of yours?" The high doma chuckled, "Where is Analere nowadays?"

"Helping the sick and diseased on Pleat. Said she wouldn't

be back for a while."

"I have been to Pleat Isle before," Albon seemed to shudder. "At least she is bringing Inta's practices to those people. Spreading the Four and the Many wherever she goes, receiving their favor."

Ultiir grimaced at the thought of Analere helping some pox-covered simpleton in the Nokys. "I have plans in the works to help the kingdom prosper. That should bring me favor with the gods." He tried to read the many parchments and saw that people were invoking the Four more than usual. "What's this?" He motioned to the mess.

"It's been hard since the war ended, even though that was fifteen years ago. The king …" he trailed off.

"My brother hasn't been doing the best. It's okay. You can say it, even the slaves in the fields are."

Albon stood. "I am not afraid of the leaders of man." He gave a letter to Ultiir. It was nothing but scribbles. "Some are preparing a pilgrimage. The king will need to be ready for hundreds if not thousands of worshippers."

"I'm sure we can accommodate that. I'll tell the council tomorrow."

"The king came in the other day," Albon stacked some books, "talking of his blessing for his feast and other matters. The slaves are hard at work getting the domaton ready, I'm sure the palace is abuzz with excitement."

Ultiir handed a book to Albon. "Excitement, yes."

"Walk with me." Albon stuffed some papers into the sleeves of his robe. The halls were busier, with people crying out to Meret for answers, giving thanks to Rana for bringing autumn another year, or cursing Ritera for taking a loved one. Some of the lesser doma were giving speeches or consoling weeping worshippers. Albon found a dark room where a slave with a gold necklace was sorting parchment. "Send these out." The high doma gave the papers from his robe and the slave nodded before leaving out a back door. "Messages to the high doma of Rowan and Terrop."

"I didn't realize you spoke after the split all those years ago."

"Emmett of Rowan was questioning the practice of idolatry as he always does. Averitt of Terrop and I are in agreement that whatever helps the common man to cope with this life is a good thing."

Outside the room, they stopped in front of a large mural. Ultiir knew what it was. Her fire hair lit the night as thousands fought beneath her feet, the goddess Matstia, one of the Many, leading a revolt from the sky above against the elven rulers, an elf-king's head in her hand. *Is she smiling upon me?* "How many complain about food?" Ultiir asked. Albon tilted his head. "Complain about harvests? The roads turning to mud? About the king?"

"Well," Albon stuttered, "there are a few complaints."

"I thought you didn't fear kings?"

The high doma straightened up. "Everyday someone complains while wagon loads of grain and fruit make their way through the city to the palace. Farmers blame His Grace for the lack of slaves and the lower yields from the harvest. They're worried we're going to be like Rowan. Slaves gone and the lowest man having to work the fields. I always tell them, 'Rowan and the other kingdoms have turned against the Four and the Many. Did they not use slave armies when at war with Veltoora? Our Majesty would never turn from them or live in sin.' That seems to calm them."

Ultiir listened with his brow lowered. "They wish him

gone?"

Albon slowly nodded. "Some even say they want a Vandes king back, though no one today was alive when the Betrayer spurned his people."

Ultiir thought of Valor the Betrayer. *What will my legacy be? Saving the kingdom from the destruction Hurvir caused? Stopping the wars and feeding the people?* A smile appeared on his face. "That's worrisome," he lied.

"Some also claim that King Hurvir has been cursed, the reason unknown, something he did in childhood. The destruction wrought by the war with the Rainvealandians and the famine that followed. I've heard his seed was tainted as a boy. The reason he has no trueborn sons or daughters from his many wives and only a bastard born from a whore."

Cursed by the gods. The child I could give Sophie. He had to hide his excitement as he said, "Awful." Albon was shaking his head, but no disgust touched his face. "But some true." He waited for the high doma to react. To talk of gods and kings. Nothing. "Most could've been avoided had he not gone to war. I loved my sister dearly, but it was no mite noblemen who killed her, just some merchant." He pictured sweet Philla's face. He was merely five when she died, but he missed her. She would always play at sword fighting with him in Goldfield. "Ealna would still be ours and not in the hands of the Maermen, we could allow slaves to be brought in. The food borne from harvests could feed families. Towns and villages wouldn't have burned." He waited. Nothing again. "All Hurvir."

Albon's eyes were watching Matstia, his fingers traced the rebels at her feet. "Some blame lies with the Rainvealandians."

"Of course." Ultiir waited to speak as a lesser doma and an

audience passed. "I wonder how these people would react if Hurvir were gone."

Albon spun around, his eyes bright. "Gone? Is the king sick?"

"It was merely a question." Ultiir took a deep breath. *I cannot let him know. The other councilors would have my head, my brother too.* "People often wonder if their life would be better with a different king, though that's not always the case."

"Some people would be happy and others sad."

Ultiir remembered the old high doma, Belfen, and the gray hairs that shot out of his nose and ears. That old man was always kind to him. Ultiir barely knew Albon. "What would you do if the king were gone?" He didn't want to use the word 'dead.'

"Whatever the laws and customs say."

"A bastard king?"

"Bastard?" Albon asked, his voice echoing in the hall.

"Hurvir's bastard in Rowan. Would he be the next king? Would the people accept him as their ruler, or would they turn to someone else?" Slaves made their way through the hall as Albon thought, his brow wrinkled, and Ultiir concealed his smile. *I need your support,* he wanted to say, *I need the support of the gods.*

"I believe you are next in line if the bastard does not declare himself in front of the lords, but I'm no expert in the laws of man."

Ultiir looked at the elven king's headless body behind Matstia. "Could you imagine? Me as king."

Albon took a step back. "The bastard will probably declare for his rights. What bastard wouldn't want to be king?" Now, Albon seemed to wait for a response. Ultiir didn't give one.

He stared at the mural. "These are dark questions you ask. The thought of your own brother dying must fill you with dread."

"It does." Ultiir walked to the grand chamber. Stepping over those who knelt in prayer. "But these are questions one must ask as chief consultant to the king. I must be ready for anything."

"Of course." Albon's voice was emotionless, but his lip slightly curled, his eyes darting around the room. *He doesn't agree.* He looked at the lesser doma that wandered the halls. *I need to find support elsewhere.*

"It was good speaking with you." Ultiir told the high doma as they found the front entrance.

A young girl with dirt on her face came to Albon with tears. "The water of life is empty, Your Holiness."

"Sweet child," he held the girl's face, "come." He went to where the Montla's water idled in a stone trough. He muttered a prayer, and the water refilled. "Vigura always sends life to us." The girl bowed, then knelt to pat water on her cheeks. Albon came back to Ultiir with a smirk. "I hope you pray to Meret for peace and your brother's health."

"I will." Ultiir stripped and donned his gold-stitched tunic, brown trousers, and pointed shoes before finding his copper knight outside.

"Did the Four help you in your journey?" Lovis asked as they went down the steps.

"They did not. I don't think they'd look kindly on what I want to do." The slaves and his other guardsmen came with the litter. "I need to speak with Lord Urses and tell him I need candidates for a new high doma." The knight nodded. Ultiir stretched his neck once in the sedan. *So much to do.*

Tundavik

They had traveled for days on horseback, Devro atop Fariage, Mar on Meadow, Raimund with Brun, and Tundavik with a skinny mare named Bera. Everything they needed was in the saddlebags. Food, clothes, daggers and knives, stakes for tents. It wasn't much, but it would last until Udello. The Gorthair people smiled when Devro and his knights vacated the castle and the city; the Rowai knights cheered when they left to go back to the capital and out of hostile territory. The cliffs and rocky hills gave way to flat plains and farmland. Coastburg was the first city they reached, and some celebration about the hanging of two Gorthair was underway. Dunniage was next. The Garden of the Four rising above the shops and homes, almost like the black cliffs in Gereduss. All port cities. Now they were riding south to Sea Snake. The only seaport in Terrop.

"We should've sailed." Tundavik grumbled.

"His Grace isn't fond of boats." Mar smirked at the young boy. "I don't think he's ever been on one."

Devro patted Fariage's side. "And I'm not going to start now. What's wrong with going by horse?" Bera shook her head as they walked through a black cloud of flies.

Raimund led his horse out of the way of an approaching

cart. The driver, with a piece of hay in his mouth and a straw hat to protect against the sun, waved at the four and said, "Have a happy Samosay day."

Raimund smiled back. "At this rate we're going to miss your father's feast."

Devro rode out in front. "But he'll still be happy to see me." The knights both stared into the distance. *At least they know Hurvir's true nature.*

They camped on the coast that night. One last sleep by the ocean before they headed east inland. Mar stoked the fire. Raimund cooked a rabbit he captured. Tundavik's nose filled with smoke. The burning scent of the cherry tree reminded him of desserts in Attrima, but he held his head. It had ached since entering Dunniage. Sleep didn't seem to cure it, only growing worse the more they traveled. He knew it was a good thing he was traveling to Viguran once again. Seeing the home of his people. His family. Ritaeum. He just thought his heart would ache instead of his head. The prince was reading from some old leather. Tundavik sat beside him. "What's that?"

"Some Rowai rubbish." He closed the book, and dust sprang from the pages. "About my grandfather's rebellion against his father. All lies. Talking about how monstrous he was. Don't they know how lucky they were my grandfather decided surrender was the best choice? He would've slaughtered them all."

"For resisting rebellion?"

Devro threw the book down. "What else should he do? His mother was murdered, and the people and the chancellery chose the king's side instead. How do all other rebellions end? A song and dance?"

"Mercy is always an option. My men and I didn't kill every Rainvealandian we saw, even if your father would've wished it."

"Maybe you should have." Devro took a piece of rabbit from Raimund. Mar whiffed the smell of the fire. The horses whinnied beside them.

"I don't think, even with all the hate in his heart toward the mites, that your father would have massacred all of them. What he did in Jorbstah was bad enough." Tundavik could still hear the pleas of those destined for death. "Just don't forget mercy." He took a small piece of rabbit and laid his head on his pack.

"You're trying to teach me how to govern, but I was trained since birth, and you haven't lived in Viguran for years to see how much worse the kingdom has gotten."

"And whose fault is that?" Mar added. Devro opened the book and hid his face, eventually falling asleep.

Tundavik's head throbbed as he and the others put away camp at first light. The waves crashing ashore sounded like he was playing in a thundercloud. The sun burned his eyes. Blue specks appeared in his eyes as quickly as they disappeared. *Udello is close,* was what he told himself. *That city is teeming with a thousand dakens.* They ate some berries as they rode south. Sea Snake only took a little over an hour to reach. The first sight was a galley being rowed into port. A carrack, with blue sails with a red snake twisted and hissing, guarded the port in the Seler Bay from any pirates or Rainvealandian attack.

Sea Snake wasn't much, certainly no Attrima or Rowan, not even Gereduss or Coastburg. Only a few clay homes and shops surrounded the port. The ships in the ocean taller than the tallest building. There was no grand domaton, only a doma who preached on the corner, with some man proselytizing in an unfamiliar language across from him. It sounded vaguely like Delerous, but was much harsher. Tundavik didn't think he had ever heard it.

"Looks the same from when the last time we were here." Mar told Raimund and Devro. "Terrop's *western pearl*." He gestured at the clay houses. They were no match for the elven marble of Vigur or the bricks in Gereduss. A sailor spat as they rode by. Wiping away any spittle. Others were smoking some leaves, more drinking and telling stories of women bending in positions nearly impossible to impress their lovers. Probably all lies. Tundavik had sailed in the West, catching and selling fish up and down the coasts; the women were never impressed.

"Best we steer clear." Raimund stopped Brun on the road, the others following. "I've heard nothing but bad things."

"In Sea Snake?" Tundavik raised his brow. "What bad things would happen in a town like this? There's nothing going on but dockworker gossip."

"The ship is here for a reason."

Mar yawned. "What a fitting end if I were to die in Terrop. I've been all over Adedor and tried my best to avoid this lousy excuse for a kingdom." He looked around the town once more, taking a deep breath. "Throw my body into the ocean; I don't want these people to touch me."

Devro chuckled. "We shouldn't stop anyway. Any detours and I'll miss the feast."

"May the Four guide us." Mar turned Meadow between the houses. "Are you going to follow? We need food." They relented and followed the knight into town, past quiet shops and small warehouses. A river ran right through the center. Not the Ters-Veck, that was farther south, but the Red Snake. It was small, not fit for boats, but the people filled buckets for drinking or to cook or bathe.

"You take stallions?" Mar asked a baker.

The woman was old, her flesh sagging, but she wore a glorious smile on her face. Enough to make even the saddest happy. "This close to the border?" She had a Terropian accent, a bit like the Rowai, more different from the Vigurites. "I'll take any coin you have."

Mar dropped from Meadow, Raimund as well. Devro sat on Fariage, watching. Tundavik dismounted Bera and grabbed the reins of the others, tying them to a nearby post. Eyes peeked out of wood slats over windows. Either they were afraid of newcomers or wanted some horses. He rested his hand on his new sword while Mar and Raimund found the bread they wanted and counted the coins. The prince overlooked all. Straightening his back and stretching his neck to look more regal. Higher than all.

He looked too much like his father. His blond hair, striking blue eyes. Tundavik could picture him older. Muscles and all. Leading troops to massacre innocents. Just like his father.

"It's good to walk the same roads as the common people." He called out to Devro. "So you know if a stone is upturned or roots are breaking through."

"These aren't my people." He rode Fariage over. The chestnut horse neighed as he approached the others. "I don't care if the people of Terrop are starving as long as my people are fine."

"A good way to make allies." Tundavik rolled his eyes as he took Fariage's reins and brushed the gelding with his fingers.

"You could always practice." Devro looked at the cobble below. The brown stains from dirt and shit. Water and piss flowed into the latrines. A naked family bathing in the Red Snake. Tundavik held out his hand. "Show them that rulers actually care. That they understand." Devro sighed as he kicked his leg over and dropped off his horse. A stray dog, fur matted and growing every which way, barked. "Not so bad."

"I guess not." Devro muttered.

The ground shook with every step Devro took, but no way a skinny child could cause the world to shake. People ran as quickly as they could from whatever was approaching the town. They hid in their homes and dove behind counters. "Well, this looks like it was a mistake." Raimund said to Mar as they found their swords. A cloud of dust and debris was heading toward Sea Snake from the east. Men were shouting from the carrack, bows being readied and smaller boats being dropped to send in infantry.

Dust settled, and a dozen men on horseback held up shields and spears. They were clad in green-dyed armor, their helms painted green, and their horses with green stripes near their eyes. It looked like they had just risen from the steppe. A man and woman, who looked to be a couple, and a few guards emerged from a nearby house that was painted white. The man wore a blue cloak with a red snake hugging his body, the woman with a dress that had a white bear and a red snake intertwined.

"Should I get back on Fariage?" Devro asked, sounding like a scared toddler.

The woman and man came face to face with the lead horse, its rider towering over them like a great oak. "I didn't think you would be visiting us after our last tribute?" The woman said. "I didn't take Greenriders for liars."

"Greenriders?" Mar said. "This far south?"

"The Maermen aren't fond of us," the rider said in a deep voice that echoed. "They confiscated our goods as soon as we crossed their border."

"So you traveled all the way here to steal more?"

"As you can see," the man with the blue cloak said. "We have protection now." The small boats were coming ashore, men with leather armor and clubs slowly making their way through the brackish water. "But this does not need to come to violence."

"Unless you wish it to?" The woman said.

"The last time we were here, we could've destroyed this marsh you call a home," the Greenrider said, "but we took pity. Now you threaten to fight us, Cada?"

Cada, the woman, laughed. "It won't be much of a fight. The king himself sent these men. The Maermen and Rowai won't have to worry about Greenrider raids any longer."

"I think I need to get on Fariage," Devro whispered.

"If you do not give us food and coin, we will blaze a trail to the Asara. Is that what you want? Deaths on your conscience?"

"As long as you leave Sea Snake alone."

The man in blue said, "We do not want anyone to get hurt. Why don't we talk it over? I can send the men back to the ship, and you can send your men to the water with some poles to fish."

"Fine, Sidoro, lead the way."

Sidoro led the rider into the white house while the armed men drifted away. "Should we be leaving?" Raimund asked. "I would like to get to Vigur in one piece."

"Travelers?" Cada overheard and walked along the wooden planks over the streams. "Heading to Vigur? I think I was invited to the king's feast, but I turned him down."

"Why would he invite you?" Devro chuckled.

"Why you?" She brushed her dark hair behind her ears. "Come from Rowan, have you? I assume since you don't look like mites. I guess that means you know about the Greenriders."

"We've heard of them." Mar said as he packed his sword and food away. "I don't understand why they'd come to Sea Snake of all places. Don't they usually stay near Caiag Rock?"

"They've grown bolder."

"Then you should send the men to fight while the leader is busy and their guard is done." Devro said, finally atop his horse. "That's what I would do."

"The townsfolk wouldn't appreciate that." Cada said.

"We really shouldn't stay." Raimund said. "Not with all that's going on."

"Oh that?" Cada laughed. "That was nothing but banter. Sidoro will clear it up and send them on their way. They think they scare us, but we have the backing of an army, and our people would die for us."

"That's always important," Tundavik said to Devro, who was clutching the reins of his horse and ignoring everything.

"Sidoro has a way of resolving things without bloodshed. That's why I like him." Sidoro and the Greenrider leader emerged from the tent quickly enough. Like this had happened many times before, and they both knew exactly what the other wanted in negotiation. Cada turned to her husband and clapped her hands. "Are we dead?"

Sidoro laughed. "Not yet. The Greenriders are going to go

back to Maertan once I get them passes. Until then, they'll stay and fish."

"Not our favorite food," Les said, "but it will do."

Devro huffed and pulled Fariage down the road to the east. "Guess we're leaving." Mar said.

"Enjoy your journey." Cada waved.

Tundavik caught up with the prince first. The road traveled along the Ters-Veck, more wagons and people appearing as they rode. "Didn't want to stay and find out how tentative that peace was?"

"My father is called the 'Warrior.' The Greenriders are lucky they don't go east over the Asara or my father would crush them."

"Well, the kings of Rowan and Maertan have been trying for years, not sure your father would fare better." Bera whinnied as a child ran near her legs.

"He would do more than that, Sidoro." Devro pushed his hair from his eyes, and touched his crownless head. "Letting an army come in and make demands like that? They'll keep coming back. The only way to stop it is to crush them."

Tundavik's head hurt again. The Ters-Veck roared to the south, cutting through the land and splitting the Rainvealandians from the Veck'kop. Nothing but grass ahead, not a single tree. Ritaeum was on his mind, as well as his bloodied hands. "Perhaps force isn't always necessary."

Raimund

Udello rose atop the foothills. The dark wood houses and shops towering over the walls. The mighty Ters-Veck roared as riverboats clogged the waters. He could hear the port sing the song of sailors from this side of the wall. It was loud. Much louder than the quiet roads behind them. He almost missed Sea Snake and the Greenriders. "Finally here," Raimund said.

"The worst city in the world." Mar kicked his mare forward.

"And why is that? What about Sea Snake?" Raimund entertained the knight even though he knew the answer. They said it at the same time.

"No brothels."

Devro snickered from behind. "I'm sure you can find one or two whores once dusk falls."

"Maybe I'll just stay outside the city tonight." Mar said.

"We already decided I will stay with the horses while you enjoy the *comforts* of Udello."

Mar flung the hair from his eyes. "How dreadful. Sure you don't want to join us? Some groomsmen will be happy to care for the horses."

"I'll take you to your inn and then come back outside," Raimund said. "It's better that way."

"The city won't let us carry swords." Tundavik said atop his mare. His hair was pepper and salt, once brown and now turning gray. His face had a few wrinkles, but he still looked young. Though his eyes always looked sad, even if he were laughing and drinking. As if something were missing. Mar had said he knew why the Duke Vandes wasn't a duke anymore, but he kept that a secret. *A first.* Tundavik pointed to a small group of houses and shops and a large building that looked to be an inn. "Perfect place for you, Raimund."

"Why don't we all stay here?" Devro asked.

Raimund didn't hesitate. "You're far too important. Your father would have our heads if we got you all the way to Udello just for you to be knifed in an inn."

"Maybe," Mar said quietly.

"I would let you stay out here, Mar," Raimund said as he pet Brun, "but I don't think you can go a day without your cock in someone's mouth. Our things would surely get stolen."

"I could make it a whole year."

Raimund rolled his eyes and gave a laugh. "I doubt you could swear that on the Four."

"I would swear to you." Mar smiled. "I hold you in much higher esteem than the Four and the Many."

Once they reached the small cluster of houses, they dismounted, and Tundavik went inside the inn to find a room while Mar spoke to a young, fat stable boy. The boy seemed mesmerized by the silver horse coin in Mar's fingers. "We don't usually accept Rowai coin, but ..." the boy trailed off. "I don't think my da will mind." Mar flicked him the coin, and the plump hand ran his finger over the engravings. "You can keep them here all day today and even tomorrow. I'll make sure no one steals anything from ya," the boy said. "But we sell them to travelers if ya don't come back."

"We'll be back." Mar rubbed the hilt of his sword, *Attana*.

"The innkeeper," Tundavik started, "is a bit crazed, but she accepted my coin and showed me the room for Raimund. You can toss your things in there."

"You don't think she'll steal from us?" Devro asked. "Especially if she found out who I was."

"Sometimes you have to trust people," Tundavik said.

"Can I stay out here?" Devro said as he looked at the towers over the wall. Raimund nodded to the others that he would wait with the prince near the stables. Mar came by to grab *Valkyr* and smaller knives Raimund had tucked away. Tundavik stuffed a saddlebag to hide coin underneath.

"Do you remember Udello?" Raimund asked. "We didn't stay here long, but the king and queen were kind to us."

"I remember. Do you think Arvon still has that bakery near the domaton? He always had the best bread, better than the palace kitchens."

"We'll be sure to look. It shouldn't be too far from where Gofrei wants to meet." Raimund said. He thought he felt eyes on him, but when he turned it was just the stable boy admiring his coin.

"It's been so long since we've seen him. Do you think he's changed?"

Raimund shook his head. "I'm sure he's the same fun lord who can buy you a boatload of wine from the West and play cards until his hands are numb." Raimund sighed. Lord Gofrei Geary was never his favorite person, always using his coin to make Devro happy when he sat on the King's Council and could have convinced Hurvir to allow him back. A lord who always spoke of his glory and prowess but never showed it, much like the other lords in Viguran. Truthfully, Raimund didn't want to go back there, especially the capital. *If only I could disappear into the mountains.* Instead, back to King Hurvir and his mood swings. His yells. His raised fists.

Tundavik and Mar eventually came back, and the four went to the city. The stone walls guarded by knights along the top and at the gates, confiscating any weapon a traveler had, promising to give them back. "You can search me, but I've nothing." Mar told a young guard. "We've been to this city enough times to know the rules." The guard did a quick check and let them into the capital of Terrop.

The people moved about the city like grass blowing across the Maera Steppe. Markets were open and swarming with people and pigs and bugs, beggars roamed the streets asking for coin or bread while thieves grabbed whole purses before disappearing into alleys barely large enough for one man, and shopkeepers shouted over the noise to draw customers. The buildings were newer than those in Gereduss. Polished wooden beams framed the houses, and the shops were made of stone but each painted a different color. Some blue, red, orange, yellow, and a few splattered with every color resembling rainbows.

Raimund wished the streets would part as they made their way through the crowds, but no such luck. Some spat, others cursed, but eventually the four reached the crest of a hill. Raimund saw an even larger crowd gathered at the bottom. He knew why immediately. A moat and curtain wall separated royalty from peasant. The people waved as a wagon led by a team of horses rolled by, guards pushing and beating anyone who dared get too close.

"Maybe I should present myself and we can get a nice room

there." Devro gave a bright smile and pointed at the castle. "I am a prince, and these are Queen Sophie's parents. She was always kind to me."

"You barely know her," Mar patted his horse and smirked, "though I wish *I* did. How Hurvir got so lucky I will never know."

"Try being a king." Tundavik said.

Mar's eyes grew wide, and sarcasm washed over his words. "I never thought of that. Maybe I'll pray to the Four."

"Shouldn't we find Arvon's bakery?" Raimund said, wanting to get away from the crowds. "If I remember right, it's near the domaton."

They turned down a road full of scurrying rats. Someone turned onto the same road, then another. Raimund let himself breathe as others followed. They must have been looking for a different path to take as well. The alley led them straight to a massive four-pointed structure made of marble, the only one in the city. Much nicer than the stripped and looted one in Gereduss. All kinds of people were on their knees, bowing low in the dirt-covered streets, praying to the four statues that adorned the four points of the star. Idolatry was forbidden in Rowan, and seeing people pray to statues reminded Raimund how long he had been away. "What do you think they pray for?" Devro asked as he tried not to hit the people with his bay.

"Ale and cunts." Mar said. "That's what I pray for when I see a domaton."

"Probably for the Four to send the mites to Veltoora," Tundavik said. "The changing of the faces is happening today south of the river."

"I've always found the Rainvealandians know how to feast."

Mar said.

Devro laughed. "My father's feast will be greater than any festival the mites throw."

"I'm sure it will be the greatest thing since the birth of man." Mar smirked. "This way, just around the bend."

Raimund grabbed for his sword hilt, forgetting it was gone, so he kept his eyes sharp. A person in the alley was still following them. He cursed to a Northern god and got in behind Devro. They turned the corner, and the whole city got quiet. The street was empty save for drunkards and rats and pigeons. Mar led them to the end of the street and stopped. The person was still following them. He was the only other person on this street, his steps getting louder on the cobblestone.

Then he walked by.

The man reached into a hidden pocket on his tunic and pulled out a key before going inside a wooden shack. Raimund let his breath out again. He wasn't paying any attention to Devro and the others until Devro said, "It's gone."

Raimund turned and saw a blackened building where the bakery used to be. The buildings around had char marks. Mar shook his head. "The best thing in the city gone, well after Tuck's Tavern that is."

"I can't believe it's gone." Devro said. Raimund could tell he was holding back tears. It was their first stop after King Hurvir sent them away. Devro was only seven, and Mar and Raimund were naïve to think it would only be for a couple of months.

They found another bakery, there was no shortage of them in the city, and shared a loaf of bread filled with raisins. Every once in a while they would have to shoo away a beggar or a drunk. The crowds had died down as the queen and king had reached their riverboat and sailed away.

They found an inn by the port. Bonfires raged across the river in celebration. Riverboats made their way upstream and downstream, clogging the Ters-Veck. Devro, Mar, and Tundavik were happy to have a room after days of traveling. Raimund could hear Mar's snores before he left the building.

***

Raimund made his way outside the walls. Alone. He had rarely been alone since Hurvir had sent them away. Unfortunately, he had to spend the night at the inn outside the city. The wood was clearly decaying, with pieces falling off and rotting to black. He stepped over an old gray, fat cat and went in. There was a whiff of mildew, and the walls seemed to be sweating, but the inn was better looking, with blue carpets and even velvet chairs, which were probably stolen from some nobleman's house. Old men with wisps of hair emerging from every orifice played cards and shouted at one another, a man with no leg begged for scraps from the cook, and the innkeeper, who only had one eye, was counting coins.

Raimund asked for a drink and sat alone in the nearly empty inn. "How long you here?" The innkeeper asked.

"Only a night."

The woman squinted her eye. "Only one? Just traveling through?"

"On my way to Tharet." Raimund lied, not wanting anyone to suspect he was traveling with a prince.

The woman spat. "Why anyone would want to go to that mite-infested city is beyond me. It will be a blessing when the king's done with them." She held out her hand. "You give me an extra silver, and I can make you breakfast." Raimund nodded and gave her the horse coins. A confused look washed over her face. "A Rowan are we? Is this the same silver we have in the Asara?"

"I suppose so."

The innkeeper trained her one eye on him, staring into his soul. "I guess it'll do." The coin disappeared into her ragged cloth. "Go upstairs. The third room on the right is yours."

As Raimund made his way down the hall, he noticed that most of the rooms were empty. *Good.* He didn't need any surprises, and perhaps he would actually get some sleep tonight.

He watched out his small window as the portcullis was lowered to enter Udello from the west. Anyone who would mean Devro harm had to have entered the city already. He ran a finger along *Valkyr*, the steel icy to the touch. The bed was small, his legs dangling over the edge, and it seemed to be infested by small bugs, but that didn't matter. Nothing mattered to him except the quiet. He could hear the occasional dog bark or vomiting from the tavern next door, but the inn was silent. The old men must have finished their card game.

After he drifted to sleep, his mind dreamed. He was standing over a fire, eyes looking back at him before they melted away. Udello faded into the distance as he was whisked away to the mountains, snow trapping his knees. *Help me!* he tried to call, but no words escaped his lips. Before he knew it he was drowning. The snow turned to water, which pushed into his mouth and filled his lungs. *Not like this.* He jumped from the seafloor and landed in a tree.

The sun shone over this tranquil place, where the birds sang, and the leaves rustled. A billowing creek called to him, and he made the mistake of going to it. A large shadow blocked the sun. Raimund looked up at nothing but the clouds and sky. *I don't want to leave.* He was standing on a map, looking over the cities and towns and rivers and bays. Red stretched across Adedor, then Khruhesh, finally Eotros and the rest of the known world. *Valkyr* landed at his feet.

Wake up.

Raimund's eyes opened. He was still in bed at the inn. He squashed a few bugs he could feel on his chest. His room was dark because of the new moon, but bonfires across the river looked like stars. *A fine Rainvealandian celebration.* He stood, lit a candle, and put his face near the glass, condensation forming from his breath.

"Only one bed."

Raimund whipped around and saw a shadow at the door, something in its hand. Raimund quickly found *Valkyr* with his eyes.

"There was supposed to be more of you. I've been following you since Rowan. Where's the others?" The man stepped into the moonlight. He was wearing all black, a hood covering his head, and he was holding a dagger. "I won't 'urt you if you tell me where the boy is."

Without thinking, Raimund lunged for his sword, but the assassin jumped in his way and stabbed the dagger toward Raimund's face. The knight caught his wrist and squeezed until the assassin's wrist cracked and the dagger thudded to the ground. The man kicked Raimund's shin and brought them both down. They crawled to the dagger, punching and kicking whatever they could find of one another. The assassin grabbed the dagger and raced to the door. Raimund yanked on the black cloak and kept them together.

It was the assassin's turn to whip around. He plunged the dagger into Raimund's torso. He could feel it slip between his ribs. Raimund cried out in pain before punching the assassin to the wall, giving him a bloodied face. Teeth rattled to the floor. Raimund let up to find his sword, but the man wrapped himself around Raimund's back.

No one could move. They were each fighting each other's strength. Blood dripped down Raimund's leg, leaving a warm trail of stickiness. He jumped back, crashing into the wall with the assassin on his back. He stood and went to the bed. The assassin groaned but stood as well. Raimund finally found *Valkyr*, turned, and shoved the sword into his throat, ripping out the other side.

Raimund brought back *Valkyr* with the sounds of gushing blood and the fresh smell of death. He took heavy breaths as he dropped his sword and crashed to the floor; the dagger sticking out of him.

Bertin

Why would I want to see the place I'm going to winter in? I'll have more than enough time to explore later." Bertin told Wilclef, who had woken him from a terrible dream about drowning.

"Captain's order," Wilclef smiled. *What prince takes orders from a captain?*

Bertin let Sir Gordo and Wilclef lead him to the helm of the ship, where Captain Lirk stood with Sir Robalt and a few of the ship's smelly crew. The ship was named something in the Delerous language, but Bertin and his guards, only the three who came with him, called it the *Voyager*.

"A real beauty." Lirk pointed over the calm Dìvara Sea, much better than the rocky waves of the Western Ocean. Bertin looked with tired eyes. Vaandet, the capital of Telemaw, looked much better than the cliffs of Gereduss or the rocky shores of Decaas back in Agaal. A colossal statue, bigger than even the palace in Vigur, loomed over the docks and piers. A few fingers were missing, but it looked to be made of solid bronze and held fire in its hands. The city behind the statue rose and fell with the small hills and valleys along the shore. More ships and river vessels continued onto the river that lay to the west of Vaandet, the Ginosa. Bertin had enough time on their weeks-long journey to study every map the captain had aboard. The prince could now name the major cities, some trading routes, most of the rivers, and every mountain range. When they sailed through the Urva le Strica was when Bertin stopped counting the days.

As they neared the city and the crew was running in preparation to dock, the houses and shops came into view. Rows and rows of dense buildings made of clay and brick and stone as far as the eye could see. The shadows shaded the heat from the streets below, and Bertin could make out people crisscrossing every which way.

He dabbed his brow as the air had gotten stickier and he sweated too much for one person, let alone a prince. Wilclef continuously dabbed his own brow with a handkerchief until it started to turn brown. The shipmates pretended not to notice, but Bertin saw how they snickered behind the prince and his entourage's backs.

As the ship docked and the captain and his crew disembarked. Bertin and his men followed closely behind. Below was a veiled woman with a few guardsmen and horses. The guards carried flags with a scorpion. "Kingsmen." Wilclef whispered.

They all slammed their spears onto the ground as Bertin made sure his small gold crown could be seen. Some passerbyers stopped before being ushered off by the guards. The woman offered a parchment, the sheer orange veil hiding the details of her face, but Bertin could hear jewelry clanging together. The wind picked up as she cleared her throat, a bit of sand blowing over them. "Lakin Hasíb la Untura is thankful that you would make the long journey from your kingdom to meet him," she said in a thick accent, "and welcomes you to his kingdom of Telemaw. His Descendant of Emperors will gladly feast and entertain with you tonight if you would so accept."

Bertin nodded, trying to keep his eyes from rolling. "Of course I accept. I traveled a month to meet him."

The woman bowed her head. "His Descendant of Emperors welcomes his friends from the north."

The guardsmen showed Bertin and his guards to their horses, and the woman led them on a white mare. Gordo leaned toward the prince. "North? Who's going to let him know we are not Heller?"

Bertin whispered back. "I don't think that matters much."

The streets were more crowded than Bertin could see from the ship. There seemed to be no order, but everything worked. Children darted in front of horses but were never hit. Carts either carried goods or important-looking people who used fans to cool themselves. Women shopped at bakeries while travelers hawked wares from the other side of the desert. Some shouted in Delerous from atop crates and had piercings in their ears and noses. *The Three Kings,* Bertin thought back to his studies about the western religion. He figured they were shouting about the end times or calling for prayer like the doma did in Rowan.

Eventually, they turned their horses down a long arcade wide enough for fifty carts side by side. In the middle were various statues of shape and style; all the men had crowns. The supposed 'Descendants of Emperors'. At the far end of the arcade was an ornate building made of granite and limestone, with a domed roof and flags of scorpions everywhere. Hundreds of people walked the shops along the arcade. Some watched as Bertin with his crown passed, but he didn't feel unsafe like he did in his own capital. He had never heard of the Telemese turning on their monarchs.

Many women wore veils and dresses of different colors, some red or yellow, others blue or green. The woman who led them was the only one wearing orange. Bertin even saw some women bowing their heads as she rode by. The men also wore long clothes to cover their skin. They mostly wore baggy white shirts and trousers with a hat only exposing their faces to the heat. Others also wore veils like the women but not sheer. Children ran chasing one another; Bertin even saw some stealing from merchants. They darted under horses and through people's legs into back alleys no bigger than two men abreast.

The buildings were all dusty and covered in sand. Bertin held a cloth to his nose. A Telemese guardsman saw him and gave a bright grin before speaking with a heavy accent. "Sandstorm season, Your Highness. Agaales is spreading the winds throughout the desert." He pointed to a large circular building to the east. "King Agaales' temple. The winds are always rough during His months."

Robalt smiled at the temple before marveling at a collapsed building of brick and plaster before being pushed on. "Ruin?" Bertin asked.

"I'm not sure, but hope so." The knight took a deep breath and then coughed up dust and sand. "To think, some of these buildings have been here for over a thousand years. Not constructed by elves either, like our ancient buildings, but by humans." He shook his head in disbelief. "Wondrous."

Bertin rolled his eyes but smiled. *I guess only girls and ale make me that happy. Am I turning into Sir Mar?* Bertin shuddered. *I hope not.*

Their host stopped at the foot of a hundred steps to the palace atop a hill. A palanquin was brought and the orange-veiled woman climbed aboard. "Your Grace." She patted the spot next to her.

Bertin was glad to jump up with her. He could barely see her face, but knew beauty was hidden under her veil. "If only we had this in Gereduss." He said to his guards before the big men carried him and the woman up the stairs, the guards following on foot.

"Do you enjoy the palace?" Bertin asked the woman. She only nodded. "I think you'll like it more with me here. I hope your king is more fun than the stories I've heard."

"What stories?" She asked in her thick accent, the words slow like honey.

"We only hear of him disciplining those of his house who embarrass him. A cousin of his who was banished for having an orgy in the ruins of the palace in Salvalone. Hopefully, he doesn't discipline me."

"His Descendant of Emperors is a kind man, a just man. He would certainly not admonish a man of your stature."

Bertin straightened his back, trying to keep his head from bobbing as the men carried them up the steps. "I think we will spend a lot of time together this winter." He wanted to believe she was blushing, but the veil hid all.

The door was as large as a hundred knights stood atop each other. It was made of solid oak, and he wondered where they got the wood. The orange-veiled lady stepped off the palanquin and motioned them to a smaller door, more human-sized, where they entered the palace. Bertin felt like they were going in a circle as they crisscrossed many small halls and chambers. He kept on the orange lady, never falling behind.

"His Descendant of Emperors apologizes for the inconvenience," she said, "but the use of the grand doors is only allowed during the changing of the seasons and when a new king is crowned."

"Unfortunate I'm not important enough." Bertin almost ran into a marble wall. "I'll just be glad when we get to the throne room."

As if his wish was granted, the woman turned right, and they were in a marble and bronze chamber that echoed with every footstep. Pillars encircled with gold kept the large domed ceiling above their heads. Blue and orange stained windows lit the entire room. A stone seat atop a marble base rose on the other side. Images of scorpions decorated the throne as if they were about to attack. A dozen guards stood in front of the marble with spears.

Bertin and his guards were told to stop while their escort continued across the room. He straightened his crown and wiped his brow. The sound of stone sliding thundered into the chamber. Another dozen guards came out, these in all black armor. Behind them, a tall, skinny man with dark features wearing a pointed gold crown found his place on the throne.

A herald cleared his throat and shouted with his deep accent that made it almost hard to understand. "King Hasíb the Sting, Descendant of Emperors, Keeper of the Desert, Leader of House Èmaw, and Greatest of the Ginosa is pleased to welcome you to his palace."

Bertin stepped forward. "And I, Prince of Rowan, am —"

"How was your journey?" The king said. "Any trouble on the seas?"

"No … um … not at all." Bertin stammered. "It was just very long."

"Long, don't I know." Hasíb laughed. His accent was not as bad as the herald's and a little better than the orange lady. *Maybe a sign of education.* "I've never done the journey north because I hate sailing. In fact, I've never been farther north than the *Urva la Stria.*" He said the words in his southern dialect. "The furthest I've been from this palace was a trip east to *Rainvilon,* I believe you call it, Attamek."

"My sister has spent time in Attamek." Bertin tried to make conversation. "Mostly in Suktir."

"I will say I was surprised when I received the letter from your father asking me to show you my ways." The king rubbed his long black beard. "I think I am the first *Denemic* king to receive word from the north."

"My father has always had respect for the kings of Telemaw and the way they keep the Saysyki away."

King Hasíb swatted that away like a bug. "The *Agariloni* are a backward people who believe taking land this side of the, uh …" he paused to translate. "Ginosa will bring them greatness. It is my job to put them down like the dogs they are." The king took off his pointed crown, handing it to a nearby servant. He descended the marble steps and unveiled the orange woman. "Thank you, Farzia, for welcoming the guests."

"It was my pleasure, Father." She bowed, and Bertin gulped as he saw her beauty. She looked nothing like her father except the same color hair. Her skin was darker, and her eyes pierced through Bertin. *Is this a ploy to get some marriage alliance? Not that I would complain.* He tried not to stare at the newly unveiled Farzia, but her looks were magnetic. *I've been talking to the princess this whole time, and she seemed to enjoy my company,* he smiled to himself.

"Why do you not show the prince's guards to their quarters?"

"Tì patro." She bowed her head once more and gathered Wilclef, Gordo, and Robalt.

The king grabbed Bertin's shoulders. "I will show you my favorite view in the whole of *Denemi.*"

They left the guardsmen behind and went to a spiral staircase behind the throne room. The ascent was steep, and Bertin was tired of walking up steps when the king pulled a latch and opened the door to a balcony. Bertin followed onto the limestone floor and took in a better view of the city. He could see atop every hill and into the valleys. The city wall lay to the east and was made of bricks of limestone the size of wagons. Bertin smiled at the sight. At the thousands of people below, all going about their day. *Rowan doesn't have a view this nice. Only grass as far as the eye can see.* The wind picked up, and Bertin rubbed sand from his eyes. Beyond the city wall, a cloud of sand and dust blew westward toward Vaandet.

"Agaales is never happy." Hasíb pointed to the sandstorm. "Do not tell the dicaré this, but he is not my favorite of the Three Kings." The king laughed and rested his arms on the wooden railing. "It is nice to have the respect of a northern king. Most of us feel no one hears news from this part of the world. Do you know how often we must fight off Kruheshian pirates and slaver ships from who knows where?" Bertin shook his head. "We protect *Adèlon* and no one notices, but at least I get this." He motioned to the city below. "I have also heard great things about your father. They tell me he reconquered *Marobol* when the peasants revolted."

"Yes, it was an ugly time. My grandmother, the queen regent, was killed."

Hasíb spat. "I hope your father made them pay for their crimes. If my people rose up against me, I would not stop until every one of them was put to death." He clenched his fist at Vaandet. The sandstorm moved closer, and the skies darkened as the sun moved behind the cloud. The city quieted. Bertin had never heard thousands of people be so silent.

"So this is normal this time of year?"

"Like I said," Hasíb pointed to the same temple as the guard before, "blame Agaales."

"How long will Vaandet have to deal with the sand?" He didn't want to spend all winter inside, breathing dust.

"Until Notoro's winds begin."

"It will be interesting staying here and seeing how the people react. I'm not sure I can handle that much sand. I've only ever seen it on the coast."

Hasíb let out a quiet laugh, as if he didn't want to disturb the peace. "I hope you get used to it. *Lìsn Biresdea* is only accessible by sand."

Bertin held his breath for a moment. *Did I hear that right?* He remembered the maps he had studied. "Lisan Biresdea? In the middle of the Delerous?"

"Oh yes," the king shook his head, "I do not think you will be much help if you stay in Vaandet. Your father wanted you to learn. What better experience than helping with the protection of the city?"

"I don't have much training in fighting off bandits and thieves. I thought maybe you wanted a marriage alliance."

"You want to marry me?" The king's laugh pierced the air.

"I am flattered, but my wife is on a trip to Edio and will be back soon." Hasíb rubbed a tear of laughter from his eye. "And my daughter, excuse me for saying, would not want to marry some northern prince; she wouldn't even fuck one if I demanded it." *Then what am I doing here?* He wanted to say. *Please do not send me away. Please.* "You will have little trouble with bandits. *Adèkhas* have been attacking traders and settlements in the desert. They began in the *Kitìb* and have spread east. Lìsn Biresdea may be their next target."

"Adèkhas?" Bertin went through his memory trying to find the word in any of the books he read.

Hasíb laid his hand on Bertin's shoulder. "I believe you call them elves."

Tundavik

The daken changed Raimund's bandages for the second time today as the morning sun washed over them outside the inn on the outskirts of Udello's walls. "I can do this myself." The knight winced as the daken secured the white wrap into place.

The daken wore a white overcoat that stretched to his black shoes, and he had a blue cap atop his bald head. "I'm sure you can, but can't ever be too careful." The daken threw the old bloodied bandages into a latrine and handed Raimund his tunic and extra bandages. "You can change your dressings from now on. I hope not to see you again." He said with a smile, as if it were the funniest thing.

Mar helped Raimund to his feet, shaking his head. "Sad that a knight of Viguran was almost bested by some hired killer. He looked like the wind could blow him over."

Raimund massaged his ribs, wincing as he did it. "He got worse. I'll be cleaning *Valkyr* for days." They grabbed their bags and headed to the stables. Tundavik could hear Bera whinnying from inside and saw Devro brushing his horse in the yard.

"I still don't understand why anyone would attack you." Mar said.

"I already told you," Raimund said with a deep breath, "he was looking for Devro. It was a good idea to have him stay in the city. He said he's been following us since we left. Maybe that's why I felt someone was watching us."

"Don't give yourself too much credit." Mar said.

"He probably stayed near the horses because he thought we'd come back." Tundavik looked around the little town against the wall. The people were going about their day, shopping and cutting wood and weaving blankets. No one paid them any attention. That was good.

"Who do you think sent him?" Mar asked.

"Maybe Gofrei has some explaining to do." Tundavik said, trying to remember if he knew this Lord Gofrei Geary. If all accounts were true, Lord Gofrei seemed like Mar with more power. A drunken, spoiled, lazy man with too much gold.

"You think the King's Council invited Devro to his father's feast after sending an assassin after him?" Mar said. "Just kill him at the feast."

"Maybe things changed," Raimund said.

Devro came running over like the child he was with a large smile on his face, seemingly naïve to the world. "Does this mean we're ready to go back into the city?"

"Let me give the stable boy my pack. For enough coin, he should watch all our belongings for the day." Raimund went into the stables.

"Is he going to be all right?" Devro said as he watched Raimund holding his side.

"Just a scratch." Tundavik said. "Nothing to be worried about, but you should stay close." They weren't meant to leave the city walls this morning, but Raimund never meant them at the inn, so they had to go looking for him. The one-eyed innkeep had already called a daken and was cursing about the blood when they found Raimund.

Mar patted Devro's horse. "Where did Gofrei say to meet? With any luck, it will be in a tavern. I need a few drinks before the ride to Vigur."

"Some inn at the port. It's supposed to be the most magnificent on the river." Devro answered.

"I was hoping for something less conspicuous." Tundavik rubbed his eyes. He had slept terribly, every sound waking him from drunkards on the street to Mar snoring. If that assassin were smarter, Devro would be dead, Tundavik knew. They had no weapons to defend themselves. He looked around the farmhouse and the fields. No one paid them any mind, at least he thought. He hadn't seen the assassin yesterday or any day before that. How many more could there be? The thought of eyes always on him reminded him of his old home, Ritaeum.

"You find the fat kid?" Mar asked as Raimund exited the stables.

"Wasn't there, and I even gave him a silver piece." Raimund shook his head. "It was some old man instead. He told me he would watch over our stuff like his life depended on it."

"It might." Mar commented.

"He even swore on Vigura."

"Nice man." Mar gave a mocking smile.

The four left their horses and their weapons to the stable hand, though Tundavik had a hard time trusting that. He kept an eye over his shoulder, but the hand brushed the horses and didn't take a sword to market, so that was good. He even saw the fat boy from yesterday, missing a hand and crying. Raimund commented he didn't know what all that was about, but Tundavik thought it had something to do with the silver coin.

The city was bustling as ever. It reminded Tundavik of Attrima, except Udello didn't have a sea breeze or salt in the air. He thought about how worried Glodsteil would be, probably thinking Tundavik had drowned at sea. Maybe one day he'll return and bring the dwarf a cart of salmon from Ortan. He smiled at the thought.

The port was packed with workers, sailors, and fishermen. Fish and crab were slung around, crates were unloaded from the river boats, men called out offering discounts on ferry rides across the river to see the festivities. A caged wagon rolled past, holding what appeared to be Rainvealandians who were pleading their innocence. A doma gave a sermon to a crowd of people, yelling about Veltoora and Vigura's wrath. Another across the street was offering his services in assisting peasants in their pilgrimage to Vigur.

Devro smiled as they pushed themselves through the crowd of people. An ornate stone building painted purple cast a shadow on them. Fish fountains dotted the plaza in front of it. Pillars swirling with color held the ceiling and created archways to the central courtyard. Men were wearing only the finest tunics with gold seams and buttons made of rubies. The women wore silk dresses with their hair styled high above their heads in the latest fashion. Guards walked the perimeter, pushing the less desirable away and shooing away merchants trying to sell fake jewelry.

Tundavik looked down at his clothes. His boots were ripping at the toe, his trousers were covered in dirt, and his tunic was missing buttons and ripped seams. His hair was matted and sticky with sweat. It didn't help that they smelled like horses everywhere they went, that even the beggars kept their distance.

"We need to have a word." Tundavik pulled Devro back before he confronted the guard. Raimund and Mar stayed back as well. "We need to talk about the assassin before we go dance with Gofrei Geary."

Devro looked dumbfounded. "Gofrei? Why not tell him about the assassin? He's smarter than he lets on, probably knows what to do."

Tundavik looked at the two knights and back at the young prince. "Lord Gofrei may have had something to do with the attack." Devro was going to protest, but he closed his mouth. "No one else knew we would be in Udello but Gofrei and the council. This assassin just makes his move the day before we're supposed to meet with him. It's all highly suspect."

"Maybe the assassin didn't want me to see Gofrei. Did you think of that?" Devro said as if it were the smartest thing. Tundavik had thought of that, but why not see Gofrei? All the stories had made him out to be a drunkard who somehow got too close to a king. "And I don't believe Gofrei would hire an assassin. He told me war stories. Lord Geary always rode into battle before his house."

"I think it would be best if you waited outside." Raimund shifted and winced. "Just until we figure things out."

"And miss seeing a friend?" The prince crossed his arms. "Not happening. I will see Gofrei and will face anything he throws at me. Which won't be assassins."

Tundavik looked at Mar, who shrugged, and Raimund, who shook his head in disappointment. "Just stay close to us. We don't have weapons to protect you."

"And he doesn't have weapons to attack me."

They entered the inn and spoke with the owner. She grimaced but sent them down a hall lined with landscape paintings of Terrop. A few of the Asara Mountains on the northern border, covered in snow; some of flat fields and dense forests; others of the Ters-Veck, the lifeblood of the kingdom. They entered through a gilded door. Large windows with iron bars filled the room with light from the courtyard. A middle-aged, clean-shaven man wearing gray clothes sat at a wooden desk. Mar shut the door behind them and locked it.

Lord Gofrei looked at Raimund a second too long before saying, "I wasn't expecting all of you to join Devro on this visit." He studied Tundavik's face, his eyes searching like an owl. "I don't believe I know you."

"Tundavik Vandes."

"Vandes … Vandes …" He tapped his chin. "Are you by chance a descendant of House Vandes of Ritaeum?" Tundavik had to force a nod. Gofrei showed off his yellow teeth and looked at the others with a smirk. "I hope you've been doing your studies, Devro. This man probably has more royal blood than you."

"Enough. The de'Tro family has been on the throne for almost two centuries." Tundavik didn't have to look at the bastard to know he was eyeing him. Tundavik cleared his throat. "We didn't come to exchange pleasantries."

"No, you didn't, it seems." The dark-skinned lord turned to the knights. "Mar, still keeping the brothels warm in Gereduss?"

"Every night. Unfortunate we left."

"And Raimund," Gofrei paused, "it's been far too long since we've last seen each other. Every time I visited Gereduss you were never there."

"I was in the city, but made sure not to be at the palace when you arrived. I don't like you." Raimund didn't mince his words, and Tundavik couldn't help but snicker.

"That's never been a secret." Gofrei's head swiveled around the room, his eyes locking on the barred windows and locked door. "But I *do* have a secret for you all. That's why I called you here."

"Does it have to do with my father?" Devro asked.

"Very much so." He forced a smirk while he was glared at. "You see, the King's Council is full of those who play their own games. Any other time, there are fifteen different plans that all collide with one another into a burst of flames until your father deals with it." He paused. Tundavik knew it was to drag out the story. "It just so happens that many of the plans this time have one goal. To bring down the de'Tro dynasty."

It was as if all the air was sucked from the room. The only noises were the muffled sounds of birds and people outside.

"Kill a king." Mar stifled a laugh. "Did none of them see what happened to Rowan just twenty years ago? The throne falls, a queen is hanged, and the whole kingdom goes to shit."

"They saw," Gofrei went on, "but they also saw what Hurvir did during the same time. War with the Rainvealandians and thousands upon thousands dead. Thousands more from the famines that followed. An increase in spending that the decreased population brought on by Hurvir's wars cannot pay for. Rowan collapsed when they had famines following the wars with Nowexerts. The King's Council is terrified of what could happen in Viguran when the peasants miss a day of bread."

"They're worried for their heads, not for the peasants." Devro said. Tundavik watched the boy. *Surprisingly calm considering he just found out his father is to be assassinated.*

Tundavik leaned in. "When is it to happen?" The lord cleared his throat and played with his fingers. "Are you going to say?"

"I would rather not, but since I must." Now everyone leaned in to hear the foolish lord speak. "On his feast day."

"I believe that is blasphemous." Mar mocked before putting his hands up when Devro glared at him. "I'm just saying killing the Four's anointed one on the day of his birth will not go over well with the High Doma."

"And you're sure all the councilors want this?" Raimund finally spoke up from behind them.

"Well, if any of them have changed their mind or had reservations, they haven't told me."

Raimund quickly crossed the room and put his hands on Gofrei, backing him into the window. "All councilors?"

"I can only … do so much when … faced with that much … support." Gofrei coughed, and Raimund relaxed. "I have stalled as much as I can. They wanted to do it on Vigura's Feast, and I tried to make them wait until Swallow's. They want it done soon so they can deal with the coin issue and give people their food."

"Noble," Mar quipped.

Gofrei continued. "I came here to warn you. I knew they were going to kill you the moment you entered Vigur. The council thinks I came to 'escort' the queen's parents. They have no idea we're speaking, which means you can go live your lives somewhere peacefully."

Devro sighed and spoke to Raimund. "Back away from

him." The knight obliged. "So, we should turn back to Gereduss? Back to a life of exile."

"What else is there?" Raimund said. "At least King Bartel should offer you protection. Maybe invite you to the capital."

Mar laughed. "I think death would be better than that city."

"No." Devro silenced the room. "We must challenge these councilors who think taking my father's life will fix their problems. We will march on Vigur before the feast and save my father."

Gofrei's eyes went big. "That would mean war."

"That's what kings do." Devro stood as straight as a wall. "They fight their enemies until they come out on top. That's what I'll do."

"Y-you cannot just de-declare war." Gofrei said with wide eyes. "You need supplies, allies, weapons. You have none of that. I came here to warn you. I don't want to see you all die, not even Raimund. Marching on Vigur with just the four of you will surely mean not only your father's death but your deaths as well."

Tundavik sat back watching them discuss war like children. He thought back to Ritaeum; his wife's face flashed in his eyes, then the king's. He had a silent fit of laughter. *I guess you didn't live that long after all, Hurvir.* Tundavik pictured his children playing in the forest. Laughing as the guards chased them up and down the trees. His eye twitched from a headache.

"I would rather go to Veltoora," Mar was saying as Tundavik tuned in.

"If Devro wishes to avenge his father," Tundavik said, and the children quieted, "then that's what we'll have to do. I was a lord for many years. I still know people in Viguran. If that means a detour to see Ritaeum again, then so be it."

"You want to go to war?" Raimund asked, stunned.

"He doesn't have a choice." Devro said. "Unless he wants to go scurrying back to Attrima and never see his home again."

Tundavik didn't know what he wanted. A dead Hurvir made him happy, but the possibility of Devro on the throne worried him. *A child. A child raised on beatings and whores. What a terrible idea that would be.* "Gofrei, who is the Duke of the Lands of Asara?"

"David Rely."

"Then I can get you allies." Tundavik smiled, though he didn't know what for. He smiled the last time he went to war too, hoping to bring glory to his family's name once again. But it took everything from him.

Bertin

The storms are our enemy during Agaales' reign. We worry about the heat when Baraga takes the throne." Safír had said in a slightly different accent than the king. He was their guide through the Delerous Desert. Bertin and his three guards rode on camelback with Safír in the lead along the Empire Road, which wasn't a road at all.

Bertin had asked him where he was from. "*Cìdinalo. Salvalone.* King Hasíb, bless his ancestors, will tell you lies that Vaandet is greatest." Safír smiled and showed his yellow teeth. "But you have never seen Salvalone. That is a city that makes emperors."

"Have you visited the ruins?" Robalt asked. "The ruins of the empire?"

Safír laughed under his beige clothes that kept the sand and heat off him; only his eyes could be seen. "Of course. Maybe I can take you there once this business in Lìsn Biresdea is finished."

Robalt's back straightened. "That would be greatly appreciated."

Bertin's one-humped camel swayed with every step she took. Bertin had felt queasy at first, not as bad as Sir Robalt, but after five days of travel on camelback, he started to like it. The camel huffed and hummed, almost sounding like a horse. He had never seen a camel before. At first, it scared him, kicking at Gordo sideways. Now, he named his Marobol, after the Delerous word for Rowan. He slept near her at night and spent all day patting her back.

Marobol grunted, and Bertin looked ahead. A sea of sand stretched in front of him for hundreds of miles. There was no quick escape. Safír scanned the horizon, looking for any trouble. He seemed to be made of muscles, which Bertin found calming, and his eyes were dark as if they had seen war. *Just like father's eyes.* Gordo's hand seemed glued to the pommel of his sword. "Still nervous?" Bertin asked his chamber guard.

"Brigands like the desert," Gordo looked behind them, "and now there are elves attacking cities. Not a safe place."

"When was the last time you heard of an elven attack?" Robalt asked. "They don't do that in Rowan."

Wilclef snorted. "We drove them out; that's why." He rubbed his stubbly chin and said, "The Pywaln Uprising? Those mountains could never have been recaptured by the Rainvealandians."

"That sounds right." Robalt said. "I guess it makes sense the elves would revolt now. The mites made it seem like elves could do anything they wished, even conquer humans. Like humans haven't driven the elves into hiding for over a thousand years."

"Should make whatever fight there is easy." Gordo puffed out his chest.

Safír shook his head. "Cluo was retaken during Baraga's reign. The adèkhas attacked from the east in the last of Notoro's months. It is said they thought *Jorbson* was attacking.

The king, bless his ancestors, was rightly worried, and called for any in the Kitìb to take up arms." Safìr patted his curved blade. "We drove them out, but not east. West. The elves attacked villages and towns along the *Hayaa* until they disappeared into the desert. Some travelers have seen them moving farther west. That is why the king fears for Lìsn Biresdea. It will be a bloody fight."

"The king, bless his ancestors," Robalt added, "said Lisan Biresdea was a fort for the emperor that they would go to if Salvalone was in danger."

King Hasíb had sent them at night from Vaandet when the sandstorm passed. The city was quiet, save for the camels. Wilclef had protested the move to Lisan Biresdea, and Bertin prayed to every god King Hasíb would see the error of his ways, but he listened to no one and couldn't understand the issue. "Lìsn Biresdea is where the emperors went for safety. Seeing the city defended from an adèkhas attack would be an honor." The king of Telemaw said. "You can explain our practices and training to your father so he may never worry again." Bertin wanted to say goodbye to the princess, Farzia, and her beautiful, large eyes, but she had disappeared into the palace, not wanting to commiserate with a *northerner*.

Safír nodded. "It is not as defended as it once was. Thousands more pass under the statue of Aldrico than ever before. I've heard rumors of the oasis drying."

Bertin chuckled. *A liar for a king? Why am I not surprised?* "Just the place I want to go." He kept laughing to stop his worry. "I could have been making Sir Mar proud in Vaandet, but no. This king," Bertin made it sound like a curse while Safír gasped, shook his head, and made a gesture with three fingers, "decided to send me to a potential siege in the middle of a shit long desert."

"Nothing will happen." Wilclef said as his camel swayed. "You'll be able to enjoy the bathhouses and cooling rooms."

Bertin said. "You believe that?" Wilclef didn't answer. Bertin found his pouch made of rabbit skin and took a swig of water. He wiped his brow. *The heat or nerves? Why not both?*

Safír yelled out, "The Three Kings have blessed us." Bertin looked up and saw the sliver of a date palm. *Water.* The camels didn't pick up their pace like horses, but they reached the oasis soon enough. Bertin refilled his rabbit skin and washed the sand off his clothes to keep from itching. The camels drank next to him as he washed. Robalt and Wilclef bathed while Gordo and Safír stood watch. Anyone could descend on them. *No oasis is safe. Maybe I should have turned King Hasíb down. Then where would I be?* He pictured Farzia. Her beautiful smooth skin and long black hair. Her orange veil that added to the mystery. *If only I could be there. She would change her mind if she spoke to me more. Saw the greatness everyone in Rowan sees.*

It was Gordo's turn to wash while the others filled their skins and wrapped cloths around their skin. Safír did not move. "The sand washes me." Was all he said. Bertin wondered what their escort would smell like when they reached the city.

"We should stay here tonight." Bertin suggested as Gordo clipped his sword belt to his waist. "The camels will be happy."

"No," Safír said, "it is too dangerous. An oasis attracts people you do not want to meet."

"We've been sleeping on the sand for days. Wouldn't it be nice to use a leaf as a pillow?"

"We must journey farther at night, away from the heat." Safír did not argue often, but he was stern. "Let us continue."

Wilclef patted Bertin's shoulder to come along. Touching the trunk of the date palm, he thought, *what I would give for a wooden bed.*

The sun had started to set when they left the oasis. The dunes and rocks created shadows that grabbed at them. Bertin licked his lips, which had become wet from the water. "How big is the oasis in Lisan Biresdea?"

"The largest," their guide said. "The city sits atop the isles in the water, and the Así oasis is close too."

"Enough to swim in?"

Safír smiled. "Yes, the children do it all the time."

Bertin kept thinking about Farzia as the sun fell and a piece of the moon rose. *We could've been watching the stars. Telling each other the names of constellations. Swimming naked together in the oasis.* He looked at the night sky with a grin, but it wasn't the same without a beautiful woman. Some stars blinked at him; others shone bright all night, as if they were staring at him. The moon and stars did very little to light the way, but Safír knew where he was going. "Notoro's star always shows the way. It points to Cìdinalo from anywhere in Denemi. We follow that from Vaandet and we reach the oasis."

Gordo was drifting off to sleep, but kept waking when his camel jerked. "I thought we would be there by now."

"You slow us down." Wilclef snickered. "Always snoring."

"Funny," Gordo said, "I seem to recall you not even making it through our first night."

"Tomorrow." Robalt called out. "We'll be there tomorrow? Right, Safír?"

"I believe so."

"It can't come soon enough." Bertin rolled his eyes. "I'm tired of dumping sand from my boot." He looked around the desert, only making out dunes. *No bandits, no elves.* "Why don't we stop here?"

Safír stopped his camel and checked his surroundings. "There is no protection. We must find some rocks."

"We'll be fine." Bertin jumped down from Marobol onto the sand. A cloud of dust rose around him. "We have tents."

Safír sighed but agreed. They got their tents from Azma, the camel carrying all their belongings. The tents weren't what Bertin was used to. They popped up some sticks and laid a cloth over the back to stop the wind, leaving the front exposed to the sand. The camels bent down. A well-earned rest from the day's travels. Wilclef took the first watch, to the complaints of Safír, and the rest went to sleep.

Bertin lay awake looking at the stars. He made out the constellation of the Rowan tree and thought of home. When his father and mother showed Baldewin to Aveline and Bertin when he was just born. The ugly pink the baby was. He smiled at the thought. His father had never smiled so big, at least not since Bertin was born, he was told. King Bartel now had two heirs. Aveline cried to Blis that night about her place in the world while the lords and chancellors celebrated the coming of another male child. Then their mother jumped to rocks.

He sat up and saw Wilclef's back. He was huddled in a blanket near the camels to escape the cold night. Bertin shivered as he kicked through the sand. "Did you think we'd be in the middle of the desert when my father told you to accompany me? I bet you'd change your mind if you knew."

"It is my duty to protect you." Wilclef said.

"You know you don't have to lie to me."

Wilclef sat up and sighed. "My honor is the most important thing to me. I would never let your father send you anywhere without my protection. Not Gereduss, not Viguran, not the desert."

"I'd rather play in sand by the water though."

Wilclef nodded. "That I agree, even with my hatred for beaches."

The moon was shrouded by a cloud, casting the world below in shadow. His protector's face disappearing save for the white of his eyes. Bertin knew Wilclef had failed before. Failed to stop the queen from jumping to her death. He would never fail again.

"Do you trust this king?" He asked when Wilclef looked at him. "Trust that he's not sending me to my death?"

"You've heard the stories. The House of Èmaw care only for themselves, not even their own people like them." Wilclef played with the sand. "They've been plagued with revolts, both elvish and human, as well as border wars with the Saysyki since the tribes united. He tried to make it seem like the elves had never attacked before. That is worrying." Marobol huffed. "The Alhya River gets raided almost every year by the ancient ones. This isn't much different. Hopefully, the travelers are wrong about Lisan Biresdea. That no one is coming to attack it." Wilclef shrugged. "But who knows?"

Bertin watched Safír's chest move up and down. "He was supposedly in Cluo and saw the elves attack along the Alhya, but wasn't the one who saw them go west. Even he could be lying."

Wilclef grabbed Bertin's shoulder with a dropped face. "Not to worry. You will see your father again, I promise."

"I'll wake Gordo so you can rest."

"No. Let everyone sleep." Bertin didn't argue and crawled back to his tent.

Sometime in the night Safír had taken over for Wilclef because the guide's screams woke them. "We must hurry!" Safír was throwing together his things and packing Azma. "We need to find rocks!"

Bertin sat up and watched as his guards did as they were told. "What for? Bandits?" He began to take down his tent.

"Worse." Safír pointed east into the darkness. *"Ih la Mat."* His words were mysterious, like he shouldn't have spoken that name. "Storm."

"I don't see anything," Robalt said.

"That does not matter." Their guide was climbing onto his camel. "It is coming. We must find rocks."

Bertin put his things into the pack atop Azma, but still saw nothing. *Can this man see in the dark, or has he gone mad?* Gordo helped Bertin to Marobol, and the others climbed their camels as well.

"Follow." Safír made his way into the night, making sure not to climb the towering dunes. His camel began to trot as Safír yelled and kicked at it. Azma and the other camels quickly followed suit. Bertin bounced with every step Marobol took, wanting to vomit. Safír kept shouting, and the camels kept following, making more noise than before. They were scared.

A bit of light began to peek from the eastern horizon. *Sunrise already.* But the new light helped him see what Safír was worried about, and what he wasn't lying about. A wall of dust and sand as high as the Aita Mountains in Agaal rolled over the dunes with nothing to stop it. It looked like a wave ready to break apart on the shore.

"Ih la Mat." Bertin said to himself.

The camels ran, but there was no outrunning the solid wall of dirt. "Find rocks! Quickly!" Safír shouted, but the desert was empty. The sky seemed to turn back in time. The sunrise only helped for a few minutes before it got dark again. Wilclef pointed to a small cluster of rocks and shouted over the increasingly loud sound of the wind. Safír changed direction, and the camels followed.

Bertin didn't dare turn around. He didn't want to see the encroaching wave, but he knew it was close. Sand whipped at his face, and the wind bellowed in his ears. *I will not let sand kill me.* The rocks doubled in size as they approached. Marobol was racing. He heard a crack and then was flying into the sand. Marobol cried out in pain, and Bertin saw she had tripped over a rock sticking out from the ground. Safír was almost to the red, jagged boulders, and his guards turned around for him. Bertin climbed to his feet and went to the camel. She tried to stand but kept buckling. His heart pounded against his chest, trying to break free.

He looked up.

From the ground to the sky, a straight line of sand and wind stretching miles across descended on him. His guards called out from a distance.

There was nothing. It was only blackness. He lifted his wrappings to his face as the whole world vanished from him. He breathed as little as possible, for every breath filled with sand. Even with his mouth and eyes covered, he could feel the grains making their way into his lungs and into every wrinkle of his skin. He took a peek from his wrappings and couldn't see his arm in front of him. The wind screamed at his ears. He couldn't hear his men or Marobol. Only the sound of sand pushing into him and the occasional pebble hitting his head, feeling like a punch from a tourney fighter. He decided there was no reason for him to be stumbling in the dark. He lay down on the sand and wrapped himself like a cocoon. *I can make it out of this. I am the heir to the throne of Rowan. They would laugh at me if some sand and wind killed me. Farzia would laugh at me.*

***

He didn't know how much time had passed. When he opened his eyes and took off his wrappings, sand fell from every crevice. Then he saw Gordo kneeling over him. "He's all right." Bertin tried to sit up, but his body fought against him. He was sore. He was thirsty. The sun was beating him down. Wilclef ran over and poured water from the skin into his mouth. Bertin smiled as the coolness spread throughout his body. Relief. Robalt and Gordo helped him to his feet. He stumbled, but finally stood.

The camels surrounded them, but Marobol was not there. He saw Safír wiping blood from his curved sword. Bertin knew what had happened. Safír must have seen his look. "She was in pain."

"I know."

Robalt was wiping sand from Bertin's clothes. "We saw some travelers in the distance. Lisan Biresdea can't be that far."

"If you're ready." Gordo said.

Bertin only nodded. "You can ride Azma," Safír told him. They carried him to the camel. Bertin's legs stung as he sat.

"How long was the storm?"

"Too long." Wilclef answered. "Maybe two hours or more."

Bertin shook his head in disbelief, sand falling all around him. "I'm still alive."

"Why wouldn't you be." Gordo made sure that Bertin had more water. "A bunch of sand won't take the Prince of Rowan."

"We should hurry before Ih la Mat returns." Their guide said. The guards nodded, and the camels began their journey.

Bertin kept his eyes closed for most of the ride, praying for rest. If Azma were more graceful, he might have fallen asleep on his back. Robalt kept him company. Telling him about the darkness he saw when the storm passed over the rocks. The camels were scared, but stood strong. Safír looked Ih la Mat straight on. The rocks had kept them from being pelted by pebbles and sand and the harsh wind. Bertin rubbed his head where little bumps made themselves known.

"We were worried." Robalt told him. "Getting caught in any storm is dangerous, but this…" his voice trailed off. "It stretched to the Four's domain. I've never seen anything like it. Not even the great waves from the Western Ocean compare."

Bertin opened his eyes, and the light burned. "I'm glad you all are all right as well." Tears formed, but not from sadness or happiness, from the sun. His vision was blurry. Barely able to make out who was in front of him.

The sand beneath the camels turned from smooth to hard, like a road had been carved between the dunes. Safír was visibly happy with a smile. Wilclef and Gordo looked relieved. Robalt said, "Finally."

They passed an outcrop of rock and between two large sand dunes. When they emerged Bertin saw another statue of a man. And a city beyond.

"We must pass under Aldrico," Safír said.

He called for the camels, and they followed. The statue of Aldrico rose above a limestone wall. The flat roofs of town just barely seen and disappearing as they went closer to the gate operated by a dozen guards with spear points that reflected the sun. Safír handed a guard a paper and said, "*Alre noi invila volentar.*"

The guard looked at the paper and then back at the company. "*Uto hamali lasci.*"

Safír nodded and told them to give the camels over to the handler. They grabbed their things and said goodbye to their companions. *If only you were Marobol.* Bertin thought as he patted Azma. The guard ushered them onto a small boat made of reeds. It didn't feel stable. Not like the riverboats in Rowan. The gate was opened, and the oarsman moved the boat toward an arch on the closest isle.

The city was built on the oasis, as was said. Reed-made boats clogged the waters between the isles. Clay and limestone buildings lined the shores. As the boat passed under Aldrico, Safír said, "Do not look up. It is bad luck."

Bertin didn't look up, but back at the closing gate. The so-called fortress had only the wall and waterways to protect it, not much different from any other city in Adedor. He could see men walking with spears, but only a few, not enough to handle a whole horde of elves. He didn't feel any safer in Lisan Biresdea than he did in the open desert. And he hoped the king was wrong.

Ultiir

U rses de'Marisco handed Ultiir a parchment. The small corner of the palace was dark, but a stained window nearby lit the names of all Urses had found. "I did countless hours of research to find the most popular doma in the realm." Ultiir read it in the light of a yellow-stained window. "The top, Ulte Vandos, is well respected, but—"

"—but a Ritae." Ultiir finished the lord's sentence. "That won't work." Never had a Ritae person been elected High Doma; only those of Veck'kop descent were allowed, and that wouldn't change now.

"There is the doma of Forecreak. The birthplace of your grandmother and not too far from your own lands." Urses said as he rubbed his nose and leaned on a column.

"I know of Maller. I used to see him as a child."

"If I may, what of the doma in Goldfield? I believe his name is also Urses."

Ultiir shook his head, reading the names on the list. "I can't be too obvious. Anyone from Goldfield would give me away. Anything else about Maller?"

Slaves and pages hurried down the corridor. Ultiir didn't wish to be seen by many people, especially if they saw the parchment. Sir Lovis was to tap his metal boot if anyone important enough came by. "This Maller has preached the importance of following the king's laws. I've also heard of a sermon he gave that denounced bastards as demons from Veltoora who Vigura will punish when they pass. Rumor has it he has a few of his own. I believe your mother is fond of him."

"Hopefully, I could make him see reason if he was the High Doma." Threatening a head of his religion would garner him no favor with the gods. *If I must,* he thought.

"I must say," Urses wiped a dirty hand on his black cloak, "this is rather dangerous. If anyone else found out you were trying to overthrow the High Doma ..." he paused. "I think there would be a revolt on your hands."

"I fear we'll have a revolt regardless." Ultiir folded the parchment and stuffed it into his tunic. "There will be supporters of my nephew."

"Even if he's dead?"

"Especially." Ultiir looked behind him. Sir Lovis was whistling a song about a knight riding a dragon into battle. "They'll never have seen if he were a good ruler. In their head he would have been perfect, the second coming of Valor the Iron. But you and I both know he would cause nothing but hardship."

The Lord of Keeland nodded. "Like his father."

"Any revolt will be put down quickly, and they will see that I am a good ruler, giving them bread rather than taking it."

Sir Lovis tapped his foot. Urses disappeared into the shadows as Ultiir turned to leave. Lord Masson walked by, waving. Ultiir smiled and said to Lovis. "Might we go to my chambers?"

Ultiir and Lovis went down the long corridors lit by stained sunlight, and climbed stairs to reach his bedchamber. Sir Lird and other guards stood around watching the slaves as they cleaned.

Ultiir lay on his bed once in the room, not caring if his golden cloak wrinkled. *Only a few days. Then, my brother will be dead. I wonder how Father feels about this, his miracle child killing the heir.* He drank some spring water and ate a bit of bread he still had from yestermorn. *Hurvir should never've been king anyway. Had Wyclef and Olmar not died …* He stopped his train of thought. No need to soil the memory of brothers he never knew.

"I am sorry, Father."

There was a knock at his door. Ultiir stood, brushed his clothes off, and said, "Come."

Sir Lird brought in Sufar, an old man, wearing brown robes to signify he was a slave. "My lord," the slave said, "your brother, His Grace, has invited you to hunt in the Ritaewood."

Ultiir nodded. Sufar, who had been his slave since coming to Vigur, slipped the linen and blue overgarment onto Ultiir, then pushed the knee-high boots onto his feet. "Send for me if a member of the King's Council needs me." Sufar bowed his head at the words. Sir Lovis came in behind Lird and followed closely behind his lord as they made their way to the stables.

Cipan's hooves dug into the dirt as Ultiir rode his black stallion on a narrow trail. Sir Lovis was behind him, riding his spotted mare. The shouts and screams of hunters sang through the thick canopy of the Ritaewood; squealing boars belted their calls for death, dogs barked for the meat from the bone. *Who doesn't love a hunt?* He thought with a roll of his eyes. His horse broke through some loose leaves, and a lake glistened in the sun. Vigura's Wrath. A tent of red and gold was off to the side. Banners whipped in the wind, owls with a bundle of wheat in his talons.

Hurvir sat on his great white mare, the sun bouncing off the horse's coat. Named after their mother, Rila, the mare ate a carrot from a slave. Dozens of guards stood about. *Waiting on me. How kind.* Ultiir never liked hunting. It was dirty and bloody and reminded him of the forced hunts he had to do as a child, trying to kill the boars that ravaged the wheat fields around his home of Goldfield.

"My king." Ultiir said, bowing his head while on the saddle.

"Fuck the formalities, brother." Hurvir laughed. "It's a hunt."

And with that, a horn blew, shaking the trees awake. The guards mounted their steeds, huntsmen and their dogs set out into the thick wood, and Hurvir called for Ultiir to ride beside him. They would take in the views of the forest. Hurvir was too old to hunt.

"Are you ready to eat boar and deer at my feast?" His brother asked. "If we're lucky, we'll have some elk too."

"Lord Dovi Lyons has ordered birds from Eotros and horses from Kruhesh. We don't need these dirty meats."

Hurvir waved a tan-gloved hand. "Nonsense. It is a feast in Viguran, so we'll eat food from Viguran."

"I guess both will do." The wood was thick, the grass blotchy from lack of sun, wildflowers grew in bushes, small animals ran as the giant horses trampled. Hurvir called out for the guards to move farther away. *That means a talk.*

"I regret we didn't do much together when we were younger." Hurvir said, his mare trotting over dead branches.

"Not much time left."

"You are older than me, had more responsibilities. Goldfield was fine with Analere."

Hurvir waved his hand. "That place was awful. There's a reason I haven't been back since my coronation, though I do feel slightly bad when Mother comes to visit. So frail." Hurvir stopped Rila, his guards quickly stopping all around, their chains rattling. The king dismounted. Ultiir watched from atop Cipan while his brother picked up a red leaf. "Samosay is sending autumn toward us." He smelled the air. "Things used to be easier back when I was younger. A new king. Full of strength and pride. The kingdom was united once, when we were at war in the South." *And starving,* Ultiir thought. "The Flewthlands didn't yearn for independence; the governors of Redington allowed us to use their port; even the Lodean scrambled down from the mountains to help in our struggle. Now, the kingdom is divided. More than ever."

"You've put down rebellions in the past. You can stop more."

Hurvir laughed. "Remember when the old Lord Blume wished to attack my ships at sea?"

Ultiir chuckled, his sweat not from the heat of the day. "You aren't planning a war, are you?"

"I'm too old to fight." Hurvir patted Cipan, Ultiir looked down on his brother. "They used to call me 'Hurvir the Warrior.' Now, I'm just an old man with a poisoned seed. No trueborn sons to carry on my line. You don't have any either. What would our grandfather think that the name de'Tro dies with us?"

"There's still time." Ultiir trotted forward, trying to get away from whatever Hurvir was feeling.

His brother looked at fallen branches. "I heard you saw

my wife." Ultiir didn't move his head, only facing forward. "Gossip travels. Is this why you haven't married?"

"Queen Sophie is twenty-two years younger than I am." His cheeks were red like the apples on the trees. "I did not know her for most of my life, so she would not be the reason." *Our marriage would be grand. I would've given her sons to be proud of.* "I just haven't found a good woman," Ultiir said. "And I have many years left." Ultiir wiped his brow as Hurvir huffed. "What is this, brother? Are you sick? Dying? Do I need to be prepared to sit upon the throne?"

Hurvir sighed. "Fifty-seven years ago, I was born. I believe it was Swallow's third day that month. So much has changed. This kingdom was still weakened from the war a century before. Then the Nowexerts came, then we fought the Rainvealandians. Yet, I still have no son. Only a bastard." Hurvir kicked Rila to quicken her pace. "I intend to grant Devro all my rights and privileges, name him Lord of Goldfield and heir to the throne."

Hurvir sped past on Rila, leaving Ultiir with no time to speak. He wiped away tears that had been forming as boars screamed out in pain.

***

"The bastard." Ultiir wanted to shout, but couldn't risk gossip spreading throughout the palace, so he just talked to himself. His face burned with either anger or sadness; he couldn't tell. Hurvir wanted to plunge the kingdom into another war. Another war caused by him. Thousands could die. *All because of that poisoned seed.* "He wants to make a bastard the king? Upending hundreds of years of tradition."

"I have a sense you're angry." Gofrei was at the door with Sir Lovis and Sufar.

"I'm sorry, my lord," Sufar said quietly as he bowed his head, "he insisted."

Lovis spoke up. "He said it was urgent. I told him you were busy, but he said it had to do with matters of the state."

Ultiir waved them away except for the Lord of Montlahead. "Please tell me it is done."

Gofrei swayed on his feet. "About Udello—"

Ultiir threw a goblet to crash against a decorative sword. "The bastard should be dead. Hurvir is going to name him his lawful heir. He claimed he did not want rebellion but now he is going to get it. Bastard children from all around the realm will rise up and demand their fathers give them what they think is theirs. The lords who do not wish to see a bastard climb so high will take up arms against Hurvir and Devro." Ultiir took a swig of water. His brow was sweating and his heart pounding. Taking a few deep breaths, he said, "What of Udello?" *Do I really want to know? Did Gofrei betray me to a bastard child?*

"I parlayed with the Margias, as I was told by the queen, and heard a strange rumor that the bastard had left Gereduss and was riding to Vigur. I assumed he would show up in Udello, but he never came."

Ultiir rubbed his temples. *Convenient.* "You think my assassin killed him?"

"Or Devro decided against seeing his father. Maybe we'll get lucky and he's sailing west as we speak. Though I heard of a scuffle outside the walls. Some inn had a murder. Maybe …" he trailed off, pulling forward a wooden chair to sit.

Ultiir couldn't show his true feelings on his face, how little he believed Gofrei and how angry he was that his bastard nephew was still alive. The feast was too near for Ultiir to have doubts about Gofrei. "I guess we'll find out when the king sends for his son."

"And why would we let him do that?" The lord leaned in to whisper. "Your brother will be dead in the coming days, will he not?" Ultiir nodded. "Then the message will never be sent. The bastard, if alive, will think nothing of it, and won't be here to invoke the Bastard Law. You, my lord of Goldfield, will be king."

"Then let us hope he is dead." He rubbed his legs through his brown trousers. "And hope no lord rises in rebellion in the name of the king's son."

"Why would they? The Bastard Wars devastated this realm, they want to repeat that? Every lord's bastard crawling out of the shadows like last time, untold numbers dead?" Gofrei shook his head. "No, the masses will cheer your name when you depose the Warrior, the one who has brought so much pain and misery to their lives. They will name you savior."

Ultiir smiled. "No one knows you are here yet?"

"The Margias decided to stop in Clear Port for the night. Absolutely unbearable, the lot of them, wanting to meet as many lords and ladies as they can before the feast. The reason we're late." Lord Geary picked at his nails. "We stayed in Tharet for two whole days touring the city to see how the old mites' homes were being demolished to make way for the Veck'kop. I couldn't get away fast enough. Told them I had things to take care of, and doubtful they miss me much anyhow, I believe I drank all their wine stores. And the only people who saw me enter this palace were Lovis and Sufar. Both can be killed." Ultiir's eyes grew big but Gofrei laughed it away. "Was a joke. I think this plot has stripped you of humor."

"Regicide and fratricide aren't humorous things."

"They can be." Gofrei stood. "I will be by the docks until tomorrow, so I can make a lavish entrance." He brought over Ultiir's tossed goblet and straightened the blade. "I hope the Four smile upon us during the feast, otherwise we'll end up in Veltoora." The door opened, Lovis standing guard. "I can't spend eternity with you."

Before the door closed, Ultiir said, "Lovis."

His stiff guard came in. "My lord?"

Ultiir walked over to the fire. Images of war and revolt danced in the flames. "You will protect me?"

He heard a small huff. "Of course, my lord, with my life."

Sophie

Sweating under her burley, Sophie dabbed her brow. It wasn't hot out; in fact, the autumn breeze that Rana blessed them with kept the day cool, a far cry from the heat of Anreo's summer. The sweat came only from nerves. She stood on the steps of the domaton, the great four-pointed building towering over the homes nearby. Thousands of knights, household guards, and city watchmen created a perimeter to keep people out; vagrants and miscreants had been tossed away from the steps. The high doma was giving a speech behind her. Telling the lesser doma their roles.

Her stomach twisted when Hurvir finally strode to her side. *He will die today.* What worried her most was her own life. Would the councilors let her live? If Ultiir had any say in the matter, she would wake on the morrow, but if others' wants and needs took precedence? She would end up failing her parents. Failing her ancestors.

"My queen." Hurvir kissed her cheek, the same one he had beaten so many times. He wore a fake smile as lords and ladies passed. She saw too many to count. Lords from Viguran and of the court she knew well, but lords had come from far and wide. Northmen with their skin paler than snow, Deleri with their entitlement of being descended from emperors, and others from the central kingdoms. Rowai and Maermen, Awarites and Plajulish. Comforting was seeing the lords from Terrop. Enne Veytet, Duke of Ladau; Uma Bray, Duchess of Cedawr; Hilar Ecole, lord mayor of Tharet; and dozens of other lesser lords and ladies. It almost felt like home. Like she was a little girl again at a feast in Udello, being fascinated by the moat that surrounded the palace and wanting to explore the world.

There was no better sight than that of her parents. The only other king and queen to celebrate Hurvir's feast. King Anvrin and Queen Evna. Her father wore a white cloak, as bright as the snow that topped the Asara; a dark tunic with a white mountain etched to the front; and a golden crown he only wore on special occasions. Her mother had a silver crown encrusted with sapphires atop a white veil, and a long green dress with sleeves that brushed the ground. Keeping tears at bay, she embraced them when they finally made their way over the cobbled streets. "Welcome back to Vigur." Hurvir shook her father's hand. "You haven't been since the wedding."

"We've been waiting on a child." Her mother interjected. "I pray Frya is good to you next year." Hurvir only smiled. He had surely heard the rumors about his poisoned seed, and even the goddess of fertility couldn't fix it. "It's good to come to this city anyhow. We should have made pilgrimage years ago and prayed for peace."

"Your mother," Anvrin started, "is worried the mites will invade Tharet. Free all their Rainvealandian brethren." He looked to the Lord Mayor Hilar. "I tell her not to worry. The more mites we push out and crush, and the more Veck'kop we move in, the lower chances of Rainvealand involvement."

"No talk of war or mites." Sophie smiled. "It is my husband's feast."

"Of course, my darling." Evna said. "It's been too long." She embraced Sophie once more. Hurvir turned to talk with some island lord, and her mother whispered in her ear. "I have a healer from Teeraj that does wonders. He may be able to help with pregnancy."

Sophie watched for Hurvir's eyes, but he was busy laughing. "I do not think this king can be helped."

Her father took Sophie aside, away from her husband. "Viguran yearns for a prince. My advisers tell me the people pray to the gods for a successor."

"Your child would be most beloved." Her mother said.

"His brother is the Lord of Goldfield." Sophie tried to find Ultiir in the crowd, but he was missing. *Plotting.*

Anvrin huffed. "A wifeless and childless brother. Just pushing the problem of succession further along."

Sophie blushed, thinking of Ultiir's desires. *What would my parents think if they knew what Ultiir wanted from me?* "I know how much you want a child from me, and trust me I have tried many times over the years, but there is a bastard successor."

"The gods laugh at bastards." Her father's brow lowered. "The last time a bastard sat the throne of Viguran, war broke out. And I'm sure Hurvir fucked more whores than the one in Caiag Rock."

"Father." Sophie made sure Hurvir was still occupied. *I know he did and still does.* "We should talk about this some other time."

Evna pulled her husband's sleeve. "I see Peliz." Sophie followed her gaze to the Grand Duke of the House of Awaran.

"We should greet him."

Anvrin yanked himself away. "I would rather fall in a pile of shit than speak to that man who thinks himself above me. Thinking the mites should hold Tharet."

"Not here." Evna pleaded. "Maybe he wouldn't care so much about Tharet if you two spoke."

"Go, father." Sophie pushed them to Peliz. Her father's face was red, but her mother was able to get him over to the Grand Duke. Closing her eyes, taking a breath, she tried not to think about what was to come. Then Hurvir snuck up behind her.

"We should make our way inside." He held out his arm.

She nodded and grabbed it. As they went into the domaton, she only thought about how nice he was acting. *Maybe if he were like this all the time, he wouldn't die today. Maybe we would already have a child, and my parents would be happy with me.* She remembered her fear. *I cannot die today. I will not.*

The many lords and ladies filed into the grand chamber of the domaton, all beneath the southern eye of Meret. *Watch over me on this day. I beg of you.* Shuffling past lesser doma and the slaves that washed their robes, the king and queen found the dais where Albon was waiting. Sophie had often called on Albon for strength while in Viguran, much nicer than Averitt, the high doma of Terrop. He knew everything and more. And he knew what Hurvir had told him in confidence. The perfect person to lead the king in his final prayer.

Once the room was silent, and the hushing had stopped, Albon cleared his throat. "Thank you to all who could be here today. Before the feast begins, I must give the blessing from the Four and Many." Albon closed his eyes, followed by the lesser doma, then the people, at least those who believed in the Four. "I pray to the Mother above, Meret, to heed our words and give the other gods our thanks. We are in an era of peace; our lands are strong with harvest; the people full from the bread you give. We thank you, Meret."

"We thank you, Meret." The audience echoed as they opened their eyes, but not Sophie, not even with Hurvir's arm around her. *If the people were so full, the council wouldn't be planning to kill the king. I've given bread to the poor. Please spare me*, she thought to Meret.

Albon read from a parchment certainly given to him by her husband. "Over a century ago, the Betrayer destroyed this kingdom, bringing death and destruction to those within. But, by the grace of the gods, the de'Tro dynasty was born, and the lineage was strong. Now, we have King Hurvir de'Tro on the throne, and he has ruled with strength and by the sword. Vanquished his enemies and destroyed armies. Viguran, and this holy city, would be gone if not for King Hurvir. We must all thank the gods for sitting him upon the throne." Albon motioned his hand.

Hurvir turned and bowed to the crowd, to applause and reverence. He took Sophie's hand and made her turn too. Overlooking the lords and ladies, she spotted Ultiir. The Lord of Goldfield was in a serene-like state. As if he were floating above all. His eyes glistened. *Has he been crying? Crying for his brother? Me?*

Once the cheers died down, Albon cleared his throat. "I will lead the final chant." The high doma took a burning candle from another, and his eyes looked to roll back. Sophie had only seen the final chant once before, at her wedding. The high doma would call for a more sacred blessing. The one given when the Four fought back their enemies of Veltoora. Back then, the final chant brought mountains crashing down and rivers to dry. Today, only the breeze came through the hole in the domed ceiling.

Albon trembled as he shouted. "We alwn rásta te gren of goade tu gaim ar fiannes armè." The lesser doma took up the chant, even some in attendance who knew the old words. Sophie waited for the world to shake. But the gods had other matters that day, and she could sense Ridara's presence; the goddess of death hovered over her husband.

Once they made their way outside the domaton, the lords and ladies piled into carriages and wagons and palanquins. Commoners stood along the road, cheering or jeering depending on their view, as the nobles sliced through the city streets to the gates of the palace. It wasn't a far ride, but the winding roads made it feel like sailing a river. Hurvir rode ahead, making sure to be the first one at his feast, surely to change clothes. Ultiir was close behind. They made eye contact as the slaves helped them through the palace gates and to the convergence of the Montla and Ritae, life and death. Where the feast would be held. The king's brother cozied beside Sophie.

"Did you enjoy the ceremony?" His eyes were red to match her dress. "I found Albon's words spoke to many of us."

"It was lovely." She spied Hurvir speaking with some lord. *How much longer?* She thought as she rubbed her head. "I didn't see you until Albon was almost finished. Did a lord or lady catch your eye?"

"Only one lady caught my eye." Ultiir smiled, and she blushed. *He won't kill me. He couldn't live with himself. I think he truly wants me to be his queen.* "Lord Gofrei arrived earlier from Udello. He was telling me of his travels. The rivers were calm as he followed your parents here."

"I need to go back someday, not that it's changed much, but it was my home." The lords and ladies filed through the gate and found their seats along the river. Sophie took a deep breath. She had to calm herself. "When was the last time you went to Goldfield? Seems you're always at the palace."

Ultiir waved a hand. "Sometime last year. Only because a small slave revolt broke out. I said hello to my mother and left soon after."

"And the reason you hate that place?"

"The same reason my brother and sister do." He gulped. "Not much fun remembering the past. Let's look to the future. Wondrous things await us."

She said, "Is that so?" as they arrived at the hedges that marked the feast area.

"Just wait and see." Ultiir disappeared into the crowd.

Lord Gofrei Geary was caressing some lady from a small hamlet. When he saw Sophie coming near, he shooed her away. "My queen." The lady said scurrying, and Gofrei echoed the salutation. "How may I be of service?" He said, plucking an out-of-place leaf from a hedge.

"I heard you were in Udello. I hope my parents welcomed you with warmth."

Gofrei walked under the arch to where the tables were spread, slaves scurrying away, the breeze from the river convergence making his robes flow. "Your family were gracious hosts, though I only met the Lord of Tenestar, your other brother was supposedly hunting Lodean in the mountains."

Sophie said, "Prince Arin enjoys a good hunt." Gofrei's smile didn't meet his eyes. He sat on a velvet chair and stretched his arms. Sophie sat beside him for a moment, waiting for the king to appear. "I heard from a very close friend at the Udello court you disappeared for some time. Lost at a brothel?"

The Lord of Montlahead hiccuped. "I wished to see your wonderful city. The palace moat, even the Little Calu River outside the walls, all beautiful country. Your father is very lucky to hold those lands."

"And the Lord of Goldfield knows about this absence," Sophie wondered while looking for Ultiir in the crowd, "when you were to make sure my parents arrived without harm?"

"Good thing they aren't children."

Hurvir was behind a tapestry that told the story of the de'Tro family, almost time for the feast to begin. "Sir Achen also told me you arrived a day before my parents. The wind must've been fast on the Montla-Ritae; you could've sailed all the way home in record time." Gofrei said nothing; he picked at his teeth.

As she made her way to the front of the gardens, where the head table was ready with plates and goblets, Lord Tedbalt Masson strode beside her. "My queen." He bowed his head. "Excited for the food? I hear the crown bought birds caught in Saamrakaa; they claim the feathers have special powers. The women sew them to their backs for eternal youth." The old lord smiled. "Shall we try?"

Sophie covered her eyes as the sun shone into them, the shadow of the palace facing the east. Ushers directed lords and ladies to their seats while guards walked the perimeter of the gardens. The smell of a dirty river mixed with the fresh smells of bread and baking ham. "And the spices are said to heal you. I don't trust the machinations of Saamrakaa'i."

He looked at a small cut on his middle finger. "I should try that." Lord Tedbalt gave a knowing smile to Sophie; all she did was nod. The old lord was always kind to her. *Maybe he sees his daughter in me?* It wouldn't surprise her if Ultiir had told the entire council that she knew the plan. Glancing at the crowd, she couldn't find Lord de'Marisco. The sneak. Somehow he had found himself on the King's Council, and she worried he would want to silence her. *Does death await me?* She pushed away the thought. *No. Not while Ultiir lives.*

A squire stepped out from behind a white tent, his hand on his pommel, his back as straight as a sword blade. "The King Hurvir de'Tro the First. Ruler of the Dominion of Viguran, Watcher of the Veck'kop, Protector of the Kinglands, Lord of the Glybelm, and Defender of the Nokys."

Hurvir emerged from the tent. He wore multiple layers of tunics and robes and cloaks. His tunics were silk, gold thread stitching the blues and yellows together. The robe atop was purple, hanging to his boots, the owl of his house embossed on the upper left. His red cloak dragged along the cobble path below, and his head was adorned with a crown made of a hundred jewels. Sophie could see his neck flexing to hold the weight. The crowd bowed, then cheered for his feast. He stopped them only when he sat. Once the crown was removed from his head, he motioned for his queen. She walked to the table, kissed his hand, and said, "My king, my husband." And took her seat.

The eyes of the crowd focused on her husband's every move. Where he placed his hands, what his eyes were drawn to, how he wiped dust from his face. Once the jesters came out to perform, and the food that followed, the gardens got loud once more.

The tables all matched, in straight columns with white plates and golden goblets. Slaves and servants and cooks moved in and out of conversations, filling the lords and ladies with wine and beer, with summer sausage and faraway birds. The convergence of the rivers was filled with laughter. *Is this what Vigura imagined when he landed on this place? The most powerful people of His kingdom enjoying opulence. People in chains not a foot away.* A slave master slapped a small girl's hand when she tried to eat a crumb of bread. *Better than a whip,* Sophie thought before being distracted by her food being brought out. A fowl from the east, drinks from the west. She found comfort in the flatbread on her small plate, made fresh every day in the palace kitchens.

Sophie ate the large breast of a bird and slurped down some wine from Baragio. She couldn't look at her husband. His hand reached for hers, but she moved it away. *Do I want to see him die? After everything he has done to me?* Shaking her head, she finally found Ultiir's eyes. They were locked on her; nothing else at the gardens mattered. *Always watching.* In the crowd, Tedbalt was enjoying food with a woman too young for him, and Urses rubbed his scarred nose. Other lords of the council were enjoying the music.

A slave girl poured more wine for Hurvir. The jesters juggled as the people conversed with one another. Oblivious to what was about to happen. Hurvir choked on laughter as a jester dropped a ball under a lady of the court's skirt. Fumbling his way into her breeches. The king took a long drink. Sophie took a breath. She stuffed her face with the next platter of rice from Eotros and salt cod. Ultiir's eyes weren't on her any longer. He sat with a smile. Urses watched the head table where Hurvir and Sophie sat. Tedbalt had stopped flirting. Lord Geary drank wine, paying no one any attention. He looked as if he had no stake in anything that was about to happen.

A soft touch caressed her fingers. With the help of the gods, she willed her eyes toward her husband. Hurvir was dabbing the corners of his mouth with a napkin, a sticky blue substance not coming off. She felt around her lips with her tongue. Nothing. *Thank you Meret.*

With no time to react, the goblet in Hurvir's hand crashed to the ground. The jesters stopped their jokes. The band stopped their music. People stopped their conversations. Ultiir came running over as Hurvir convulsed. Sophie stood and held the king's head. "Help." She screamed. Tears rushed to her cheeks, from sadness or thankfulness, she could not say. Hurvir tried to open his mouth to fill it with wine or water, but the stickiness was too much. The blue goo stretched to block his breath. The king was flailing. Slaves and servants, Ultiir and other lords, all ran trying to help by turning him on his back and calling for dakens. Guards didn't know how to solve a problem that didn't require swords. And ladies in the garden screamed.

The blue substance oozed from Hurvir's mouth. The flailing stopped, and his head fell to the table, the crown toppling off his head and rolling along the brick below.

King Hurvir de'Tro the First was dead.

Raimund

ho travels the Swallow Pass?" A voice cut through the crisp air. Three men emerged from behind a rock face atop their black steeds. Knights who wore all white armor from head to toe that glistened in the noon sun, the reflection blinding Raimund. Their cloaks fell to their feet, also white. And an off-white bear, barely noticeable, was stamped in the middle of their breastplate.

Mar whispered, "I assume we're here," and dismounted. "We have been traveling to reach Whitehall. We urgently need to speak with the lord." Raimund almost forgot what it sounded like for Mar to be serious.

"State your business." A young-sounding knight said.

"This is the king's son." Mar gestured to Devro, who stiffened his back. "He would like to see Lord David."

The young knight took off his helm and let his red curls fall. "Forgive me." He gave a half bow. "The King Hurvir de'Tro is dead. I am sorry for your loss."

"You believe him, Pollard?" One of the other knights asked. "This could be anyone."

"The duke will know me," Tundavik said. "He will vouch for us."

Devro didn't move. He sat still while Fariage danced about. "I have come to claim my crown, and demand Lord David speak with me."

"Lord David is busy," the red-haired knight said, "but he did have love for your father. I will let you speak with him." The knight put his helm on again, reflecting the sun into Raimund's eyes. The other knights rolled their eyes but moved along with Pollard. "Sir Rye, go forward and tell Whitehall of its guests." He turned to the group shivering in the Swallow Pass. "Follow."

Not long after they found the end of the pass, a large meadow greeted them when they left the rocks. Whitehall was large for a mountain village. Raimund could make out a bakery, a blacksmith, two inns, a tannery, and numerous other stone houses and shops. The only thing he couldn't find was the keep. Then the young knight pointed to David Rely's home and place of governance.

The keep was made of wood. It was rotten and obviously infected with termites. Boards were falling, and nails littered the ground. There was a blanket covering one side, and burn marks showed that there had been a fire. The wood-constructed parts poked out of the mountain, but Raimund could see windows and air holes throughout the rocks. *It's larger and more secure than I thought. Hopefully, that stops an attack.*

Sir Pollard dismounted his horse and called over a stable-boy. The boy was skinny and long-legged. He gathered the reins of all the horses and walked them toward the stable, somehow never losing control of the five horses. Whitehall was a small village, but the largest they've seen since leaving Udello. There was a masonry with strewn bricks all about;

a bakery with the scent of bread and sweets filling the air; a tannery with hides hanging and drying; there was even a tavern and drunk men wandering out. None of it was especially nice. All made of wood. Plopped in the middle of a large valley with mountains on all sides. Raimund wondered what lived atop the mountains in the snow.

One of the other knights, Sir Howe, galloped back to the pass in case others journeyed through. Sir Rye came out of the keep and hobbled over to Pollard.

Before the knights were done with their conversation, Raimund leaned over to Devro and said, "This doesn't need to come to war."

Devro's eyes glistened with tears that wouldn't fall. "My uncle killed my father, you heard the knight. It is his fault. I am not the one choosing war. The throne is mine with the Bastard Law."

Raimund let out a sigh that had been building since Udello. They had made their plan to see Lord David Rely and had journeyed through the Asara Mountains. Past forests and rocks and streams. Journeymen and merchants had whispered rumors of a dead king, but no one believed it, but now a knight told them.

"My father will see you now," Pollard said and led the way to the keep.

"I hope I didn't say anything that would offend him on our journey," Mar whispered to Raimund.

"You didn't talk much."

"Oh," Mar nodded, "then I must have thought those things." He patted Raimund on the back. "I heard what Devro said. Maybe you'll see your first war. It isn't anything like the stories, not fun at all. A lot of shitting and bleeding and dying." Mar gave a large smile. "But maybe you'll make a name for yourself."

Raimund looked at his sword. The sunstone gave off a faint glow. *I don't need to make a name for myself.* He had never known war. Didn't live in Viguran when they fought the Rainvealandians, and the North was too tired after the Sixteen Great Wars when he was born. He just hoped he wouldn't die. "I'm sure the King's Council will change their mind."

"The naïveté," Mar laughed.

The inside of the keep was no better than the busted and rotting outside. Wood still fell, but the farther back you got, the more stone gave a look of put-togetherness, where furs covered the ground to keep their feet warm and large empty fireplaces sat ready to burn. Pollard disappeared into a back room and came back with four black fur cloaks. "Made from the finest bear." The four wrapped themselves in their new cloaks, the nicest things they've seen since setting foot in Whitehall. "Wait here." Pollard went farther back.

Raimund could hear a commotion behind closed wooden doors. The hinges seemed to be on their last life. The door swung open with an echoing *creeeek* and out came over a dozen people. They all wore the same bear fur cloaks and made a line directly across from Raimund and the others. Men and women, old and young, stared at them. Raimund could tell who were the servants and pages and who were considered important. The servants had confused looks, while those above them wore a regal look. Their chins raised and eyes focused.

From behind them came an old man. His hair had already fallen from his head, and he walked with a limp supported by a cane. He huffed and wheezed as he climbed the two steps to his wooden chair covered in ripped velvet. Pollard and some other white-armored knights stood to his left; a young girl, around Devro's age, stood to his right. *Maybe a new wife for the old duke.*

Lord David Rely looked them over with squinted eyes. He raised a frail finger and pointed at Tundavik. "I know you. I never thought I'd see you again."

"How are you, Lord David?" Tundavik said.

The duke's face seemed to flush with emotion. His frown became a smile and he seemed twenty years younger. "Where did you disappear to all these years? Every lord and lady has questioned it for over a decade."

"Attrima."

"West?" David laughed. "I always liked the West, much warmer than my mountain home. That's where I sent one of these two's sister." He pointed at Pollard and then the girl to his right. *So a daughter,* Raimund thought. "Yvanne was just asking me why the Prince of Viguran had returned. She says she remembers when you came here a few years ago," he said to Devro, "a young boy then."

"I have something I need of you." Devro said before Tundavik stepped forward.

"We want to ask you something, but we don't want to give your shoulders more weight."

"Nonsense." The duke waved a bony hand. "You've come to ask me something. And it must be important, or why else would the Duke Tundavik Vandes come back to Viguran?"

"I am not a duke. Not even a lord."

"You are to me." David smiled, and Raimund saw Tundavik smile and choke back what seemed to be tears. "I always liked

Adile, you remember that."

Tundavik cleared his throat. "We heard from your son that King Hurvir is dead."

"Not a king no more." David chuckled. "I figured you would be out celebrating in the streets, Lord Tundavik."

"I would, but I have more important matters." Tundavik never looked at Devro, but Raimund did. The prince swayed and wiped sweat from his brow. "Before the new king is crowned, Devro here would like to cite the Bastard Law."

"He wishes to be king?"

"It is my birthright." Devro said just below a shout.

Tundavik put a hand on the prince's shoulder. "He wants to continue the de'Tro dynasty and legacy. We came to you because the King's Council has shown they've no problem assassinating kings."

"The rumor is," David started, "that the king choked on his chicken." He gave a shrug and a cunning smile. "I've no reason to question it."

"You know what would happen if Devro cited the law. The council won't give up. It would lead to war." The room went silent. Only David Rely's wheezing could be heard. "We need your help ..."

Raimund tuned out the talking. He felt eyes on him. His eyes darted around the room, looking at the line of people. *Not many here, who could it be?* He stopped at the young girl standing near her father. *Yvanne.* Her eyes were green and inviting. She wouldn't take them off him even as Raimund made eye contact. *What does she think? Does she wish to speak with me? Some other things?* He cleared his thoughts of the girl, who was obviously half his age. Her eyes stayed on Raimund until she smiled.

Then other eyes were on him.

"Raimund?" Tundavik said.

The knight's eyes widened. "Yes."

"Tell Lord David about the armies."

"Of course." Raimund coughed. "I would lead the armies in battle unless you had a better alternative. Unfortunately, there are not many men to lead, but with your support we believe other houses, large and small, would join our side. Put pressure on Vigur to capitulate. Sir Mar would also lead the armies with me."

"Like you said, I don't know about *armies*, but an army could use some leadership. Have you fought in wars, Sir?" the duke asked. Raimund shook his head. "Why won't you, Tundavik?"

"I'm too old."

Lord David let out a sound that was a mix between wheezing and laughing. "Too fucking old? I'm too old. You are half my age and led the successful campaign along the Bezir. You sacked Panscar. Sacked Suktir." Tundavik winced at the words.

"I would advise, as I hoped you would." Tundavik straightened his tunic. "We need someone who finished off the Nowexerts as an adviser too."

"Only fought for a short time—"

"—I can do it." Raimund interrupted the duke and stepped forward. "I can beat the King's Council. Mar and I are excellent fighters. You all know strategy. Together, we can place the rightful heir on the throne."

The room was silent again. He glanced at his son and daughter and then at the advisers. "I would need something."

"Anything," Devro said. "You ask and you shall receive."

"It is a big ask. You probably should've waited til you heard." The duke wiped his nose. "If you are to be king, you will need a queen." Raimund nodded in understanding. *Always in it for themselves.* "As you can see, my house is not very wealthy. Trade routes run north and south of us, the Lodean like to sabotage our mining operations, and our ground is not much for wheat. I have married off sons and daughters to lords and ladies from the Kormat to the Kash, from Vatona to the Flewth-Vet, and everywhere in between. What I lack in resources I make up for in potential fighting men. I need just call my children home." He coughed into a handkerchief. "I have never married a child to an heir." Devro cleared his throat. "My daughter, Yvanne, is around your age. Prime wedding and birthing age. You must make her a queen."

Devro's jaw had opened slightly. Tundavik and Mar turned to the prince. Raimund already knew the answer. "Of course." Devro said. "When I am crowned—"

"No," David interrupted, "before we begin a war."

"Even better." Devro bowed to Yvanne.

"Then we will have a feast and a wedding." David clapped and stood. The young girl smiled and then stared at Raimund, her eyes burning like a fire.

Yvanne

Leaves rustled as she walked under the line of oak trees above the cliff just outside the keep, Whitehall was quieting for the night. The moon cut through the stale autumn and lit the entire town. Yvanne looked over the cliff at the clearing below. Leaves had turned red. The sunflowers had hidden away while the moonflowers basked in the light. She pulled her cloak tighter with gloved hands. Come tomorrow, she would wed a bastard boy and be on her way to becoming the queen of Viguran. *A queen. What would Mother say about this?*

As she walked along the only nice part of town, toward a picnic area that overlooked the meadow, she saw a dark shadow leaning against a rail. It was larger than her, but she wasn't afraid. The shadowed figure gave off a warmth. She could feel the air changing on her face, like the spray of the ocean. The shadow's face turned to her. It was him.

"I knew I would find you out here." She smiled at Sir Raimund. The knight threw back his hood to reveal his shaggy black hair and the pale face of a Northerner. "Where did you say you came from?"

"I didn't, my lady." He gave a half bow.

"One of my sisters lives in Taidem. Have you been?"

Sir Raimund nodded. "I lived there for a time, long before I came to Viguran."

"My father never told me outsiders could be knights, and my doma claims only a Veck'kop can guard members of the royal household."

Raimund squeezed the railing. "Is there something you need, my lady?"

"Yvanne is fine. I'm not the lady of Whitehall yet, nor queen." She played with her fingers as the knight's energy warmed her. "You're the man who will lead the armies. Are you scared?"

"Who wouldn't be?" he said curtly.

Yvanne stood beside him, clenching the chilly wooden rail. It creaked. "I understand why you might mistrust me, but I'm not trying to pry." She bit her cheek. "I know who you are."

"Sir Raimund, obviously." The knight cocked his head and smiled.

"*What* you are."

The knight stepped back and rested his hand on his sword. The glimmer of a red-tinted jewel caught her eye. "Why so cryptic?" Raimund said.

"I know what will happen if your secret gets out. Because the same would happen to me." She fingered the necklace beneath her cloak. "Éithrio aren't so common here; I knew the moment you arrived you had a power like mine." Pulling the locket out, she showed the knight the inscription. *For my darling daughter.* "My mother gave this to me before she left. It is my most prized possession and something I could never be without." She opened the locket, and inside was a mineral that reflected the light from the moon. It shone red all by itself. "My sunstone."

"How did you know?"

"I can sense it somehow." She put her necklace away. Raimund dropped his shoulders and looked over the valley once again. The warmth died down. Yvanne said, "I'm not sure how, but I always know."

"I guess it's good we found you then. Does your father know? Brother?"

"None but my doma. She has been with me since birth, teaching and caring for me. She says I shouldn't tell others, but," she paused, "I trust you. Sharing the same power means something to me."

"At least I know Devro will be taken care of when I'm gone."

"You think there will be war?"

"Why wouldn't there be?" Raimund gave a nervous chuckle. "Maybe we should be in the vanguard. The King's Council wouldn't stand a chance if we just burned the palace with them in it."

"Then be hanged and quartered." Yvanne said. "I think a queen and knight of the realm deserve a better death."

"It's late, my lady, I should find Sir Mar and get to sleep."

"Are you together?"

Raimund chuckled. "Mar is only a friend, and much too promiscuous for me."

Yvanne laughed with him. "I will see you at the wedding then." The leaves crunched under his feet as he left. "Your secret is safe." He nodded back at her. *The wedding. Becoming a rebel queen. It would sound more romantic if I read it in a story, instead of possible war breaking out all over the kingdom. Not even Whitehall is safe,* she thought as she made her way into the warm keep to sleep.

Usually she would get up with the sun, but Helge had to

wake her today. *Why can't the old crone ever give me a few moments to myself?* Yvanne couldn't help but smile as the old woman whisked around her room, grabbing at any dresses she could find. "We'll need to comb that nest you call hair." Helge said.

"Of course." *Was it all a dream? A queen? An éithrio?* She shook her head. *It couldn't have been.* "Shall we pray?"

The doma stopped with a handful of dresses. She straightened her back and gently put the clothes on a chair. She reached out a hand and grabbed Yvanne's. "We call upon you, Mother Meret. We ask for your safety and for you to hear what we have to say. I pray Yvanne becomes a wonderful wife and queen."

"And I pray that Whitehall be spared from the upcoming battles."

"Thank you, Mother Meret, for hearing our needs and wants." Helge sat on the bed and stroked Yvanne's red hair before finding a brush. *She's combing harder than usual.* Yvanne thought as her hair ripped from the doma's hard hand. "That was foolish last night." *Of course, she knows.* "Anyone in town could have seen you."

"But they didn't, and nothing happened."

"I don't know why you had to tell that éth …" The doma silenced. Yvanne knew the doma couldn't say the word. It was too dangerous. "There was no reason for that."

"I know. But I haven't felt a power this strong in years." Yvanne went over to the mirror, and the doma followed. Hazel eyes stared back at her. "It gets lonely after a while. Not being able to tell people. No one to talk to."

"You can talk to me."

"Still." Yvanne plucked at her brow. "You can't always be

there for me."

"Did you read from the Book of Samosay like I told you?"

Yvanne nodded, trying to remember the exact words in the thick book. "Sam the Sayer was blessing lords and ladies that traveled with him on their quest to find flaming arrows needed to defeat the savages."

"May he bless you this day."

"Bless me with flaming arrows?" She laughed while Helge's face was flat. Yvanne took the brush from Helge and pulled at her tangled hair. "Enough of this. We talk about my teachings every day, but this day is different." She smiled at the dresses. "Will I sit on the throne in Vigur?" Yvanne asked the old woman who could see the future.

Helge sighed. "I wish you wouldn't ask those types of questions."

"You can tell me. I won't ask anymore."

The old doma stood and brushed her hand against Yvanne's Book of the Four. "This is a gift from the gods. I should not abuse it." Yvanne could feel the warmth radiating from Helge as she pulled on all the energy around. She believed her power came from the gods; Yvanne wasn't sure. "You realize what all this means? If I see you in Vigur, then that means a war has been fought, the kingdom torn apart, countless dead. This will not be easy."

"I know." Yvanne couldn't imagine how anyone could support a council that usurped the throne, not even from a bastard. "It's only fun to learn what the future has in store."

"Dangerous." Helge took a deep breath, her eyes closed, and her hands trembled more than usual. The warmth felt like a fire. "I see you walking through the gates of Vigur."

"In a week? A year?" Yvanne pursed her lips.

"You know I can't see that far."

"Oh, I must know, doma." Yvanne grabbed the old woman's wrinkly fingers.

"Stop." Helge pulled away. "There is no reason to fret about an ever-changing future that can change with every step you take. I can't see past Swallow's Feast in the spring. This war will last at least until then. What happens next I do not know, but if I see anything too concerning, then I will tell you. I promise."

"Swear on the Four?"

Helge stepped back and then said, "Fine." Yvanne finished with her hair and called for her handmaid. "Good luck today. I will see you later for the feast." Yvanne waved the old crone off as Jacka came in. She watched Helge go with guilty eyes.

"All finished." Jacka said hours later. "Just in time for the feast." Yvanne looked in the mirror. She had makeup on that made her even paler, and her hair was tied atop her head like massive stones. When she stood, Jacka had to stop her from toppling. Yvanne's dress was blue with white stitching, a bear at the bottom near her black shoes where the gown fluttered out across the floorboards.

"This was my mother's." Yvanne told her handmaiden.

"I didn't know. Would you like me to find another?"

Yvanne gave a slight smile. "I love it. She wore it the last time the prince was here." *During the famine when Queen Sophie brought us food. I hope people remember me that way.* "Have a fun night, Jacka. It's not every day that we get to feast."

"It's not every day we crown a queen." Her handmaiden grabbed Yvanne's warm hands. "I just know you will be the most amazing queen Viguran has ever had."

"You don't have to butter me like I'm a piece of bread. I'll take you to court or wherever I end up."

"I was being serious." Jacka gave a tearful smile. "I didn't know your mother; I was so young, but I know she would be proud based on the stories I've heard."

Yvanne clutched Jacka's hand. "Let's feast."

***

The main hall was filled to the brim. Peasants, knights, advisers, cooks, and servants scurried around the room. They were as finely dressed as they could be, wearing tunics and trousers. They had their nicest leather for boots. Some even wore hats made of feathers from faraway lands. Lands Yvanne had never heard of. Tables were dressed and chairs straightened. The servants had laid out plates and cups. At the head of the room, where her father's seat normally sat, were two chairs of blue velvet. Yvanne had never seen them before, but the velvet wasn't ripping and the seat backs were decorated with wood carvings of owls and bears.

An old bearded man was handing some of her father's knights new surcoats. She went closer and saw an owl in flight like Sir Raimund's armor. *I guess the prince has a larger following now. Seems like war is as inevitable as Helge says.* Others, like Sir Loc, stood with the normal white bear on their chests and surcoats. "Ready for tonight?" Loc said to her as she passed by. "You look beautiful if I must say."

"Thank you." Yvanne blushed. Sir Loc had always been kind to her. "I am nervous but excited." Jacka followed in step. Yvanne let her go mingle with her friends when she saw her brother.

Sir Pollard was sharpening his blade as if he actually used it. "You may cut someone," she said.

"Not if they don't get in my way." He sheathed his sword and pushed his red curls from his eyes. "I guess tonight is the last time I can poke fun at you. Now you can remove my head if I so much as look at you wrong."

"As if I would do that." Yvanne laughed. "But don't think I haven't thought about it."

Pollard looked at her dress; his eyes widened at the bear at the hem. "Mother's. I can't believe you're old enough to fit in it."

Yvanne fluffed the dress and smiled. "I wonder what life would be like if she were still here." Yvanne tried to think of her mother every day, pretending she was still in the keep helped soften the sting she felt when she remembered she had run away.

"Well, father probably would've found another by now." Pollard said as he twirled Yvanne, the white bear spinning as if it were dancing. "She would be back in her home."

"Maybe we would be with her."

"Then you wouldn't be becoming a queen." Pollard shrugged. "We wouldn't be about to go to war."

"There's still time."

Pollard played with his sword pommel. "No. When the bastard marched into Whitehall, we lost any time we had. The King's Council will find out and send whichever lord in the Lands of Asara is loyal to them, and the fighting will start. Guess we'll find out which owls' talons are sharper. The one with gold or the one in the mountains. I have my bet."

Yvanne looked into her brother's eyes. The same as hers. "Will you fight?"

"If I'm commanded to."

"So I become a queen and risk losing my only full-blooded brother." A lump grew in her throat. The realization of never seeing her brother again made her want to run away and hide from the wedding, but she couldn't disobey her father. *And becoming a queen is what fairy tales are made of.* "I don't want to lose anyone else, not after Mother."

"The Four will decide my fate. Live or die. Nothing I can do." He shrugged again.

Her father stumbled over to his children. Pollard steadied Lord David. "Talking about the marriage? It's about to begin."

"I'll go to my place," Pollard said and disappeared along the wall of white-clad knights. His eyes lost. *Will that be what it's like if he dies? Just another knight.*

"My darling," her father brought her back to the moment with a hug.

Yvanne looked at her father's wrinkled skin and sunken cheeks. *Only a few more years.* "I will make you proud."

David Rely laid a liver-spotted hand on his daughter's shoulder. "I am already proud of you. Since the day you were born. My last Rely." He clutched his cane. "Yes, it will be nice when you are queen, but there will be a war. I'm not sure if you're prepared for what's to come." *Everyone keeps saying that,* she thought. "But I know you will do what you think is right to save this kingdom from destruction." Yvanne hugged her father, letting her cheeks stain with tears. "Let's get ready."

Knights lined the walls. Owls on her right, bears on her left. The peasants, in their nicest fashion, stood all across the room, mostly wearing smiles. Everyone from Whitehall was invited. Yvanne waited near the entrance to the keep while

Helge got into place. The bastard prince came from a back room, followed by his knights and the old Lord Tundavik Vandes. Devro wore a purple tunic fastened with silver. *Not exactly like the fairy tales, but he will do. Helge has said that King Hurvir was a strong man. A warrior. Has this child ever even held a sword?* She smiled at the bastard. Before the night was over, he would be her husband. *They will sing songs about the queen from the Lands of Asara.*

Devro joined her side to walk to the doma. When Devro's bony arm wrapped around hers, they began. Every eye was on them. All staring into her soul. All questioning. "Will she be a good queen?" "Can she lead us during a war?" "Who would want to marry a girl from Whitehall?" Yvanne gulped. The room was silent except for their footsteps and the creaking wood.

When they reached Helge, Yvanne's father came over. "Please present the dowry before the gods." David gave a pouch that clinked with coins to Devro. Her father bowed his head, and Devro passed the dowry to Sir Mar. "Now, before the Four and the Many, Hurvir de'Tro the Second, you must recite the rights of every marriage"

Devro cleared his throat, and it sounded deeper than before. "Under the watchful eyes of the Four, I have chosen to marry. Before Meret, I have taken Yvanne of Whitehall as my bride. Before Samosay, I promise to protect her. Before Swallow, I swear to uphold her honor. Before Vigura, I vow to keep her from the dangers of this world and the depths of Veltoora. Before the Many, I claim these oaths to be true."

Helge smiled and nodded a rigid head at Yvanne. "Do you accept the wishes of the Four and your man?"

Everyone watched her; she could feel the eyes boring into

her neck. Her father suppressed a cough, and she could feel the warmth from Raimund. "I accept the wishes."

"Then by the grace of the Four and all other gods beneath them," Helge shouted to the room, "I pronounce that Yvanne Rely, daughter of Lord David Rely of Whitehall, and Hurvir de'Tro the Second of Viguran, now joined together until their dying days." The mountain roared as the room erupted into cheers and shouts. Devro kissed Yvanne as quickly as he could and waved to the crowd. The knights with owl insignias caught her eye. The Lands of Asara in open revolt, declaring for a child. She bit the inside of her cheek as she wondered how many in this room would never return.

Bertin

ertin had to stand guard atop the walls of the city. The desert was below; the wind creating new dunes and destroying old ones. He wanted to go to a bathhouse to wash the filth off of him from traveling, but the commander thought that was nonsense. "The king said you are here to protect the city. Prince or no, you must walk the walls." Commander Abrezo had told him. So walked the walls he did. For two days. Every night he saw Wilclef, Gordo, Robalt, and even Safír. Other than that, he was on the limestone brick.

Bertin was to watch for elves. For any change in the Delerous Desert that was unnatural. For suspicious travelers. He watched and saw only humans. Humans trading wares from Kruhesh, humans crying to get into the city and out of Ih la Mat, humans dying in the heat. No elves. *I'm beginning to think this king wanted to get rid of me. And I thought he wanted a marriage alliance.* "Curse him to Veltoora."

A shirtless, muscular man with a spear tapped Bertin on the shoulder. *"Parti drent."* He had a tattoo of a scorpion across his chest, ready to attack.

"What?" Bertin had not grown accustomed to a different language. The people able to talk without worrying what they say, snickering behind his back. There was a Delerous quarter in Rowan, full of statues to their gods, where they all laughed in their language. The only time Bertin went they threw oranges at his head. "No *Del'us*," he said.

The man gave a sour look. "*Adantè* Abrezo wants to see you."

"Have the Four blessed me with reprieve?" He said in a sarcastic tone.

"Maybe the *Re'as Totti Sopro*." The Kings Above All. Bertin had heard that more times than he could count.

Bertin rolled his eyes and walked along the sand-blown walls. Kicking dust as he went. Guards stood along the wall, having come from every corner of Telemaw to help protect the ancient city. He looked over at the city below, hearing the sounds of children running and playing. A reed boat made its way to an isle. *Any other time of year, this city would be nice to visit.* A sandstorm had battered Lisan Biresdea the day they went under Aldrico. The entire city stayed inside for hours. This time though, Bertin didn't have to lie in the sand. He could eat, drink and talk. He worried about another storm as big as Ih la Mat, the smaller ones didn't scare him as much. *Maybe the elves won't attack because of the sand. Maybe the city will be spared.* That is if the king and Safír even told the truth of the elves moving west from the Alhya. He didn't talk to other travelers for confirmation.

A small tower where the north and east walls met was where Commander Abrezo stood. He was giving some command when Bertin found him. "I guess I can leave now?" Bertin wanted to get this conversation over with before it began.

Abrezo smiled. "I thought it was past time I showed you

our defenses." The commander went through the armory first. Shields and spears to be used at the gate; bowmen and crossbowmen along the walls, swords ready if the city was breached. "But that could never happen. Not since the Èmaw conquered the desert a hundred years ago." That didn't make Bertin feel any safer. They continued along the wall until Emperor Aldrico Onte's statue loomed over them, casting a cooling shadow. The gate was busy below. Traders carrying goods from Rainvealand and Salvalone. Abrezo pointed to a few holes where rocks or hot sand could be dropped. "I believe you call those murder holes." Bertin nodded. "Apt name. Not one elf will get in without them losing ten more."

Bertin thought about his childhood. He had entered Rowan after spending a week in River's Meadow and saw an elf hanging from the gate. "Rowan has not had to deal with hordes of elves in decades. The occasional one here or there." Abrezo's eyes narrowed. Bertin tugged at the collar of his new baggy shirt, which the commander thought would keep him cool. "What did King Hasíb do to upset them?"

"Upset them?" The commander laughed. Other guardsmen turned to see as if it had never happened before. "Adèkhas are savages. They burn and rape wherever they go. They need no reason."

"I've heard the same said about the Gorthair."

Abrezo's brow raised. "An ancient race as well?"

Bertin waved away the subject. "Not important. What else do you have to show me?"

The commander kept pointing out small details he said would help with defense. Bertin had to pretend it was interesting. *This city is going to fall, isn't it? I need to get out of here, but where would I go? The king sent me as far away from civilization as he could.* Abrezo stopped as a sandstorm moved farther north. He held out his hands as if a fire were near. "It warms me."

"Are you from Lisan Biresdea?"

"Salvalone. The greatest city in the world. I've seen your city, Rowan, as well as Edincassone. Salvalone is even greater than those."

Bertin held back a chuckle. A city of a ruined empire versus the largest cities in the known world? "My guide told me about Salvalone. He told me he would take us there if all goes well in Lisan Biresdea."

"You won't be disappointed." The sandstorm swept over dunes and rocks. Hopefully, no travelers were out there. He never thought he would worry about sand, but the darkness that engulfed him still gave him nightmares. "How was Vaandet?"

"It was fine." Bertin didn't know how to answer.

"The last time I was there, they were still rebuilding from the Saysyki attack. Those Agarian bastards don't seem to know what a river border means. We have elves in the east and always the threat of Saysyk in the west."

"But you win the wars."

Abrezo walked again. "Even the mightiest armies have fallen to lesser ones. King Hasíb, bless his ancestors, has held off many attacks. I do not think we can hold forever." They reached a landing with wooden steps leading below. "You have done enough patrolling for today. Do you still want to go to the bathhouse?"

Bertin had to keep his excitement in check. "Of course."

"There is one near the Palace of Sands. Best in the city."

Bertin gave a small bow and pranced down the steps.

"About time." He said loud enough for the commander to hear.

He made it to the water and flagged down a boat. The poleman said something in Delerous and held out his hand. Bertin found a copper piece Safír had given him and threw it to the man before getting on the reed boat. *"Zentra Ira."* Bertin had quickly learned those words to get to the center isle of Lisan Biresdea; he wished to see his guards before going to the bathhouse. The Four and the Many knew that they needed to be cleaned as well.

The poleman nodded and pushed off. The water was shallow, and Bertin could see the sand beneath getting kicked up from the pole. Small boats choked the canals that went east of the main body of water. People and goods were shipped all around the city. Bertin could tell the wealthy from everyone else by the covered boats that went by. Sometimes servants would be fanning the elite even in the shade.

Bertin held his hand up to keep the sun from his eyes, but it didn't help with the heat, and supposedly it got even warmer when Baraga's season—*summer*—came. Going over the water sent a gentle breeze to help cool him, but when he got off on the center isle he got hotter. Just yesterday, a sandstorm blew through. Today, he saw people cleaning their homes and shops of all the dust that had layered the city. He dodged carts and kids, smiled at a beautiful woman baking flatbread, and said hello to the men pushing carts and trading wares. Everyone returned a smile. He didn't know if they were genuine or because they remembered he came into the city wearing a crown, but it was a welcome reprieve from the hostility of his home.

He reached the small limestone building he was staying in.

The lord of the city, Lord Abia Èmaw, had personally seen to their accommodations when Safír showed his papers and Bertin wore his crown. The lord didn't seem like he wanted much to do with Bertin, so he sent him to the walls and gave him a shack to live in. There were much nicer houses all around the city. All owned by the elite and other members of House Èmaw. Bertin grumbled when he first saw it, but at least it kept them out of the sandstorms.

He opened the wooden door on squeaky hinges and saw his men playing cards. Safír was tying up packs with goods he had bartered from around town. The interior was covered with a layer of dust. No one bothered to clean after the sandstorm yesterday when another would surely happen soon. The windows were holes that could be covered with wood. The room was lit up by the sun, but the shade and cool breeze from the oasis made it livable.

Bertin's men had lost all outward respect they showed to their prince. They cursed at one another instead of bowing. Bertin plopped down on a wooden stool. His neck burned from being in the sun. Safír must've noticed because he handed Bertin a cooling gel that came from some leaf that grew outside the city walls. "Thank you." He again noticed Safír's bags. "What are you doing? Going to market?"

"The market in Salvalone."

Bertin stood and wiped the gel from his fingers. "You can't leave for Salvalone yet. What about Robalt seeing the city?"

"He said we may be here for a while." Robalt put down his cards. "We can go later. Lisan Biresdea is full of desert guides."

Safír finished tying a knot. "It is true. There have been murmurings of the Adèkhas in the desert. I am not sure when His Lord Èmaw or Adantè Abrezo will let you leave. It could be months when I thought it would be days."

Bertin was at a loss for words. *Am I more upset about Safir leaving or rumors of an attack?* "If an attack is about to happen, then we all need to leave. I need to be safe."

The air was sucked out of the room. Wilclef left the card game and said, "Both your father and King Hasíb would be furious."

"What are we going to do?" Bertin turned red. "There are only five of us, four if Safír leaves. They have dozens of men with spears and bows and shields. If they can't hold the city from a pack of elves, then why should we help?"

"Your father," Gordo drank some water, "wanted you to learn."

"I'm sure he thought I would be spending my days in the desert on a wall." Bertin rolled his eyes. "He thought King Hasíb would let me in on meetings. Maybe try to broker a peace with some rival faction. Get a marriage alliance. Not thrust into a potential war. He wouldn't have sent me if he believed that." At least, that's what Bertin told himself. "He especially wouldn't want me dead."

"You won't die." Wilclef said. "That's why we are here."

"A hundred elves pour over the walls and you think you can protect me?"

Robalt pointed to his sword. "I am always ready. We have protected you on the road all over Rowan, even in Gorthair territory, where they would like to see your entrails pulled out. We can protect you from some elves."

"There's a reason humans are dominant on Adedor," Gordo said. "The elves fight worse than shit."

"They took Cluo," Bertin said, referring to the city on the

eastern edge of Telemaw.

"Only for a couple of days." Safír chimed in. "His Descendant of Emperors' men and the peasants of Cluo were able to take it back." Bertin's guards agreed before Safír continued. "But that does not make Lìsn Biresdea safe. The elves will put all their might into taking this oasis. If not for water than to embarrass the king, bless his ancestors."

"So we can come with you?" Bertin asked.

Safír shook his head. "I would not want Adantè Abrezo after me. And the adèkhas may lie south of here. It is too dangerous."

Bertin's shoulders dropped. "More dangerous than staying here?" Safír did not make eye contact. "Tell the truth."

"I must leave." As Safír walked past, Bertin grabbed his arm. He pleaded with his eyes. "I would leave if I were you."

"Nonsense," Gordo said. "Here we have a wall. Out there are storms."

Safír grabbed his packs. "I would rather take my chances with Ih la Mat." He left out the door, and Bertin followed. "I will leave the camels with you except for Azma and Alíf. You will have three." Safír started to put his belongings onto a cart. "The Empire Gate is not so well guarded at night. Stay away from there. That is where the adèkhas will attack. Sail under Aldrico, grab the camels, and head south when the sun falls. The guards will not question travelers at night."

Bertin was shocked. "Why not wait to leave with us?"

"I do not want my head cut off for helping the Prince of Marobol escape."

Before he could think, Bertin wrapped his arms around Safír. "Thank you for taking us through the Delerous. We wouldn't have made it without you." He stepped back. *A hug?*

I'm turning into a boy again instead of a man.

"That is what the king, bless his ancestors, paid me to do." He grabbed his cart that would eventually be emptied onto Azma. He smiled and said, "Be safe."

Safír pushed his cart and disappeared into the crowds.

Bertin turned back to the house. His three guards were standing at the door. "If you feel this is right," Wilclef began, "then we will follow you."

"But I think you're wrong." Gordo added.

Bertin smiled at them. "Then we leave tonight."

"I'll go to the market for food." Gordo said.

Wilclef said, "I'll pack our things and see how to get a boat."

"I'll go to the bathhouse." Bertin could smell himself. "Then I'll come help."

"You'll need protection." Robalt said. Bertin nodded, happy one of his guards would smell better. If the elves attacked, he would need a sword to guard him, and he still didn't trust the smiles worn by the peasants.

Bertin and Robalt made their way through the narrow streets until they found a reed boat to take them to the Emperor's Isle, just across the water to the east. "Are you sure we should be this far away from the house?"

"I thought you said we were safe here."

Robalt watched the pole push them across the shallow channel. "You never know." They sat in silence as the poleman quickly crossed the water and dropped them on the sandy bank.

The Palace of Sands loomed over them once off the boat. Most of it seemed intact, but some sandstone bricks had fallen in. The main residence was atop a small hill, so it overlooked the oasis. Three walls encircled it with rounded towers and arrow slits every fifty paces. Guards surrounded the fortress, forcing passerbyers away. It was still a fortress. *Probably the only part of the city that could withstand an attack.* A dozen scorpion banners hung from the balustrades. He could see men inside with better-looking armor than even Abrezo.

"Amazing." Robalt gasped. "The emperors of old used to live here. Now, this is where the Èmawi lord lives."

"Would have been much better accommodation." Bertin scanned the area and saw a large limestone building with steam bellowing out the windows. "And I would say that's the bathhouse."

It didn't take long to enter. Robalt had to leave his weapon at the front, which he argued over, but once inside he relaxed as the steam hit him. They stripped off their clothes and scrubbed themselves in a small room, leaving brown dirt and water all over the floor. Once he was done, he found Robalt in a large pool.

"Next door is a cooling room." His guard told him. "We should go there next."

Bertin said nothing. He laid his head back and relaxed in the water, letting the warmth wrap around him like a blanket. He could hear others walking barefoot and stepping into the pool, but he didn't care. The world was finally silent. *Like back home. Why did I have to be sent to a place experiencing revolts? Why not North Ferga like Aveline, or Decaro like Baldewin?* He could hear his father's voice telling him it was because he was to become king. *I would have learned more at Hurvir's feast then coming to a desert.*

Once he had sweated enough, Robalt jumped into the cooling pool, splashing some ladies who laughed with him. Bertin stayed in the heat even as Robalt left to find his clothes and sword. He did not care how pruney his fingers and toes got. He didn't have to worry about anything. *And tonight we will begin to Salvalone for safety.*

He heard distant screams. Bertin opened his eyes and saw men and women getting out of the pools to investigate. He stood and walked barefoot over the stone floors, finding a towel and drying off before putting his baggy clothes on. Robalt was nowhere to be found. Bertin went back to the pool chamber, but only naked people were scurrying behind columns or fitting through back windows. *Everything's all right,* he told himself. *Robalt will be back soon.*

He went to the front of the building and was about to turn the doorknob when it burst open. Robalt clutched a bloody sword and pushed Bertin farther back near the pools. "They've come." Was all he said over and over.

"The elves are here?" Bertin wanted Robalt to say no, but the guard said nothing at all. He didn't want to believe it. Just five minutes before the world was silent, now it was full of screams. Men and women and children cried out from beyond the door. Those in the bathhouse hid behind benches or statues. Robalt's sword was ready to kill anything that came close.

Arrows filled the room. Everyone inside jumped for cover. Robalt pushed Bertin to the ground, his chin cracking and nose bleeding as he hit the stone. He watched as the door was engulfed by elves. Some Telemese guards followed behind but stood no chance. The elvish spears and swords stabbed right through their necks. The bathhouse owner was killed. People were running everywhere, their pink soles from the hot water carrying them to small windows or their deaths. Screams grew louder as the elves went through the rooms, killing everyone they saw.

Robalt pulled Bertin to his feet and went to the other side of the pool. There was only a wall behind them and a statue of an old emperor. Some people were hidden behind, wincing with every scream. "I will get you out of here." Robalt told Bertin. "We said we would leave tonight, and I plan to do just that."

The elves in gray armor moved like snakes. There were half a dozen of them killing as they went, slithering and striking with venom. As they drew closer, Robalt gripped his sword. "Do not come near us." The elves smirked and moved like specters. "On my honor as a knight, I will kill all of you savages if you touch a hair on his head."

Commander Abrezo was thrown forward out of nowhere. His face was bloodied and puffy. "We've been told the lord had a special guest," one elf said in the common language.

The commander nodded and pointed at Bertin. "Yes, yes! That is him. The prince. Prince of Rowan. A good hostage … he would make a good hostage."

"The prince?" A male elf looked at another, and they conversed in their language.

Robalt dropped his shoulders before taking a deep breath. "That is right. His father, King Bartel, will bring his entire might if you harm the prince. As will I."

They didn't listen to the threat, and whisked their swords around. Robalt lunged and caught one off guard, stabbing him in the throat, blood shooting into the pool. Another elf, tall and lanky, locked swords, and they parried one another's blows. Bertin didn't want to watch but couldn't keep his eyes away. *I will not be a coward. I will see the elf who kills me.* Another elf came into the bathhouse and was shouting in their ancient tongue. The fighting between Robalt and the tall elf did not stop. They seemed oblivious to the world. Block and hit and parry and hit. Robalt was holding his own much better than the Telemese guards.

"Enough." An elf with a pointed helm said in a guttural voice. He pushed a spear, and it impaled Robalt in the chest. Bertin's guard choked and dropped his sword. He glanced at Bertin, and tears rolled down his cheeks. The helmed elf kicked Robalt off the spear and into the water below. The pool turned red.

An elf grabbed Bertin by his hair and stared into his eyes. "Lucky for you, *maryr,* the lord of this city has already surrendered, and our leader wishes to see you."

Ultiir

Ultiir stood over his brother's lifeless body. Alone. Beneath the domaton in the stone crypt lit only by candles and the resting places of the many High Doma. Waiting for his body to be brought upstairs for all a commoner to see. The daken and lesser doma had made him more handsome than in life, his skin tighter with blush for more color, with his eyes closed and lips stern, a tint of blue. *The poison.* His torso and legs were wrapped in red robes, the golden wheat stitches catching the candlelight. A fake crown adorned his head, painted silver, and the sword he used during the wars, Red Wrath, lay on his body, his fingers wrapped around the hilt. Instead of death, he smelled like roses.

Just like when father died. I never realized how similar they looked. Once Hurvir was dead, it became clear to Ultiir what he had done. Killed his brother. He didn't sleep for days, wondering how history would remember him. If Vigura would welcome him to feast or cast him to Veltoora. Wondering if he'd be a righteous king. All his confidence was stripped away the moment blue oozed from Hurvir's mouth. The daken had made a hole in his stomach hoping to get the poison out. It was of no use. Hurvir was dead. Ultiir was responsible.

Now, Ultiir and his sister, Analere, were the last legitimate de'Tros. The bastard might be out there. He didn't worry so much about Devro. What boy would lead an army days after their father's death? He would be inconsolable. *As I should be, but I am king. The moment Hurvir died, I was king.* He had done little since, only arranged the funeral and investigated the cooks and merchants that brought the food to the feast. Two slaves had already been executed. They were the ones who brought Hurvir his food and drink. A cook was in the dungeon, a merchant had run and guards perused. He drowned in the Ritae.

If anyone suspected members of the King's Council, they did it quietly. Gossip in the court was not as prevalent as before. Once a king dies, the small matters of marriage and affairs become trivial. Ultiir had noticed that both Lords Zazí and Hirons were watching him closely, but they kept their mouths shut. Lord Durcy was foolishly seen celebrating the king's death with a toast, which overtook the court for a day, with the landed lord now rotting in a dungeon until he repented. Some commoners also celebrated the king's demise. Getting drunk and dancing in the streets as if the world began anew. They were hanged.

Albon had said some final words for His Grace. Some ladies cried. Ultiir had stood silent within the confines of the doma. It was a small funeral. Not too many prying eyes, but now the king was being readied for the commoners to gawk at him.

Ultiir didn't want anyone else to see his brother, but he was king, and the few commoners who loved him deserved to say goodbye. He thought of the Four welcoming Hurvir to feast with his ancestors. His father and older brothers and Philla and Analla all looking down on Ultiir as a kinslayer. *But I didn't give Hurvir the poison; I didn't even buy it. I just knew about it. Didn't rebel against him like my father against his father and brother. I only watched it happen.* That's what he told himself every night.

The stone door opened as Ultiir wiped away tears. The now dowager queen, Sophie, with braided hair tied close to her head to show she was in mourning, and draped in a red dress to preserve her modesty, came to see her dead husband. "Did I intrude?" Her voice was sad, but the emotion didn't reach her face. Now the two of them were alone with his dead brother's corpse.

"No." Ultiir felt his hair to make sure it was combed back. "I've already said my goodbyes and prayers. Just seeing him before the peasants are allowed."

Sophie grabbed Ultiir's hand; her skin so smooth he tried hard not to blush. "The realm will surely miss him." He saw lust in her eyes. *She wants this marriage soon, to consummate.* "I dreamt the gods allowed him at their feast."

"Hopefully your dream is true," she said. Ultiir's breath quickened. Her skin was the beautiful color of the Veck'kop, her eyes small and angled at him. Wanting him. "I enjoyed Albon's prayers."

He had to come up with something to say, to distract his mind and body from her fluttering eyelashes. "I pray he will allow us to marry."

Sophie smiled. "My parents will surely push me to you. What will the commoners think?"

"What does it matter?" And he put his lips against hers. Feeling the suppleness, caressing her body.

She pushed him off. "Not here," she said, looking behind her. "Someone could walk in and see us. We don't want to cause a scandal."

Muscles relaxing, he cleared his throat. "You're right."

A knock. Albon stood in the doorway, a brow slightly raised. "Your Holiness." Sophie bowed; Ultiir did not give him the pleasure.

"My Lady Duchess." Albon bowed his head, addressing her by her lesser title now that the king was dead. "I did not expect to find you both here. The lesser doma are getting anxious; they wish to display His Grace's body for the people. Droves of commoners line the streets."

"They can wait." Ultiir's jaw was tense. He didn't like the word *droves*. Hurvir had caused too much harm to the kingdom for *droves* of people to come see his poisoned body.

Sophie took hold of his hand once more. "They deserve to see their king, may the Four watch over him, before he is taken to Goldfield for the queen mother to bury him." She rubbed his fingers. "He has been monarch for almost four decades."

Mother losing another child. Now, she's stuck with me and Analere. He chuckled to himself to stop from thinking of her. The thought of his mother crying at the sight of another death hurt his head. "Fine. Be careful with him."

"Of course." Albon called in the lesser doma, who carried a flat litter where they carefully pushed the king's body. They tried not to step on the loose rocks that lined the crypt.

The litter disappeared up the stairs, and Ultiir said, "No one can lay a hand on him."

"No one will." Albon calmed. "My doma have much practice with this. The four who stand guard will let nothing happen."

"Thank you," Sophie's soft voice said, "Your Holiness. Shall we make our way to the palace?" She asked Ultiir.

He watched Albon's face. The High Doma wore a smirk. *This is the man who will crown me, a man I trust for naught.* "We have much to discuss."

"I hear the crowning will happen soon." Albon said. "Has news come from Gereduss?"

Ultiir didn't know whether Devro was alive or dead. *No matter. He isn't here to cite the Bastard Law.* "Nothing. I fear my nephew may miss his father's funeral and my crowning."

"Come." Sophie pulled Ultiir away. Leaving the High Doma alone in the crypt to clean where Hurvir was. *Plotting.*

They rode in a steel carriage back to the palace, through hordes of people, the guards shouting for the peasants to move. Ultiir heard crying and shouting. A mix of emotions he wasn't expecting. "Some are actually sad."

"Is that a surprise?" Sophie said. "We do not live in Rowan; here, kings and queens are loved."

"The city was under siege because of my brother. Thousands across the kingdom starved or froze in the winter or were murdered by outlaws. I saved them."

Sophie rubbed his shoulder. "We're almost to the palace. There, you don't have to worry about what they think. You are king. You will wear the crown soon, and the High Doma will bless you in the name of the Four."

Ultiir let out a held breath. "Do you think the Royal Court will allow it? Your son-by-law still lives." *Hopefully not.*

"You will make them." Sophie said, and Ultiir leaned his head in for a kiss, which she gave to his brow.

As they disembarked their wagon, Dele came running from

the palace doors. "My king." He bowed low and out of breath. "An emergency session of the King's Council has been called."

"What for?" Sophie and he said together.

"News from the Lands of Asara, Your Grace."

"What news could possibly warrant an emergency meeting? Has Duke Rely and his five knights revolted? Stop shipping their ore through the passes?" He tried to make light, but no grin appeared on the page's face.

"You should come." He stood aside. "The lords are waiting."

Ultiir left Sophie. Going through the maze of halls, passing the throne room and the kitchens. When they arrived at the council chamber, Ultiir entered to bows and greetings. The new seating arrangement was already decided. Ultiir sat at the head. Urses at his right side as the chief consultant. The new chief informant, Edel de'Viere, sat across from Lord Masson.

Tedbalt was reading a letter inches from his eyes, his lips twisted like he had eaten a lemon. "No good," he mumbled.

Lord Hirons cleared his throat. "Your Grace," Ultiir was still getting used to that, "we have received a message from David Rely, the duke in the Lands." He shifted his eyes down, avoiding eye contact. "He claims the bastard prince is still alive, and that his daughter, Yvanne, has taken him as husband, becoming the rightful king and queen of Viguran."

Ultiir's eyes seemed to be stuck open. He couldn't do anything, almost forgetting to breathe. *It's happened. The worst that could, did.* Lord Zazí filled his cup. Ultiir couldn't drink. "Demands?" He croaked.

Tedbalt said, "For you to abdicate, for Devro to be crowned, the King's Councilors to be replaced. An investigation into whether we committed regicide, and you," he frowned at

Ultiir, "fratricide. Though Sophie can remain as queen mother."

"Also," Gofrei spoke up, "your nephew seems to have sent a message to the High Doma."

Smart. Devro could never come up with that on his own.

"Then we must act quickly." Ultiir stood, letting his red cloak flow. "Lord Urses, word on this Maller?"

"He is to arrive in the coming days."

"Then I will deal with Albon later." Some questioning looks flashed on the lords' faces. Ultiir ignored them. "I must be crowned tomorrow before news of the Lands spreads."

"Your coronation should happen in Goldfield, not here." Tedbalt said.

"We don't have time. The proper coronation can still take place, my vassals can pay homage, I can see my mother, but tomorrow I will be crowned in front of the court." He thought of an open revolt by lords who supported Devro. "Will the lords of the court follow me?" He looked at Edel.

The young lord looked surprised. He shuffled some papers, trying to figure out what to do with his hands. "We won't know."

"Find out."

Edel bowed his head. "Yes, Your Grace."

"Can you ready knights and armies?" Ultiir said to Lord Hirons.

"You can call upon your personal levies. I will start writing to lords across the Lands of Asara, try to stop David from mustering a strong force. Also, the Eastlands and the Kinglands. We'll want to keep any rebellion contained to the mountains."

"I'll have my men double their patrols on the city wall, and along the rivers." Gofrei said, spinning a coin. *Not very serious.*

"I will also need a wife. And it seems my nephew has a soft spot for the queen dowager. I feel she would make a perfect bride." There were no looks of surprise, only consternation from Tedbalt. "Perhaps Devro will decide not to attack if his mother-by-law is my wife. They've always had a good relationship. She is also very popular with the peasants."

"And young." Gofrei said.

"I can give her a child, something Hurvir couldn't do." He noted Tedbalt's grimace.

"Your Grace?" Alan Hirons said. "I think we as councilors deserve the truth." Only a bird chirping outside the stained window could be heard. "Is what this letter says true?"

"How would Lord Rely know the goings-on of the King's Council?" Lord de'Marisco said. "I seem to recall he decided against coming to the feast due to his ailing health."

"There are rumors." Lord Zazí spoke up. "A frenzy of letters and riders followed the king's death."

Ultiir rubbed his temples. "I think you all know the answer and don't need me to tell you. You can believe whatever you like. That your new king killed his only surviving brother while our mother still lives, or that Hurvir choked on a peacock's feather, or that a slave who was hit one too many times decided to poison his drink. I do not care. But I must know if these questions and doubts will affect your performance?" Alan gazed at his twitching fingers, and Henk rubbed his bald head before they both shook their heads. "Good. I need sleep." He went to the door while the councilors stood and bowed. "Ready the court for tomorrow."

✳✳✳

The next day was abuzz with excitement. The councilors and servants had been moving about all morning, going between the old elvish manors in the Noble Lands, gathering every lord of the Royal Court. Servants had been sent to decorate the throne room. Tapestries of every color hung from banisters, showing every king of Viguran. From Valor the Iron to Hurvir, skipping the Betrayer.

Ultiir looked out. He stood in a small room behind the throne. Lords and ladies were packed into the room, standing between the towering brick pillars that held up the limestone ceiling. Sophie was next to him as dowager queen, Tedbalt as the chief daken. They waited for Albon. "It's beautiful," she said.

"I need it over with." Ultiir tapped his foot. Urses was standing in the front row, a smirk never leaving his face. The other councilors were getting into position. *That must mean we're ready.* He couldn't count, but there would be at least seventy lords and their wives, several young pages and older servants, ladies-in-waiting, and many guards. No Albon.

Ultiir snuck behind Sir Lovis. "Where is the High Doma?"

"I've received no word," his household guard said. "I have asked a few other knights, and they have no news, Your Grace."

"Do not worry." Sophie came to straighten Ultiir's collar. "He will come."

Ultiir was wearing a long mantle of fur, different from the normal silk cloak. It was purple, with gold stitches and decorations. Bushels of wheat lined the cloak from toe to neck. It was heavy. Ultiir hated the feeling that he was being pulled to the ground. *The crown will be much heavier.* He brushed his hair from his eyes.

"Your Grace," Lovis said.

Albon came through the door, three guards from the doma, swords at their side. "We will wait." Tedbalt said and pushed Sophie from the room to take their places to the right of the throne. Sir Lovis drew closer to Ultiir, his hand resting on the sword hilt.

"Where have you been?" Ultiir tried to keep his face from going red.

"I had important duties in the domaton."

"More important than crowning your king?"

Albon laughed. "I have one king, and he does not wish to be crowned by me."

"Do not make this day a spectacle." Ultiir motioned to the three guards. They had a four-pointed star painted on their breastplates. His feet dragged him even closer to Lovis. *I will not die before the coronation.* "Crown me and be done. Your gods will wait."

"I received a message in the night. At first I thought it was a forgery." Albon closed the door to a crack, the mingling of lords getting quiet, and pulled a parchment from his sleeve. "You have been charged with regicide. The gods may wait, but my justice will not. I cannot crown you while another calls himself king and invokes the laws of this land."

"Those are lies, and Devro must be in this palace when he invokes such laws." Ultiir's head was throbbing.

Albon looked up as if he were looking to the gods. "I believe there may be some truth. Our discussion in the domaton, your brother now dead, you moments from being crowned. It is suspicious."

Ultiir came face to face with the High Doma. "I am the heir. It i by law that I am crowned, bastard or no."

"I am here to make sure you are not crowned with just vile accusations against you. To take you to the dungeon if need be. I do not wish to sic my guards upon you," Albon said, "but they fight with the Four and the Many guiding their hands."

"Quiet your tongue," Lovis said with gritted teeth and unsheathed his sword. "The gods' men will never defeat a man knighted by a king, and Sir Lird and others are right outside that door to cut you down."

Ultiir put his hand on Lovis' leather armor. "This cannot come to violence. Not on the day of my coronation. Albon, it is treason that you come here with blades and threaten me, but I do not need you to put a crown on my head. I have hands. They give me power."

Lovis held out his sword while Ultiir flung the door open, dragging the heavy mantle behind him. Albon put up his arms to stop his men from advancing.

The court went silent. Lovis followed to the center of the room in line with the other knights of his household, standing in front of Ultiir, who was in front of the throne. Some whispers spread when Albon did not follow, others about the guards the High Doma brought. Ultiir nodded to Lord Masson, who would give the words. Tedbalt looked concerned but cleared his throat and shouted. "The King Hurvir de'Tro the Warrior has been sent to feast with the Four and the Many. At times this happens, which brings about a new era of Viguran. A ruler may die, but the king lives on."

He grabbed a sword the length of his leg, the Gods' Harvest, used by Rickart the Maker when he was bringing the kingdom of Viguran together, and presented it to Ultiir, who took it and placed the tip on the red carpet below. "The gods oversee the transfer of this city. This holy place. The place where Vigura walked among us, and the land that surrounds it, to a successor." Ultiir was watching attendants sneak into the room. Whispering. Small gossip began in the back. *They know of Devro. I just know it.* He locked eyes with the old lord, willing him to go faster.

Tedbalt continued, "The laws of this realm, made under the gods, have made the succession clear." This was the time Albon would have given Ultiir his crown. To show the audience he was the rightful successor, but the High Doma was a coward. Ultiir turned to the throne. The crown was a magnificent pile of jewels waiting to show off the wealth of kings. Sitting on the throne, laying the sword across his legs, he lifted the heavy crown above his head and placed it on him. There were a few gasps.

Then Tedbalt gave a shaky shout. "I give you the King of the dominion of Viguran, Watcher of the Veck'kop, Protector of the Kinglands, Lord of the Glybelm, and Defender of the Nokys. King Ultiir de'Tro the First."

The audience clapped and shouted, "Long live the king."

Tundavik

The old doma cleared her throat. Tundavik could hear from the other side of the door. He had decided not to go in, no point in seeing a new king crowned. The real coronation would be in Vigur. *If we win.* He rubbed his hands together to warm them. Whitehall was getting colder with every passing day. Helge shouted over the sound of applause, "I give you the King of the dominion of Viguran, Watcher of the …" The town was empty outside, eerily familiar. He grabbed his head as a headache racked his brain.

The doors flung open, and the peasants who had watched spilled out. Knights joked and took off their surcoats. Devro and his new queen came out. They both wore gilded iron as crowns. Not as fanciful as the crown the new false king would have on his head. The bastard stood with a newfound mightiness. "A woman has never crowned a king in Viguran," he sneered.

Yvanne patted his arm. "Some women do it in other kingdoms."

"We're not in *other kingdoms*. We are in Viguran." His face turned into a pout. "I'll get crowned again in Vigur." He changed his face to a smile as the new king and queen greeted the peasants and knights and advisers.

Tundavik rolled his eyes at Devro as Sirs Mar and Raimund followed behind. "That messenger from a few days ago, who told us about Ultiir's coronation, told him that his uncle crowned himself." Raimund said.

"Devro thinks just like the false king," Mar started, "that he's higher than the gods. I had to convince him to let the old woman crown him."

"They are family." Raimund muttered.

Tundavik watched as Yvanne greeted the people, shaking their hands. "The people will love our new queen, it seems."

"I doubt anyone can be as beloved as the queen dowager." Mar said, then nodded in understanding. "I forgot you haven't been here. Queen Sophie from Terrop came in and fed anyone who asked, and prayed with them to the gods. Some rumors say she fucked young virgins, so they knew what to do when the time came." Mar must've seen Raimund and Tundavik's twisted faces. "I'm not saying I believe it. I'm sure Hurvir's previous wives had a lot to do with any salacious rumors that attached to the queen."

"Let's hope that doesn't run in the family." Tundavik said. "Devro will have to decide on his successor," he whispered, "in the unfortunate case he is killed."

Raimund's voice also dropped to a whisper. "There was the incident in Udello. If Ultiir can get that close to him outside the realm."

"Who knows what he can do here." Mar said. "All things we'll need to discuss."

The Duke of the Lands of Asara came out of the 'throne room' and embraced his daughter and new son-by-law. "It is time this marriage was consummated." He roared, visibly holding back a cough. The crowd cheered, and Yvanne and Devro were whisked away to their bedchamber deep in the mountain.

"I think that means it's time for sleep." Tundavik said. "Fetch me if anything goes awry." The two knights nodded.

Tundavik found his small bedchamber within the mountain that he shared with Mar and Raimund. Thick fur lay atop his bed so he could stay warm as the nights grew colder. He stripped down and crawled under what looked like bear fur. It reminded him of his new cloak. The old lord stared at the ceiling and its rotting wooden beams. *War is about to begin. Let's not end like last time.* He fell asleep.

***

A cool breeze washed over him. The darkness of the room turned to the dark of a forest. Towering trees surrounded him. *Ritaeum.* A small light glowed in the distance. It called out to him in a language he didn't understand. His boots pulled him against his will. Tundavik stumbled over the roots that poked from the ground. His eyes were still sleepy. As the light grew bigger and brighter, the world came into view. Death was everywhere.

A young girl with a twisted neck dead in a pool, a man bleeding out. He turned and saw himself. His eyes fell as his face collapsed in on itself. Then it was Devro, choking and calling out for his father and mother. Tundavik ran, but he was getting nowhere. The voice from the light screamed at him now. Pulling him into the whiteness. His nails dug into the ground, but it was no use. He was yanked into the light. He felt nothing. Saw nothing.

194

Then, his head trembled. A noble tree, taller than any mountain he had ever seen, crashed into the world below. Earthquakes rippled and volcanoes erupted. The entire world was killing itself. Falling into itself.

Then it was quiet.

A voice pierced the air as he found himself back in the dark forest. "You will not reach the light of the world until you find the forest." The image of a naked woman with etchings on her body clouded his vision. Her skin a map of raised bumps that looked like slithering snakes waiting to strike. "Bring Ryobas to the forest. You mustn't waste time. Nhamcaryn is coming, and with it, the end of your world and those you love. You mustn't waste time."

***

Tundavik woke with a knock on his door. A knight with a bear surcoat opened it. "My lord, they are waiting for you."

His vision was blurry and his voice was hoarse; images of Ritaeum filled his head. The sounds of his wife and children. The sounds of his people. His breathing quickened so much he felt like he was about to faint. "Adile?"

"Excuse me, my lord?"

Tundavik sat up, his head pulsing, and calmed his breath while he wiped the sweat from his brow. "Who are you?"

"Sir Robern, my lord." The knight held his head high.

"I am not a lord." Tundavik stood to find his clothes, resting his hand on his heart. It wanted to fall out of his chest. An old shirt was lying on a chair. "What meeting?" He said as he dressed, his hands shaking.

"The king and his council. They are planning what to do

next."

"Lead me there," Tundavik gulped from the nightmare.

They wandered into the hall outside his door. *Might as well be catacombs.* There was no light except for the torches. The walls were gray rock, and moisture dripped from the rocky ceiling. Some wooden beams held the mountain up above them. He wanted to inspect them for cracks, but decided he'd rather not know if the Asara was about to collapse. The corridors looked like the mines he had seen when he was young. The mountains were full of them. Backbreaking work to get whatever precious ore for some rich, fat bastard to flaunt. The keep in Whitehall already looked stripped of iron or coal or whatever may have been there.

The darkness reminded him of the woman who called out to him. Of the horrors he dreamed. "I need fresh air first." He said to Sir Robern, who only nodded.

He was calm again once the fresh air hit his face. Smelling the cookfires for morning, and seeing the people go about their day brought him joy. The air was warm today, even though Meret would bring winter soon. He smiled at the thought of Glodsteil, the dwarf in Attrima, who closed up shop when Agaales' winds blew over the harbor. *Wonder if Whitehall comes to a halt in the winter?* He then realized he hadn't seen snow since leaving Viguran all those years ago; maybe something good would come out of this detour.

His stomach gurgled as the smell of fresh bread wafted through the air; he probably didn't have time to eat. The lords and knights and whomever else were waiting for him. Even the lady in the forest waited for him.

His head ached. *Strange dream,* he thought, *if it was only a dream. A message from the gods?* Remembering the dream sent chills down his spine. Nothing good can come from this dream. *Maybe Adile's ghost will be awaiting me.*

"Do you have bad dreams here, Sir Robern?"

The knight looked surprised. "Nothing unusual. The occasional dream of a family member dying, then that happening a few days or weeks later. The gods must wish for me to see them again."

"I haven't had a dream like that in many years." *Not since that night in Suktir when I dreamt Ritaeum dead.* He didn't want to have awful dreams again, but his dream last night and the awful pain in his head worried him. "I'm ready." He spun on his heels and walked back into the catacombs.

Sir Robern took his turn to stand guard by the door after opening it. When Tundavik entered the room, David Rely, Raimund, Mar, Devro, and Arold, the swordmaster of Whitehall, sat at a long table. Pollard and some other guard stood in their blinding white armor at the edges of the room. The men were passing around a parchment, Devro with a beaming smile. He ripped the letter from Mar's hand and looked like a child who'd been given too many sweets. "Read this."

Tundavik took it, saying, "Important?"

At the top he saw the words 'King Hurvir de'Tro the First' and wondered if the dead were rising from the Ritae. Before he could finish, Devro pointed to the middle of the page. "He has accepted me."

Tundavik didn't understand how someone as cruel as Hurvir could do anyone a kindness.

David stood with a wobble and said, "The dead king, may the Four watch over him, seems to have legitimized Devro," the duke coughed, "before his death. At least the parchment bears his signature."

Tundavik scanned the note. It was true. "And you believe these words?"

"What does it matter?" Mar said. "Real or not, it has the king's seal and signature. It looks like the parchments he signed while alive." He leaned back in his chair. "Only the lords need to believe it's true for Devro to gain support."

"It will put any mutterings about the Bastard Law at bay," David said. "The trueborn heir need not present himself to the court to claim succession. He could be in the wetlands of Eotros and still be king upon the death of his father."

"Who sent it?"

"Lord Geary." Raimund didn't sound as amused as the others. "A messenger came in the night."

"You don't think the people will support Ultiir anyhow?" Tundavik asked.

"The people will support whoever has the larger army." Raimund laid his hands on a map that was sprawled out on the table, showing the whole of Viguran. "And right now we have only Whitehall for certain and assume the rest of the Lands will follow Lord Rely."

David panted. "I have begun recruiting for our cause. I've had letters sent to the Lords of the Peaks, the Lowlands, the Crossing; telling them to support their liege lord. The other dukes have surely got messages by now. I sent word weeks ago to the High Doma, Albon, telling him of Ultiir's transgressions. Even the kings of Rowan, Terrop, Maertan, the governors of Redington, the House of Awaran. I am hoping to gain stronger allies."

"I've been telling them all morning," Raimund started, "that it will not matter how many people we get to our side if we cannot pay for the levies."

"It is their duty to follow me." The duke said before a fit of coughing attacked. Pollard came over and whispered in his ear; David shooed him away. "I give them protection from invaders, the Lodean, meddling from the king; and they support me in battle. A fair trade. And if we must, the mountains are home to some of the most beautiful land this world has seen; a knight can become landed, and the peasants can be sent to live with them. I sent word to the other dukes as well. Of course, Lord Blume stopped his father's rebellion, so who knows what he'll do. Lord Adyn Gallient is young and untrained. Lord Valles in the Woodlands has sent word in the last month of ominous things in the trees. If he handled whatever ghosts were haunting him, then he might join our side."

Raimund let David cough some more. "I think we should meet with the bankers in Redington."

Tundavik finally sat. The wooden chair was wobbly, and the table smelled of mildew. Mar sat across from him, Raimund next to him, Devro at the end and David at the other. Arold, the swordmaster, whom Tundavik knew little about, sat to his right. It wasn't anything like the King's Council in Vigur, which Tundavik had seen once. There were no stained windows, nor mosaics on the walls. No columns. No arched door with black metalwork. This room was wooden, the same as the chairs and table. It was warmer as it was built farther into the mountain. A fire crackled in the corner. *Where does the smoke go?* Was Tundavik's only thought before the swordmaster finally spoke, "I am inclined to agree with my Lord Duke. It would be a waste of precious time to go to Redington."

"If we don't get support," Raimund sighed, "we'll need to hire mercenaries."

"Those aren't cheap." Mar said.

Tundavik asked, "What does Devro think?" Heads at the table swiveled to the young prince—no—king. Devro was rocking in his seat.

"I think," Devro said, "that Lord Rely is right. My father has legitimized me and named me heir. Once the rest of the kingdom hears of this, there will be no one left to support my uncle. He'll be seen as a usurper. Go down in history like Valor the Dark." Tundavik saw Arold wince at the name 'Valor.' "Redington will always be there, and the bankers will probably send us money once they see I am winning against whatever rebellion Ultiir tries." Tundavik had never seen the child so happy. *I guess a father's acceptance will do that. Too bad he's still naïve.* "And if my uncle decides to throw down his arms and support me, then I can name him Lord of Goldfield once more." *So naïve.*

"Yes, Your Grace," Arold said. "Though I agree with Sir Raimund that we need support."

"Pick a place and send me." Mar said. "I can get anyone to do anything for me."

"Preferably a powerful ally." Tundavik said. "We have to hope that Lord Rely's vassals will answer his call no issue, so look outward." He watched as Devro's eyes scanned the map, looking at the borders and the names of the duchies and cities. Tundavik's old shirt was scratchy on his neck. The sooner out of this, the better. "Also close by," he added, eyeing the capital of the Eastlands.

Devro said, "Riverton." Tundavik nodded.

"Good choice, Your Grace," Arold said.

"I've known Lord Gallient a long time," David wheezed. "He shouldn't be too hard to convince."

"Mar and Raimund, you can go." Devro said.

"Someone will need to stay by your side." Raimund's eyes were wide. "We cannot let you get hurt."

"I'll be fine, Sirs Pollard and Robern and Firo are close." He stood and looked at the flatness of the Eastlands. Tundavik did too. Seeing how easy it would be for Ultiir to send men over the fertile steppe. He followed the Three Rivers from their sources in the Asara to the Nokys. *Easy to send riverboats with armies.*

"Perhaps we send some men with Raimund and Mar," Tundavik said. "In case of attack." Arold nodded. *Maybe he sees what I see.* "Also, if the Duke of the Eastlands tries anything grave. We must assume Ultiir is also gathering support, promising whatever he can. I think Lord Rely should continue to send messages for support, especially lords in the Flewthlands; they have a knack for revolt."

David cleared his throat. "Your being seen is important, and while I don't think you should go to Riverton in case of battle, Winterlake would love to see you. Lord Vandes and the king can wait in the foothills of the Asara until word comes that Riverton is safe." There was nodding around the room except for Raimund, who stared at Redington on the map.

"So it's settled." Devro clapped, his faux-gold crown almost falling from his head. "Sir Raimund and Sir Mar will go to Riverton and get the Eastlands on my side, Tundavik and I will go to the edge of the Lands, and Lord Rely will continue to write for more support. Hopefully, a quick end to Ultiir's coup."

Sophie

Ultiir tensed as he finished inside her then fell over panting. Sophie dried her brow of sweat from the fucking and the wool sheets. She flipped her hair back and rubbed Ultiir's chest. "News will spread." *Especially among my 'council'.*

"Let it." Ultiir kissed her hand. "I don't care what anyone thinks, only you."

"The new king and queen dowager fucking until the sun rises is sure to bother some, especially the doma." *What would my parents think? But they want me to be the queen, and Ultiir needs me to calm him.*

"Fuck the doma."

Sophie's eyes widened. "The Four will not be happy with that. Kings and queens are supposed to be subservient to their most devout."

"I will pray." Ultiir quietly chuckled. "Why do you care what others think? You act as if you're the first queen to take the new king as husband."

"But we are not yet married." She sat up, her hair falling down her back. "When?" She wished for the marriage to be over to make sure Ultiir took her as his wife. She couldn't be sent back to Terrop or her dowager lands and embarrass her parents.

"Whenever Albon decides, he will serve his new king."

"Or Maller of Forecreak arrives?"

She saw Ultiir's chest sink. "Maller? How did you find out?"

Sophie gave a sly smile as she grabbed Ultiir's trousers from the floor and wiped herself clean of him. *I do not need a child at the moment. Then I could never be rid of Ultiir.* "You act as if the queen knows nothing. I have people, the same as you and Hurvir before. I knew every detail about the nights he would visit the King's Brothel. The women. The positions. I am not helpless."

"So I shouldn't visit any whores?" He smiled as he sat up, smelling of sweat. "I will not hide anything from you, and especially not fuck any other woman than you." He reached an icy hand to rest on her back. "Maller will be here soon. He had to pay his respects to my mother and the dead king in Goldfield."

"You're sure he will marry us?"

He laughed. "You seem to be looking forward to it as much as I am."

"Of course," she said with no emotion. She only needed Ultiir to marry her to not be cast aside. She was entrusted with uniting Terrop and Viguran, and that was what she planned to do. "The only reason I did not tell anyone of your plan was because you said we would wed."

"Shame we couldn't wait to consummate the marriage the lawful way. You were just too beautiful today."

She slipped into her nightgown and draped a black cloak over her shoulders, rolling her eyes at Ultiir's comment, but making sure he didn't see. "Not again." She said, shaking her finger. "Not until we are officially married." She didn't give him a last kiss as he leaned in. Instead, opening the door and almost hitting Sir Lovis, she left in silence.

As she exited Ultiir's bedchamber, she saw two young slaves whispering in a corner. Giggling like the girls they were. Snapping her fingers at them, she said, "And what purpose do you have to be in this wing of the palace?" The girls bowed and quickly shuffled away. *Now, even the slave quarters will be abuzz with gossip. Before long, the whole of Vigur will know.*

She walked as quietly as she could. Hoping the whole place was asleep. Making her way through slave stairs and dark corners, she eventually reached her wing of the palace. Sir Achen nodded. "Thank you," she said to her guard. It took much convincing to let her leave alone at night, but a guard must obey his ruler. She sneaked past Renna and Amalla's room, hearing the girls giggling about something. She fell onto her bed and dreamt of her dead husband.

As she woke to the curtains being opened by her handmaids, she could only think about Hurvir. Even though she was happy he was not here anymore, here to beat her or lash out at her, even ruin her as he gained pleasure, she still wept. She had cried over her dead husband. She had cried at the thought of blue poison oozing from his mouth, his lifeless eyes staring at her, judging her. *The Four know Ultiir told me. They know I did not stop my husband from being murdered.* She laid a hand on her forehead, whispering a prayer to Meret. *Not a very dutiful wife I am.*

"A bath, Your Grace?" Renna said as Amalla found a rag.

"Isn't it a little early?" Sophie yawned, her mind still racing with thoughts of Hurvir and Ultiir. *I must play nice with Ultiir. He killed his own brother. What horrors could he inflict upon me?*

"Your parents wish to see you, Your Grace."

"My parents?" She quickly sat up. "Is everything all right?"

"Yes," Amalla strode over to fix Sophie's bedsheets. "They only want to talk."

Sophie nodded and went about her normal morning routine. A bath, her hair brushed. Eventually, a slave brought up some buttered bread and goat cheese. Her handmaids dressed her in a red gown with yellow stitching. It hid her legs from the world, and the neckline showed no chest. Renna tied Sophie's hair under a red veil. A modest widow in mourning.

"Sir Achen will escort you, Your Grace," Amalla said.

Her knight took her down the main stairs instead of her preferred side steps. *The whole palace is to see me depressed, as any dowager queen should be.* Lords of the Royal Court and their wives stood at the bottom of the steps, all staring at her. She straightened her back. Lady Alba of Midriver's eyes were full of contempt. Other lords and ladies whispered as she passed. *Ultiir. I wonder if my parents know? Would they even care?* Sir Achen took her outside so the slaves and masters could watch her. *Gossip spreads faster than a plague.*

Her parents stood near the bank of the Montla, looking at the Cliffs of Iron. She never appreciated the scenery as much as she did now. The flatness of Udello was nothing like that of Vigur. Rivers cutting smooth lines to divide the city from the surrounding mass; the snowcapped mountains in the distance, ever looming; the cliffs and bluffs that were sprinkled near the water, some bare, some wooded. The best view in Udello was of the palace. No mountains or cliffs, only a river over a mile wide making Rainvealand look so far away.

The guards bowed as Sophie hugged her mother. "You're

leaving." Sophie noticed they were wearing gray tunics and trousers, not at all the clothes of her family.

Her father embraced her and then straightened his crown. "Vigur doesn't seem the best place for kings at the moment. We will go to the Ritae Docks in a few hours."

"Won't you stay?" Sophie held back her tears. "For me?"

Evna brushed Sophie's hair from her eyes. "I'm sorry, daughter. We must get to Udello; we visited the king, we saw Ultiir crowned. There is nothing else for us here."

"We would take you back," Anvrin said, "but you have dowager lands to see to." He looked out over the water. "As well as a new king."

"Rumors." Sophie squeaked.

"No matter." Her mother said. "If Ultiir will take you for his bride, then you must stay. You must do whatever it takes."

"Then stay for the wedding." *Don't leave me. Not with Ultiir.* "I'm sure no expense will be spared. It will be grander than my late husband's feast. Food and drink from every continent. A place of honor for the bride's parents."

"Enough, Sophie." Her father turned back to her. "You are a woman grown. You do not need us to help you. An heir. That is what's needed. You marry this new king and produce heirs for him. The Margia line will be stronger than ever. The two Veck'kop kingdoms ruled by our descendants, perhaps one day joining them as one. It is a glorious thought. Our family rising from Dukes of Vecca to kings of great realms to emperors of the Ters-Veck. You must stay. Your brother will do his duty in Terrop, and you must do yours here."

"Mother …" Sophie held tears while looking at Evna.

"Your father is right, my sweet." Evna rubbed Sophie's hand. "We will not stay away long, and you can visit Udello once you are remarried."

Sophie stepped back, taking a deep breath of fresh air, watching fish jump out of the Montla. Her parents embraced her in silence. Eventually they left with their knights and pages, leaving her to stare over the river. The river of life. The place where Vigura raised the first man. The first man with thoughts of his own, feelings of his own. A man who did what he wanted. He didn't have parents to listen to. Vigura put him into this world and let him do whatever he pleased.

She traced the palace's shadow with her eyes. It cast a darkness over the cliffs and bluffs around the rivers, keeping her cool as the morning sun rose. Smoke bellowed from bakeries and homes in the city getting ready for the day. *This land could be mine. Not just my dowager lands in the Eastlands. All mine. Not even my parents would control it.* She smoothed her dress, and Sir Achen escorted her back into the palace.

They made their way inside, lords and ladies eating breakfast in the Noble Lands. Smells of fresh bread and cooking ham and eggs and morning ale filled her nose. Sophie stopped at the large wooden doors of the throne room. Black iron trim.

"Is the Royal Court in today?" She asked her guard.

Sir Achen shook his head. "Still in a period of mourning."

The guards in front of the doors wore surcoats with owls. "Does the king know you wish to enter his throne room, Your Grace?" A knight with a boyish face asked.

Sophie ignored him, and Achen glared the boy into submission. "Tell me if someone wishes to enter." Stepping forward, the young guard opened the creaking doors. "Stay." Sir Achen bowed his head.

The throne room was empty. Tapestries removed, carpets

rolled up, no servant or slave to be found. The guards shut the large wooden doors behind her; the thump echoing through the columns and the large ceiling. Stained windows lit her with different shades. *So quiet.* No roar of the river or lords conversing with their wives. No moans of pleasure from Ultiir. No yellings or beatings from Hurvir.

She walked down the aisle. Imagining the crowd that appeared for Ultiir's crowning. All clapping and cheering. Instead, calling out, "Queen Sophie." Her parents beamed with happiness that their daughter would become the most powerful woman in Adedor. Her brothers jealous. Hurvir and Ultiir were nowhere to be found.

Reaching the steps to the chair, she took a deep breath. *No one is around to see.* She climbed the stairs slowly, one foot in front of the other, making sure not to trip. She wouldn't want to embarrass herself in front of her imaginary lords. Her silver diadem clung to her hair, but the crown of Viguran would strain her neck, the jewels weighing down her body. That's what she wished for. The heavy burden of that crown. Her Queen's Council wouldn't be about gossip, but about rebellion and politics and trade. Lord Masson shouted out that she was the protector of the Veck'kop. That she ruled from the Ters-Veck to the Flit River, controlled the islands of the Nokys and was lady of the Glybelm.

She sat.

The velvet hugged her. The handles cold on her arms, her feet just dangling above the floor, the crowd cheering as she was crowned as queen, no king needed for her to rule. She took a breath of power.

"You look good," Urses said, emerging from the shadow of a brick column, then bowing. "My Duchess of Aele."

No queen.

"Lurking are we?" Sophie didn't stand. She wanted to feel what it was like to rule from her newfound throne.

"Enjoying the quiet." Urses rubbed his nose as he ascended the steps, his blue cloak bouncing. "You may cause a scandal sitting in that chair. What would Lady Abre say? Your now-dead husband?" He drug his fingers across the metal armrests. "Another scandal so soon after …" he stopped.

Sophie smiled. *Thinking he can threaten me?* "Apparently, mine and Ultiir's pleasure cannot be hidden." Urses circled the throne like a hawk with prey. "You'll be glad to know our new king will take me to wife in the coming days."

"Yes, after Maller shows his face so Albon can be stripped of his duties."

"You believe the other doma will go along with the plan?"

Urses stopped in front of her, holding out his hand to take hers. She declined. Standing on her own, she puffed her gown and began her way to the door. "Ultiir has noticed things about His Holiness that would get common people killed," Urses said, "especially in your homeland." Sophie gave a questioning look. "You've read your histories. Udello was filled with smoke for months as the mages were put to fire."

"Ultiir is going to accuse Albon of witchcraft?" She gave a small laugh. "And when the conclave sees no proof?"

They stopped at the door; the guards conversing and their boots clanging on the other side. "Your soon-to-be-husband is no simpleton. He has two eyes, and a king's word is law, unless the doma want to be banished to Pleat to deal with the plague."

"I'll be interested to see the outcome." Sophie knocked on the large doors and the guards opened it. Achen with a grimace toward Urses.

"The lords would never let you sit there, not you or a daughter, even if she were Ultiir's." Urses bowed his head before leaving. *We will see.* The lord of Keeland turned back around once he was down the corridor. "It seems Maller of Forecreak has arrived." Sophie took a deep breath at the thought of another marriage.

Bertin

e's coming." Lord Abia Èmaw said before the door was thrown open. Gala came in wearing Telemese leather, showing off his yellow teeth that looked like fangs. "Kuslu wants to see the lord now." His voice was melodic. It didn't match his rough face and bloodstained knuckles that he used to beat Bertin and the lord. "I'll be back for you." He told Bertin.

Lord Abia Èmaw, the lord of Lisan Biresdea, had spent the days crying and pleading with the elves whenever they checked on their prisoners. He had given up the city in less time than Bertin could blink. Bertin told him what he had seen in the bathhouse. *Robalt is dead,* he remembered the pool running red. *Idiot. Had to fight the elves who cut through the Telemese like it was nothing. Of course, he died.* His hand moved to dry tears, but there were none. He had had nothing to drink for days. At least he hoped it was days and not weeks. He lost count.

They left the room, and Bertin fell into a pile of dust. The sun cooked his cell from the tiny window above him. He wore only white, baggy shirts; stained pants that ended just above the ankle; and no shoes, causing his feet to burn as the scorching sun heated the stone floors. He was locked in a wooden cell in the western tower of the Palace of Sands. Ih la Mat had battered the city since morn, dust and sand sticking to the limestone walls. The elves had leaped over the walls and attacked the Èmawi lord and his guards before pushing through the rest of the city. Abrezo, a laughable excuse of a commander, surrendered when the palace fell, then was killed and thrown into the oasis. *Coward. This was the man chosen to lead the defense of the city?*

He felt his tongue. Dry. Worse than when he was in the Delerous Desert with Safír. He didn't know how long he could go without water. *Rowan is full of streams and rivers, and here I am regretting not drinking more at home. I should have never left. Told father to fuck off.* He lowered his head. *I wonder if this is what Grandmother felt like when the People's Chamber had imprisoned her. Helpless. Hopeless. There is nothing I can do.*

Abia had turned to Bertin with a bloodied face when he was thrown into the cell. "The Prince of Rowan." The lord spoke in Delerous, pleading with his captors. Later, Gala, their elf-guard, with dark skin and towering height, told Bertin what Abia had said. "Will you let me go now? I promise to keep my cousin's armies at bay. There will be no war. I gave you a greater gift than myself—just a lousy lord—I gave you a prince of one of the most powerful kingdoms in Adedor. His father will give you anything you desire to get his heir back." It was his fault Robalt was dead.

He wanted to cry, but just like before, no tears came. His eyes burned, and his throat got drier. His heart was beating so fast he could hear it. He couldn't cry and could hardly sweat. "Water." He said to no one. The palace was no more than twenty feet from the oasis, and he couldn't reach it. He may never feel the coolness of water again. Never cry again.

Splashing sounds came through the window. He pulled himself up to the iron bars and saw kids playing in it. The elves watched but didn't harm them. Probably waiting to kill them like predators watching prey. Other than that, Lisan Biresdea was dead to the world. It was as if the desert had swallowed it. There were no bakers, traders, butchers, or tailors. The streets were empty, and the channels were free of boats. The water actually looked clear without humans always rowing over it. He could see the statue of Aldrico watching the city. Probably crying at his fortress falling to elves.

He wanted to go home so badly his chest ached. *After I find Wilclef and Gordo.* He had waited for the door to swing open and his guards to be tossed into cells, but they never came, and Bertin assumed the worst. *No. They are not dead. I won't believe it.*

Bertin had fallen asleep when the door opened and the Èmawi lord was thrown back in his cell. Gala fumbled with the keys. "Your turn." He opened Bertin's door and pulled him out. Bertin tried to see if Abia was beaten and bloodied, but the lord crawled into a corner to sleep.

Gala pushed and pulled him through the corridors of the Palace of Sands. The interior was the same as outside, all sandstone. It was ugly, not like the wooden fortresses of Rowan. He remembered it had been built over a thousand years ago. *Robalt.* The windows showed the elves patrolling below on the three curtain walls. Some wore elvish armor, while others wore stolen Telemese plates. He could see that the scorpion banners across the city were gone. Bonfires set all across the Emperor Isle. Gala pushed him harder when Bertin got lost in the scene outside.

"What does this Kuslu want?" He asked the elf.

Gala responded in his singsong voice that didn't match his look. "Don't think because some say you're a prince that you get to speak. You are a prisoner here."

"It was only a question. Abia Èmaw didn't look to beat up, so I was curious." His vision went black then fuzzy as his head smashed into the wall, and Gala smiled.

"Beat enough for you?"

Bertin could taste blood, and his neck ached. He didn't say anymore as they made their way up the spiral stone steps. Down a short corridor was a busted door that was ornate with iron and gold. Some elves were stripping it as they went by.

Inside were a few elves surrounding a table. Bertin could make out a map of Telemaw, the oasis of Lisan Biresdea and the Ginosa where Vaandet rose above its banks. A female elf with purple warpaint across her cheeks tapped a spear. An elf with a short sword on his hip turned.

"Well, if it isn't the Prince of Rowan himself." He nodded at Gala, who stepped back. "That Èmaw told me you met just a few days ago. Arranged for you to stay in a shack." He moved closer. Bertin didn't know much about elves; Blis had skipped that part of their lessons. But what he did know was that this elf, Kuslu, was from a southern band. His skin was darker than Gala's, and his voice more guttural than melodic. Blis didn't fail to mention the Pywaln Revolt. *This elf probably took part in that.* "He didn't have many nice things to say about a foreign king sending his son to help with *Oléman* problems. And you didn't even help with the city's defense. My *mehét* tell me you were in a bathhouse. They found you naked with your guard," Kuslu said as Gala snickered behind him. "You're allowed to speak. You are a prince after all."

"I have nothing to say."

"Ioelena," Kuslu said to the female elf, "some water." Bertin's ears perked up as Ioelena, the one with the warpaint, brought over a small cup of water.

She then spoke in the most mesmerizing voice Bertin had ever heard. "For the prince." Her words were like silk. They flowed over him and made him comfortable. He took a drink and instantly felt relief, but craved more. The elf took the cup and his chances of getting any. *Maybe if I talked.*

His throat seemed to open up with the water. "I only want to know what you plan to do with me?"

Kuslu smiled. "You think we're going to kill you? Cut off your head and send it to your father? We would not resort to such human savagery," he said it like a curse. "I will personally write a letter to the king of Rowan, explaining to him that you are safe and under my protection. The only things I need are coins. Then you can go back to your fields."

"Money?" Bertin shook his head. "My father took back Rowan when the fields were on fire. He led his armies to Bardekan and sacked the city to end the war, the first time in almost a thousand years," he added. "What makes you think he will not sail the hundreds of miles and bring you to your knees?"

Gala said from behind, "He seems to think his father is invincible. Shall we put it to the test?"

Kuslu ignored Gala. "I have heard all the stories an elf can of King Bartel of Rowan. Killing his own people to take back a throne. How noble." Kuslu motioned to the room. "This is what protects us from your kind. This fortress was built to protect emperors from other humans. What makes you think an army can take it?"

He can't be serious. "Your army took it."

"We are elves," he gave a smirk. "And not mine, King Blaenda's army."

"And where is this king? I would like to speak to him."

"No human can lay their eyes on the king," an elf from behind Ioelena said. He had light skin but dark eyes. Like evil was crawling its way out of him.

"Quiet, Ryfor," Kuslu said. "King Blaenda did not come with us. He rules in Anha Jorbstah."

"At least my father led his men into battle." It was Bertin's turn to smirk. "He didn't cower away in a castle while they died."

"The king has many things to worry about," Kuslu said to Bertin before speaking in elvish to calm down Ryfor, whose eyes were bulging with anger. "He recruited me from *Anha Jorbstah.* I had led the revolt in the Pywaln and the reason the city is back in elvish control." *Of course. An elf can never be content with what he has; he must take and take. Age must've taught him how to bring down fortresses.*

As if Kuslu read Bertin's mind, he said, "I was born when the last elven war took place. My parents had fled from Anha Jorbstah to *Mi'aral,* the land of dwarves. I took Anha Jorbstah back from the Rainvealandians to give it back to our ancient brethren."

"And now you've spread west for what? You don't control the land from Cluo to the Nokys. There is much to take over there."

"*Oléma* is weak." Ryfor piped up. "They have been weak since the empire burned to ash, and we plan on showing *Mi'tor* that we are not weak anymore."

Kuslu didn't quiet him, but agreed. "This fortress that once housed emperors and their wives now houses a wealthy lord whose only power is his cousin, the king. We have shown Hasíb and all rulers of Mi'tor that we are to be taken seriously once more. We are not the elves of old, nor the ones in your storybooks. No, we revolt, and most importantly, we win."

An elf came into the room and spoke to Kuslu. They discussed something at great length until Bertin's legs got tired from standing. Kuslu said something to Ioelena and Gala.

"We will have to speak more some other time." Kuslu told Bertin.

His guard left the room, and Ioelena grabbed her spear. She turned Bertin and pushed his back.

"What's happening?" Bertin asked as some other elves followed Gala down the hall.

"Gala will be busy for the next few days." Ioelena's voice was soft and would've been comforting had it not been for the spear at his back. "I will be your guard."

They walked through the corridors, and Bertin could see a group of elves dressing themselves in stolen armor. Gala was shouting at them in elvish. He couldn't watch long because Ioelena wouldn't let him. She poked and prodded him like he was a bull, or maybe just a cow. *A weak calf.*

He walked into his cell without objection, not wanting to be thrown in like Abia. The lord's mouth was slightly open when Ioelena left. "They didn't …" he touched the dry blood on his puffy cheeks. "They beat me. Said awful things to me."

"I assume you deserved it."

Abia only rubbed his face. "Where is Gala?"

Bertin looked at the barred window but saw nothing

unusual. "It was too quick. Gala left, and Ioelena is now our guard. Maybe your cousin is good for something."

"May Baraga guide him." The lord laughed. "If they changed guards to a she-elf, we can overpower her and get out of here."

"And go where?" Bertin turned away from the window. "There are elves patrolling all across the city, and Ioelena has a spear. We don't."

Abia Èmaw didn't speak the rest of the night. Bertin could hear commotion outside and smelled smoke, but he didn't care enough to look. *Probably another celebration,* Bertin thought as he wished for more water.

The lord had snored all night as elves sang below his window. Bertin couldn't sleep. *At least they don't plan on killing me, though it'd be better than rotting in this place.*

The door swung open, and a tall elf with long white hair came in. Ioelena behind him. They went to Abia's cell and woke him. Ioelena watched Bertin. *Is she worried we'll fight back?*

"What're you doing?" Abia said as if he were still asleep. "I don't want to go anywhere with you."

The tall elf put his hand on the lord's forehead. "Relax." His voice was soothing. "My name is Sharet, and I am here to guide you to the Dragon."

"Dragon?" Abia seethed. "I do not have time for elvish savages and their tales of ancient beasts. I never met an adult who believes in dragons. They are children's stories."

Sharet held a glare at Abia. "I am merely a guide. You will see the Dragon, but we must go." Abia struggled, but Sharet easily dragged him out of the room. "No. No." The lord shouted and kicked, but couldn't get away. "Leave me be.

I demand it." He locked eyes with Bertin, tears welling up. "Please help me. Tell your father I never meant you any harm. I cared only for myself, but no longer. You must help me. I am sorry for what I did. You must help." His voice trailed as the white-haired elf dragged him into the corridor.

Ioelena stayed behind, staring at Bertin.

"What's he talking about?" Bertin asked. "A Dragon? A guide?"

"You will see." She nodded toward the window.

Bertin looked out and saw hundreds of elves surrounding a bonfire in the middle of the street. One stood on a wooden crate and shouted, though it sounded like singing. The other elves called back. Bertin strained to see, the stone hurting the tips of his toes. The elves parted like a wheat field, and Sharet went through. Behind him was Abia.

The lord still fought, but he had no chance. Bertin followed the path and saw the bonfire. His eyes widened. "Tell me what's going to happen?"

"I am sure you can figure it out."

He whipped around. "You can't." *Did I just say that? Do I really care if the man who got Robalt killed dies?* He didn't have time to think. "King Hasíb will descend on Lisan Biresdea. On you. Isn't that why Gala left?"

Darkness partially hid Ioelena's face as she laughed. "You know he won't. Humans care little for one another, and Gala is riding to Vaandet either to treat with the king or to cause trouble. The lord's cousin will be too preoccupied to attack us."

Bertin gulped. *Kuslu said he wasn't going to kill me. He wouldn't lie. But elves always lie.* He looked out the window once more and saw Lord Èmaw crying as he was being tied to the stake. "Please." That was all he could think of saying.

"It is too late. Sharet will guide him now."

Sharet began shouting below. *"An draca ar eb alvori. An draca ulé behnani jenén bynai."*

Bertin dropped from the window and buried his face in his arms. He finally began to cry. *Am I crying for Abia or because I'm next? I will die in a few short days unless father sends the coin. I'm next.* He could feel Ioelena's eyes boring into him. Lord Abia Èmaw screamed as the air filled with the smell of burning flesh.

Raimund

Raimund saw the castle and the surrounding homes and fields as his army crested a hill. Riverton wasn't anything special, much smaller than Vigur and not as beautiful and rocky as Gereduss. The surrounding land was almost pleasing to Raimund. Flat grass and shrubs stretched for miles instead of the jagged mountains that cut him off from the world. The Asara reminded him too much of home. The Eastlands of better times. Cows and wild buffalo roamed along the Samosay River, farmers pushing them away from their fields of wheat and barley. A large wooden wall encircled the castle. Wood and dirt huts surrounded the lord's keep, smoke rising from chimneys, the people going about their day. *Perhaps they haven't heard of us after all,* Raimund thought as he assumed the Duke of the Eastlands would be waiting with an army. *May the gods keep us from having to use ours.*

He wasn't sure if a battle broke out if he would win. The men making up the army were peasants or vagrants from Whitehall and the surrounding lands, a few here and there that followed as the troops came into their town. A few knights led the way. They weren't considered leaders like Raimund and Mar, but they had more experience than the rest of the men combined. Sir Hilo was older than David Rely and fought the Nowexerts in the last years of the war. Sir Riron, a year older than Devro, was newly knighted, after squiring in Greatbath. A large range of ages. Probably not the strongest. *Hilo may break if the wind catches him wrong.*

No one from Winterlake had come, much to Raimund's worry. Devro and Tundavik had stayed behind near the town where Lord David Viero reigned. The mountains had turned to hills that had turned to flat steppe when they descended the River Pass. People had gathered on the dirt roads of Winterlake to see the army of five dozen march through their towns, and the new, young king. Questions arose. "Have they come to attack?" "Are they to war?" "The bastard king has an army?" Raimund paid them no mind. His mission was to gain allies, and while bringing an army through someone's village wasn't the best idea, Lord David of Winterlake greeted him and declared for Devro. *Will he keep his promise?*

Raimund sighed at the thought of leaving Devro so close to Winterlake, where anyone there could bring him harm, and he sighed at the harm he was meant to bring to Riverton. Mar said, "Worried?"

"Are you not?"

Mar chuckled, his armor rattling. "I've been in wars before, fought numerous battles."

"But these aren't the Rainvealandians, or more Glybelm raiders, nor Nowexerts."

"I'm not that old." His friend laughed.

"I know." Raimund stopped on the hill, the men behind following suit. He could see the farmers below herding their families inside. Some carried clubs or held hoes as weapons. Others disappeared into the fields. It wasn't a foreign army that descended on them, but a Vigurite one. "These are your people. Viguran hasn't fought between itself in centuries, and we're leading the cause."

"These aren't my people." Mar motioned to the Eastlanders below. "My people are in Ruwy, where my lord father rules and my brother hunts. My people are in the Asara, where Devro tries to play the king and Tundavik scoffs at him. You're my people." His eyes were gentle as they watched Raimund. "I'm not fighting against you."

"So that makes it easier to kill strangers?"

"Am I supposed to lie?" Mar turned his face away, facing the keep below. "Unfortunately, it does make it easier." Mar clicked his mouth for Meadow to get going. Raimund told Sir Hilo to wait on the hill until they returned.

The Duke of the Eastlands, Adyn, was young, near Devro's age. Raimund had been told that all of Allean Gallient's older sons had died during the war with the Rainvealandians, but he wasn't expecting Adyn Gallient to be this young. His face still had the fat of childhood, his chin was bare, and the stirrups on his saddle were higher than anyone else's around. His horse was black. The duke's back was as straight as a sword. A woman in green sat on a white mare beside him; her hair was graying, and her eyes dark. A row of guards stood about them. Raimund and Mar greeted them. Brun snorted as Raimund took his place across the Duke.

"What is the meaning of this?" Adyn asked in a high-pitched voice. "Coming to my home with an army? Messages were flying in from Winterlake all morning, Lord David thought we were being attacked."

Yet he declared for Devro, Raimund thought, remembering that and trying not to worry about Devro and Tundavik. "We have come in the name of King Hurvir de'Tro the Second. He wished to be here, but we weren't sure it was safe." Adyn's horse sidestepped. "We are not attacking."

"Then why bring an army?"

"A precaution." Mar said. "The false king may have already sent word to you. We weren't sure what would be waiting for us."

"And you think this would endear me to you?" Adyn made his voice deeper, trying to show strength. Raimund had spent too much time with a teenage boy to feel anything but humor at the situation. "What makes you think I would declare Eastlands in open revolt against Vigur?"

Raimund took a breath, pulled out a copy of the parchment legitimizing Devro, then passed it to a guard to give to Lord Gallient. "The late king, may the Four watch over him," he hoped that was right, "has declared Dev — Hurvir the Second his lawful son and heir. Ultiir has usurped the throne. The Eastlands would surely like to see law prevail."

"Law?" Adyn laughed and looked at the woman next to him. "The dead king," he spat, "did not follow the law while he was alive. Annulment of marriage is to be granted only if the wife has committed adultery. Yet, I believe he had two annulments granted by his corrupt High Doma. My sister," he pointed to the graying woman, "Lady Annue was the first in the history of this great kingdom to be besmirched by her kingly husband. The first royal annulment. And you expect me to honor his word, to side with his bastard child. What will the bastards born throughout this kingdom think if Devro is allowed to take the throne? They will petition their father for lands and titles not rightfully theirs. Do you know how many illegitimate brothers and sisters my father sired across the land? You want them to come here asking for a birthright that is not there's?"

Raimund was about to speak, but Mar spoke first. "I'm sorry, Lady Annue, for what the king did. He hurt many people during his reign, but Devro is not his father, and Ultiir was his brother's chief consultant for many years. Either way, you must choose to support a de'Tro for the throne, should you not?"

"Did Ultiir send an army?" Adyn's eyes were focused on the men atop the hill. Lady Annue leaned over to her younger brother and whispered in his ear. *Maybe she'll have a soft spot for Devro,* Raimund thought as he gulped. He looked at the army behind him. Men were joking around, laughing, probably telling stories of the glory that was about to be bestowed upon them. He glanced at his sword. *Valkyr.* The Northern god of death. He said a silent prayer to avoid any fighting, any death.

The young Duke of the Eastlands looked at Mar than Raimund, eyes full of thoughts; he nodded at his sister. The former queen of Viguran had a deeper voice, making her sound wise. "I would rather support another Valor to take the throne than any de'Tro."

Raimund's stomach sank. Brun whinnied. Adyn said, "We will retreat back to my castle, keep the Eastlands out of whatever war you are planning, and pray to Meret that you do not attack us." The guards formed a line in front of the young duke, while Adyn and Annue disappeared inside their wooden castle walls. The village had gotten quieter; he wondered if they could hear what was being discussed.

Mar and Raimund rode away from the keep, staying on the dirt roads between the farms. "What now?" Mar asked.

Raimund slowly turned to Mar, his heart wishing to burst from his chest. Was Riverton that important? Maybe if they went home, Adyn would look at them more kindly. Ultiir might attack first. Or Devro and David would complain that Raimund let the Eastlands slip through his fingers. "I guess war."

Sir Hilo wobbled over to Raimund, seeming to strain his back straight. "Has the Lord Adyn declared for us?"

Mar whispered to a bowman. "Start a fire. Riverton is all wood."

Raimund put his helm on, tightened his gauntlets, and dropped his visor, then cleared his throat and rode Brun the length of the men. "Listen here." The soldiers quieted. "The Duke of the Eastlands has denied Hurvir the Second as rightful heir; he has sided with the false king and against the laws of this land. Your king sent you here. He had hoped Lord Gallient would see the truth in the matter, but in case he did not, you were sent to take Riverton by force. To show the whole of Viguran and the conspirators in the capital that our demands are not to be taken lightly, to be met with laughs. Who is with me? Who is with me as we take this castle and deliver it to our king?" The crowd erupted. Raimund kicked his horse, Mar followed with the few others on horseback, the footmen behind them, the bowmen setting up atop the hill. To battle.

Before they got to the town below the keep, arrows were loosed on them. Shields went above the heads of the footmen, Raimund following suit. He heard the pinging of arrows. Each one could mean death. Through his visor, he saw the villagers running toward the walls of the keep; if they opened the gate, he could lead a charge straight to Lord Gallient's bedchamber. Whizzing came overhead, but no arrows hit him. He turned and saw the bowmen from the Asara loosing lit arrows; the fire hitting the wooden walls. *Mar has been in battle before,* he thought, *and I haven't.* He couldn't worry about himself at the moment. This was the first strike. If he should fail, lords across Viguran and beyond would laugh at the thought of Devro as king, a boy who couldn't capture one castle.

Footmen from Riverton came running out from another gate Raimund couldn't see. Brun crashed into a few. He cried as his legs were cut and bruised, Raimund stabbing with his spear, Mar as well, and the other men on horseback. The men wearing white bears and owls on their tunics clashed with the men from Riverton, wearing surcoats with three winding rivers. They fought with swords, axes, spiked balls, and shields. The clanging of metal, the screams of death that followed, drowned out the screams of villagers.

Rocks and arrows came from the walls. He saw men dumping water on the fire caused by arrows, some falling as more arrows hit them. He quickly swiveled his head. *No one around.* He freed one hand from his spear and raised it slightly; just enough but not too obvious. The energy pulled around him. His fingertips felt heavy and hot; if he wasn't careful, his gauntlet could catch fire.

He waited.

An arrow buzzed overhead, and he flexed his hand as if he were dropping something. The arrow hit the wall, and a fireball erupted from it, men screaming as they burned, the wood quickly catching fire, embers starting smaller fires. No one seemed to notice, maybe the bowmen did, but the chaos on the ground protected his secret.

More men were spilling out from behind Riverton, some other gate. *Why does this place have so many? It wasn't supposed to be so defended.* He didn't need answers; all he needed was to win. He lost his spear as it stuck in a man wearing mail, breaking the shaft in half. Raimund had to hold on to Brun as tight as he could with his legs to stop from falling, his thighs straining as they gripped. Reaching for Valkyr, his hand burned, and he transferred the heat to his sword. Valkyr turned a slight red. He chopped and cut as if he were going through a thicket, men falling all around from the burning slashes they received. He circled Brun around to catch his breath and to get a clearer look at the battle.

The bowmen on the hill had no trouble; they set fire to the tips of their arrows and loosed. Men atop the wall were yelling for more water to stop the blaze that spread with every arrow. Mar had Attana in his hand, slicing from atop his horse. Sir Hilo lay dead, being trampled under hooves and metal boots. Sir Riron was holding his own against two men; apparently, his training was worth it.

A horn bellowed from behind the walls. The fighting seemed to pause. Mar pulled Meadow away from the fighting to see what was happening. There was a low rumble, like the world was shaking, as if they lived in the West. The gate on the other side of Riverton must've opened wide, unleashing its forces like a wave. Hundreds of horses spilled out. They rode over fields of wheat, spears coming down, all wearing chainmail. Pebbles shook beneath Brun's steady hooves. Raimund's breath quickened. His vision blurry from dripping sweat.

He made his decision.

"Retreat." He shouted as loud as he could, kicking Brun

to ride fast. He galloped over the grass, shouting, "Retreat."
Some of his men began running back to the hill while the
bowmen littered the countryside with arrows of fire to slow
the attacking cavalry. The world was shaking violently now.
Riverton's cavalry, led by the young Duke of the Eastlands,
began smashing into the owl and bear soldiers, the three
rivers men running back to the safety of the walls. "Retreat."

He saw an arrow fly and hit Meadow in the chest. She came
down hard, Mar flinging from her back, flipping as he hit the
grass. Raimund pulled the reins, turning Brun, still yelling,
"Retreat." He could feel the doom behind him, the cavalry
destroying anything and anyone they came across. *Must get
to Mar.* Sir Riron was running, but stopped at the knight who
lay on the ground. *Don't be dead.* Was all Raimund could
think. Brun slid to a stop above Mar.

"How is he?" Raimund shouted.

"I hear breathing." The young knight said as he took off his
helm. "Let me help." He lifted Mar and his armor to Raimund;
they laid him across the back of Brun.

"Get on." Raimund said over the crying death of Meadow.

Riron nodded, and that was the last thing he did. An arrow
burst through his mouth and nose, blood and chunks spewing
onto Raimund's leg. He had no time to think, so he kicked
his horse and ran. The cavalry were still killing and stabbing.
Raimund said, "Retreat," his voice going hoarse. "Retreat." He
was still yelling as he reached the hill. Behind him, the horses
and remaining footmen stopped. They weren't following.
Their fields burning. Smoke filled the sky.

"Retreat." Raimund wheezed.

Bertin

The walls were brown. Bertin had been looking at them for days. *Getting closer to death.* Death. That was his only thought. Lord Èmaw was burned alive, and Bertin would be next if the king of Rowan didn't send money or arms or whatever Kuslu wanted. *Why would he? He didn't save his mother or sister during the flames. Why would he save me in some faraway kingdom?* Bertin didn't want to think awful things about his father, but his hope was dwindling as the sun burned him through the barred windows.

I am going to die.

The door banged open. Bertin jumped every time, counting the seconds until his death. But this time it was just Kelltar, a bulky elf with large arms and legs ready to crush anyone who came near him. The elf reminded him of the men in the tourney fighting ring in Gereduss. Kelltar came every other day to empty Bertin's bucket of piss and shit. If the bucket was full, Bertin could count on not seeing Ioelena until it was gone. Kelltar always had a small dagger on his belt, but he never had to use it. *Where would I go?* All Bertin did was stare at the wall. Not acknowledging the elf. Kelltar grabbed the bucket and left the room.

Ioelena came in moments later. Ever since Gala had left

for Vaandet, Ioelena had watched over him. She was nicer, which wasn't saying much. Bringing water and snacks so he wouldn't die of thirst or hunger. She even talked to him. She closed the door behind her and sat on the floor across from Bertin on the other side of the bars. A flatbread was half-eaten in her hand. She gave Bertin a different one. It felt like a thousand pounds when he took it, but he loved every bite. "You have not eaten much." Ioelena's voice rang like a melody.

"What do you care?" The flatbread was soft in his mouth. He could feel his stomach thanking him. "I'm dead, anyway."

"You look alive to me." Ioelena gave a sweet laugh. "Why would we kill a prince before the king has even written back? Our message to him is probably weeks away." She munched on the bread; he could see a white cream smeared in it. He drooled. "You mustn't worry."

He swallowed the rest of the bread hard. "All I do is worry," he said with a dry mouth, thinking about his death. Bertin wished he had paid more attention when his father would bring him and his siblings to the domaton. Maybe believing that he would feast with the gods upon his death would make things better. He hadn't cried since Lord Abia Emaw's death. His energy sapped. He didn't cry when thinking of his dead grandmother, whom he never met, nor his mother. *Is she feasting with the gods or have the fish picked apart her bones?* He shuddered. He wanted nothing more than to cry, but no tears would come. Before he thought it was his dehydration, now he wasn't so sure. *Ever since Mother jumped from the cliff, death has surrounded me. Ever since I got on that ship to Vaandet.* The memory of Robalt being impaled by a spear flashed in his mind, searing his insides. *Wilclef and Gordo are probably dead too. Now, I'm dead.*

Ioelena picked at her bread, a small piece of some seasoning stuck in her front teeth. "How was the king of this place? Hasíb is his name?"

"Fine."

"Was he a great warrior?" Ioelena cleaned her teeth. The paint under her eyes had been washed off, so she didn't look as angry as before. She actually looked nice, but Bertin knew elves weren't nice. They were monsters.

"No."

Ioelena rocked her body in the heat of the sun. "And your journey through the desert? Ours was a tough road, the sands always shifting, hiding from soldiers and caravans, fighting human bandits who thought they could rob us. It was funny to see their faces when they saw our ears." She touched the point of her right ear. Bertin was waiting for her finger to bleed, but it never did. "Did you fight anyone?"

"I don't fight."

"Surely a prince would fight?" She giggled, and for a moment Bertin forgot she was his captor. Her laugh sounded sweeter than a bird's call. "Your father did not train you? Kuslu has read from some manuscripts kept in this palace. Most talk of the empire, but a few speak of your kingdom. Is it not one of the most powerful?" She asked as she took a bite of bread.

"It is." Bertin sighed as he watched her pick the bread slowly, savoring every bite. He had devoured his, couldn't even remember what it tasted like. "I didn't always listen to my father when he trained me."

"Why?"

Bertin shrugged. *If I had actually listened and trained, I would be able to cut myself through these elves, find Salvalone, and sail back home. I spent too much time practicing with whores and ale.*

"I trained to fight in Mi'rallen," Ioelena said as she wiped the sauce from the bread off the corner of her mouth. "It is a beautiful place. It had mountains as far as the eye could see. Waterfalls flow over great rocks. Birds always sing, even in the winter. Does Rowan have mountains?"

"You didn't look at a map?"

"I merely follow. The leaders read the maps and tell us where to go."

"Like dogs," he mumbled.

"What?" Ioelena cocked her head. "We have leaders and we have followers. Humans do as well. Can you point to Mi'rallen on a map?"

"Of course."

"And who taught you that?"

"Blis, he was my teacher."

Ioelena didn't take her eyes off Bertin's face. *Do I have dirt smeared across my brow?* he thought. "And where is this Blis now? Was he one of your knights?"

He couldn't help but laugh, followed by a dry cough. "He's too fat."

"So he is not a fighter, but a tutor. We have those as well."

"Blis sailed to war once. Won too."

Ioelena tossed Bertin another bit of bread she had been holding onto. He gobbled it up like he had never tasted anything before. "Was he decorated?"

"He was given a place in my father's service."

"Our great warriors are touched by the Dragon. They will take out a whole battalion of elf hunters and the next morning wake with a Dragon mark along their arm. It is a wondrous occasion."

"Do you have a Dragon mark?"

Ioelena laughed as she stood, wiping dust off her pants. "I am not a great warrior. Yet."

"Don't you worry?"

"About you?"

Bertin shook his head. "About the other humans. You've taken their city, killed their leaders. You don't worry they'll rise up."

"Were the humans not given a better life without their leaders? I guess you haven't seen the joy on their faces." Ioelena muttered. Bertin scoffed at the idea of humans having joy over invading elves who happily burn people alive. "Are you worried?" Ioelena asked, her skin dazzling in the sunlight.

Bertin nodded, his eyes glazing over. "Of course. I worry about my death, I worry about Wilclef and Gordo, I worry about my father, and I worry about the kingdom when they find out their prince is missing or dead." He imagined the gleeful looks of the Gorthair and even some Brutahki. The cheers and celebrations in the streets at the announcement of his death. "Little Baldewin will be thrust into the role of heir apparent. He has never had to think about kingly things. Another revolt would probably happen once my father died." He had a newfound energy. *Must be the bread.* "I need to leave. Somehow."

"You will have to get past me." She eyed her spear. "Then there are the guards in the halls and on the palace grounds. More guards outside in the streets. The gates are full of elves." She ripped off a small piece of her snack. "Good luck," she smiled.

He laid his head in his palms. "I just want it to end. Shitting in a bucket, eating off the floor, squishing scorpions. My father will not pay the ransom anyway. Kuslu wouldn't have to think of me anymore, and you all can march on Vaandet."

"Sharet listens for the Dragon, and he will say when you are ready. And besides, Kuslu is not looking toward Vaandet. Salvalone is next."

"Salvalone?" *Safír was going there to be safe. I guess the gods don't favor him.* "The city of the Lones will be guarded tenfold what Lisan Biresdea was. I doubt their commander gives up so easily."

"Half to Salvalone, the other half hold the oasis. Simple."

Bertin laughed for the first time in days. "The elves that go to Salvalone will be wiped out. Then they'll come for this city. I saw Vaandet. The wall was weak, and the streets defenseless. The Saysyki like to wage war, so the capital has lost a lot of resources and men." He tried to remember what Safír had said. "Salvalone is one of the greatest cities in the world. The gateway to Kruhesh. Kuslu and that king in Anha Jorbstah are fools if they think it will fall quickly."

"Gala is scouting Vaandet. Making peace or trouble."

"And he won't die because the capital is weaker than Salvalone. Honestly, Kuslu should have abandoned Lisan Biresdea and went with Gala. Why would a bunch of elves want to hold a city in the middle of the desert?"

Ioelena stood and brushed dust from her pants. "As Kuslu said, this was once the fortress of emperors, and now we control it." She went to the door. "He will be pleased to know that Vaandet is so inadequately guarded."

Bertin's brow raised. "You could've waited for Gala to come back instead of getting information from me. Lord Èmaw would've been better too, but you killed him."

"Gala is not coming back. We are to meet him." She opened the door. "The king will be dead within the month."

He was alone again in the dark and sweating room. The sun shone through the windows, and he dried his brow. *That flatbread was the best thing I've ever eaten. I wonder what the sauce she had was?* He had to stop thinking about food. His stomach called out for more. There was nothing else he could do but sleep. He still hadn't gotten used to the stone floor, waking with an aching back every day. But the food tonight was lovely, and he slept, all while the worry washed over him.

Tundavik

The wind whipped over the foothills; the five in the camp huddled together near the fire, wrapping themselves tightly in their bear fur cloaks. Sir Rye stood behind Devro, who was closest to the fire, hearing stories from the two who stayed behind, skinny Rodolf and a bald man named Ed. Their rough lives in Whitehall and the Asara, Lodean attacks, the fight with the Rainvealandians. Hopefully Devro was listening. Hearing the horrors that can come if a king is too careless or callous.

It was the second night without a word from Raimund. *Surely he would've sent a rider or bird. Unless the Duke of the Eastlands is stronger than we thought.* But that couldn't be the case. He apparently was young, not the same Lord Gallient Tundavik remembered, not even the same heir. He remembered Lady Annue and the scandal that was Hurvir's annulment. *Is she there? Talking sense into her brother? Telling him to attack?* He hadn't thought about what would happen if the Eastlands sided with Ultiir. The breadbasket of Viguran, the most populated duchy in the kingdom, the most knights and manor lords. All the food would stop coming to the Lands right as winter hit.

He didn't want to think about that.

"Why did you come back to Viguran?" Rodolf asked, shivering as the wind chilled his bones. "I've heard stories about you leaving, never figured the Duke of the Woodlands would return."

"I am no duke." Tundavik saw Devro staring, wanting to know the reason he had left. "I came back to see my home. I haven't stepped foot in Ritaeum in almost twenty years."

Ed spoke up, straightening his fur cap. "You think Lord Valles will accept you as a guest of honor?"

The fire danced as the wind caught it; the men moved away from the flames. "What does it matter? Now I have an army," Tundavik gave a small smile.

The men cheered and laughed and drank their mulled wine to warm themselves. "Surely you didn't think you would be in open revolt when you set sail from Attrima," Rodolf said. "That had to be a surprise."

"Very much so." Tundavik looked at Devro. When the firelight hit his face just right, he looked like his father, the anger he felt warming him more than any flame could. "I hope to see King Devro make a better ruler than his father. I will guide him toward that anyway I can."

Devro stirred, standing and leading Sir Rye away from the heat. The men poured more wine and, as the night went on, began singing songs about hunting and women and glory. Ed's favorite being 'Where the Women Roam,' something about a paradise where naked women pick the fruit from trees. As the full moon finally came out from beyond the horizon, lighting the foothills, Tundavik stood to find the young king. Devro and Sir Rye were wrapped in their furs away from the fire.

"You may leave us." Tundavik told the knight, who bowed

and happily went to warm himself. "You'll catch a cold standing out here."

"I'm eagerly awaiting my men to arrive." Devro snapped.

Tundavik nodded in understanding. "You didn't like what I had to say."

The young king swiveled on his heels. "You always complain of my father being a bad king, how I should be better. I don't think he was perfect, but one of my earliest memories is being sent with Queen Sophie around Viguran to feed the poor and needy. What bad king would do that?" He looked at the moon. "I don't understand your hatred."

"You don't want to know."

"But I do." He clutched the furs tighter as the wind blew quicker and colder. "Do you hate the king of Baragio the same? All those who call themselves rulers like you're a Gorthair? Only my father? My dead father?"

Tundavik took a deep breath, hoping he wouldn't have to explain himself to Devro, but the boy was his king, and it was Tundavik's fault he felt this way. "I will tell you if you wish." Devro nodded.

"I was on campaign in the South." Devro gave a small gasp when Tundavik followed through. "Taking every city and village I came across, starting with Panscar. It was awful. A thousand mites, all ready and willing to die rather than see us cross, doing whatever it took, blocked the Iron Gate, dropping acid into the cave. Arrows rained down from the rocks above. Shield walls and spears lined the bridge. The only way across was by boat, which wasn't any easier. We got lucky. There was a weak point on the east bank of the Bezir, so we crossed two rivers and charged into the city, fighting from the port up the Hill of the Ancient One. The men at the Iron Gate were preoccupied, and ships on the Ters-Veck were being set alight. We had the advantage then. We took it.

"Almost the entire city burned that day, I'm sure they're still rebuilding parts of it. It wasn't a siege; it was a massacre. Sometime in the chaos, the king's sister died, your Aunt Analla. I don't know what happened." His brow twitched as he shivered. "Her body was sent back to Vigur, and I guess the king was angry we couldn't save her. Understandable. I led the march along the Bezir, thousands of men behind me. I think it was the largest campaign of the war outside of the Çesdiri's first invasion of Awaran. Anyway, we warred south, hoping to capture Suktir and Kahdar as quickly as we could and press on to Jorbstah. That didn't happen. At least not for me.

"It was the second month of the siege of Suktir, Vigura's third day that month. A messenger arrived from the Woodlands, his horse as dark as night itself, saying there had been an incident and I was to leave the siege immediately, that I was relieved of command by orders of the king, 'go back to whence you came.' I didn't want to go. But who was I to go against my liege lord?" Tundavik's eyes filled with tears as he remembered. Did he really want to go back there? To all the towering trees that kept him in the dark? The trees like his dream. Was the woman in the forest trying to tell him something about Ritaeum, or was she nothing more than a dream? *I do not want these nightmares.* "We rode through war-torn land, seeing the horrors I had inflicted on the people, but that didn't matter to me." He took a deep breath, trying to keep his voice from croaking.

"Ritaeum was smoldering when I arrived. All I saw were the bodies of my people, my servants and pages and slaves, my uncles and aunts and cousins, my wife and children. I cradled Adile's lifeless body for who knows how long. Hours? Days? Weeks? The world was only a blur. I don't even remember burying my children. My sweet Guis and beautiful Ertha. I couldn't tell you what they looked like. Sounded like." His voice was monotonous. All the emotion was drained from him again, like it had been all those years ago. "I placed Adile under her favorite tree. She hoped her body would help it grow stronger and live longer. I hope so too." His eyes were cold from the wind hitting his tears. "Your father butchered my family. Burned my keep. Slaughtered my Adile and children. All because he thought us Rainvealandians, trying to deceive him or what not, I don't know what he thought. He hated the mites so much that he attacked the home of one of his dukes.

"That is why I hate your father, for the massacre he inflicted upon my house. That is why I wish to keep you from becoming like him."

Devro looked out over the moonlit fields below. "Do you?"

"Do I what?" Tundavik's tearful eyes became venomous. "Have Rainvealandian blood? Most people in Viguran do. The empire collapsed, and the mites were driven away, but not all left the mainland. The Lanlar lived for hundreds of years along the Ters-Veck, near my ancestral home, intermarrying with our people. But would it matter if my mother was from Jorbstah? My father from Çakiz?" Devro didn't say a word. "Adile was not of my blood anyhow; she was merely my wife. My children had an even smaller drop of mite blood than I do. The day butchering innocents is the way to deal with your worries is the day I turn the blade on myself." He walked away, not wanting to look at the son of the man who had massacred his family.

When the full moon was high in the sky, lighting the whole of the camp. Tundavik awoke to the ground shaking from boots. Raimund and Mar, both atop Brun, led their army into the foothills. *This doesn't look good.*

The five in the camp gathered near the dying fire. Luckily, the wind had calmed even though the night was still cold. Raimund dropped from Brun, his face black from dirt. Mar helped a few men get their armor off, and he had a slight limp. Raimund gave an awkward bow to Devro, something he probably would never get used to, and said, "We have failed. I have failed. Riverton stays in the hands of Lord Gallient."

"What happened?" Was all Devro could say.

"Our men were no match for his cavalry." Raimund patted Brun's nose. "We lost two dozen men to death or imprisonment."

"And a few to the cold." Mar said. "Winter is looking to be hard."

"About half the army remains." Raimund said. "I'm sorry."

Devro's fist clenched. Tundavik put a hand on his shoulder. "What was the Duke of the Eastlands' hesitation? Perhaps we can plan for it next time."

Mar unbuckled his sword belt slowly, wincing as he did. "Lady Annue still holds a grudge against the dead king, not that I blame her." The knight looked at Devro. "I think you'll find your father made little friends; Lady Annue, Tundavik here, his suppression of revolts in the Flewthlands has done nothing to endear him to Lord Plume, I fear we have limited options. David Rely is the exception."

"But Ultiir is his brother." Devro sounded shocked. "Are they happy that he committed murder?"

"I doubt Lady Annue and her brother were that upset." Mar answered, then turned to Ed. "Where's the wine?" The man brought him the now-cold drink.

Devro stood as tall as he could. "Tomorrow I will march done these hills, look Lord Gallient in the face, and demand he support me or be put to death."

Tundavik heard Mar choking on his wine, stifling a laugh. Raimund took his gloves off. "We just tried that."

"Seeing the king will change his mind."

"It's all right." Tundavik said. "We won't win every battle. We weren't as prepared as we should've been, thinking that the duke would support your claim. That blinded us. We'll have to find our allies in lesser lords in the Lands, nothing wrong with that."

"Except now all of Viguran has seen us lose a battle." Devro whined. "They will see Ultiir as stronger; they will support his coup and throw me to the wayside."

Tundavik rolled his eyes. "A battle is just a battle. The Nowexerts conquered half of Adedor but still lost the war."

Devro threw his cloak back. "We go back to Whitehall in the morn."

Raimund, Mar, and Tundavik all stood together as the men collapsed to sleep or huddled for warmth. "The men weren't ready." Raimund whispered. "I don't think we would've won anyhow, but their training was inadequate, to say the least."

"I don't think they could ford a river if needed." Mar said. Tundavik didn't want to just hold the Asara Mountains while the rest of Viguran moved on with a new king. *I have to think of something.*

Ultiir

A s I've said before," said Lord Avre, "the roads in the Woodlands are needed to move armies about. I've heard haunting stories from my people. Trees attacking. We need armed men to investigate these disturbances."

The king sat on his velvet throne; the softness coddling Ultiir as he watched over the lords below. The throne room was filled to the brim with lords and ladies and onlookers and servants as the lords of the Royal Court begged and pleaded and fought for what they wanted. But Viguran was nothing like Rowan, where the lords had more say in how the kingdom was run. The Royal Court in Viguran was merely to keep the lords and barons happy throughout the realm. The king had final say in all matters. *Ultiir* had the final say.

"Does the Woodlands still believe in ghosts?" The lord of Shipton asked, Ultiir had forgotten his name in all the business of the last few weeks, and the lords began laughing at Lord Avre.

"The horror on my people's faces …" Avre said until the laughing drowned him out completely.

Ultiir held up his hand. The knights in front of the throne shouted, "Quiet!" and the room silenced. "I will have Lord

Lyons look at our finances, but we have a revolt in the Asara; the crown sees that as most important." Lord Avre bowed. Before he went back to stand in his row, Ultiir called out, "Why has the Duke Valles not declared his support for me as king? The Woodlands sit quiet even though Riverton was just attacked and the Lowlands descend into fighting."

Lord Avre cleared his throat. "I am sure my lord duke has sent a letter. Perhaps it has not arrived, my king. My lord duke, as I have, surely heard stories of the terror coming from the trees. We've heard of many dead." Ultiir rolled his eyes, not wanting to hear the same drivel, and motioned him away.

Lord Tedol of Raior came forward. "Your Grace." He bowed, as was customary when the king presided over the Royal Court, before turning to the other lords. "My Lords, the Eastlands is aflame. Not only was my lord duke's home attacked, but there have been reports of slave revolts along the Three Rivers. This is not something I wished to happen." He swallowed. "But I propose taxes be raised to pay for defense." There were jeers from the other lords. "Levies are not free; we do not use slave armies for a reason. I hope you will hear me out …"

The Royal Court erupted into debate and name-calling. Ultiir drowned it out. As king, he could do whatever, tell the lords that taxes were to rise, or tell Lord Tedol to jump in the Ritae. He cared neither way. His levies would be paid for, and this rebellion, as seen in their defeat in Riverton, would be over quickly. Sophie, who he forgot was next to him in a small wooden chair, leaned forward. "You do not have to entertain them." He told his soon-to-be-wife. "The dowager queen doesn't usually listen in on the Royal Court."

"I hope not to be dowager queen for much longer." She

smiled with her sweet lips. Ultiir blushed; letting Sophie sit at his right side during court would not do much to quell the rumors of their late-night adventures. Ultiir silently laughed. *Let them gossip. The pleasure is better than any glares from a jealous lady.*

"Soon we will wed." He spoke as quietly as he could while the debate raged.

"You keep saying that."

"The High Doma is a difficult man. He doesn't like to come to the palace to meet, prefers I go to the domaton."

"He is a devout man." Sophie said. "The Book of the Four says that the rulers of man mustn't make demands of the religious."

"He will come." Ultiir stood, and the room quieted. *They decided on nothing.* A page, Adyn, whispered in his ear.

"The doma of Forecreak is here as requested."

Maller had been in the city for days, but Ultiir couldn't be too obvious. Not yet. "You may continue this debate in my absence. I will ask for updates on the morrow, but I must ask about the act of attainder. Is it finished?"

Lord Harle, a middle-aged giant of a man from Highriver, bowed. "The bastard rebel and all those who join him, including the Duke David Rely, have been attainted. Their lands and rights revoked, waiting for new lords to be named."

"And this has been sent?"

"All across the realm." Lord Harle said. The lords around him were itching to get back to the debate. *Worried I'll raise taxes without their consent. As if I wish to be so unpopular.*

"Then you may continue your discussion. I have matters to attend to." The lords bowed as he disappeared into the corridor behind the throne, Sophie staying to watch the debate.

He rubbed his head as he walked through the palace halls; sweat had made his hair sticky. Adyn led him and the guards that followed up a side staircase, only used by slaves, into the depths of the palace, an area never seen by Ultiir, the walls gray stone. *Must've been used for defense before the walls were built.*

The corridor led to a small chamber, webs hanging from candles and door handles, lit only by an arrowslit. "Your Grace." Maller bowed as Ultiir entered, his guards as shadows. The doma was older than Albon, graying throughout his brown hair, more wrinkles on his face and saggy eyes. He wore a brown robe and looked to have crawled out of a hole. His hair frayed, his skin dark but not from the sun, a slight stench about him saying he didn't know how to bathe in the River Fore.

"Your Holiness." Ultiir nodded his head, fluffed his cloak, and sat on a rickety chair with torn fabric. Maller stood. "You must be questioning why I called you here. I know we haven't spoken in many years."

"Yes," Maller wheezed. *Not a good sign,* Ultiir thought, *I'll need you for the remainder of my reign. However long that is.* "You don't get to Goldfield much, and definitely not Forecreak," Maller said as he tapped his fingers. "I wondered why I was called, but assumed it had to do with your coronation? Perhaps the traditional visit to Goldfield after a de'Tro is crowned?"

Ultiir didn't know how to say it. *If Maller tells the other doma, if Albon finds out, if lords and ladies across Viguran learn of this* ... he let the thought go. He was king, the High Doma may not traditionally be chosen by the sovereign, but he could change that. There was no law against it. "You would be wrong." Maller's ears perked as Ultiir whispered so not even the gods could hear. "As king, it is my duty to protect the realm from any threat. As you can see, I have to deal with an open revolt in the Lands of Asara, a bastard who claims the throne, throwing centuries of tradition into a pigpen. He has not come to Vigur to declare the Bastard Law. He has not come to swear fealty. The bastard didn't even come to see how his uncle is doing, to see his father before he was buried in Goldfield." Maller had stopped tapping his fingers; they brushed his chin as he soaked it all in. "Devro had the idea in his head that he would be king, probably to pass the time of his banishment, and now threatens to plunge the kingdom into war. I was lord of Goldfield, the heir. My brother, may the Four guide his journey, never wavered in that. In fact, I spoke to him days before his death near Vigura's wrath, where he affirmed his position." He hoped Maller wouldn't see a small lie in a sea of truth.

"All that said," Ultiir wiped his brow, feeling the coolness of his crown in his hand, "the High Doma refused to crown me. For the first time in our history, I had to put the crown atop my head. I saw it as an affront to the gods. I do not want to seem greater than they, but Albon forced my hand. He has taken the word of a bastard over the lawful heir, to fan the flames of rebellion, potentially getting thousands killed."

Maller finally sat, the chair swaying, and said, "That is serious."

Ultiir nodded. *Now's my chance.* "I remembered the fondness I had for you when I would visit Forecreak as a child. I wish for you to put your name in as Albon's successor. Become the High Doma and help spread the Four and the

Many far and wide."

"But Albon has not died nor stepped down." Maller's face contorted. "A king cannot make these decisions; only the gods."

"I have terrible news." He took a deep breath, trying not to twist his nose at the stink of the doma. "I have witnessed Albon use dark arts." Maller audibly gasped.

"That accusation," he struggled over the words, "that would mean death. You would need proof; you would need to alert the doma across the kingdom."

"All in time." Ultiir thought back to Albon and the water; it filled from nowhere after being depleted. "I know how serious this is, but I cannot let an éithrio guide our people toward the work of Veltoora. Because I witnessed it, I will need to arrest him. Sooner rather than later."

"And you wish me to take his spot? Will the doma accept me?"

"Better you than that abomination of a man."

Maller stood, his brown cloak falling to his dirt-covered bare feet. "Then I will do it. I must. I cannot let this evil stand anymore in the domaton. In the most holy city of this world."

Ultiir stood and shook the doma's hand. "I will remove Albon; you must go to the domaton and tell them this news. Tell them you will lead them." Maller nodded and stumbled out of the room muttering, "Yes, my king." Ultiir tried to hide his smile from the guards, whose eyes had gotten wide from eavesdropping.

"Have Sir Lovis tell me when Albon has arrived."

An older guard bowed his head and answered with, "Your Grace."

***

It wasn't long after his meeting with Maller that Lovis found him. "The High Doma awaits you in the kitchens as requested." Ultiir couldn't help but smile as he walked down the stairs from his room to the ground level, guards and lords and slaves all bowing their heads or curtsying as he passed, trying to gain favor. He wondered if they would continue their bows once Albon was gone. *Time to find out how much influence the High Doma has.*

Guards already stood outside the kitchen doors. Slaves and servants and cooks scurried about, getting food ready for the hundreds of people in the palace. The area was hot from the multiple fires. The smell of parsley, rosemary, garlic, and cooked lamb wafted in the air, making Ultiir's stomach groan. *A nice celebratory feast once I've finished. The gods couldn't have planned it better.* The High Doma was tasting a stew, telling the cooks to add more salt and pepper, sneezing as they did. He bowed his head at Ultiir. "My king, I'm glad you invited me to supper; your cooks are marvelous." The men and women who made the food blushed, or maybe it was just the heat.

"I hoped we could talk in the room over," Ultiir said as Albon followed. *Not as hard as I thought.* They entered a dark room, cabbages by the hundreds filling the shelves. "Let no one in." Ultiir told Lovis, who handed him a candle for light, then left to stand guard. The door was shut, Ultiir set the candle on a nearby shelf, the shadows dancing on Albon's face, making him look like the evil mage he was.

"What is the meaning of this?" Albon said, whatever nice demeanor faded away. "You demand I come here after I said you were not the king, after I said I would wait for the bastard to show, bring me into a cellar beneath the palace? I have never been treated with such disgrace."

Ultiir felt the small crown on his head. "But I am king; you couldn't *not* have listened, especially after the fuss you made at my coronation."

"I know of Maller." Albon must've hoped Ultiir would take that like a punch in the gut based on his smug smile. "Confusing why you would call for the doma of Forecreak, but now it makes sense. You need an ally. Who better than someone you knew as a child, surely better than me. But you should know that no doma will support you interfering in the business of High Doma."

"Do you know what happened to the High Doma when Valor the Savior took back control from the de'Beys?" He waited for an answer, but Albon only watched him. "He was stripped of his power because of his support of Cuis de'Bey's coup. Drowned in the River Ritae and hung from chains over the city walls for twenty-three days, the same number of years the de'Bey's ruled."

"There is no coup attempt against you, only a question of succession, and I only wish to hear from the bastard before making my decision."

Afraid, Ultiir laughed to himself, *and I thought he would push back more.* "No. You're right. No coup. But there is a precedent for the king to remove the High Doma."

Albon cleared his throat, the light from the candle casting his long shadow on the cabbages. "Have you read the Book of the Swallow?"

"Of course," he said through gritted teeth, "it was long ago, but I have read it."

"Then you'll remember the visions Swallow received when

the forces of darkness were locked away in their cages. The forces of Veltoora once again pouring over this world. Bringing the end times and death of all those who live and breathe. Cities falling into oceans, mountains crumbling to nothingness, rivers drying, hunger spreading, the world collapsing. Perhaps Swallow's gift of forethought was not about Veltoora; perhaps it was about us. We move away from the gods, they retreat into the heavens. Mankind bringing about the end times. And I know what you're going to say, 'What man could turn mountains to dust?' That is if you read it literally, like many past doma. You.

"The gods forsake those who kill their kin. They turn their backs on those who turn their backs on them. You and your lust will bring about the end of this kingdom. This kingdom named for Vigura; this holy city named for Vigura. The Four and the Many will not help you when the forces of Veltoora are at your doorstep and you beg and plead for mercy. And I will watch from my holy place as the city I love falls to ruin. I hope it was worth it to you to kill your last remaining brother and gain so much power."

Ultiir held back a smile. *He thinks himself more powerful than me? I will show him. I am the king.* "You talk of Veltoora's wrath as if it has not already been set upon us. Everything you describe: cities falling to ruin, people starving and dying, all came to be. My brother caused two wars with the Rainvealandians that destroyed countless villages, burned many fields, killed thousands upon thousands of people. Yet you claim I will be the one to bring about collapse?" Ultiir's face burned red.

"The man you supported for so many years wrought more destruction on us than since the Betrayer. To pay for his transgressions, the Four cursed him. His seed was poison no matter how many wives he took, and only by fucking a whore was he able to have a child. An illegitimate heir to the throne that would bring shame upon this kingdom you claim to be holy. I am sparing our people, *my* people, from the darkness you are describing. And you will not be able to sit in your chamber of opulence and watch the world collapse because you are not the High Doma anymore. Those who practice the arts of Veltoora are not welcome in my kingdom."

Albon's eyes widened as the king stood. His shadow dwarfed the High Doma, like a beast come to feed. "I will not have traitors in my midst. I will not have éithrios close by. You claim you do not fear the rulers of man," Ultiir took a deep breath. "Fear me." He called for his guards, who came in with their spears. "Arrest the High Doma on charges of witchcraft. Bind his hands, brand him, and parade him about the city before taking him to the dungeons." The guards looked at one another. Ultiir bore his eyes into them, forcing them to obey his order. Sir Lovis stood with his hand on the hilt of his sword. The High Doma said nothing as he was led from the room, going to be seen as a traitor to the people. An enemy from Veltoora.

Ultiir didn't hide his grin as he and Sir Lovis made their way out of the kitchens and outside the palace, workers gaping at what they just saw, but hurrying to get back to their chores. He wanted to see Albon dragged away. And he did. The High Doma was trying to pull free as guards stripped him and dressed him in tan robes. There was commotion, some not understanding what was happening, but one look toward Ultiir told them their king had sanctioned this.

A young guard, short and baby-faced, ran up to them. Lovis

used his metal gauntlet to stop him from getting close to the king. "What is the meaning of this?" Lovis asked with a tight jaw.

The guard was panting like it was a hot summer day. He took a few breaths before bowing. "Your Grace. My king." Another breath. "Lord de'Marisco has requested an urgent meeting with you and the other councilors. Someone intercepted a message."

Ultiir motioned for Lovis to back off. "The war? Revolt?"

The guard wheezed. "It is about the Lord of Montlahead, Gofrei, Your Grace."

Bertin

ertin woke to Ioelena coming in. She opened the cells and stood like she was waiting for something. Her eyes sparkling and her skin glistening in the sunlight. "Get up." She sang to him.

Bertin did as he was told. The elf tied his hands together. "I'm guessing Kuslu wants to see me?"

"No," she gestured for him to walk. "He wants to thank you." They left the cell and found the hallway. "He knows how difficult it can be to be locked in a cage. No prince should have to endure that." Through the windows, the city looked much quieter than before. *I wonder if Wilclef or Gordo made it out? Maybe they're still fighting to save me.* He didn't hold that hope for long.

When they made their way to the short grass below, he could've cried. He hadn't stepped out of the palace in days. Only limestone for a floor. He wanted to throw his boots off and run over the grass and into the oasis. Feel the sand on his soles. Elves walked the streets with humans nearby, some frightened, others looking like they wanted to fight back against the invaders, others like it was just another day. Smoke from fires rose over the water. *Celebrations or killings? Maybe the Telemese have revolted.* "Offerings to the Dragon."

She must've followed Bertin's gaze. "The Dragon calls for food and flesh so he may fly again."

"Human sacrifice? There hasn't been a burning in Rowan for hundreds of years." He looked into Ioelena's starry eyes. "And you wonder why people call you savage."

"We also burn cows and pigs or even clothes. Not everyone of those is a human. Whatever the Dragon calls for."

"And who knows what the Dragon wants?"

She pointed to a proselytizing elf on the street, humans and elves passing her, some listening. "*Rainík*. They speak to the Dragon through flames and air."

Bertin watched the elf, who yelled out in both her language and the common language. She held a rock shaped like a serpent, and fire shot from her fingertips. It swirled upward, to the amazement of those below. "Éithrio." He said under his breath.

"What was that? Sounded like Archel." He gave a questioning look. "Northern elvish."

"Like a mage." Bertin said as he stared in amazement, just like the other humans. He had never seen a mage, only heard stories. Blis would tell about the éithrio using their magic and dwarfish and human slaves to connect the Ters-Veck to the Nokys. How they controlled the early kingdoms that arose from the ashes of empires. How they were all killed in the massacre before another was carried out hundreds of years later. Éithrio were outlawed. The Telemese had probably never seen magic before either. *At least that's what their eyes say.* "Is that allowed?"

"Allowed?" Ioelena's mouth gaped like he had asked the stupidest question she had heard. "They are rainík. That is what they do."

Another rainík was shouting his religious words, and gusts of wind seemingly from nowhere pushed behind him. His baggy clothes flapping and adding drama to his speech. Passerbyers gawked or ran aside. "Are there a lot in Mi'rallen?"

"Mi'rallen is not the only place elves live, but yes." She smiled at Bertin as they watched the magic. "Rainík also live in Pywaln and Sruhq. Even in hidden towns in the *Efryn*."

"I do not know your elvish speech."

"Seàs. I speak Seàs of lower Adedor. And Efryn is your Ters-Veck."

Bertin gave a laugh of disbelief. "I have never seen an elf along the river. They were pushed out a thousand years ago."

"Slaughtered." Her eyes went dark for a moment. "I said hidden towns. In the mountains, in the forests, under the ground. All over." *Underground? Why do I feel like she's telling the truth?*

"So your kind came here to take the city and sacrifice humans for the Dragon?" Ioelena opened her mouth to interrupt, but Bertin continued. "Is that why you're here? To spread the rainík's views?"

"I came to show humans how weak they really are."

Ioelena led Bertin to the water, and cut his hands free. "Enjoy," she said.

The many reed boats that clogged the water had vanished; only a few remained. The water must've been playing tricks on his eyes because he thought he saw an elf and a human laughing while rowing over the oasis. Zentra Ira looked abandoned across the canal. Elven patrols walked the streets, but there didn't seem to be any humans over there. The temples of the Three Kings were being stripped of jewels and gold, just like the domaton was in Rowan during the flames. The grand statue of Aldrico at the gates to the city didn't look as shiny as before, the sun not reflecting off the bronze, but instead showing every crack as if it were ready to topple over. His fortress in the desert had fallen.

Bertin put his toes into the water first, much cooler than the surrounding air. He didn't even strip off his clothes before diving in. Ioelena shouted, but she couldn't stop him. His hair floated above his head like nothingness. His cracked skin healing. Emerging from the water, he didn't spit any out but instead swallowed, not caring if he got sick later. It didn't matter. It was the best bath he had ever taken. "You were to only feel the water." Ioelena said to him, and Bertin could see she was trying to hide a smile.

"I needed to wash off the stench of elf."

Children had joined him as he rubbed the water over his skin. Some were splashing, others laughing. He never thought he'd hear a child's laugh while armed elves stood nearby. *But the elves are laughing too,* he thought as not only Ioelena was giggling at the playing children but so were a few of the elf guards, their smiling faces in stark contrast to the swords and spears they held, the children's parents laughing along with them. *This is the oddest city I've ever been in.*

After he splashed a few of the children, he sat on the bank to dry. "Did all the elves come to prove humans weak?"

"I didn't ask." Ioelena gripped her spear and stood.

"I don't hate all elves, you know? There aren't enough in Rowan for me to feel any way about them."

"Yet you have the *stench of elf,*" Ioelena mocked. "You hate us even if you do not know us."

"And you hate me, but you don't know me."

"My Archel brethren are from what you call Rowan. They called it *Atha Bàn*, you stole it from them."

"And what is this?" Bertin motioned to the city around him, controlled by elves. "Revenge? Maybe we've no reason to hate each other at all."

Ioelena only laughed. "Please tell me about a time when the elves pushed humans from their home." Ioelena's eyes bore into his. "You do not know how we feel because you still hold on to a kingdom created in the ashes of ours. You live in a palace created by our ancestors." Bertin heard shouting behind him from the rainík but kept his eyes on Ioelena. "I do not come here for no reason, nor to do what Kuslu wishes — to bring down the successor to the empire."

Bertin stood and looked into Ioelena's sparkling eyes. "Why then? Wouldn't you rather have me in your beautiful Mi'rallen than fighting a war?"

"My brothers, Encayn and Lufa, brought me here. One day in Mi'rallen we went fishing; my father told us not to go. We were too young." Ioelena audibly gulped. "Encayn would not have it, so we left. The fish were large and plentiful that day. I think Lufa caught five or six. When we were done and heading back home, humans came upon shore.

"There were three of them. One for each of us. Encayn grabbed a small knife he used for fish, and Lufa found a stick." Her voice tightened. "The humans did not like that. I watched as they found their swords and hacked Encayn to bits. Then one defiled Lufa before cutting off his hands and feeding him to the river. I only watched. Could do nothing to save them. I would have been raped too if not for my father and some of the others spotting the hunters. The elves descended on the humans. I watched that too. So much blood for what? What did my brothers do wrong to deserve that? To the humans, it was merely a game. They hunted for sport and laughed as they did it. I am in Telemaw to make things right. First this kingdom falls, then the others.

"This *is* revenge. This is what Lufa and Encayn would have wanted."

Bertin looked down at his sandy feet. "And if you don't succeed?"

Ioelena straightened her back. "Then the Dragon will unite me and my brothers once more."

"What's this?" Bertin heard a sneer from near the palace. Ryfor stalked across the grass with two other elves in mail. Despite the sunlight, Ryfor's eyes were clouded in shadow. "Has the prince escaped?" He laughed, and the others joined in.

"Kuslu wanted him to see the city. To see how the elves are treating the people." Ioelena said.

"To see the sacrifices?" Ryfor had a jagged blade in his hand. *Is that for my head?* Bertin scratched his neck as Ryfor pointed to bellows of smoke. "That's right, Prince, your friends are out there. Their skin is charring and blackening while they scream in agony." He came closer, his steps uneven. *Has he been drinking? Western wine is probably better than even the water in Mi'rallen.* "I wonder how the Dragon would feel if a human prince were sent to him. Would he accept you or burn you a second time?"

Ioelena spoke up. "You know only the rainík know what the Dragon demands. If Bertin was to be a sacrifice, we would know."

"Bertin now?" Ryfor's blade found Bertin's throat. He could feel a trickle of blood leaving him. "How would the king feel if he knew Kuslu was giving his prisoners good treatment? King Blaenda would seethe and say how the humans have never been kind to elves. So why should we show them any kindness?"

"It's only for a few minutes." Ioelena said.

"Our king spent decades in a slave colony on some island near Mi'aral, and we're letting our most valuable prisoner waltz around the palace? He is not a prince here. He is nothing." The jagged blade nicked Bertin's throat once more. Ryfor stepped away, and Bertin put a hand to his throat to stop the bleeding. "You are only a sacrifice."

Ioelena was pushed, and Ryfor and the two elves in mail grabbed Bertin by his arms and drug him across the grass. Ioelena shouted in Seàs. It was of no use. Nothing she said stopped Ryfor and his friends. They left the palace gate and found the nearest pile of wood. It was still smoking from another sacrificial burning. "Please, no," Bertin yelled repeatedly. "You do not want to do this." *I guess I really am dying. And here I thought things were changing.* He clattered across the logs when the elves threw him.

"Enough." Ioelena put a dagger to Ryfor's throat. The passerbyers stood in as much amazement as when the rainík were shouting. "You do not decide the sacrifices. You will desecrate our way of life if you do this. The rainík will shun you. Kuslu will release you of duties."

Ryfor smiled as he pushed Ioelena to the ground, and the other elves grabbed her dagger. "Do you care for this human now? You are not of sound mind."

Bertin had not moved. He lay on logs and awaited the fire. *Maybe I'll even see Ioelena's brothers. I can tell them she still loves them.* Ryfor came over and pulled the prince to his feet. "I guess your father won't see you again. I wonder how your ancestors treated mine? Did they even allow them to be imprisoned? To touch grass or water once more? I bet they bashed in elven children's heads in front of their parents." Bertin shut his eyes. He remembered only Ioelena's starry eyes, her comforting voice. *This will calm me until the end.*

But it didn't happen. Instead, the ground rumbled and crashed with the words, "What is the meaning of this?" Bertin was surprised it was in the common language. He figured the Dragon would have a slimy speech, but it wasn't the Dragon speaking, just another elf.

An amber-colored stone shone on Sharet's belt as the ground split Ryfor and Bertin from everyone else. Small plants and vines twisted and grew from the new cracks in the ground. Sharet parted the crowd with no problem. Bertin could see humans running scared and elves looking on curiously.

"Are you rainík?" He shouted the question at Ryfor, who did nothing. "Answer me." The plants grew taller and reached for Ryfor's feet.

"I am not."

"Then what is your business at an offering site?"

"To scare the prince." Ryfor's voice was meek now.

"Kuslu told us no harm was to come to him while he awaits word from Rowan, or are you disobeying an order? You know how the Dragon feels about disobedience." Sharet's stone glowed with the threat.

"This prince does not deserve our respect," Ryfor spat. "He doesn't deserve the dignity of being ransomed. His ancestors slaughtered ours." The elvish crowd murmured in agreement. "Sharet, you are descended from Archel. Where are they now?

There is a reason you have lived on Mi'rallen all your life."

"Do not speak of my brethren." Sharet came closer; his body seemed to enlarge with rage. "I was there all those hundreds of years ago. Saw the massacres and the pogroms. I know exactly what happened to the Archel and who was responsible."

"Then why do you shout at me?"

"Because the Dragon has not claimed his flesh." Sharet's voice quieted. "I will happily watch him burn for the Dragon, but it is not his time."

"Then when?"

Sharet sighed. "We are finished with the conversation. Take the prince back to his cell."

Ryfor glared at Bertin as Sharet made his way back to the palace. Bertin could see his eyes clouding in shadow even more. The elf yelled as he brought down his sword toward Bertin's hand. The last thing Bertin remembered before he fainted was plants wrapping themselves around Ryfor's legs.

Yvanne

She felt odd, like she had begun a new life. There was Yvanne from before, before the marriage and after the marriage, before the crown and after the crown. All throughout her childhood, her father held court in Whitehall. She sat and observed. The people of the Lands came to him to discuss their problems. Coyotes or wolves attacking livestock, neighboring farmers and ranchers killing or stealing a cow or sheep, the Lodean descending from the mountains and raiding their village. Lord Rely passed judgment. Usually giving the person a few coins to pay for the damages.

Now she held court.

The keep was still the rotted wood smelling, mold growing home under the mountain, but the great room was outfitted with new furnishings to represent the Rely's ascent to royalty. Her father had dug deep into the mountain to find old family treasures to pay the seamstresses of Whitehall handsomely for their work.

White bear tapestries had golden crowns added to the heads. Newly made rugs had owls taking flight sewn into them. A lewd painting of an owl and bear mating had even been hanging in the back, something Yvanne had removed.

Purple and red were the colors of choice. Yvanne looked like an orchid wearing a long purple gown with streaks of white, making her look paler than usual. Red carpets and rugs thrown about in no particular order, and purple veils from Yvanne's mother's closest hung as decoration.

She didn't like any of it. Yes, the room looked better than it had before the fire broke out and caused half the keep to burn and rot, but it reminded her how much had changed in such a short amount of time. She missed the humbleness of her father's keep. Now, it was made to show the people of Whitehall that the Rely's were becoming wealthier, more powerful, superior to them in every way.

With the newfound power, came bigger problems. Some shepherd on the other side of the Asara had traveled to Whitehall instead of Vigur to complain of Terropian soldiers on this side of the border. *Wherever that is.* She thought, trying to picture which mountains belonged to Viguran and which to Terrop. A farmer was mad that the water in his irrigation canal was being used by people in the Eastlands. A young girl even complained of no rain. *Some things even a queen cannot fix.* Yvanne thought as she told the girl to go to the local domaton and pray. Lord Emallen Reck had traveled from Midvalley to pay homage to Devro, though the king had already left, and he grumbled as Yvanne took his oath. "I will have patrols in the Northern and River Passes. Midvalley men are strong and will not fall to the false king."

"Thank you, Lord Emallen." The lord bowed and disappeared with his entourage. The hall was empty. Only her, Pollard, and Sir Loc were left. She stood from the chair made of stone, noting how much it hurt her backside, wondering what it would feel like to sit on the actual throne, to have all the power in the kingdom instead of only her father's duchy. There was a shadow at the door, and she sighed. *Another.* But it was merely her father. He always looked worse in winter, at least as long as she'd known him. His skin got grayer and the wrinkles more pronounced, his gait was slower, and he seemed to limp as his joints ached from the cold. But it was only autumn. Meret hadn't dragged the world to winter yet.

He bowed his head, however much he could before it hurt. "Seeing you like this almost brings tears to my eyes." They embraced, Yvanne feeling like she was holding her father from falling. She wasn't ready to let go of him. Her mother had been gone for years; she didn't want to lose her father too, to become an orphan as she ascended the throne. *I need you,* she wanted to say. The words caught in her throat. "I think the whole realm will delight in you as queen, even more than the dowager queen."

"Thank you, father." She kissed his cheeks, forgetting her worries about him. The great David Rely had faced death before and won. This will be no different. He will see her sit the actual throne in Viguran, beam with pride as she makes righteous judgments and carries out the king's prerogative, giving him even more grandchildren than her other sisters.

Pollard walked over, resting his hand on the butt of his sword, wearing his bright white armor and fur cloak. A peak of his red curly hair could be seen under his nasal helm. "Was there any doubt how popular she'd be?" Pollard said with a smile. Her father wheezed and found Lord Emallen to thank for his support. Her brother leaned in to whisper. "One reason they're trying to steal you away."

Yvanne fixed her tilting diadem. "Steal me?"

"Take you from your home to Vigur. Away from your

family."

"If you're worried I won't bring you, then you're wrong. You have a place at my side."

"You really want to leave?" Pollard took off his helm, his curls falling. "You just have to wait, the not-lord Valles and his knights and the bastard," he whispered, "they'll see how much the common people and lords alike are fond of you and use you. Use you to fight their war."

"It's our war."

"Because father said so? Have you not heard his stories of fighting with the mites? Thousands dead for nothing? Who cares who the king of Viguran is?" Yvanne pushed Pollard toward a corner, trying to keep others from hearing. "Ultiir or Devro, both would've left father as Duke of the Lands of Asara. I would've stayed a knight. You, the—"

"—last daughter. I can't even inherit Whitehall when father dies. I have nothing. Devro and his men at least brought me something."

"You really want this?"

Yvanne thought of her mother. Gone. Her father. Close to death. Her brothers and sisters, who have moved away and started families and taken lordships. Her brother, Albert, lord of Canniage and heir to the Lands of Asara. *I would be nothing. Just another lord's daughter to be married off to another lord far away. At least here I have more power.* "I do. And you know it."

Pollard sighed but nodded. "Well, okay." He began for the door. Yvanne slowly followed, her purple dress flowing on the creaking wood below.

She heard the butchers shouting as they chopped their meat, saw them pouring salt to dry them. In a few days, men and women would journey into the mountains to collect the snow and ice atop the high peaks. Once winter came to town, they won't need to travel at all. Wagons were being unloaded of wheat and barley. The storehouse inside the mountain next to the keep. All preparations for winter. *I need to ask Helge how difficult this year will be. Hopefully Meret has mercy on us.*

Some children ran in from where Nopra's Pass cut through the mountains to the Eastlands. "The army is coming." They skipped and shouted.

"This can't be good." Pollard told her. "A messenger would've arrived if they'd taken the city or were laying siege."

"Which means they lost."

Pollard nodded. "Perhaps your life as queen will be cut short." His eyes were low, like he really believed Ultiir himself would march into the Asara and take her head. The thought of being queen for only a few weeks saddened her as well. *At least mother isn't here to see my failure.*

The townsfolk gathered around, waiting as rocks shook from the mass of soldiers streaming up the road. First, she saw Raimund—actually she sensed him first; the energy radiating off him hitting her harder than before—then came Mar and Tundavik. Devro, with his small crown, looked troubled riding his horse. *He's as worried as Pollard. Worried he will die like his father.* She took a deep breath. "My lord husband." She said, making sure her smile was large and sincere. "I worried."

Devro dismounted, and a stableboy took his horse. Raimund and his energy disappeared into the keep. The men hugged their wives or parents or found the bakery. Tundavik shook his head and found her father. "Lord Gallient had dozens of horses." He told the old duke. "I've never heard of the Eastlands having such a formidable cavalry."

Her father coughed and rubbed the whiskers on his chin. "Ultiir may've been quicker than us, foresaw our move, set some men with horses."

"And Gofrei didn't tell us?" Tundavik and David continued to talk while walking into the keep.

Yvanne gave another smile to Devro to get his attention. "My lord husband, I'm sorry for your loss." She wanted the young boy to like her; she didn't need him to cast her away from someone else like his father did to his wives. And she wanted to like him. She wanted to be there for him, like she was taught all her life. *I've always been a good daughter, I can surely be a good wife now.*

The boy waved a wand. "Tundavik says these things happen." His face was still sad, he seemed not to take comfort in Lord Vandes' words. "I'll have to make a new plan."

"You and your councilors will have much to discuss." She saw the Lord of Midvalley standing to the side. "While you were gone, Lord Emallen of Midvalley took his oath to you, my husband, bringing men that will surely join your side." Devro continued past Emallen Reck. Yvanne turned to the lord. "He will meet with you later." She hoped that was enough to make him feel not slighted.

Devro changed the conversation, probably so he didn't have to discuss his defeat. "Has your body changed at all?" It took a moment for her to understand what he was asking.

"My time to bleed still has not come," Yvanne whispered in the hopes it wouldn't anger him. But Devro was young, and all he did was grimace at her words. "We will find out soon enough, and if I am still without your child, then we will try again."

"Gofrei?"

Anything but the battle. "My lord father received a message yesterday. The false king is planning to take the dowager queen as his wife."

Devro stopped walking before the doorway to the keep. The knights who stood guard carefully watched him, Pollard waiting behind Yvanne. "Even she has turned her back on me." When he stepped forward, so did the entourage that followed. He put a hand up. "I wish to be alone." He went into the keep, leaving Yvanne to stare at the guards around, hearing the cries of mothers and fathers mourning the loss of their sons.

***

Her bed was cold. As was the whole of the keep. A fire raged in the front of the room, the heat filling her dark chamber. Yvanne never felt as cold as the others in Whitehall. When the winter hit, she would bring the energy that flowed around her into her body, warming her insides as if she were a dragon. Others would complain about the snow and ice. She would sweat. Energy rippled around the fire, strands going into her room and escaping under the door or cracks in the rock. Yvanne held her hand out, and a few strands came to her, her fingertips glowing a soft red. She didn't know why, but she could sense the energy in all the fires of the keep. She knew when the baker woke, when the smith lit his flame, when the cooks gathered in the kitchen for breakfast. Helge was the only one she could talk to about it since she valued her head being attached to her neck too much.

Raimund. I can talk to Raimund. She hadn't seen the knight since he came back from Riverton; she hadn't seen most who had come back. Dinner had been uneventful. The council convened and held talks well into the night. She ate only with Jacka, talking of the future as Queen of Viguran and watching the light of the sun disappear behind the mountains.

Raimund's energy pulsed a little faint at the moment. *Outside.* When he was in the keep, she knew by the way the strands of the world broke in three, some flowing to her and to Raimund, smaller pieces finding Helge. Now, most of the energy around fluttered through the air to her. Lifting the furs off her and wiping her brow of sweat, she found her night shoes and opened her door. The keep was silent except for the many fires throughout and her father's snores in the bedchamber down the hall. She followed the energy being pulled. It was only a slight tug. *Trying to warm himself.* She stopped taking in strands so that they might go to Raimund. More of them shot through the keep and through the cracks to the town beyond.

Sir Rickart stood at the door and gave a nod. "It is late, my queen. Is there something wrong?" He looked behind her and then at the door. "Do you need help?"

"I am fine. I just need some fresh air."

"Let me come."

She put her hand up. "Is Sir Raimund out there?" He nodded. "Then I will be fine." The knight said nothing as he took his post as guard.

Yvanne followed the strands until she found Raimund by the town well. "Cold?" She whispered, not wanting to disturb the townsfolk sleeping, or wake the cold vagrants at the doors to shops. "It will only get worse as Meret sends winter."

"I don't get cold easily." He said and then added, "not

because of what we are. I grew up in Irto, deep in the mountains along the Faskyd. Every winter was hard, and the snow piled up larger than most men." He looked into the well, the bucket a hundred feet below. "But also because we're different."

She yanked on the energy being put off by the fires, a lot according to the smoke that filled the air, feeling the warmth spread throughout her body. "My husband didn't seem to mind the loss in Riverton, but I know it is a sad thing losing your first battle."

"I knew we weren't ready." Raimund spoke freely. "I wished to find money to pay for trained knights, but the rest wanted to go headlong into a fight. I fear the future if we don't get more men."

She looked around; only the two of them seemed awake. "And if you use your power?"

The knight shook his head. "I already used too much, luckily no one saw anything. It's too dangerous for us to do that. We wouldn't have to worry only about Ultiir if others found out."

He was right, of course. The last éithrio spotted in Viguran helped burn siege engines when Vigur was being attacked by the Riorska, he was hanged the next day and his body burned to the cheers of a besieged city. "It is odd how much our talents are hated. We are known as a 'gift from the gods' but the people treat us as if we crawled straight from Veltoora to strangle their children and kill their mothers."

"It was a different time." Soft snores came from a house. "We can still help if needed; you can protect yourself if Ultiir's armies find their way here; I can help on the battlefield even if we lose."

"You mustn't blame yourself." She rested a hand on Raimund's arm, his sleeve soft. "My father told me stories of the men he led during the fight with the Rainvealandians. During the first war, the men didn't know what they were fighting for. There was no glory to be found, no one needing saving, no empire that spanned two continents. He told me how untrained they were. The men who fought the Nowexerts either never made it back or were too old and too troubled to fight again. Then Awaran was invaded. The men felt invigorated; someone needed their help."

"The Savior of Vikry," Raimund muttered.

"What?"

Raimund shook his head. "So I need Ultiir to butcher innocents to win this war?"

"It may help." They both chuckled at the dark thought. "You just need something worth fighting for. To crown a bastard may not be enough."

Raimund's eyes darted around the town, looking at the houses and empty shops. "The people of the Asara like you more than Devro. Maybe you could invigorate them."

"Women do not lead men into battle."

"Mertha Vandes begged to differ." Raimund gave a shy smile; Yvanne could see the warmth filling him. "After Maller's Trial and the death of her mother, she controlled Caiag Rock ..."

"... leading armies across the steppe." Yvanne nodded. "That was hundreds of years ago. I have only left Whitehall once before. Never even visited my mother's homeland, never seen Vigur, certainly not Caiag Rock or the Maera Steppe. I have no military training. If you asked Pollard, I'm sure he would do it."

"Not to be rude, but the men do not like Pollard as much as they like you."

"They would feel I was being condescending. Who wants a little girl telling them to go to war, telling them to kill and pillage and be a strong man for the family?"

"It's merely a thought. I can travel to Redington if need be. Get coin from the governors to hire Northern mercenaries and pay the knights to leave their lands." Yvanne pulled more energy to her, her cold, bare hand getting hotter and turning red like a piece of metal in fire. It didn't hurt. "Just a thought," he repeated. She didn't know how anyone would feel if she suggested this. *A woman rallying support.* Then she thought back to what her father had said: "I think the whole realm will delight in you as queen, even more than the dowager queen."

The energy flowed toward her.

Ultiir

"Can you believe this?" Ultiir stalked around his bedchamber, the fire in the hearth causing his brow to sweat. Sophie lay naked in his bed, wrapped in silk sheets. "Who does he think he is to go against me? Did he think he would never get caught?" Ultiir fumed, fire whipped atop wood, thick smoke going up the chimney.

"Lord Geary would visit Gereduss from time to time." The dowager queen said. "Perhaps we should've seen it coming." He knew she didn't want to talk about Gofrei at a time like this. Her eyes were low, lashes fluttering. She couldn't help but stare at Ultiir's naked body as he hovered over the fire. *Treason is far more important, but just barely.*

"I will have Sir Lovis take his head. Mount it in the throne room for all the lords of the court to see what happens when they betray me."

Sophie patted the soft bed. "Don't worry about it so much. The Lord of Montlahead will be taken care of, and you won't have to think of him any longer." She brushed her fingers through her beautiful brown hair. Wanting him. He stayed by the warmth of the fire, but imagining the warmth she could give him stiffened him. Sophie's smile widened before she walked to him, rubbing her breasts on his back, massaging his chest. "I should have said something sooner; this is my fault."

He kissed her fingers. *She will be my wife in the coming days. The mother to my children.* His smile was wide. "You cannot blame yourself for Gofrei. He's always been a drunken fool."

"I spoke to Lord Geary during Hurvir's feast, may the Four guide him. Friends in Udello told me he had disappeared for quite some time. He claimed he was seeing the sights." She grabbed his head so their eyes connected. "I can only assume he was writing or talking to the bastard. If I had told you, then he would already be in a dungeon cell."

Ultiir stepped away, pinching the bridge of his nose. "I do not blame you. It's not like I let you in on council secrets." His dark shadow shifted in the sword above the mantle. "But you are right. Had you told me he would be in a dungeon at least for questioning, but now he has committed treason against his king, gone against me for months." He grabbed his underclothes and slipped on his tunic and trousers. "Now, he will die." He left his bedchamber before Sophie could stop him. *Seduce him.*

The palace was eerie. The elves that once lived here probably loved the quiet. Built away from the city below. Elven etchings ran along the wall of the corridor. Some lettering he couldn't read. Sir Lovis followed, stretching his arms after being awakened by Sir Lird. They made their way down a hall of paintings, the eyes of dozens of past kings staring down at him. Judging him. Slaves bowed as they went down the grand staircase. The halls were dark. Shadows danced in corners where torches hung. *Perfect timing for my brother's ghost to come back. Kill me,* he chuckled, *I hope you see it my way, brother. The good of the kingdom comes before any one king.*

His private study behind the throne room was small, only a desk and a chair and a few cabinets to showcase the very best of the crown. Jewels from across Adedor and Kruhesh. Minerals from the Asara. Crowns of old and crowns of new. The heavy jeweled monstrosity sitting on the desk. A decorative crossbow and bolt were on a table behind the desk, where moonlight would hit if it weren't cloudy. His red cloak hung from the back of the chair. Clasping it on, he turned to Sir Lovis and Lird, a younger knight but just as strong. "You will protect me?"

Lovis, dressed in plain clothes but still with his sword, said, "Until the day I die."

"Let's not make that today." He sat.

"My king," Dele's high-pitched voice came through the door, "the Lord of Montlahead has arrived." Ultiir motioned him in. Lord Geary had bags under eyes, his pupils getting smaller. He was wrapped in a gray robe to hide his under-clothes. "You know it's late?" Gofrei stretched. "Not even Lendia herself is awake."

"Your Majesty."

"What?" Gofrei's eyes narrowed. He jumped as the door slammed behind him, Sir Lovis standing in the corner, Sir Lird by the door.

"You address your king with 'Your Majesty', or have you forgotten?" Ultiir stood, letting his red cloak fall to the floor. "Spent so much time declaring yourself for another that you forgot I was king?" Gofrei quickly looked around. The windows, the doors. All barred and locked. "You forget who wears the crown of Viguran? Who represents all kings that came before him?" Ultiir gestured to the jeweled crown, which sat on a cushion on his desk. "A thousand years of kings. Thousands of plots. Yet you think yourself special? Think you can follow a false king, a bastard king, and not get caught?" He kept the emotion from his voice. No use in getting angry. Not yet. "Treason is still punishable by death while I rule."

"Whatever you have heard," Gofrei's voice dropped, "it is not—"

"—don't lie." Ultiir interrupted, wiping hair from his face. "Your punishment will be far more severe if you lie."

The Lord of Montlahead only shook his head. "It is not true. I have not declared for the bastard. I have declared for you. Only you. We worked to depose Hurvir. For years we planned. Why would I turn on you now?" Ultiir watched Lovis from the corner of his eye. The knight's face was unreadable. Stoic. "Who told you this? Who spread these vile rumors?"

"It does not matter."

"Was it Urses? That man is cool and calculating and seeks to undo all you care for. He would rather your reign turn to shit than see the people of Viguran prosper." Gofrei's brow glistened as the candlelight hit it. "I will fetch him." The lord moved to the door, but Sir Lird barred his exit. "You cannot do this." He turned back. "You kill me over gossip and rumors, and you will lose Montlahead. My young son and wife will welcome Devro. The bastard will send riverboats down the Montla before Meret's Feast even arrives."

Ultiir sat at his desk again. A painting over the door showed Tiro the Fifth being hanged. King Valor the Blessed had found out that Tiro was planning to assassinate him. *We treat traitors the same,* he told the kings of old. He held up the note addressed to Devro. "This is my proof. Not rumor. Not Urses. Your own words. Telling the bastard and his rebels that my late brother legitimized his son. Luckily, the court had passed an act of attainder, so no true lord loyal to me would dare follow him, but I know you sent it. Your name." He pointed to the signature and shook his head. "So naïve to think you wouldn't be caught, that you signed these messages with your name." The parchment fluttered in the windless room. *Ghosts don't haunt me,* Ultiir thought as he felt a breeze on his skin. Gofrei was staring at the crown, at the parchment, at Ultiir.

"So you will imprison me? Kill me? I have sent messages telling dukes and counts and manor lords of Devro's legitimization. You only got one message out of dozens. The kingdom will turn against you swiftly. For regicide. Fratricide. Usurpation."

"That's a nice world you live in. A world where people listen to tradition instead of the army at their back. The many lords of Viguran will also receive a letter denouncing this as a forgery. A forgery written by a rogue lord on the King's Council, who had a fondness for drunkenness and fucking. A lord not to be trusted. And they will listen to me because I have the larger army."

Ultiir's hair whipped around his face, the flames on the candles licking the walls. Sir Lovis took a step back. "You will not take me." Gofrei's hand raised. The wind from nowhere picked up as if Ultiir were out in a storm. *Am I surrounded by mages?* Ultiir thought as his eyes went wide. He wondered why the mages didn't all get together and overthrow him. Why they stayed hidden with this much power. *At least I have witnesses this time. Now the council and the city will see I am not a liar.*

Gofrei continued to fling around papers and books and candles. "You will let me leave this palace and make my way to Whitehall, or you will not live to see the morrow." Ultiir nodded at Lovis, who ripped his sword from the sheath and went to hack Gofrei, but the knight was thrown against the door as air crashed into him. Ultiir went to his knees to keep from being blown over. Sir Lird found his sword, but it flew out of his hands, and he started choking. The young knight grabbed at his torso, seemingly to dig his way to his lungs. Gofrei made a fist, and Lird crashed to the floor. His eyes dim. Dead.

This is not the day I die, Ultiir thought as he looked around the small room. The crossbow sat on the table by the window. Gofrei was turning to face Lovis. Ultiir found a bolt and prayed the crossbow worked. Lovis was trying to stand, but was being pushed down by the invisible force. "Stay down." Lord Geary was saying. Ultiir and his knight made eye contact. Lovis was able to kick Gofrei in the knee, who yelped and crumbled. The wind stopped.

Ultiir loosed the bolt.

The Lord of Montlahead faced the king. The point of the bolt sticking out of his neck, blood splattering the floor, Gofrei gurgling and choking. His head was cut off. Sir Lovis stood with the bloodied sword.

The study had turned red and had already begun to stink of death. Ultiir didn't know how others would take this. A councilor being killed without trial, but he didn't care. He was king.

*****

"I have received word from the domaton—" Lord Edel de'Viere gasped as he entered the council chamber. "Your Majesty." He bowed at the sight of Ultiir near the stained window, Lord Geary's headless corpse lying across the table. Lovis and Ultiir had moved the corpse in the night. A perfect sight for the councilors to see. The other lords of the council stood as shocked as Lord de'Viere as they arrived one by one. Urses was last. Ultiir saw shock wash over his face for just a moment.

"Sit," Ultiir said, and they obeyed. "What of the domaton?"

Edel let out a dry cough. "The conclave has voted Maller to take over emergency duties. The actual vote should take place in the coming weeks, maybe while you are in Goldfield."

Ultiir nodded. *These lords fear me. How things should be.* He smiled before grabbing a brown sack from the floor and setting it on the table by the body. Ultiir could almost taste the blood that stank in the chamber.

"I have made my decision regarding Redington." The lords were looking at the sack instead of their king. "We are to invade and reclaim the city." Lord Zazí, the cupbearer from Redington, nearly dropped the glass of wine he was polishing. "The city will need patrols and the port reopened to slaves, especially if the reports of slave rebellion are true." Lord Hirons nodded. "Now, I am sure you all are wondering what this is." He waved his hands over the body as if it were a feast. The lords didn't look especially hungry this morn.

Lord Masson scratched at his whiskers. "It is very obviously the Lord of Montlahead. You have acted on this matter without the consent of the council."

"The king doesn't need us to deal with traitors." Alan said. The chief commander wouldn't look at the body, only over it or to the side while his breathing quickened. "How did he take it?"

Ultiir pushed his chair back, the wood scraping the marble floor, before standing. "He declared himself innocent." Lord de'Marisco laughed. "I wanted to bring his body here because it seems our kingdom has forgotten the severity of treason. All these lords and ladies choosing sides. But there are no sides. The king is king, ruler above all, answerable only to the Four and the Many. All these people think it is not treason if they go with the bastard and deny me my throne, but I want to remind them I will have their heads." He motioned to the cloth sack. Red coloring the bottom. "I need someone to take this to Whitehall."

"Dele will be up to it," Lord Lyons, the chief collector, said. "We can hire a wagon for him so he doesn't have to ride. I'm sure I can find the money."

"Not Dele." Ultiir cracked his knuckles. "Someone important. A lord of this council."

"And risk being captured?" The chief ambassador, Lord Verrier, said. "That's preposterous."

"Is it?" Lord de'Marisco whispered. "Dele would be killed if he brought Lord Geary's body. A lord may survive the war in captivity. I trust His Grace will free us once the Lands are no longer in rebellion."

He heard Gofrei's voice. *Urses would rather I fail, wouldn't he? A dangerous man who doesn't realize what he just did.* "Perfect Lord de'Marisco. You can go."

"What?" the lord said as Ultiir brought the sack of a head to Urses, slamming it down on the table for the bloodied skin to squish and crack.

"If you are able to," Ultiir paused, "come back. If the bastard captures you, then I will be soon. I have already sent word to Lord Drogue de'Vil that he will be named Duke of the Lands of Asara. He should march closer to Swallow's Feast."

"That's months away."

"The winter will be tough. Don't freeze." The king found his chair again, overlooking the lords and the gaping hole in Lord Geary's neck. Muscles and tendons and blood and bones staring back at him. The wood table staining. Lord de'Marisco bowed as he stood to leave, his eyes darting to the other lords. None spoke.

Raimund

"My lords and good sirs, I arrived as fast as I could." The messenger dropped to one knee in the great room of the keep in Whitehall while gasping for breath. "Lord Firgo Pan of Greatbath greatly desires your help. Joint hosts of men from the Kinglands and the Eastlands have descended on the town. The walls have been surrounded. Siege engines have been built."

None of this should be happening, Raimund thought as he shook his head at the news. *I should've gone to Redington before any fighting broke out. Now look at us, not even enough men to help some village.*

The messenger continued, "Lord Firgo fears if Greatbath falls then the Crossing is next, eventually the entirety of the lowlands and the Duke's Pass will overrun with traitors who support the false king."

Devro presided over the meeting in the stone block carved to be a chair, now a throne. Yvanne stood to his left, Tundavik to his right. Mar and Raimund were a step below, garbed in their metal armor that never seemed to come off, and surcoats with a crowned owl taking flight. The messenger handed a note to Raimund, the seal nothing but a large building. The bathhouse after which Greatbath was named. He gave the letter to Devro. His king. The boy half his age read the words, his chin raised trying to command respect.

"I feel for the lord of Greatbath." He took a moment. Raimund could see the boy thinking about what to say. "Lord Firgo is a fine man, but I do not know if Whitehall can help." The messenger had his eyes on the ground, not making eye contact. "Our fight in Riverton was not a great success, but I'm sure Lord Osbern of the Crossing would be glad to help, Lord Amil of Duketon as well."

The messenger cleared his throat. "Lords Osbern and Amil have both said they await your word. Greatbath will fall if you do not send support."

Tundavik was swaying, Mar was picking at his fingers, Yvanne was watching her young husband, Raimund squeezing his sword hilt before pushing his black hair from his eyes. "Perhaps we should converse." Raimund said. The quiet room stared at him, the messenger making eye contact, his blue eyes held in tears for his home. "Your Grace," Raimund thought to add.

Devro nodded. "Good idea. Leave us." He told the messenger, who backed away with a bow. The room was silent again, everyone waiting for the next to speak. Tundavik stepped away from the throne. "What are you thinking?"

"Just what I told him," Devro said while tapping his fingers on the black stone chair, "Lord Osbern and Lord Amil are closer."

"You cannot leave your people to massacre." Sir Pollard spoke up from near the door. Tundavik's eyes widened in surprise. Yvanne slowly shook her head at her brother, telling him no. The knight stepped back with a red face, either from anger or embarrassment; Raimund couldn't tell.

"He's right." Mar said. "Greatbath is loyal to you, so why would others join our cause if they are not guaranteed protection?"

Devro let out a whine. "It's far away, in the lowlands."

"Riverton was farther." Mar rolled his eyes. It hurt Raimund to hear talk of Riverton. He had failed, and it looked like they were about to fail Greatbath as well.

"I say no," Devro said before slouching in his seat. "But I guess I will hear what you all think."

David Rely had not come to see the messenger, but Raimund thought that the old duke would definitely disagree with Devro. The Lands were still his. Greatbath still his people. He didn't know if anyone could convince the young king to go. Raimund was about to mention Redington when, to everyone's shock based on their raised brows, Yvanne spoke.

"I have been to Greatbath many times. My mother believed the bathhouse could rid anyone of any sickness, and she took me there when I was a child. The Lord Firgo Pan has been lord for as long as I can remember. We cannot let the city fall. We do not know what your uncle's army will do. Will they accept surrender? Will they loot the city? We cannot give them the chance. I say we march."

"But we will leave Whitehall defenseless." Devro said with a raised voice.

Raimund huffed, "As I've been saying, we do not have enough men for this war. Like Devro worries, who will stay in Whitehall if we take troops to Greatbath? What if this is a trap set by Ultiir to lure us to the lowlands while he brings a host up the King's Pass? We'll be a mountain away as Whitehall falls. No matter how many lords of the Asara come to our aid, we will be outnumbered if the Kinglands and the Eastlands join together."

"I know what you're going to ask," Devro sighed, "you must forget Redington. We have all the things we need right here, and I need you to lead my army."

A breeze from the open windows reminded Raimund that winter was on its way. It sent a chill down his spine. "I failed in Riverton." His eyes dropped. *All the men killed or captured because of me.*

"That doesn't mean you will fail everywhere." Devro said, acting like he had given sage advice. "I need you by my side." There was a hint of begging in his voice, like a son talking to his father. Raimund stepped back. Never getting his way. *I guess it's time to see Greatbath fall,* he thought as he shook his legs.

"We haven't heard from Lord Geary in quite some time. Who knows what Ultiir is planning." Mar said. He stared at Tundavik, who was watching out the window. The messenger was pacing. The townsfolk went about their day. "Lord Vandes?"

"I think, Your Grace," Tundavik took a deep breath, "you are wrong." Mar nodded. Raimund could see a sly smile on Yvanne's face. "We all agree that leaving Greatbath for Ultiir's taking is a bad idea. Except you. We went to Riverton because we thought we could win, but we didn't. The false king's levies march on Greatbath because they think they can win. Let's show them they cannot. They cannot march into the duchy loyal to you. They cannot attack your people without reprisal."

"So leave Whitehall without an army?"

"I can stay." Tundavik said. "Lord Rely is also here. Leave

a dozen men, some of Lord Emallen's, and we will stop any attack through the passes."

Devro scratched his chin. "And you all agree?" Tundavik, Mar, and Yvanne nodded, even Sir Pollard. Raimund joined in, letting the thought of Redington go. *Maybe we can still win without their help. Maybe.*

Yvanne stepped forward and curtsied to her husband. "I wish to go."

Devro's eyes narrowed. "Go?"

"Like I said, I've known Lord Firgo for a long time, and I know Lord Osbern and Lord Amil as well. They have declared for you, but may take more kindly to seeing me."

"It's far too dangerous." Tundavik said. "What would your father think?"

Raimund could see anger and fear on Pollard's face. "If she goes, I can protect her." Raimund said before he could think. *Dumb. What will they think? She doesn't need my protection anyhow,* he thought as he traced the stone on his sword hilt, the same stone in Yvanne's necklace.

"If you're guarding her, then you're not leading the army." Devro said.

"I can leave her with you when I go to Greatbath."

Devro shook his head. "She can come." He said, to Yvanne's obvious surprise. "I'm sure the lords of the Duke's Pass would love to see her, but Sir Loc can guard her." Raimund didn't make eye contact with anyone, but he could feel Mar's eyes on him. Pollard stepped forward to protest. Wanting to protect his sister. Devro shook his head before the knight could speak. "You must guard your father, not Yvanne." Devro rubbed his eyes before climbing from his seat and venturing deeper into the tunnels. Pollard's face was red.

***

The town was abuzz that night as Tundavik announced the king's decision. The messenger was gleeful. Even happier when Devro let him take a horse back to Greatbath. Crates were being loaded with weapons, food, blankets, and bandages. The bakers were hard at work making more bread. Seamstresses patching clothes. Raimund was to make sure everything was packed correctly and tightly. Enough supplies to last until the Crossing. Enough weapons for a battle at Greatbath.

He didn't know what the future held. *Will I fail like Riverton? If Lord Gallient is leading his cavalry into the lowlands, I just might.* He didn't want to think of his failure, but he kept remembering the men who screamed as they died while he retreated, his hand glowing red with fire that could've saved them. *No. I would've burned them. Then they me. I can't even use my power in Greatbath, nor can Yvanne.*

"Make sure that hardtack is mixed before dawn." He yelled at Gia, the baker's apprentice, who was loading fresh bread into baskets. She bowed her head and ran off.

Tundavik snuck up behind him. "You really want to go to Redington?"

Raimund pulled his eyes away from the mess that was people packing. "Coins win wars."

"Not always." Tundavik smiled. "I wonder why you think the governors will support us? Why wouldn't they direct the banks to send money to Ultiir instead?"

"Hurvir was a believer in a greater Viguran, and Redington would be the first of many kingdoms and cities to be 'reconquered'. The false king was his chief consultant for a decade.

Surely, he agreed with his brother. If the governors think Ultiir will try to invade …" he let the thought linger.

"And Devro doesn't believe in reuniting the empire? Most kings of Viguran have wanted nothing more."

Raimund jumped behind a wagon to keep a crate of swords from falling on a young man's head. "Better watch yourself," he said, helping to secure it in the cart. He strode back to Tundavik. "Hopefully, we can talk him out of it. Especially if Redington gives us coin."

"I'm not sure about all that." Tundavik was watching the setting sun, pink and orange filling the sky. "But I do agree we need more men. Maybe we'll hear of lords in other duchies declaring for Devro." Tundavik walked with Raimund as he surveyed the pack animals. "I am curious though," he spoke slowly, "why you were so quick to want to protect the young queen. You spoke up even before her brother could."

Raimund blushed, but didn't look at Tundavik, and didn't like what he was implying. "She needs protection, and I failed in Riverton. I figured Mar could lead the fighting just fine."

"Just be careful." Tundavik's tone implied treason again.

"It is not what you think." He said plainly. Hoping to put to bed any rumors that may flourish. Tundavik patted his shoulder and went on his way.

As the sun disappeared, and the moon rose, the packing came to a halt. Some still filled crates, but most of the men and women disappeared, some into their homes. Others into the tavern or behind shops for what could be the last fuck of their life. Raimund sent a couple on their way after finding them by the well. Lord Rely was told of the plan, which he agreed to, though it took convincing to let Yvanne go, and he found men to guard his keep while the usual knights left.

Pollard sulked. But Sir Loc was glad to be going to battle and had said, "I can finally show off the skills I learned while fighting the Greenriders in Maertan."

Tundavik and Devro and Yvanne talked of Lord Osbern, and a little of Lord Amil. But Raimund could tell the lord of the Crossing was the more important of the two. Mar was nowhere to be found, but finding Mar was easier than finding grass in the Maera Steppe.

The tavern was busy with men who had come back from Riverton, who would leave in the morn for Greatbath, and those who would miss them. The barkeep was busy. Ale and mead flowed, men stumbling around drunk. He even saw a basket of lemons, probably stolen from a grove near Riverton. It was the most lively Whitehall had felt since Raimund arrived. The barkeep, Jovian, Jo for short, was laughing and joking, handing out goblets and tankards and refilling when needed. Raimund could hear the cook in the back and smell smoke.

"Sir Raimund," Jo said, out of breath but wearing a smile, "what can I get you?"

Raimund shook his head. "Mar?"

Jo pointed to the end of the bar. "Been celebrating life with the lot of us. Swell fellow, I call him." Raimund smiled in agreement at the barkeep as he made his way to his friend.

"Preparing for death?" Raimund asked Mar, who had just finished a tankard and asked for more.

"If that's what drinking means, then all the time." He wiped the corners of his mouth. "I thought you were packing?"

"Without you." Raimund stood in a corner, trying to stay out of the way of the drunkards and the cook.

"Sorry." Mar drank his new ale. "I was too busy buying

drinks for everyone." He shouted, and the bar erupted in cheers. Even Jo clapped, happy his bar was getting so much coin. "Hope the king doesn't mind." The knight's eyes were glossy. He really had been there all day. Raimund would probably find him in the morn, as he often did in Gereduss, hiccuping from his drinks. "You know," Mar said, lifting his tankard of ale, "through all the excitement we never toasted to the king's death." He said it quietly so the other patrons wouldn't hear, not that they could over their laughter. "You promised we would."

Raimund chuckled to himself, placing two bronze coins and calling for some ale as well. "You're right." Mar gave a smile that said, "I always am," and cheered Raimund's cup when Jo set it down. "To King Hurvir," Raimund said, "may he rot in Veltoora."

"And regret every decision he ever made in life." Mar added, and they drank. "I hope before he died he saw how cursed he was, cursed by all his wars and the way he treated people loyal to him, cursed to only birth a bastard. A bastard who's following his lead, taking us to war." Mar ate a hard piece of bread. "I miss the Devro of old. The fun one. He's trying too hard to be king, to always be right. Making rash decisions and not listening."

"He never listened." Raimund laughed, remembering when the boy was younger, doing whatever a prince could.

"He didn't listen about bedtime or not to play with swords or balance on the ledge of a balcony. Now, he doesn't listen when it comes to people's lives."

"I should be drinking more with you, especially if we find what I think we're going to in Greatbath. A dying city." Raimund burped after finishing his ale. Mar played with his, staring at nothing but his past life. "You think this war is a mistake?"

Mar waved a hand. "I don't really care. As long as we're not captured and forced to live in a dungeon, or sent to some mining colony, or put to death. I stopped caring long ago."

"I know." Was all Raimund said before ordering more to drink.

Bertin

Sunlight shone in Bertin's hand. He couldn't take his eyes off it. *A crippled king. That's what I'll be called.* His little finger was gone; not even a nub remained. His third finger had a scar from the sword Ryfor used. Bertin was terrified his entire hand would be gone, but the elf only wanted to toy with him.

Bertin stood near Ioelena in Kuslu's quarters. The elven commander was busy outside shouting orders, but even his yells sounded like a sweet song. *Have bards heard elvish voices? They would all quit if they heard Ioelena's speech.* He hadn't noticed her beauty until his near death. Her eyes shone like candles; her skin looked as soft as blankets of fur. *Now she wouldn't even look twice at me. Nor would Farzia. I'll never have a queen as a cripple.*

"They aren't going to grow back." Ioelena said as Bertin gazed at his hand. "Besides, it was only your small finger."

"And the tip of my third." He didn't want to defend himself. She had seen war, probably has more cuts and bruises hidden under her clothes. Bertin had never fought. Never needed to. That was what Wilclef and Gordo and Robalt were for. And now he lost a finger and a half, and his guards.

"I am sorry." She sounded sincere, and Bertin chose to

believe she was.

Kuslu quickly came in and found his desk. Scrolls and parchments littered the table. Inkblots and feathers showed how many letters he'd been writing. Bertin saw maps of the desert in Telemaw, the arid lands of Saysyk, and the peninsular mountains of Agaal. *Are they planning on attacking the whole of the West? Not even with their rainiks would it be possible to beat them. And they better pray to their Dragon that Baragio doesn't get involved.*

"Sharet has sent Ryfor to cleaning duties." Kuslu's canorous voice rang out, dropping Bertin's guard. "Let me apologize for his behavior. Ryfor is young, born only during the Nowexerti Wars. He is zealous and has an intense hatred of all things human. It won't happen again."

"In my home, Ryfor would be hanged and desecrated for harming a prince, but my father won't be too mad that I'm damaged. It makes me look strong." He lied. "He and I will be even happier if you send me home. Preferably today." Kuslu smiled and looked at his maps. Bertin followed his eyes to Salvalone. The once mighty capital of the Delerous Empire, the center of the world for hundreds of years. Then the elf focused on Vaandet, markings and drawings of a planned siege stained the map.

"Like our idea?" Kuslu asked. "I'm heeding your warning about Salvalone and focusing on Vaandet. Once that's over, we'll have options. Agaal to the north or Saysyk to the west." He spread each map out and faced them to Bertin. "What do you think?"

"I'm no strategist," Bertin took a deep breath, "but Saysyk is obvious. It's a backwater country. Poor and less populated. Agaal will have ships along the coast if they get word of the invasion. I don't even know if the Saysyki have ships."

"My thoughts as well." Kuslu said. "Your father must have taught you many things about Mi'tor."

"Blis was my tutor. Now he teaches my younger brother about kingdoms and history and fishing." He had forgotten Blis and Baldewin were on Decaro. *Have they caught anything? Have they made it back to my father?* "I didn't listen to most of it."

Kuslu looked like he wanted to laugh, but stopped himself. He pushed the maps to the side and opened a small chest with a scorpion emblem, left over from the Telemese. "This is a note from your father. It got here quickly—a fast pigeon." Bertin gulped but stood straight as he could. "You're lucky this came after Ryfor tried to kill you. I may have let it happen." Bertin saw Ioelena's head jerk to Kuslu. "Your father isn't going to pay the ransom. He isn't going to send ships or men to come save you. He abandoned you to imprisonment."

"You're lying." Bertin said before he could stop himself. *That's not true. It can't be.*

"Why would I lie? I only got coin if he paid. Now I'm stuck with you." Kuslu put the note away.

Bertin shook his head in disbelief. *He avenged his mother and took down the People's Chamber. He wouldn't leave me with elves. His heir. His firstborn son.* "Then why not kill me?"

Kuslu shrugged. "You are one of the few humans to give us information about kingdoms and rulers and armies. Maybe you have some potent things to tell us."

"I told you I don't know much. Everything I know is ten-year-old-information."

"Ioelena can judge what's important and what's not." He spoke in Seàs to Ioelena and before he knew it, he was ushered out of the room. He didn't notice anything as they walked through the corridors. The walls and floors and other elves blurred past him.

He was in his cell before his thoughts broke. The moon was full and lit the room better than the candles. "I'm sorry again." Ioelena said. She handed him a skin of water and a flatbread.

He threw the bread onto the dusty floor and stared at the wall. "You don't mean that."

She knelt at his eye level and tried to get his attention, but he wouldn't give her the satisfaction of looking. "I mean that. The Dragon knows what's in my heart and mind even if you do not."

His eyes watered at the sound of her voice. Like he was in a crib and being comforted by his mother. "I guess my father thinks Baldewin would make a better heir." He dragged his fingers through the dirt. "Lord Èmaw is dead, Robalt, Gordo, Wilclef. My father sent me here and now doesn't care if I die." Bertin looked at where he used to have a small finger. "I don't have any more information to give. All I told you was what I was taught, and that is common knowledge if you know anything about the world." Ioelena's eyes were shimmering. "Why don't you kill me?"

Her eyes widened. "I wouldn't."

"Just tell yourself you're avenging your brothers. That's what made it okay to kill all the other men and women, didn't it?" Ioelena slowly stood, her eyes sparkling more than usual, like she was holding back tears. Her shadow engulfed the wall behind her. *At least I won't die wondering what father would've done. Maybe if mother were here, she would talk sense into him. But it's too late now.* He closed his eyes, ready for death. He wasn't scared like when Ryfor was about to light the pyre. *Ioelena will do it quickly. Maybe it will be painless.* The door slammed.

She was gone.

***

He dreamt of a feast. A long table stretched for miles in either direction with him at the center. It took a while before he noticed he was the size of the palace in Vigur, along with three other shadows the same size. He looked down at his feet, where the table was set with pigs and chickens and vegetables. His father had a broken crown on his head, Aveline had streaks of red across her face, Baldewin was pouring a goblet of water over his head, gasping for breath.

He turned his head and saw Robalt with a stab wound enjoying a turkey leg while Gordo with a smashed head picked bones from a live hen. Ioelena was talking with his mother. Ioelena's neck was cut. Her voice came from the wound instead of her mouth. His mother's face was destroyed, nothing like he remembered. All the beauty cracking and peeling. Small pebbles embedded in her skin. They began to call out "Bertin." Pulling him closer. Making him smaller.

***

He woke with a fright. The sun had appeared with orange and yellow rays of morning. His chest ached as his heart beat too quick for comfort. *Just a dream.* He had to repeat that thought many times before he began to believe. *I may be close to dying, but that was a dream.* Images of his dead friends and family replayed in his mind. He tried to tell himself it wasn't real, but he couldn't take it. But he felt sick. He found his bucket of shit and vomited into it. "A dream." He said as he wiped his mouth.

Kelltar came in with a dagger on his belt. Bertin backed away from the cell door as the bulky elf opened it. He wanted to attack him. Maybe hit him over the head with the bucket, grab the dagger, and fight his way out of the palace. *Can I do it?* Kelltar grabbed the bucket and glared at Bertin, the muscles on his head throbbing. *No, I don't think I can.*

"You know Kuslu sent Ryfor to tend to the horses and camels." The elf dumped the contents of the bucket onto the stone floor. Bertin jumped up and into a corner. "Ryfor was right. Kuslu is too much of a coward to kill a human prince." He threw the bucket at Bertin, knocking the air from his lungs. "I am not a coward." Kelltar said as he pulled out the dagger. The small knife had elven writing, and the blade glowed blue when the light hit it. The elf used his enormous arms to pin Bertin against the wall. He didn't fight back. Just like with Ioelena. He didn't want Kelltar to be the one to kill him, to stab him and let his body soak in his own shit, but he saw no other way to leave Lisan Biresdea. *Maybe father will regret this when he receives my head on a platter.*

"Enough of this." Ioelena yanked Kelltar, and he stumbled over his own weight into the piss and shit and vomit. "I am tired of Bertin being threatened. If Kuslu wanted him dead, then he would be dead." Kelltar was yelling in elvish, probably cursing, wiping the excrement off his arms and back. "Now, get out before I throw you from the top of this palace." Kelltar cursed some more and left the room. "And bring another bucket to clean your mess." She shouted after him.

"I don't understand." Bertin let out the breath he was holding. "I wanted you to end me, I didn't mind that Kelltar was doing it."

Ioelena shoved him against the limestone brick. "And I am tired of you begging to be killed. Stop talking about it and come with me." She carefully left the cell and Bertin sighed as he followed.

They wandered through the corridors, up some stairs, down some others. It grew narrower as they went. Like this part of the palace was not as important as the rest. Ioelena found a small wooden door and pulled Bertin through. He looked up and saw Wilclef. His guard stared at the streets below, his wrists tied together with a rope.

"You're alive." Bertin said with a scratchy throat and tears in his eyes.

Wilclef smiled and came to embrace him, but his hands were tied. "I'm just as surprised as you. The elves didn't take kindly to Gordo and me and our swords."

Bertin turned to Ioelena and pointed at the ropes on Wilclef's wrists. "Will you?"

She rolled her eyes but cut the ropes. Bertin embraced his guard. He could hear Wilclef sniffling. "I thought I was going to have to explain to your father that you died." Wilclef studied Bertin's face. "I thought I was about to die when elves snatched me from my cell and dragged me here."

"Cell? You've been locked away too."

"Most of the fighters have. Locked near Commander Abrezo's quarters, unless they died like the commander." Wilclef wiped his eyes and pulled at the skin around his nails. "Gordo is dead. Cut down saving me."

Bertin nodded. "Robalt died protecting me."

"As was his duty. An honorable thing." His guard looked at Ioelena with questioning eyes. "And now she brought us together. What's her plan?"

"I don't know." Bertin said while turning to the elf.

She sighed and threw up her hands. "I was tired of you going on about death and not wanting to live. Hearing your cries is enough to drive people mad." Bertin smiled at her, and her face turned red. "I also felt bad after the letter."

"Apparently, my father is not saving me." Bertin said to Wilclef. "They asked."

"Then it's us two." Wilclef patted Bertin's shoulder and then saw the prince's hand. "What happened? Did you get this during the battle?" He studied Bertin's nub.

"Some elf tried to kill me, but that's been happening since we got to this oasis."

"Then we need to leave." Wilclef dropped to a whisper, but Bertin knew Ioelena heard.

"Leave?" Ioelena said, answering Bertin's suspicions. "This visit is not so you can escape; it's to let Bertin speak with someone close to him."

"But you've already broken the rules, I presume," Wilclef said while gesturing between Bertin and him. "I doubt your leader wants a prince and his guard talking to one another. What will happen if he finds out?"

"Probably kill you," Ioelena's eyes darted across the room as she thought, "and me. But you will definitely die if you try to escape. The best thing you can do is stay put until we move on Vaandet. Maybe Kuslu will send you on a ship north."

Wilclef's mouth was agape. "You don't really believe that. Your kind has held us captive for weeks, and you think this

Kuslu will just free us when he takes all of Telemaw?"

"Won't he need me for Saysyk?" Bertin chimed in. "Agaal? You all aren't done with me. Unless my father decides to save me. I'm stuck here."

Ioelena pursed her lips. "I cannot let you leave. I'm sorry."

"You say that a lot, you know." Bertin's voice rose. "How much more apologizing will it take before you realize that you're not actually sorry? Have you spoken with Kuslu about me? Did you try to stop Lord Èmaw from being burned? Stop Ryfor? All you do is say sorry after the fact. You have never actually helped me. Now, it's time I helped myself." Ioelena's eyes fell to the floor as she shifted her feet. *Will we even make it out of the city?* There was a window behind Wilclef. They were only a few stories high, with limestone jutting out down the wall either by design or decay. *Maybe we can climb.*

Wilclef and Bertin didn't get a chance to test it. To see if they could escape Lisan Biresdea with their lives. The door burst open, and in came four elven guards. Ioelena was pushed against the wall. Wilclef was slammed to the ground. Bertin was tied by his wrists and felt a gust of wind knock him to his feet. He saw an elf with a bright blue stone in hand. *Éithrio.* He also saw Kelltar in the doorway smiling.

The three were dragged to separate places. Bertin lost sight of Ioelena and Wilclef in the maze of steps and tight corridors. He was back in his cell with Kelltar gripping the bars. "You're still lucky Kuslu wants you alive. The other two don't have such luck." The iron bars seemed to bend with the elf's squeeze. "I will try to convince him to see otherwise. Kuslu should have let Ryfor end you, then we wouldn't be in this mess."

Ioelena and Wilclef. Two more gone. He shuddered, thinking of how the elves would kill them. *Will they make Ioelena's quick? She is still an elf. But Wilclef.* He didn't finish his thought. It was too much. Too much death.

"Hopefully, this is your last night in this world." Kelltar sneered. "If Kuslu agrees, then the Dragon will burn you tomorrow." The elf left with a slammed door behind him.

Bertin pictured the window for the rest of the night. *What could have been. If only we moved faster.* Ioelena's spear was leaning against the wall. *When Kelltar makes me walk to my death, I can grab that. I can kill him or probably die trying.* His face froze. He had never killed anyone. *But I've killed rabbits and caught fish. Elves are not human. They are savages who deserve to die.* That's what he told himself as he imagined Kelltar's blood smearing the spearpoint and the walls behind it, shivering.

There was a smash outside the room that woke him. The smell of ash and burned flesh flooded his cell. *Wilclef must be dead,* he thought as he stood. *Let's get this over with.* His eyes stuck on the spear. *My only chance to escape this city and get back home. I can do it.*

The door creaked open. Ioelena, with purple paint on her cheeks, and a bloodied dagger in her hand, wheezed. She fumbled with keys and unlocked his cell. "Are you coming?"

Yvanne

Yvanne was watching the pack mules. Their owners calming them and giving them carrots or oats. A layer of frost had covered the ground as winter drew nearer, fires rippling in the chimneys throughout Whitehall. Sirs Rye and Howe protected the wagons from thieves, Sir Groel guarded the Swallow Pass that night. Once the snow fell thieves.no knight would need to guard any pass. Whitehall would be cut off from the lowlands. She didn't know if that was good. What if another village needed their king like Greatbath? It would take the whole town to dig a trench in the snow, not counting more snowfall making it all the harder.

The moon was waning. Closer and closer it was getting to its monthly rebirth. Yvanne felt her stomach. She hoped to give Devro a child soon, lest she end up like Lady Annue, a once-youthful-queen who was sent back to her father's home. She wanted David to see his grandchild. He didn't get to see most of his family except on large occasions, the last one apparently being when he married her mother. *I will show him what a true daughter should be. Let him enjoy seeing me and Pollard and my child before he dies.* The thought chilled her bones even as she warmed them. That would be the next time she sees all her brothers and sisters and their husbands and wives and children. When her father dies.

Men and women streamed out of the seam-busting-tavern. All hollering from drunkenness, kissing and fondling, trying to find a quiet place in the cold. Raimund, holding Mar, followed along. She waved at the knights, who paid her no mind. "It's getting colder, my queen." Jacka had come outside, wrapped in fur. "I worry for your health."

"Don't." Yvanne smiled at her handmaid. "You seem much colder than me." Jacka's body was shaking, teeth chattering. Yvanne was able to warm her body. The stone on her necklace shone ever so faintly. "Let's go inside."

***

She slipped into a bath drawn by Jacka, hot coals underneath to warm the water. "Is it too hot?" Jacka asked. Yvanne shook her head. She could still burn, but soaking in all the energy from the coals and the hot water tickled her entire body, clearing her head. "Thank you for the bath, Jacka." Her handmaid bowed her head. "I hope you stay warm while I go to Greatbath."

The handmaid's eyes dropped. "Am I not to go with you? Who will dress you? Clean you? Make sure you eat?"

Yvanne grabbed Jacka's hand. "It is too dangerous." She took the smooth scrubbing rock from Jacka. "And I clean myself." The stone glided over her wet skin. "Men who do not have the luxury of a handmaid will surround me. I don't want them to see me differently."

"But you are different. You are their queen."

Yvanne smiled. "They don't need reminding." Jacka's head

was low. "Can you find Helge for me? I would very much like to pray."

Jacka nodded. "I will also pray for you while you are gone. I will pray for Greatbath and your safe return." The handmaid left, leaving Yvanne with the hot water lit by candles. It was more relaxing than watching the pack animals or worrying about the future. Her stomach still felt empty. Maybe if she wished hard enough, life would sprout like a flower.

There was a knock on the door, but Helge was not the one to come in. Devro did.

He looked slightly away at the sight of her nakedness, acting as if they hadn't spent the night together after their marriage. Holding out her hand, he took it. *Why had he come in?* Her belly was still small, no child if that's what he wanted. "Have you taken up Arold's offer to train you in the ways of the sword?"

Her husband chuckled. "If Mar and Raimund couldn't get me to do it, I don't know how Arold would."

"A king should lead his armies, should he not?" She traced the lines on his hand.

His eyes were shrouded in shadow. "I am not sure I could. I'm not my father, nor Raimund. Even though he lost in Riverton, he is still a better leader than I could ever be."

"You just have to practice."

Devro looked at her stomach submerged in water. She shook her head in response. "Should we try again?" Devro asked. *Father will see my child.* She gave a quick nod before they kissed, eventually sending Helge back to her bedchamber.

***

Devro was out of breath while watching the fire; Yvanne was hugging herself. *So young to have all these worries. A child. A kingdom. A war. If only I could help more.* She clutched at her bare stomach, wishing she were far enough along to feel a kick. She wanted to know so badly. Nothing. "I'm sure your seed is strong." She wanted to be comforting, but didn't want to remind him of his father.

"I do not worry about that." He found a fur cloak and wrapped his naked body, which was covered in goose bumps. "I know I will give you a son. My heir." He sat on the bed and smiled as he rubbed her stomach.

Yvanne crumpled the blankets into her lap. "Is it the war? I don't know how it would be possible for any ruler not to stress about battle. Especially if they are fighting their own uncle."

Devro sighed and plopped his head on the bed, his blond hair fraying. "I'm not very good at this. Not as good I thought I'd be. Tundavik or your father or even my knights have to speak sense to me; sometimes I think they'd rather hit me. It'd be faster." Yvanne rubbed his chest. He startled at first, but calmed at her touch. "I don't want to mess this up. To start a war for no reason."

"You believe your uncle killed your father?" He nodded. "And took the throne even though the king declared you his legitimate heir?" Her young husband nodded once more. "Then there is a reason to fight. Win or lose, and I think we can win, Ultiir stole what was yours."

"You think we can win?"

"Of course. The Asara is as rife with rebellion as the Flewthlands; we just don't do it as much. The Lodean regularly go against the crown. My father has said no to frivolous demands from the crown for decades. Marching through the passes isn't easy, and if we can get others on board. All those who feel wronged by your ancestors. If you promise to make their lives better. The Lodean, the Ritae, the Del; you already have Lord Vandes and half the lords of the Asara; only the Four know who else your father has hurt. We can get allies. We can win."

Devro gave a shy smile while rubbing his hand on her knee. The world got quieter for a brief moment, as if the fire in the room didn't crackle or Devro wasn't saying, "thank you." She saw the swirls of energy all around, coming from the fire, a bit from the king. They wanted to move, but it was like they were frozen in ice. Then they went on. Flowing into the world as free as a bird. She had seen this before, and it was never good. The last time was when some random traveler fell ill and died in the tavern. He was an éithrio. "I appreciate the reminder." Devro finished.

Yvanne stood, letting the blankets fall from her naked body. She went to her wardrobe and found a smock to slide over her head. Opening the door, Devro said from behind, "Where are you going?" He dressed and followed. Once in the great room, the carved stone throne to her left, she saw a crowd of people gathering by the well. Pollard was guarding the door, but he stood outside, leaving it open. She walked out barefoot. The cold morning grass, frozen overnight, crunched under her feet, poking her skin. Making her way through the crowd, she saw her father and Tundavik waiting for a trotting horse to stop. Raimund and a hungover Mar pushed their way in to see. Devro, wearing only a gray nightgown, went to Lord Vandes.

"What is happening?"

The lord pointed to Sir Groel, who had ridden from the Swallow Pass. "Urgent news." The knight said as he halted his palomino. "From Vigur."

The crowd murmured. Devro stepped forward, looking naked without his small crown. "Is it my uncle? Is it about the war?"

Lord Groel turned in his saddle. "You best hear it from him."

A baby-faced man rode from behind on a black mare. The horse snorted at the sight of the crowd, holding her head high. The man, wearing black tunic and trousers, with a purple cloak fastened to him, controlled his mare with a whisper. He obviously a lord based on the gold stitching in his clothes and his crest on the saddle blanket, a bridge being held up by a stone giant. Yvanne couldn't remember where that came from. He rubbed his nose as he was stopped by Sir Groel. Sirs Rye and Howe and finally Pollard came to help with protection.

"Pardon my intrusion, my lords." He bowed his head at David and then Devro. "I didn't mean to cause such a stir, but I bring sad news from Vigur." More murmurs from the crowd about Ultiir being dead or Sophie being murdered or Vigura coming down from the skies to smite the city. Yvanne leaned forward to hear. "Ultiir still rules in the capital, but he has sent me here with a message." The lord pulled out a paper sack. When the knights unsheathed their swords or daggers, the man raised his hands in surrender. "I've come unarmed. Nothing on me can hurt you. Physically." He dropped the sack with a thud. Flies buzzed near the opening and a stench radiated. Pollard carefully picked it up.

A head rolled out.

The crowd gasped or screamed. Yvanne squinted her eyes at the sight, Mar shook his head, Raimund stepped forward. Devro's jaw dropped. Now, Sirs Loc and Rye had their sword points in the lord's sides, ready to kill him if commanded. "I am Urses de'Marisco, Lord of Keeland, and chief consultant to the King Ultiir de'Tro." He dropped from his horse, the knights staying with him. He could only take a step forward before Pollard got in his way. Urses backed off. He went down on one knee. "I humbly ask you, King Hurvir the Second, to spare me for my treason. I wished to escape the moment your father was killed, but I could not go against the false king, else I end up like this," he motioned to the head, "Lord Gofrei Geary was slain by Ultiir's hand when the lord of Montlahead attempted to assassinate him in your name. And I could no longer sit idly by while Ultiir took the throne from the lawful heir. I convinced him to let me bring Lord Geary's head, so that you may give him a proper burial. Please forgive me."

Devro said nothing. He bent down, and to the surprise of all, picked up the rotting head. Flies and other insects made Lord Gofrei Geary their home now. His eyes were dim. Bits of his neck falling, blood blackened where a sword was used, the tongue removed. A child wailed in the crowd. Yvanne went up to Devro. He knelt in the crowd, a few feet from Urses. "Were you close?" She rubbed his back.

Devro stood. "Sir Pollard, take Lord de'Marisco to a cell." Pollard seemed frozen until Loc pushed his side.

"We don't have a functioning cell, my king."

David went to Pollard. "We will make do." Her brother nodded and dragged the lord away, who said nothing, her father following, muttering to himself.

Facing Tundavik and the knights, Devro said. "Raimund, you may go to Redington. See that the governors and the banks back us. Get enough coin to hire the best mercenaries in the known world. Tundavik," the old lord straightened, "you will lead the army in Greatbath." Her husband vanished into the keep with Sir Rye. Raimund only blinked, too surprised at everything that happened. Tundavik rubbed his head. She wished she could comfort Devro, but other than letters she did not know who Lord Gofrei Geary was or why her husband was so upset, and they had to get on with their march.

Tundavik

Lord Amil Dandalee was a fat man, his horse weighed down by his giant mass. He had needed help onto his horse, probably help down too. They rode in a long train on the road between Duketon and the Crossing. It was a winding dirt path with mountains on either side and the occasional rockfall. Tundavik worried the wagons might get hit. Raimund and Mar led the way. Yvanne insisted she ride behind them with Sir Groel. Tundavik rode to the right of Devro and a few knights and men who had been appointed guards. Lord Amil was to Tundavik's left. Singing songs and telling stories about his Duketon. He was a cheerful man, but not even a smile appeared on Devro's lips.

Lord Gofrei Geary was dead. The king had buried the lord's head in a valley of flowers below Whitehall; the valley about to die in winter just as much as Gofrei, but at least the flowers would grow back. Lord Geary was a drunkard, but Devro seemed almost as fond of him as he was of the knights who raised him.

"And my father fucked around the kingdom, sleeping with any woman who would have him, until my mother got pregnant." Lord Amil bolstered. "The doma were in an uproar; it was scandalous. They had to marry. That's how I became lord of Duketon and heir to Uphain, unfortunately Onto's Rebellion happened and I lost my rights to Uphain, no matter, the Lands of Asara are even better than the Flewthlands, and the women much more friendly in the winter." He raised his brow. Devro watched a mountain goat ascending the rocks above.

"The king never thanked you for joining his cause." Tundavik said, still Devro was quiet. "I would like to extend my gratitude, Lord Amil."

The fat lord bowed as best he could so as not to tip his horse. "It was the right thing to do. My father fought with Onto, now I fight with my king."

"Perhaps you should check on your men." The soldiers from Duketon, and the stragglers that joined on the road, were in the far back of the wagon train, protecting the goods and weapons from a rear attack. Lord Amil nodded and reined his horse around. "You will need to speak when we reach the Crossing." Tundavik told Devro. "Lord Osbern would have every right to refuse if you do not honor him."

"Honor him." Finally, the boy spoke. "He should be honoring me. I am king. Just like with Lord Amil, there was no reason to thank him for joining; it was his duty by law to follow his liege lord. Me."

"They are the men in charge of armies. How do you think we would fare in a war with only the men from Whitehall? Ultiir wouldn't even march on us." Devro kicked his horse and trotted to Raimund and Mar, putting himself in danger if an attack were to occur. Tundavik sighed.

After a few hours of silence, with shadows looming as the sun found itself west of the mountains, a cry was heard from Sir Rickart. "The Crossing lies ahead." It echoed to the back of the train. Tundavik didn't need anyone to tell him. As the pass began to open and the mountains moved farther apart, a pointed tower rose from the fields and pastures. The tower was lit at the top like a lighthouse. It was all stone, matching the rocks found in the Asara. The buildings below, some belonging to Lord Osbern and others to the people, were made of the same stone, but with slanted wooden roofs for the snow. The train split the valley in two. Commoners looked on from their farmhouses, slaves from the fields. The dirt path turned to stone and weaved its way under a stone arch gate. The portcullis was lowered. Watchtowers rose above the city walls. The only way through the pass was to go into the city or be shot by an arrow from above.

A guard dressed in leather shouted down at the hundreds that lined the street. "Who wishes to enter his Lord Osbern's crossing?"

Tundavik took a breath to shout, but Devro said instead, "Tell him it is his king." The guard wrinkled his nose but disappeared. Lord Amil found his way back to Tundavik, some knights had dismounted their horses. Yvanne and Raimund whispered to each other by Brun. *Foolish. How stupid do they think I am that I can't see what is happening?* His brow twitched. No reason to talk to them now.

The portcullis shuddered, and the sound of chains rattling echoed in the large valley. An older man with a fur-lined coat stood in their way, flanked by knights wearing surcoats adorned with a giant stone arch. The lord made eye contact with Devro and bowed, the people around him following. "My king. I am humbled by your presence. Please know that I received your letters and have had a feast cooked in your honor."

Devro, who was half Lord Osbern's size, walked beneath the gate and pulled him to his feet. "Then let's feast."

Devro invited Tundavik, Amil, Raimund, Mar, Yvanne, Sirs Groel and Rickart, and a dozen other men to eat inside Lord Osbern's tower. Most of the men and wagons stayed to the west of the walls. "Not enough room on the streets," Lord Osbern said. The men grumbled, but seemed fine when cartloads of roast chicken and duck, steamed vegetables and sliced fruit, cakes and pies were brought out.

Tundavik could hear the cheering and eating from the men as he followed the lord under the portcullis. City guards had made way for the large group, pushing people back into their homes. Everything made of stone. A perfect fortress to protect Whitehall from anyone trying to attack from the east. *And that's why Devro needs to play nice,* he thought as he saw Devro puff up his chest as they strode down the street to the great tower. Lord Osbern had his great iron doors opened and led them to his great hall arranged with three long tables that stretched the length of the room.

Inside was all stone as well, with wooden beams to hold the ceiling. Large pillars of gray rock held the tower above. Candles were the only source of light in the now-dark world. Osbern took the head of the middle table, Devro to his right, one of his advisers to the left. Devro's men sat to the right of the table. Osbern's to the left. The other tables were full of important men and women of the Crossing, Tundavik assumed by their fur hats and velvet coats. Osbern stood before the food was brought out and said, "Tonight is a special night. This is the first time a king of Viguran has feasted with us in the Crossing, and I am glad to be the lord for whom the king has come. Let us pray to Meret for a good meal." A moment of silence washed over the room. "Then let us eat."

There was clapping and banging on tables as the servants and slaves brought out trays of food. The center table got the nicest plates of marble and the silver trays. They unveiled a whole pig in front of Tundavik. Long, narrow bread was placed at each plate, and onion soup followed, steaming and warming his hands. Knives the length of Tundavik's arms cut the pig, and the butcher passed around everyone's favorite cuts.

Tundavik sat next to Sir Groel and Sir Mar. Mar was drinking the wine and kept calling for more as he tore apart pork ribs. Sir Groel was eating much nicer. Dabbing his mouth when it got too dirty. Across the table was a pretty girl who blushed at Groel. Now his cleanliness made sense. Yvanne was on the other side of Groel, Raimund next to her, and Devro farther down. He couldn't hear much of what was being talked about, but Lord Osbern and Devro seemed to get along, occasionally bringing in Yvanne and Osbern's wife for conversation. The Lady of the Crossing asked if Yvanne had a love for the arts or helping the needy. The young queen was asking about dresses and parties.

"Are you going to eat that?" Mar pointed to the untouched pork shoulder on Tundavik's plate. He passed the meat over. "Not hungry?" The knight asked as he stuffed his face. "We haven't eaten like this since Gereduss. Don't tell David, but his feast wasn't up to my standards."

Raimund and Yvanne, her cheeks obviously getting red, laughed with one another. "What is going on with them?" Tundavik asked.

Mar stretched his neck to see the queen. "Friends?" It wasn't an answer. "What do you care? It's not like they're fucking."

"Keep your voice low." Tundavik said as a slave boy refilled Mar's wine. "They have grown very comfortable with each other. I see them talking almost every day." Mar's face puzzled. "I just don't want Devro to get the wrong idea."

"You worry too much. Raimund has slept with exactly one woman since becoming a knight, and he views that as a damning mistake. He thinks the Northern gods are going to swoop down and punish him at any moment. He takes his vows seriously." Mar ripped a chunk of bread and dipped it in the soup. "I, on the other hand, lost count as soon as I reached Maertan. That was, oh, fourteen years ago, I can see why Hurvir bedded a whore in Fariage."

Tundavik nodded understandingly, mainly to get Mar to stop talking.

Lord Osbern stood, the herald called for quiet. "This feast has been a great success. I have shown the wonders of my keep to our king. I have discussed plans for the future and how best to take back the throne from the usurper." He raised his goblet of wine to Devro. "I have taken my oaths to him at this very table, wanting to get it over with quickly so that we may aid in the fight for Greatbath." There was clapping. Devro's smile proved he was pleased with himself. "Tomorrow, I will march with King Hurvir and those who follow him, along with my retinue, so that we can save the lowlands from burning." He sat as more clapping followed. Tundavik let out a breath he hadn't known he was holding. Lord Amil and Lord Osbern both backed Devro. Both protectors of the Duke's Pass. He heard Osbern tell Devro, "Of course you can sleep here tonight. I wouldn't have my king sleep in fields beyond the protection of my walls. I have a lovely bedchamber for you two to enjoy in the tower."

Once the feast was finished and the cake was eaten, Osbern directed the wealthy of the Crossing to leave, thanking them for coming. Yvanne and Devro were shown their circular room just below Osbern's high in the tower. Chambers with bunks were used for the men who didn't wish to sleep outside. Tundavik, Raimund, and Mar had a room at the base of the tower, the smells of dinner wafting in under the door.

The room was small, Mar's snoring and Raimund's constant shuffling under the furs kept him up. It was almost pitch black save for his candle. The moon wouldn't rise tonight, the goddess Lendia keeping it for herself. The Deleri believed their god Notoro made love once a month with a moon goddess, and the changing of the moon from new to full to new again was watching their child live and die. Glodsteil loved that story. Tundavik turned over to face the cold stone wall, hoping to dream of the dwarf's jokes.

*****

He was in Ritaeum, the forest dark and suffocating. The buildings all around burned with an orange haze in the sky. Bodies were strewn about like dolls, blood stained the grass, bones littered the paths. He didn't want to see this. Not again. Inside the keep, thunder in the distance, he reached for a body. His hand moved even though he wanted it to stop. There was no control here.

Flipping the body over, he saw the face, or where the face should've been. It was a hole. Hair was atop and a neck below, but no face. No innards. Only black. But he knew it was

Adile; he knew the moment his hand touched her. He cradled her in his arms for decades. Her body turned to dust and he an old man, gray-haired and with a beard that went all the way to his feet.

Children's laughter.

Outside, the laughter grew louder. The trees were dead; the ground surrounded by fire. Two people sat in velvet chairs. The laughter was coming from that place. His feet dragged him to them. He didn't want to see Guis and Ertha, especially if they looked like his Adile.

He stopped himself.

But it didn't matter. The heads of the people swiveled on their necks like owls. He wasn't staring at his kids, but at himself and Devro. Both dead, with maggots crawling from their eyes. "You must go to Ritaeum." A voice echoed as blue light blinded him. "Ritaeum." The words grew so loud he had to cover his ears; yellow fairies flew around his face like moths. He swatted but couldn't kill them. They laughed like children. Devro and his dead body stared lifeless black circles at him.

***

He awoke in a sweat.

"You all right?" Mar asked while he changed his underclothes and brushed off his tunic. Raimund was already gone from the room; the sun shining in from the window.

"Is it time?" He jumped out of bed, the cold air hitting his naked body. Winter was close, so he would have to start sleeping in furs.

"Time for Raimund to go, and for us to march." Mar came

closer, his brow narrowed. "Are you alright?"

"Fine." Tundavik grabbed his underclothes and then slipped into his trousers. His chest was wet with sweat. He brushed it off and found his shirt. "To Greatbath then."

It was nice to see the city during the day, stone sparkling as the sun hit it, the streets busy with people going about their morn. Sir Rickart had stayed behind while the others had left for the camp beyond the walls. Surprisingly, even Devro had already gone. Outside the walls, the tree line was clearly visible. The oaks, pines, and spruce all stopped midway up the mountains, snow capping the peaks ready to fall farther down, distant towers guarding the Asara. Tundavik could see his breath. He hadn't seen snow since he had left Viguran. He didn't know whether he wanted to see it again.

Raimund was handing the reins of Brun to Mar. "Take good care of him. I plan to be back by Meret's Feast so long as the passes aren't snow-covered."

Mar scratched the horse's snout. "We'll be waiting."

Yvanne came from behind with Devro in tow. "Goodbye, Sir Raimund. Safe travels." *I'll be glad that he's gone, even if it is just a short while,* Tundavik thought, *I won't have to worry about those two.* Devro embraced Raimund, whispering goodbye.

The knight made his way to Tundavik. "Good luck in Greatbath. I wish I were going to help."

Tundavik nodded. "You did nothing wrong in Riverton." He held the knight's arm, shaking it. "You came back with many men, and didn't die yourself. That counts for something." Raimund smiled, said goodbye once more, and borrowed a horse used by messengers. He entered the city to travel the north road to the Byway, where he would then turn east toward the great city of Redington.

The men were loading the wagons and horses and pack mules, dressing in their armor, whether mail or leather, grabbing their clubs or warhammers or swords. They would ride straight through the Crossing to Greatbath.

Lords Osbern and Amil got along quite well, enough to keep Amil away from Tundavik, listening to the same stories and him trying to make Devro laugh. The king seemed in a better mood than yesterday. Smiling at Yvanne, joking with Mar. When Mar led a loud and awful rendition of 'Traitor, Baiter, Fornicator' the king even joined in. It would make the day of traveling go quicker with a happy mood. The skies were better too. Instead of the gray overcast they had been traveling under, it was bright and blue. Birds sang as they flew farther south. Cows grazed the pastures, munching on cud as the host traveled by. Deer darted every which way, the occasional dead doe being picked at by carrion eaters.

The land was getting flatter; the mountains growing apart. Tundavik felt as though he could see the Nokys from where he stood. A sea of grass separated him from that reality. The road had become dirt again, dust filling the lowlands behind them, short stone walls dividing the land between farms, the occasional slave waving or farmer finishing the harvest. They filled their waterskins in the small Wolfrun Branch before it and the road diverted away from each other for a time; according to the maps, they would see the river again in Greatbath.

They followed the dirt road until they came upon an intersection. A cart coming from the north didn't stop when seeing the train. The man who drove it only said, "Don't go that way. Nothing good comes from the north."

"Ominous," Lord Amil said.

It wasn't far from the intersection when they saw billowing smoke. *We may not have a battle to fight,* Tundavik thought as his stomach tightened. Yvanne insisted on going forward to see what happened for herself. Devro led the way, a sword at his hip, he didn't know how to use it.

Greatbath was in ruins. Lord Firgo's keep lost somewhere among the houses of the peasants. Burned. They trotted carefully over the smoldering wooden remains and embers. A haze blocked the view of the road. Coins and jewelry, torn shirts and dresses, dolls and wood toys littered the ground, crunching beneath the horses' hooves. The men who followed him gasped and whispered curses. Yvanne's eyes were on the brink of tears. Devro shook his head. Lord Amil came from behind and said, "Oh dear, we were too late."

A young fellow who had joined back in Duketon ran to a mass of charred wood and smolders. He dug his hands into the soot and ash. "They were right here." He cried out. "This was our home." Other men gathered around to comfort him.

Tundavik dismounted, handing the reins to a boy named Firo. He kicked smoky pieces of wood, a wrapped cauldron, and bones. The flesh had burned off the bodies that lay across the debris-laden road. They had found the Wolfrun Branch once more, but the small river was clogged with blackened waste, bodies, soot, and ash. Lord Osbern remembered where the keep was and led Tundavik, Amil, and Devro to it. Yvanne walked with Mar and Groel through the destruction. "His seat was there." Osbern said. "I cannot believe what's been done."

"Where did they go?" Amil said. "The men from the Eastlands and Kinglands burned Greatbath and left. We saw no one on the road."

Devro kicked some embers. "Did my uncle wish to send a message?"

Tundavik followed Osbern to where the great building, with ornate marble and gold jewels built into the walls, once stood. The bathhouse of Greatbath was renowned throughout Viguran for its healing waters. No one would visit the bathhouse again. He didn't speak. Couldn't. The words were caught in his throat. He worried if he did speak that tears and screams would follow. Greatbath was in ruin just like Ritaeum. He could see Adile and Guis and Ertha among the carnage. Envisioned others coming to Greatbath and finding their loved one's dead and flesh melting from their bones.

Turning away from the bathhouse, he saw hundreds of men gathering around in what used to be the center of town. "Maybe a survivor." Osbern said. It wasn't a survivor or a fighter. It was Yvanne.

The young queen stood on a mound of dirt, Groel below her. Mar and Devro pushed through the crowd, just like Tundavik and Osbern. Amil waddled along too. She wore riding clothes instead of her usual dress, wanting to look more like the men than a highborn lady. It seemed to work. The men were enamored of her as she spoke. "Look at what they did to us. Before we arrived, we were singing songs, enjoying the blue skies, while they were raping and pillaging and burning Lord Firgo's home. Some of your families dead. I am the Lady of Whitehall, Queen of Viguran. My people have been slain. Slain by a usurper, a kinslayer and kingslayer, who took the rightful place of my husband, the king. No longer should we sing and dance. We should train with sword and shield and bow and arrow. We would never have massacred

Riverton had we won. Never have burned it to the ground. We are a decent people. People of the Lands of Asara.

"This is how they treat us. This is how they mean to beat us. But we cannot let them win. We cannot let them believe this is the way to win Ultiir's war. We must train and gather support, cut down our enemies, and march on Vigur. And we *will* march on Vigur. First, we must wait for Meret to bring winter, then Swallow spring. Ultiir and those who follow the false king will know what vengeance means. We of the Lands do not forget and certainly do not forgive. Follow me! Follow the rightful King! Together we will show the world that treachery has no place in Viguran!"

The crowd erupted in whoops and hollers. Clapping and stomping their boots. The ground shook with excitement. Devro took Yvanne's hand and cheered with the people. Tundavik clapped, watching the queen take in all her support.

Bertin

Ioelena gave Bertin her dagger, grabbing her spear near the door. "Stay with me." She said in a hushed tone. He didn't ask questions, instead, following the elf into the hall from the cell room and seeing Kelltar sprawled on the floor with a bleeding wound on his head. His chest was still moving with slow breaths. Ioelena crouched and shimmied along the wall under the palace windows. Bertin followed. He gripped the dagger so tight that his knuckles ached. *I'm ready. Ready for anything.* But he wasn't sure if he was lying to himself. He had never killed anyone, and certainly wouldn't choose a dagger. To be so close when life leaves the eyes.

"I can do this." He whispered, and Ioelena shot him a look. She said, "We must be quiet," and Bertin nodded at the elf.

Ioelena peaked past a corner and motioned for Bertin to stay. He did just that. Once she disappeared, it wasn't a few seconds before he heard an elf shout in Seàs and a thud. Peeking, he saw Ioelena. She was standing over an unconscious skinny elf, who had a dent in his head where the butt of her spear had hit him.

"Good job." Bertin said as walked over. Ioelena's eyes were full of anger, but she said nothing. He softened his grip on the dagger. *She'll protect me. I won't have to kill after all.* They found an iron door, and Ioelena went to work. She used her spear to undo the lock. Inside, a cell much like Bertin's. But Wilclef was behind the bars. Ioelena put her finger to her mouth and tried her keys in silence.

"Won't do," she tossed the keys down. "Wait here." She left with her spear at the ready.

"What is this?" Wilclef whispered. "Are we escaping? Is she helping?"

Bertin nodded. His guard had dried blood from his nose and bruising on his cheeks. "Are you alright? I thought they killed you."

"Just some scratches." Wilclef winced as he rubbed his cheek. "Some skinny elf did this and told me the Dragon would welcome me on the morrow. It seems I'm lucky that Ioelena found me."

"Me too."

Footsteps approached, and Bertin gripped his dagger. Ioelena came in with another set of keys. "These should do." The cell door unlocked, and Wilclef came out. "Both of you must do as I say if we are to make it out of here."

"And why are you doing this?" Wilclef asked. "Did you not kill your way through the city like the rest of your kind?" Ioelena left without a word.

They went to the hall, and Wilclef saw the skinny elf unconscious on the ground. He grabbed the elf's curved blade and stood over him. Wilclef pointed the blade at the elf's chest and sliced through skin and bone. Ioelena's spearpoint found its way to Wilclef's neck. He froze. "He was going to kill me."

Ioelena's voice was melodic, but her eyes were fury. "You do not get to kill my brethren."

Wilclef kept the sword steady. "Or what? You save me and

now you're going to kill me? I don't think so."

Bertin heard footsteps echoing in the palace. *They're coming.* "We don't have time for this." He pushed Ioelena's spear down, and her cool blue eyes looked like they wanted to stab him. "If they find us, then we all die."

Ioelena turned and kicked open a door to steps. Below would be the outside. *Freedom.* If they could make it past the hundreds of elves between the Palace of Sand and the city walls. Bertin went to follow down the stairs. He turned to see Wilclef still above the elf. Not moving. "Hurry." He seemed to snap his guard out of whatever trance his thoughts had put on him. Wilclef slid the sword into the elf, blood spurting out of the wound. He followed Bertin down the steps.

These must be for the servants. Bertin thought as they squeezed down the narrow staircase, just wider than Wilclef's hips. Remembering the secret side corridors he and Aveline would play in when they were younger.

A horn blared. Seemingly at once, every door throughout the palace opened. The walls shook as they shimmied down the steps. Ioelena burst through a door at the bottom, and grass stretched out. "Run."

They raced away from the elves. All three darted in every direction as the horde behind them grew. He slid on the grass as if it were a sheet of ice. Arrows were flying. Metal clanging. Bertin saw Ioelena spin in the air and whack some helms with her spearpoint, sending the elves in them stammering back. Wilclef pushed elves with swords away from him. Hacking at anyone who dared get too close. Bertin clutched his dagger. And only that. The elves tried to catch him, but he dodged their attempts. *I should've paid more attention during my training.* But there was no time to think about that. It seemed like the palace grounds were bursting with elves. They came from every gate, every hole in the wall, like roaches. Chasing.

If he could just make it to the city gate, maybe he would be safe. *Probably not. But it's a chance.* He felt a hand clasp his arm. Wilclef. His guard pulled him to the right, then the left. They had to continue to the gate or be surrounded. Wilclef parried a jagged blade and sliced with all his might. The scream was almost deafening. The elf's arm fell to the ground, and he cried, withering in his own blood. "Almost there." Wilclef said through bated breath.

Wilclef's eyes widened, and he pushed Bertin away, pointing to a grouping of houses. Bertin ran. His guard was fighting five or six elves. Arrows raining. Ioelena burst from nowhere and stabbed at her brethren's legs, making them dance. Still no killing blows. Men appeared from the homes and shops behind them. Helping Wilclef while trying to fight Ioelena. Bertin jumped through a window and closed his eyes while catching his breath. *Not too far. I can make it. We can all make it.*

"*Cestè al marad satorì?*" A squeaky voice asked.

Bertin opened his eyes and saw a young girl asking the question. Behind her stood a younger boy, rocking at the sounds of metal on metal and screams outside. "No Del'us," he whispered.

A sword found his throat. It was straight, not curved. "I speak your common language." A man of about the age of Wilclef said. "Answer my daughter. Is this the rebellion against the invaders? Are we to drive the elves back to the ends of this world?"

Bertin didn't know what to say. *Rebellion? The people can*

fight for me. He gulped at the sounds of swords fighting and arrows firing. "Yes."

The father, with his bald head, nodded and hugged his children. *"Ut mori."* The children cried and found a corner to hide in while their father went outside. Bertin saw him look to the sky before shutting the door.

He found his dagger next to him. *Time to find Wilclef, and hope that Ioelena is okay.* Bertin followed the bald man and saw the carnage in the streets of Lisan Biresdea. Blood soaked through the stone paths. Arms and heads rolled. Swords and spears and shields clashed with the screams of their handlers. He heard shouts in Delerous. More men, and some women, came from the homes with their weapons. Cutting knives, ladles, chair legs, lit torches. Anything they could find to fight the elven occupiers. Bertin also saw some humans fighting each other. Not wanting to go back to the way things were before.

A burst of flames engulfed a narrow street packed with rebels while Bertin was shaking his head. Burning flesh and screams of dying filled the air. Rainík descended from the Palace of Sands. Sharet led the pack. Stones glowed from every elven mage, and their hands flashed signs. Homes exploded in flames. Men were pushed off their feet with bursts of air. The oasis seemed to come alive as the water churned and pulled rebels under. Sharet closed his eyes, chanted in elvish, and moved his fingers as if he were writing in the sky. Others followed. Plants that weren't there before broke from the ground and wrapped their thorns around legs. Some hacked at the vines with their swords, while others had no choice but to succumb to the crushing force of the plants.

Air smacked his face. Ioelena had knocked an elf out near

him, and the air stopped. "Pay attention," she said, "or you will be next."

"No more fighting." He shouted to her over the clashing steel. "We need to go while they're distracted."

Ioelena glanced at the hordes of elves pushing into the city, driving the people back, burning and looting their homes. She nodded. "I will find Wilclef; you head for the gate."

He scurried away. Not wanting to be seen by a rainík. The sun had begun to rise over the city walls. It was quieter as he moved away from the fighting. He saw a sandstorm in the far distance. *What I would give to be back there.* He missed when his biggest problem was merely sand. Even more when it was finding Sir Mar in the crowds of Gereduss. He even missed being in that city. *A city full of people who want nothing more than to see me hanged.* He laughed at his thoughts. *Now I wish my death would be a hanging.* Shivering at the thought of being burned alive, he made his way past long-cast shadows of buildings, never stepping foot on the main road so elvish guards wouldn't see him along the wall. He crept under windows, hearing snoring inside. *If only they knew a revolt was happening on the other side.*

Bertin turned. Hoping to see Ioelena and Wilclef. All he saw was the oasis. He was the farthest he had been from the water since coming to Lisan Biresdea. The isles that rose from the oasis looked small. He started back toward the wall. The grass he had loved so well was now turning to sand. He smiled and bent to scoop up the grains and laughed as they poured from his fingers. *Never would I imagine I'd be happy seeing sand. Maybe Safír will be waiting on the other side of the gate, waiting to take me to Salvalone.* He knew that wasn't going to happen. The desert guide would already be in the city of the Lones, wondering if Bertin was dead.

A thump echoed behind him.

Bertin turned to see nothing. *Just someone waking.* But he gripped his dagger until his hand ached and the designs on the hilt were etched into his fingers. There were elves standing atop the wall. Some looked toward the desert; others looked to the fighting. He was close enough to hear them. They didn't seem to notice him in the shadows of the houses, and with the sun waking, so were the people to go about their day. They acted as if there were no occupiers. Like Lord Èmaw was still ruling. Like there hadn't been men and women burned at the stake. He wished he could live in that bliss. Others must've heard the sounds of swords as they peaked from their windows before closing the wooden slats.

Bertin turned a corner. A tall elf with black paint under his eyes smiled with teeth that looked like fangs. Bertin ran back, but the elf was quick. A dagger similar to his own was at his throat before Bertin could take two steps.

"Poor prince thought he could run away." The elf spat in his ears. "Kuslu won't be happy about you starting a revolt. In fact," he licked his lips, "I think I'll take you off his hands so you can't cause us to be delayed anymore."

The dagger found Bertin's old scar on his throat from Ryfor's sword. He could feel the skin ripping apart and warmth running toward his chest. Then he felt the warmth on his back. But he wasn't stabbed. The elf fell behind him, and Bertin saw the bald man from earlier yanking a bloodied sword from the elf's back. *"Fuleno."* The bald man cursed and then spat on the elf.

Bertin quickly snatched the dagger away in case the elf's ghost wanted to exact revenge. "You saved me." He said to the man. "What about the fighting? Is it over?"

He shook his head. "No. The revolt has just begun." His accent was deep, and he breathed heavily, making him hard to understand. "I saw this *adèkhe* follow you. I didn't think you deserved to die, so I came."

"I don't know how to repay you."

"No repayment necessary." The bald man looked over his shoulder. "But we must leave this." He spat once more on the corpse.

Bertin and the bald man, who said his name was Cellae, snuck through the narrow streets, avoiding the eyes of humans and elves. "The gate." Cellae whispered. He pointed to an iron portcullis with elves atop the limestone bricks.

"How do we get through?"

Cellae smirked. "I have no idea, but we'll figure it out."

The road ahead was basically empty; only a few people went about their day. They would be in full view of the guards if they ran to the gate. *So close. I can do it. I have to get to the desert.* Cellae nodded to follow. They took a few steps before going into a sprint. The elves above shouted and grabbed their swords. "Hurry." Cellae pushed Bertin forward. He didn't know how he was going to lift the gate. He had to find chains. *Hopefully Cellae can get inside.*

A cough came from behind. Then choking.

Bertin turned to see more death in his wake. Kelltar, with muscles bulging, had driven a sword into Cellae's head, the point poking out where his nose should've been. Bertin wanted to stop breathing. *So close. I have to get to the gate.* "Don't turn away from me." The elf shouted. "You have escaped the Dragon's fate far too long." Kelltar kicked Cellae's corpse as he went past. Bertin pictured his children hiding in the corner, then shook his head. No reason to think about that. "And Kuslu isn't here to save you this time."

Kelltar smiled as he dragged his blade across the ground. He shouted something at the elves above, and they stopped in their tracks. Bertin gulped. He readjusted the grip on his dagger. The elf spun his blade. "Time to die."

A spear whipped through the air and stuck in Kelltar's foot. The elf screamed, and Ioelena ran to her weapon, yanked it out, causing the elf to curse, and whacked him on the head until he fell to the ground unconscious. Wilclef came from behind, making his way to the elves on the wall. He fought one easily and pushed the other off the steps before disappearing into the limestone.

"Are you alright?" Ioelena asked. "We thought you were dead."

"How did you find me?"

"Kelltar and Sharet."

Bertin's shoulders tensed. He looked around the empty streets and peered at the homes and shops. No sign of the rainík. "I haven't seen Sharet."

Ioelena's eyes widened, and then quickly calmed. "We don't have much time."

The portcullis rose slowly, just enough to fit under. Wilclef emerged from a door. "I jammed the winch; that should buy us time." He embraced Bertin. "Let's go." Without warning, he pushed Bertin against the wall and shushed him. Vines destroyed the ground below and wrapped Ioelena and Wilclef's legs. Her spear snapped in half, and Wilclef's sword fell to his side. Bertin hid behind a wall, just a foot from the open gate.

Sharet walked in from the east, his shadow filling the

street. Ioelena and Wilclef struggled and yelled. Vines wrapped themselves around their mouths. "A betrayal." Sharet walked toward Ioelena. "Your ancestors look down on you with regret. Your brothers turn their backs to you." She struggled, but the vines tightened. "Saving a human? A prince? Someone descended from the very people who drove us from our lands." He spat. "You will burn tonight. Kuslu has decided your fate. Most important, the Dragon has decided your fate." Sharet turned to Wilclef. "You were to burn this morning with the rising of the sun. Do not think you have escaped the flame."

Sharet continued to talk to Wilclef. Telling him of his fate. Ioelena struggled. She found Bertin's eyes, and he could see pleading for help. An elven sword lay near the wall. The elf Wilclef had pushed from the walkway dead next to it. *The gate is open. I can leave them to whatever fate Sharet wants.* Sharet's back was to him, but he was still speaking down to Wilclef. Bertin made his decision.

He pocketed his dagger and slowly grabbed the sword. Sharet didn't turn. He pictured the rainík stabbed through the back; the blood flowing down the bricks of the street. He froze. *Pretend he is a training dummy. Just like Rowan.*

He raised the sword above Sharet. Imagining the final breath and sputtering of blood. The sword reflected the rising sun. The rainík was calling out for other elves. Bertin brought the blade down and hit Sharet over the head. Not with the blade. With the hilt. A wound opened in his head, and he was on the ground.

Wilclef made noises, and Bertin knew he wanted the vines cut. He brought the blade over and sawed until Wilclef's arms were free and he could pull the plants from his body, then Bertin did the same for Ioelena. She yelled out in her language, probably curses, and went over to the unconscious rainík. Ioelena grabbed her spear and, through a mess of tears, brought the point into Sharet's back, killing him. Bertin's eyes were wide, and his heart dropped for Ioelena as she screamed out into the morning sky. He felt guilty. He should've been the one to kill Sharet. Ioelena shouldn't have had to kill her kin. She started toward the gate.

There was a commotion near the houses. People were running. Wilclef took the blade from Bertin and found his own sword. "We must go." His jaw was clenched. An arrow landed at Bertin's feet. Another horde of elves was coming, cutting down anyone in their way. Wilclef pushed Bertin and Ioelena toward the gate. "Go." He shouted. "I will buy you time."

"We aren't leaving you." Bertin tugged on his guard's sleeve.

Wilclef pushed him off. "We don't have time." The elves were firing arrows as warnings. "We can't keep doing this. Go south until you hit Salvalone and then charter a ship to Rowan."

Bertin could barely see through his tears. He embraced Wilclef and said, "I won't let the world forget you."

"Hurry," Ioelena called from the gate.

Wilclef rushed the elves with his two swords while Bertin rushed to Ioelena. He heard metal clanging behind him. A gust of wind blew on his face, and he was being drug back into the city by an invisible hand on his ankle. Ioelena threw out her arm. Bertin gripped her and the limestone bricks. He saw an elf pulling the air like a rope with a blue stone shining from a headpiece. Wilclef's hilt snapped the elf's head back, and the wind stopped. Bertin clambered up. Ioelena fit under the portcullis, and Bertin right after.

The desert in front of them was quiet. Behind a battle raged. They ran into the sand before Bertin looked back. He saw a dozen elves overtaking Wilclef. His guard died in a fury of stabs.

Ioelena grabbed Bertin's hand, and they raced into the desert.

Sophie

Sophie watched from her carriage as some bald man yelled to a crowd below. The crowd that was supposed to be glad for her and Ultiir's wedding. Instead, they stood below a ledge of the domaton while a false preacher shouted, "Look at the money wasted while you starve in the streets. Look at the fine clothes and dresses the lords and ladies wear while you stitch together centuries-old rags. See their sneers. They think themselves above you. How? Who gave them that right? The Four and the Many make no mention of kings and queens or barons and counts. Meret heard our prayers. The people. Vigura did not raise a king from the Montla, but a peasant. Swallow watches over all living things, not just monarchs. Samosay gave us words just as much as them, and I intend to use my gift from the gods."

Sophie was to remain in her carriage as the man shouted. The lords and ladies sneered just as the man said as they made their way past the crowd of hundreds trying to get into the domaton. Maller of Forecreak, dressed in blue robes, had come to quell the people.

"Even the High Doma has forsaken the gods. He who calls himself king has installed a puppet, answering to him instead of Vigura, accusing the last of witchcraft. We watched as they paraded him through the street. Whipped, his blood leaving trails. Yet we have seen no proof. We are to take the king's word as law, but what if he turns on you?" He pointed to an old woman. "Or you? He can use his words to cast us out. Divide us. While he watches from his elven palace fucking the dowager queen, who many believed loved us. She has shown she cares more for power than her people."

Screams erupted. The city guards shoved their way through the crowd, beating those with clubs who did not move or fight back, making their way to the shouting man. "Do not forget what I have told you this day." Was the last thing he said before a club busted his teeth and nose, blood pouring as they dragged the kicking man away.

The door to the carriage opened, and Sir Achen held out a bare hand. "Sorry, my lady, for the delay. It seems to've been taken care of." People were pushed away from the domaton, Maller yelling, "Stop this madness," to no one listening.

Sophie took the knight's hand and stepped onto the cobbled street below. The domaton rose above her as if the gods were staring her down. "Hopefully, the ceremony is fast so we don't have to worry about a riot."

"Yes, my lady." Her knight in green armor said. He had to look better than his usual metal for a wedding day.

"It will also be nice to have you calling me queen again. It feels odd."

Sir Achen smiled. He had come from Aele with her all those years ago, still carrying the Vallnioc accent. It made her miss home. Her parents not even coming to her second marriage to a king. How many could say that? The common people, who had thrown flowers and cried tears of joy when the young princess of Terrop married Hurvir, were either all driven out or glaring at her. "Did they not hate my late husband?"

Sir Achen coughed like he hadn't expected her to speak. "The commoners do not know what they like or dislike. They would be cheering for you if that man," he pointed to where the guards were loading the speaker into a wagon befit with iron bars, "told them to. Because he hates you, they hate you. Simple."

Is it that simple? She brushed any dirt off her dress after making the way up the steps to the domaton. She wore a white dress with blue down the arm and at the cuff. Her diadem snug on her head. Her hair was merely braided today, no reason for an elaborate design since it wasn't her first marriage. Fresh blood lingered where the man had been beaten. Without the domaton slaves wiping it away with cloth, it would stain. The house of worship in the most holy city in Adedor couldn't have blood spilled near it, at least back when other High Domas ruled. Maller may have no power. Ultiir is the one who selected him for the election, and the conclave had almost no choice but to follow the king's wishes lest they be paraded through the streets as fiends of darkness.

"Have you been to Goldfield before?" She asked her knight.

"Never. The last time you went I was sick with a fever," he gave a nervous laugh, "I am glad I get to see it. Though I'm not sure it is the safest place to go during open rebellion. Have you heard what happened in Greatbath? The lowlands of the Asara are not that far away."

They would leave for Goldfield in the coming days, weeks if messages came in saying the bastard had marched on it, but that was unlikely. The Duke of the Eastlands seemed to be taking care of any fighting. Goldfield was where most of the lords could see Ultiir, and she would again see the queen mother. *That wretched old woman.* She knew exactly where Hurvir and Ultiir got their wild emotions from. "I'm sure we'll be fine, and you will protect me no matter what. That makes me feel secure." Her knight blushed, and Sophie chuckled to herself.

"Stunning." Lord Masson barred their way to the door of the domaton. "You look stunning." His smile added more wrinkles to his old face. He wore his best velvet tunic, adorned with purple jewels and gold-work at the seams. His coat was lined with ermine fur, and his trousers were tight-fitting around his legs. It made him handsome. More handsome had he been younger. "May I speak with the dowager queen?" He asked Sir Achen, who looked at Sophie for an answer.

"Stay close." She told the knight. "I don't want to be late for my wedding."

The old lord took Sophie's arm in his and they strolled along the stone walkways that lined the domaton's four points. As they reached Swallow's Point, he said, "I hope His Grace does not think he doesn't owe you a dowry just because you were married to his brother."

"Of course not," Sophie feigned a smile. "He has already sent wagon loads of gold to my father and extended my lands in the Eastlands."

"A fine gift." The people watched from below. Sophie couldn't help but think that man was right. It seemed as if Sophie and Lord Tedbalt Masson might spit on them at any moment. "Have you heard of Lord de'Marisco? Delivering a message to Whitehall himself. To me, it seems dangerous. He could be captured or worse, but he insisted."

Carrying a head to Whitehall, she thought. Poor Lord Geary's body thrown into the Ritae. She was just happy she didn't live in Clear Port, where a headless man might wash ashore. Tedbalt stopped at Swallow's Point, his statue far atop the domaton, the god holding a parchment in one hand and a bird on his finger in the other. Sir Achen also stopped, just out of earshot. "I wished to congratulate you in private. It's not every day a woman becomes a queen for the second time."

Why did this old man bring me far away from everyone? Sir Achen watched some pigeons. "I feel there is something more you wish to say." Sophie gave a smile, not wanting this lord to see her reservations.

Tedbalt took her hand in his liver-spotted one. "It is nothing bad, my queen, nothing to worry yourself over. I just wanted to offer you comfort and support as you marry Ultiir. He may not be as bad as your previous husband, but our kingdom heads into dangerous times. He'll of course ask for your father's support in the fight over the throne. Another army loyal to Terrop in Viguran. They could do unthinkable damage to people not their own."

"And you wish for me to stop him? To tell my father not to support his claim and my own?" She pulled her hand away; it had become sweaty in his grip.

Tedbalt straightened his spine. Growing taller before her eyes, seemingly younger. "I just want you to know that you have friends not only in Terrop, but friends in Vigur as well."

"Is this because of Lord Geary?"

"No," his jowls swung as he shook his head, "this is merely a friend talking." His voice got lower; his eyes darkened with the shadows. "If you need anything at all you can talk to me. I have sway with some lords of the court, and that is of course the place you go to change laws you think unfair."

"My lady," Sir Achen called, "His Holiness is asking for you."

"Anything at all." Lord Masson repeated. "Shall we?" He offered his hand, which she took, and they smiled and laughed their way back to the door. Sir Achen with questioning eyes. When the last of the Royal Court made it inside, Maller pushed Sophie forward.

"Ultiir is ready. He seems awfully eager."

She arched her back to get his hand off. "As am I," *to finally be queen again, and not just the woman Ultiir fucks when he feels like it.* Lord Masson huffed as he went inside under Meret's statue. She did not have to strip as one usually does when entering the place for the gods, her dress too elaborate. She would pray tonight after the ceremony.

Everyone from the Royal Court was in the domaton, just like for Hurvir's feast. It was warm from the bodies and candles. Actually nice compared to the cool morn. As she walked toward the center, to be under the gods' light in the dome, she heard whispers. Gossip. "Did you hear she supplied the poison? "Lords Ormac and Hester fled last night for the bastard." "Is that what she's wearing?" "Have you seen the king?" She tried to tune it out, but when she did, she heard Lord Masson in her head. *Support in Vigur? Of course I have support in Vigur, I've been here for years. Achen walks right behind me.* She tried to convince herself, even with all the gossip flinging about her. She had support somewhere; she just had to find it. But having support from the chief daken, a member of the King's Council, was more than she hoped.

Ultiir stood under the circle of sunlight, Maller coming to his side. The king wore his smaller crown, not wanting to heft around the many-pound mass of jewels and gold. He had on a pale violet surcoat and gold belt to cover his brown leggings, his red cloak draped to his left side with a golden clasp to keep it around his shoulders. His hair had grown longer since Hurvir's feast. Before it was short, lying atop his head. Now, it was almost past his ears. He was looking more like his brother and nephew with every passing day. As the sun hit his face and made him look paler, she could see the Bruthaki in him. Forgetting his father was once the heir to the throne of Rowan. *How different things would've been.*

She took her place across Ultiir, to the left of Maller. On the walls were paintings and mosaics. Only one caught her attention. A painting of the first marriage between a man and a woman, Meret watching from the heavens above, Samosay blessing the union. Maller was no Samosay. But she hoped Meret was watching, so she said a silent prayer to the Mother. Wishing for protection in this marriage, during this war.

"I have been given assurances that the dowry has been paid, is this true?" The High Doma asked Ultiir, who quickly nodded. "Now, before the Four and the Many, Ultiir de'Tro the First, you must recite the rights of every marriage."

Ultiir's gaze was all lust. He couldn't wait to bed her without committing a sin. Give her a child. Sophie didn't care if that happened at all. She just needed Ultiir to say the words. She would be even closer to the throne. "Under the watchful eyes of the Four, I have chosen to marry. Before Meret, I have taken Sophie of Aele as my bride. Before Samosay, I promise to protect her. Before Swallow, I swear to uphold her honor. Before Vigura, I vow to keep her from the dangers of this world and the depths of Veltoora. Before the Many, I claim these oaths true."

Maller turned to Sophie. "Do you accept the wishes of the

Four and your man?"

"I accept the wishes."

Maller shook like a peacock from Saamrakaa and shouted. "Then by the grace of the Four and all other gods beneath them I pronounce that Sophie Margia, Duchess of Aele and Princess of Terrop, and King Ultiir de'Tro the First of Viguran, now joined together until their dying days."

The domaton echoed with claps, not too loud, proper enough for the lords and ladies of Viguran. Ultiir gave her a small kiss. Smiling, the crowd stared at her; she couldn't show her true feelings for Ultiir. *A man who murdered his own brother could do untold harm to me, but I must play this game for my parents.* If only they and her brothers were here. The many faces below did not know her. They were not from Terrop and would put Viguran over a foreign queen no matter the cost. That she had learned since marrying Hurvir. She bowed her head at her ladies-in-waiting, at Sir Achen, and locked eyes with Lord Tedbalt Masson. If she were to take the throne and the power for herself, then she would need more support.

Bertin

He woke up in a pool of sweat-soaked sand. Ioelena slept under a rock, her body slowly moving with every breath. The moon was gone tonight. The only light came from the stars. He found Notoro's star. The bright yellow dot of light that Safír had said pointed to Salvalone. *We're going in the right direction. Now, to not get lost in the day.*

Bertin sighed. Ioelena stirred in the darkness. "I killed one of my brothers." She whispered, pulling her knees to her stomach. "The Dragon will not forget this."

Bertin scooted closer, placing his hand on her leg. "I'm sorry." He was trying to find the words to say. "It couldn't have been easy."

Ioelena sat up, the stars reflecting off her eyes, her voice serenading the sand. "It was easy. He had tried to kill me. They all threatened me with burning." Tears fell onto Bertin's hand. "I don't know if the Dragon would've accepted me, but now I know he will not."

"The doma say the Four always offer seats at their table."

"You wish for me to take the beliefs of our oppressors?" She shook her head. "I will not turn my back on my ancestors. They fought for hundreds of years against your kind." She rubbed sand off her hands. "The Dragon has been good to me. He breathed life into me, gave me strength and showed me right from wrong. I could not turn away from the Dragon if I tried." Ioelena looked at the stars, the reflection of her tears making her eyes a mirror. "My father told me those are the ancestors. Mine and every other elf's." She sniffled and chuckled. "My mother called him a liar and said that they were actually the Dragon's many eyes. Always watching. Protecting."

Bertin stayed silent, listening to Ioelena's cries. "I never thanked you for protecting me."

"It was my duty. I told you we would escape."

"But you didn't have to help me at all. You didn't have to bring Wilclef to me, or break me out." He looked up at the moonless sky. Wondering if they would get lost in the sand, if Ih la Mat would return. Maybe the Dragon's eyes would watch over them. Bring them to safety. "Why did you?"

Bertin could barely see her, but he felt Ioelena shake with tears. "I did not like the way Kuslu and the others were treating you. They lied to you, beat you, starved you. They would've taken away everything you cared about just to get your knowledge of human kingdoms or coin or weapons." She tightened her hand around Bertin's. "I couldn't stand it any longer. If only your guard did not have to sacrifice himself. If I had planned better—"

"You can't blame yourself. Only the other elves. Maybe even Wilclef for staying behind instead of running." He was glad he was far away when Wilclef died. It was bad enough watching the vicious stabbings, but seeing his guard's lifeless eyes would've been worse. He had already watched Robalt die. He had seen enough killing to last a lifetime. "But if he had run, the elves might've caught us. Look at us now." He gestured to the rock and sand in the dark and tried to lighten the mood. "We're obviously skilled at the mystic art of hiding in deserts." Bertin hoped Ioelena had smiled, but he wasn't really in a joking mood. He tried to forget all the death that followed him in Telemaw, but the colorless faces stared at him when he closed his eyes.

He rarely slept anymore. "We need to move."

Ioelena nodded. "They're probably close behind. Moving in the night is smart." The sand went on forever in all directions. His boots were filled, dumping them out once an hour, Ioelena's too. No matter how much fell out, more found a place. His legs were scratchy, feeling like a thousand ants were always crawling on him. *At least Ih La Mat has gone away. We don't need a sandstorm.*

Bertin knew the sun was coming before he saw any light; the heat washing over him like water. Water. He couldn't think about that; it only made his mouth drier. Ioelena stopped near an outcrop. The rocks would only get hotter during the day, but there was a sliver of shade beneath a large red boulder. "The desert near the mountains is better. More shade." Ioelena said.

He remembered the elven attack on Cluo, the reason King Hasíb wanted him to go to Lisan Biresdea. To help prepare if the elves attacked. "What happened in Cluo? Peasants and troops stopped your attack?"

"We wanted entry to cross the desert; we were denied. Kuslu wished for peace, but it would not come. We had to fight to stay alive. The peasants tried to push us out, the soldiers too. We fled down the *Alív*. Kuslu wanted to show the Oléman that we are not to be trifled with, so we attacked some villages before his idea to attack Lisan Biresdea."

"So the stories are true." Bertin wondered where Safír was now. Safe? "And Kuslu was lucky I was there. I was lucky Kuslu was there. I'd've been drowned in the oasis if he weren't."

Ioelena watched the sand, making shapes. "Your father did not write that letter." There was a moment of silence as Bertin tried to remember what she was talking about. The elf crushed a scorpion with her boot. Then it hit him. "It was a ploy so you would help Kuslu. Your father never wrote back, or we didn't receive the message."

Bertin wanted to cry, if he had the tears for it. "So, my father may want to save me. He wasn't leaving me to die." Ioelena shook her head.

"I'm sorry for going along with it. Humans have tricked my kind for so long I thought it made sense to trick you, but," she took a deep breath, "I'm sorry."

"Thank you." He meant it. Of course, his father would never let some elves get away with abducting him. He was the heir to the throne after all.

Ioelena gasped. Bertin didn't have to ask what it was; he saw it too. Four horses in the distance. Certainly elves on their backs. They dug their bodies into the rock, hoping to become invisible. The horses were trotting to the outcrop. "Do you think they've seen us?" Ioelena only shrugged. The elves answered for her.

The horses raced across the sand. There was nowhere for Bertin and Ioelena to go. She grabbed her spear, trembling. He pulled out the dagger he had never used, hoping it was sharp. *One last fight.*

As if Ioelena read his mind, she said, "I will get you out

of here. I don't care how far Salvalone is. We will make it."

As the elves on horseback came closer, Bertin could see the faces. Ryfor led Kelltar and two other elves he had never seen. "Hold steady." Ioelena said through gritted teeth.

Kelltar was the first to laugh; the others joined in as they encircled the pair, the sand and dust choking Bertin. Eventually, they came to a halt. "What is that going to do?" He pointed to Bertin's dagger. "A stab wound won't stop the Dragon nor me from getting you."

"What about from me?" Ioelena sneered.

"Enough, Kelltar," Ryfor dropped from his horse. "We have a traitor among us. The prince can be dealt with later." Ryfor took an almost hidden blade from a bald elf. "Thank you, Elron. Let us show her what happens to those who murder their brethren." The blade became invisible in the sun as he lifted it over Ioelena.

Before he could bring it down, Bertin stepped in front. "You'll have to kill me."

Kelltar laughed. A cloud of dirt rose when he jumped off his stallion. "Kuslu has decided against that. Even though you're the reason the humans are rising against us. Us? Their liberators. We've treated them better than any lord or king ever has."

"Burning people alive?" Bertin said, still wary of the sword Ryfor held.

"The Dragon calls and the rainík answer."

"And now we have lost a rainík due to her." Elron said from atop his horse.

The elf beside him said. "It is a crime to cut down one of your own."

"He was going to kill me, Erch," Ioelena said to the elf. "I had to do it."

Ryfor cleared his throat before anyone else could speak. "You helped a human escape. Your ancestors look down on you with disgust. Helping the people who destroyed our homes and drove us from our lands. Kuslu is furious. Who knows what Blaenda would think. He would have you thrown from the highest peak in Mi'rallen."

Ioelena lowered her spear. "We just want to get to the ocean. If you let us go, we won't bother you ever again. I won't step foot on Mi'rallen."

"It's too late." Kelltar said from behind. "You knew the consequences."

"And how important the prince is for Kuslu," Elron said. "Someone high-ranking who knows the movements of humans as our prisoner is a gift from the Dragon itself."

Kelltar smirked. "Some believe the Dragon sent you to help us destroy the humans, to bring about Nhamcaryn and the destruction that follows." He twirled a dagger in his fingers. "I'm not so sure."

"Which means you'll come with us," Ryfor said. He turned to Ioelena. "You can either die now or have the rainík's sacrifice you." His sliver of a sword whipped in the air. "It is your choice."

Ioelena's feet took a fighting stance. *I need the Dragon on my side for once instead of taking these elves' sides,* Bertin thought as he raised his dagger and the elves laughed. Erch and Elron dismounted their horses. Swords rose around them. Ioelena charged.

The point hit Elron before she spun it in the air and whacked Ryfor with the butt. Erch's sword flew, but Ioelena sidestepped. Elron held a hand over his stab wound and flailed his sword at Ioelena, then Bertin. Bertin jumped back. Into Kelltar's arms. The big elf let out a laugh and flicked his dagger to the prince's neck. "Just because Kuslu wants you alive," he whispered, "doesn't mean I do."

"No, Kelltar," Ryfor shouted as he dodged and attacked Ioelena with his sword.

Kelltar pushed Bertin back to fight. The horses stomped from fright, covering the area in sand and dirt. Bertin coughed. He couldn't see anything, only hoped Ioelena was doing well, and knew she was alive by the sounds of metal and shouting. He gripped his dagger. Bertin went farther into the cloud and saw a shadow. He brought the dagger down and stabbed flesh. A female voice let out a scream. As the dust died down, he saw Erch with a bloody shoulder and let out a sigh of relief. Ioelena was still pushing back Ryfor and Elron with her spear.

Kelltar sprang from behind with his dagger, slicing down Ioelena's spine as he landed on his feet. She shouted in elvish as she fell. Erch punched Bertin in the face, and he fell to the sandy cushion. The cloud had disappeared as Elron calmed the horses. Bertin felt his cheekbone and knew it had shattered. Ryfor yanked the prince to his feet. He saw Kelltar cleaning his dagger and Ioelena coughing. Her breath shallow. Her eyes cloudy.

"May your ancestors never forgive you." Erch told Ioelena. "Die knowing your lineage dies with you. *Marai amád.*" She spat. The other three elves also spat near Ioelena.

Bertin's vision was also cloudy, but not because he was dying, because of loss. *Another. Gone. My fault,* was all he could think about. He didn't notice Ryfor had hogtied him and laid him over a horse. Kelltar patted the stallion and got on the saddle. "I hope you survive the trip." He sneered at Bertin. Bertin's body burned, his jaw hurting from gritting his teeth. Kelltar and the others spurred their horses on.

Ioelena lay in the sand, a circle of blood around her. She was gasping for air. It was over. She was bleeding out. Kelltar had made sure of it. He looked at the muscly elf and shut his eyes. *Don't worry, Ioelena, I will make sure the Dragon burns him.*

The elves took Bertin on the road north to Lisan Biresdea. Ioelena bled to death with no one to see.

Yvanne

en followed Yvanne while she rode atop Snowfall. Her back was stiff and straight, not even the cold of a near winter making her shiver. *They are following me.* After seeing the massacre and charred remains at Greatbath, they left Lords Osbern and Amil at the Crossing, leaving a garrison of men from Whitehall to reinforce the city, while Yvanne led the rest back home in case anyone tried attacking from Nopra's Pass. She heard the armies' conversations at the fires on the way home. All praising her. If she didn't know any better, she'd think Devro wasn't around anymore. He tried to take credit for her actions, tried to rally the men with a speech almost identical to her own, but they only placated him. They were following her.

If only Raimund could see it. I hope he stays safe in the Eastlands; nothing good seems to come from that place. Tundavik and Mar rode near her, Sir Groel at her side, Devro a bit behind. He had talked little on the trip there and back, only a few words to keep others from worrying. But she knew how upset he was. Gofrei dead, Raimund leaving, seeing a failure at Greatbath. The second failure in the war, both while he claimed to be king.

The familiar sight of Whitehall came into view as the rocks

to either side of them opened, signifying the end of the Nopra's Pass. Her brother guarded it. He asked no questions, only watched Yvanne's face before leading them to the keep. The people of Whitehall poked their heads out of their homes and shops. Children getting water from the well skipped to their parents. Family members came running to hug their husbands and newly bearded sons. Whispers of Greatbath spread as quickly as the city had burned. Luckily, there were no cries for the dead as there was no battle.

Yvanne dismounted Snowfall with Groel's help. Helge, Jacka, and Sir Rye stood by the charred pieces of the keep. The doma wore a smile, hugged her, and said, "I knew you would return." Yvanne hugged Jacka. Her father was not outside. A knot grew in her stomach. *Dead. No, do not think that. Only slow, maybe coughing. Not dead.*

"Where is father?" She asked as Devro joined her side.

Helge took Yvanne's hands. "Nothing to worry about. A small cold has taken hold of him." The doma wasn't the best liar, not when she could see months into the future. Her baggy eyes held back tears. "He is in his bedchamber if you wish to see him."

Pollard put his hand on Yvanne's shoulder. "She tells the truth. Father is in good spirits, just a worse cough than usual."

Yvanne took Helge's hand and pulled the doma with her into the keep, leaving the rest behind to catch up. "You saw Greatbath?" She asked once out of earshot.

Helge nodded. "I saw you coming back while leading armies."

"So you can see my father? What happens to him? Do not lie to me; I know that look on your face. Tell me the truth, or I will cast you out." She lied. She would never cast Helge out, but she needed her father to be okay.

The doma took back her hand. "I do not want to worry you with visions. Like I've said, I only see glimpses, and not exactly the real thing. I saw you with soot on your face and ash in your hair leading an army of giants, and deduced what it meant. I did not see the actual events that took place. My visions could mean anything."

"Then what are your visions of my father?" She gulped, not knowing if she really wanted to know, but it was too late to back down.

"I saw him melt like snow on a warm winter day. I saw you grow into a snowcapped mountain high above all. Not exactly accurate." Helge placed a hand on Yvanne's stomach. "But I did see something I was certain of." The tears seemed to well up again, but the old lady held them back.

Yvanne squeezed Helge's hand. "I know as well. I did not bleed during the march." *An heir to the throne.* She purposely didn't think about it much on the journey, not wanting to be wrong, not getting her hopes up for the future. *Giving birth to the heir of Viguran. A son with Rely blood on the throne. Father will be elated.* They came to the door of David's bedchamber. Helge bowed as the door opened and walked away with her hands behind her back. A daken was dabbing a wet cloth on her father's face.

Lord Rely was paler than normal, almost as white as snow, sweating like it was summer in the Saipta Isles. He was under a stack of fur blankets that looked like it was ready to topple over. Letting out a wheeze, he said, "My daughter." He held out his wrinkly hand; she took it, his palm moist. "I didn't know we still had a daken in Whitehall," she said. "I remember he left when I was a child."

The daken bowed her head. "Your Grace," she was almost as young as Yvanne, "I traveled with Lord Emallen to help with the war." Her voice was quiet and soothing, things her father would need.

"What is your name?"

"Dera, Your Grace." Dera lowered her head again. She wore all white in the usual daken fashion, her brown hair tied behind her head with a white veil hiding the rest.

"Thank you for watching over him." Yvanne lifted Dera to her feet and led her to the door. "Don't go far." Dera bowed her head and waited outside the door.

Yvanne sat on the stool near his bed and rubbed his hand. "Sick?"

David waved a hand. "Nothing to fret over. Dera is good, and I've been far sicker in the past. Your mother was a good healer."

She smiled and brought his hand to her stomach. "I am giving you a grandson soon."

Her father's yellow teeth shone with a smile. "A Rely on the throne. My father could never have imagined; I couldn't imagine until Devro came through the pass." He rubbed a knuckle on her cheek, clearing his throat and dabbing his nose. "You could have a girl too. Do not discount that; a daughter in this world can do good things as much as a son. And you will have more children. I certainly did." He coughed and choked until phlegm covered his handkerchief. "What happened in Greatbath? Did Devro slay Ultiir?"

"The false king was not there, and no battle took place." His face contorted. "Greatbath was looted and burned before we arrived. There seemed to be no survivors, not even Lord Firgo."

David closed his eyes. "Firgo just had a child a year ago." He shook his head. "Such tragedy." Cough. "Devro will need to retaliate; you should've marched to the Byway or south to Montlahead since Ultiir sent us Gofrei's head. There was no reason to come back."

Yvanne watched out the small window near her father's bed. The stone around it wet from the cold. Families were singing, children were skipping, men were laughing. When she looked into her father's eyes once more, she thought, *there is one reason.* "We need more men. Raimund went to Redington, but we can't count solely on mercenaries. We need the lords of the peaks, lords from the King's Pass, maybe even the Lodean."

"Do not trust a Lodean." Her father pointed a finger at her.

"Anyone willing to join Devro can be trusted. We cannot afford to turn anyone away, no matter your feelings about them." Yvanne placed a calming hand on her father's head, feeling the fever. She had rarely met a Lodean, but the talk was always of their treachery. *But we're committing treason, are we not?*

Her father coughed again before saying, "Would you trust Lord de'Marisco? He claims he wants to declare Keeland for Devro, but he also stayed with Ultiir all this time, and brought the Lord Geary's head. Would you let him out of his cell?"

She had forgotten about the prisoner. Lord de'Marisco, the new chief consultant after Ultiir assumed the throne, was somewhere in the keep in a makeshift cell. *The things he could tell us of Ultiir.* She rubbed her knees through her riding pants. Kissing her father's head, she said, "I will come by later. Get better. You have a grandchild coming."

"Another." She couldn't tell if he had said that out of happiness or annoyance. She called for Dera, and the daken put more cloth on his head to cool his fever. Her father's coughs shook the mountain as she walked down the corridor. There were still people cheering outside, happy no one was dead; she checked a few rooms, wondering where Lord de'Marisco was.

Robet, the cook, was in the kitchen making lunch for the keep, Arold was sharpening his swords, Helge was praying with some girls, Jacka was stitching in the great room. Her handmaid was sitting by the window, watching the celebrations, patching up someone's trousers. Yvanne rubbed the stone seat. Cool. Only going to get colder. Some young boy she had seen around Whitehall was starting a fire on the opposite side of the room. "Where is the prisoner being held?"

Jacka's eyes narrowed. "Prisoner?"

"Lord de'Marisco. I wish to talk with him."

Her handmaid stood and led Yvanne deeper into the mountain, walking with the curves of the rock until stopping at a root cellar that hadn't been used in years. Yvanne thanked Jacka and turned her attention to another boy. Tiro. He was the son of Tito, the best baker in the village. *Father must've recruited more help while we were gone.* "I need to go in." Yvanne said, the boy scratched the back of head.

"But the prisoner."

"Everything will be fine, and I'm sure you'll hear my screams if he attacks. But he is a lord, not some common criminal."

"Yes, my lady—my queen." Tiro stammered.

He found the key in his boot and unlocked the door.

Handing her a candle, he said, "There isn't much light." She thanked him and went in.

Lord de'Marisco laid his head on a shelf, breathing into his hands. Empty shelves that had once been full of beetroots and garlic and cabbage stretched to the rocky ceiling. Urses' eyes squinted as the candle flame lit the empty cellar. "Warmer in here than outside." She said as she sat the candle next to the lord and hopped up on a shelf to sit. "It's nice."

"You are Devro's queen." He stood and bowed while rubbing his neck. "Never did I think you would come here." The light made his eyes dark, but she could see them reading her face. "I take it things didn't go well in the lowlands. It wasn't Ultiir's idea. Lord Adyn thought it a perfect response to the attack on Riverton. The only reason he didn't march up Nopra's Pass was because it was narrow, and he thought you could hold it. I am sorry for your people, though. So many dead." He leaned against the stone. "Lord Firgo?"

He did know so much, but how much more? Would the others feel the same as her, placating this lord so he would give details? *It doesn't matter what they think. I am queen; I have an army.* "Dead, presumably. We couldn't identify anybody."

He nodded. "Lord Adyn is young. Who knows? Perhaps if Lord Firgo is alive the Duke of the Eastlands will try to ransom him. Or he killed him without cause." He chuckled softly. "Lords killing lords. Hasn't happened in years."

Yvanne wondered if the lord was happy. If any of the lands around Keeland came under attack, he could expand. She wished she could trust the baby-faced lord, but his eyes were darting back and forth. He came before Devro but never told them about Lord Adyn's plans. "Did you enjoy it when the usurper killed Lord Geary?"

"I wish I could've told your husband and father what happened." The lord massaged his arms, flexing to get the blood flowing. "Gofrei died because he was foolish. He was sloppy. Ultiir found out he was sending letters to Whitehall and had him killed, charged him with witchcraft, apparently an éithrio."

Yvanne pulled energy to her, hiding her red-lit fingertips below her brown pants. *I knew I felt it when he arrived, when the energy stopped flowing for that brief moment.*

Urses continued, "I never wished to stay with Ultiir, but I had to be careful. I couldn't write letters. Send messengers. Getting caught and dying wouldn't be helpful. So, I took my chance when it came. Offered to go to Whitehall and present Gofrei's head. I know how hard it is for you and everyone else to trust me, but that is the truth. I want to help. Avenge Devro's father. Make Ultiir pay."

The candle was getting low; the wax falling onto the shelf. "You seem a good asset. If you know more of what Ultiir plans."

"We talked some." He nodded. "The false king—as you call him—really wants to take Redington, so he doesn't have to rely on Lord Plume's loyalty. We know how fickle those Flewthlands tend to be." Yvanne leaned forward, not caring how her father or Devro felt, suppressing any of her distrust of this lord, anything to get her and her husband to Vigur. "He has also written to lords in the King's Pass to set up a blockade to Whitehall, and, even more important, will send for King Anvrin's troops once he and the dowager queen are married." The Swallow Pass being overrun with Terropian troops frightened her, as it did her father and his father before him.

"Would Sophie marry the man who killed her husband?" The lord only nodded, Yvanne's eyes wide. *He knows too much to be locked away. I can keep him close. Any scent of treason and Pollard will happily take his head.* "I release you." She huffed. "By order of the Queen of Viguran, but only if you swear fealty to my husband and swear to tell the whole of what you know about Ultiir."

"I will swear it now and when I see the king and swear it every day until my last."

His eyes glistened in the candlelight; his young face stern. "Very well." Yvanne opened the door and gestured him out. Young Tiro raced to her with fists bared when he saw Lord de'Marisco. "It's all right. I am taking him to the king. You may follow." Tiro's mouth opened as he dropped his fists and then gave a curt nod.

The lord rubbed his legs. "I may not walk very well, and the light may burn."

"Do hurry." Yvanne smiled as she walked to the front of the keep; she could hear his footsteps following. *They will see it the same as I. We need him for information.* The celebrations, and sadness for Greatbath, had died down, but people were still milling about. Tundavik, Mar, and Devro were talking with anyone who asked them a question. Telling them about the march. Of the feast. Of the horror. Yvanne snuggled into the group, watching them shiver as she warmed herself, sensing Helge taking a bit of energy, probably for a reading.

"How's your father?" Lord Vandes asked when Katerna, a seamstress, left smiling.

"A little sick, nothing much. He'll be better before Meret's Feast."

Mar pulled his cloak tighter. "Being here for the winter has made me appreciate Gereduss a little more, even if it was a dreary place."

Before they could talk of the weather and her father, she blurted out, "I have something important to share. Do not be mad." The men watched her face, but she motioned to the door. Lord de'Marisco was shading his eyes as he and Tiro emerged from the keep.

Mar grabbed his sword hilt. "Trouble?"

"No." Yvanne stepped in front of the knight, something she wouldn't have done a few months ago. "Hear him out. He wishes to pledge his support."

Tundavik huffed. "What do we need him for? Keeland? The city of bandits? Who will they send to fight?"

"We'll need every man we can muster." The men scrunched their noses as she said it. "Ultiir wishes to marry your mother-by-law, Sophie, if he hasn't already. King Anvrin—"

"King Anvrin will send men from Terrop," Lord de'Marisco interrupted. "And Ultiir wishes to take Redington, a port closer to home."

Devro and Mar looked at one another, and her husband said, "But Raimund's in Redington."

"If he leaves before the week is over, he'll be fine." The lord said. "Ultiir is slow to put plans into action. We have talked many times since you cited the Bastard Law; I could tell you whatever he is thinking."

Tundavik shook his head. "We've been doing fine without you."

"Riverton?" Devro turned to the old lord. "Greatbath? We have yet to win a single battle; our men are being slaughtered." Devro looked at Lord de'Marisco, licking his gums. "Swear your loyalty to me."

The men shifted when the lord dropped to one knee on the cold ground. "I, Urses de'Marisco, have come here to ask forgiveness in helping your usurper uncle. I had no choice, lest I end up like Lord Gofrei Geary." Devro flinched at the remembrance. "And I humbly ask that you accept my apology and honor me with your grace." He took Devro's hand, Mar never letting go of his sword. "I swear my fealty to you, Hurvir de'Tro the Second, as rightful King of Viguran and its overseas land, that you are my liege lord, my commander, and that I shall never commit an act against you. I swear my lands and holdings as Lord of Keeland, so that my men may fight for you and honor you. I say these terms under the eyes of the Four." A crowd of people had gathered. Devro looked at their faces, at Yvanne's, who was nodding, wanting to trust the lord as much as she could. He grabbed the lord's hands and lifted him to his feet.

"I accept your terms, Lord de'Marisco, and accept the support of Keeland."

Urses gave a low bow. "Thank you, my king." There were small claps and murmurs. Urses bowed again, grabbing his cloak tight. "Mind if I find a bath?"

Yvanne patted his shoulder. He stank. "We can talk later." The lord left Yvanne to tell her husband and the onlookers the news. *News that can make them fight harder.* She cleared her throat and fixed a piece of Devro's light hair. "I have news for you. News for all." She shouted.

"Hopefully nothing too serious," he said.

She placed his hand on her stomach; already, gasps escaped the crowd. "I am pregnant." Devro's eyes darted until a smile gleamed on his face. "I carry inside me the heir to the throne of Viguran." She shouted over the heads of the onlookers.

Mar put his hands on Devro's shoulders. Tundavik smiled but focused on something else. "I carry Hurvir de'Tro the Third. The man who will carry on the legacy of my husband and his father and their ancestors. The de'Tro dynasty shall last for a thousand more years." *Thanks to me.* The crowd's gasps turned to claps, not small but large. The air grew colder as they cheered. "Your king will have a prince, and your prince will protect you for years to come." More and more cheers, those who had stopped celebrating had come back from their homes and shops. Mar congratulated Devro with smiles and laughs. Lord Emallen found Devro as well. Fathers and mothers cheering for their soon-to-be-prince. She followed Lord Vandes' gaze. He was looking over Devro's head at Urses de'Marisco, who stood at the door of the keep. Watching.

Snow began to fall on Whitehall.

End of Book One

Thank you for reading! You survived the beginnings of a civil war. If you enjoyed the political intrigue, please take 30 seconds to leave a quick review or rating on Amazon.

Click here to leave your review for A Breath of Power

Your feedback is the biggest way to help new readers discover my epic fantasy saga.

Want more updates on the series? Join the Shining Orb community here: https://theshiningorb.com/

List of Characters

Kinglands:

King Hurvir de'Tro - King of Viguran, Sophie's husband, and the father of Devro

Queen Sophie Margia - Queen of Viguran, Princess of Terrop, Duchess of Aele, and Hurvir's fourth wife

Prince Ultiir de'Tro - lord of Goldfield, Hurvir's younger brother, and heir to the throne

Rila de'Tro - Queen Mother of Viguran, mother of Hurvir, Ultiir, and Analere, and was married to King Ferrick of Viguran

Lord Urses de'Marisco - lord of Keeland and chief informant on the King's Council

Lord Gofrei Geary - lord of Montlahead and chief watcher on the King's Council

Lord Tedbalt Masson - chief daken on the King's Council

Lord Alan Hirons - chief commander on the King's Council

Lord Serle Verrier - chief ambassador on the King's Council

Lord Dovi Lyons - chief collector on the King's Council

Lord Henk Zazí - lord of the Insurgent Redington and cupbearer of the King's Council

Lord Edel de'Viere - manor lord

His Most Holy Albon - High Doma of Viguran

Lord Durcy - lord of the Royal Court

Lady Rista - lady of Clear Port

Lady Abre Volles - lady of the Queen's Council
Countess Filra - lady of the Queen's Council
Lady Betal - lady of the Queen's Council
Baroness Mara - lady of the Queen's Council
Lady Ficca - lady of the Queen's Council
Lady Rila - lady of the Queen's Council
Sir Achen - chief knight of Sophie's guard
Sir Lovis - chief knight of Ultiir's guard
Sir Lird - knight in Ultiir's guard
Amalla - Sophie's handmaid
Renna - Sophie's handmaid from Zhepatev in Masa Naq
Sufar - Ultiir's chamber slave

Eastlands:
Maller of Forecreak - doma of Forecreak
Duke Adyn Gallient - Duke of the Eastlands
Lady Annue Gallient - the Duke's elder sister and first wife of King Hurvir

Lands of Asara:
Duke David Rely - Duke of the Lands of Asara
Yvanne Rely - youngest daughter of David
Sir Pollard - youngest son of David and knight of Whitehall
Helge - local doma of Whitehall
Lord Emallen Reck - lord of Midvalley
Lord Amil Dandalee - lord of Duketon
Lord Osbern Lot - lord of the Crossing
Lord Firgo Pan - lord of Greatbath
Sir Loc - knight of Whitehall
Sir Groel - knight of Whitehall
Sir Rye - knight of Whitehall

Sir Rickart - knight of Whitehall
Arold - swordmaster of Whitehall
Jacka - Yvanne's handmaid
Tiro - a young man in Whitehall
Firo - a young boy from Duketon

Terrop:
King Anvrin Margia - King of Terrop
Queen Evna of Aele - Queen of Terrop
Duke Enne Veytet - Duke of Ladau
Duchess Uma Brah - Duchess of Cedawr
Lord Mayor Hilar Ecole - Lord Mayor of Tharet, a Terropian city with a majority Rainvealandian population

Gereduss:
Prince Devro de'Tro - bastard son of Hurvir
Sir Raimund - knight of Viguran, a member of Devro's guard, and born in the North
Sir Mar - knight of Viguran and member of Devro's guard
Tundavik Vandes - once a duke in Viguran but now lives in Attrima, the capital of Baragio

Rowan:
King Bartel Thomas - King of Rowan
Queen Rouna of Ashtree - Queen of Rowan who committed suicide
Princess Aveline Thomas - Princess of Rowan, the eldest child and only daughter of Bartel
Prince Bertin Thomas - Prince of Rowan and heir to the throne
Prince Baldewin Thomas - Prince of Rowan and Bartel's

youngest child
    Blis - teacher to the royal family
    Sir Gerg - knight of Bertin's guard
    Sir Robalt - knight of Bertin's guard
    Wilclef - head of Bertin's guard
    Gordo - apart of Bertin's guard
    Mari - one of Aveline's handmaids

Telemaw:
    King Hasíb Èmaw la Untura - King of Telemaw and leader of the House of Èmaw
    Princess Farzia - Princess of Telemaw
    Safír - traveler in the Delerous Desert
    Commander Abrezo - Commander of Telemese soldiers in Lisan Biresdea protecting against elvish and nomadic raids
    Lord Abia Èmaw - lord of Lisan Biresdea

Elves:
    King Blaenda - self proclaimed king of the elves in Mi'rallen
    Sharet - elvish mage
    Ryfor - elvish guard with a temper
    Ioelena - elvish guard from Mi'rallen
    Kelltar - elvish prison guard
    Kuslu - leader of the elves in Telemaw

A Roar of Strength

Aveline

Safe travels Princess." A man at the gate bowed after Ivlin, the pocked-face guard, showed their passes at the Gate of the Steppe in the eastern part of the city of Rowan.

That was a sign Aveline needed to raise her hood. The blue-gray cloak protected her from the peasants who meant her harm. The same ones who had destroyed the palace and the domaton and the Royal Chancellery, the ones who had children and bred hatred into them. As they rode along the newly cobbled conquest road, she couldn't help but wish she were on the western road. The palace was her home, but the western parts of the city was where she came alive. She didn't fear the peasants as much as her father or brothers feared them. She knew a few of them. Had learned from them. Even the ones who wished nothing more than to see King Bartel's head desecrated by a mob enjoyed her company. She drank with them, smoked with them, played games with them. She missed it so very much. The formalities of court always bored her.

Even as the stench of the city filled her nose, she couldn't help but feel at home. Rowan was her favorite city in the world, and nothing could change that. Zoell, another guard, saw Aveline's smile and rolled her eyes. "Wait until I bring you to Moon Bay, my princess; there, you'll be surely amazed."

"She'd be amazed at pigshit if it were shiny enough the way

she looks at this city." Bert, her eldest guard, said.

They traveled the conquest road, which had gotten considerably busier as Aveline grew. New manses and farms for the city's elite sprang up like weeds outside the city. Highborns looking for fresher air and larger lots to look down upon the poor. Inside the walls, the road had become overcrowded with people from the countryside looking for work. The road was where King Artin made his procession into the city to be crowned king. The same road her father took eight hundred years later to quell the flames that had killed Artin's kingdom. Now she took the road. But for nothing. Only arriving back from the kingdom of North Ferga. Her father would be disappointed the marriage didn't work out, but why would a princess marry a lower born lord? A Northerner at that. She always knew her father had a soft spot for Northerners from spending his childhood there in hiding while the kingdom fought, but a marriage? He almost had a heart attack when she suggested she marry a Rainvealandian prince, but he wouldn't hear her objections about going North for the winter.

To the west, jagged hills and rocks emerged from the flatness to create the River Marches, which would eventually give way to the greater Gorthair Marches. Her father had told her how the smell of Rowan had changed for the worse after the flames. The entire city smelled of rot and burning wood. Before it smelled of roses and cherries. She didn't believe a city this big could ever have smelled good, but it was a nice thought.

Her guards protected her on all sides, but tried to make it look as if they just happened to be riding beside her. *Nothing more suspicious than someone being guarded by five people,* she thought with a raised brow. The conquest road ended at the river. The Bruthak churning below. Carrying both the life and filth of the city through her heart, cutting Rowan into two.

They crossed a bridge, almost too crowded to move, near Brissa's Point, named for her aunt, where the River Crom flowed into Bruthak. From atop the bridge, she could see Amalia's Rest near the domaton. The spot where her grandmother was put on trial by the People's Chamber for crimes against Rowan and hanged, her body thrown into the river. This city and its people had caused her family so much harm, yet still she smiled at the sights of children playing, bakers kneading, crazed fools proselytizing about the end times. The Fragrance Guild wore their blue robes and gold masks and wafted perfume about the center of the city. From the domaton to the palace.

The marble palace rose above the shops and homes. A striking white. Almost blinding her as the sun reflected off its walls and columns. There were more guards and knights around the palace gates than when she left. Winter was a hard time for some, and storming the palace for warmth and food seemed like a good idea. *Did Father ever make the farmers' tax lower? I guess I'll find out if they burst into my room to steal me and my jewels.*

The crowd outside the palace gates scowled when Ivlin presented the pass and the guards bowed. *If only the guards knew that was a bad idea.* Once behind safety, Aveline dropped her hood and heard more hissing; she didn't turn to look at them. The last thing they wanted was to see her eyes. Eyes that would close tonight in the warmth of a bed stuffed with feathers and wrapped in the nicest wools in the known world.

"Back so soon?" Mari, her handmaid asked, emerging from

the doors of the palace. Aveline towered over her on her horse. "My princess," she bowed, and Aveline could tell she hated doing it.

"I guess I couldn't bear to be away for so long, and there was a bit of an accident involving Raff." She dismounted her horse, remembering poor Raff's cracked head against the stone from his fall. The red mess of blood matting his black hair. "My body is as stiff as a tree. I've ridden enough to last a lifetime. And the snow was dreadful. From North Ferga to the Sylvastist. You'd think the world ended north of the Therirock. Too quiet. I actually missed the rains of Rowan." Groomsmen found their way to her and her guards' horses before taking them to the stables.

Zoell kissed her spotted mare goodbye and said, "I think we need to visit some Telemese bathhouses."

Ivlin smelled himself, his tunic with sweat stains under the arms. "I could bathe for a month and still not get the stench of Heller off my clothes."

"Would you like me to draw you a bath?" Mari asked Aveline.

"Nothing would please me more." Dern the Third said. "Will a beautiful lady such as yourself be joining me?" Dern gave a small bow, showing off his bald and scarred head, and reached for Mari's hand but she pulled it away, much to the joy of Aveline and her other guards.

Bert slapped Dern's back as he laughed. "For that you'll need Lady Indy's house."

Aveline finally said to her handmaid, "That would be great."

Her guards all parted, Bert and Dern off to a brothel to tell of their adventures fighting imaginary monsters in the North, Ivlin and Tomas disappearing to their quarters, Zoell to practice her swordplay. Commoners watched it all from the gates of the palace. *Just let me take a bath,* she thought as she imagined the horde of people spilling over into the palace.

Aveline and Mari passed below the elven-etched columns and into the palace with bowing servants and those who had come to court. Mari told her why they had come. A few peasants who complained about the price of wheat. Envoys from Viguran to discuss politics. The lords of the Sunrise and Sunset, Darry and Rean, argued about the kingdom.

"Welcome back, Princess." Aida, another handmaid, bowed.

"Get water ready for a bath." Mari told her. "Miss your handmaids?" She asked Aveline with a drop in formality. The North was full of 'princess this' and 'princess that.' She was happy to be back around someone who didn't care about her title.

Aveline chuckled. "How could I not? Raff's hospitality was sorely lacking, and Erbat, his father, was no better." They came to a great door to the throne room. The iron handle called to her. "I should speak with my father before disappearing into my chambers."

Mari cleared her throat. "Not to be rude, but your father would think you've been sleeping in stables. You may scare away the peasants and their children."

"That bad?" Aveline sniffed herself and grimaced. "Fine."

***

Aveline lay naked in the tub, Mari and Aida trying to clean the filth off her, Mari rubbing her hair, the other her feet. Candles lit the small room. The scents of lavender and rose wafted through the air. The water had already been replaced with how brown it had turned.

"I did miss this." She tilted her head back and closed her eyes. A chill ran down her spine as the warm water hugged her.

"Did the Hellers even know what a bath was?" Aida asked.

"They're not complete savages, but being a princess comes with perks, and the North didn't seem to care if I were a goddess from their Vatya herself." She shivered as if she were still in that barren, cold land. "I had to wash myself. Which wasn't so bad; I've done it before, but I missed your touch." Mari squeezed her fingers on Aveline's head. "And only Mari knows the best way to clear my hair of tangles."

She let the candle wicks die down and another bucket of hot water be poured over her before saying, "I think we're finished. Aida, can you find me a dress suitable for an audience with my father? It doesn't need to be perfect; I'm sure he wouldn't mind if I showed up in rags. Maybe something of mother's." Aida curtsied and went on her adventure.

"A towel?" Mari walked by the tub, and Aveline pulled her closer and kissed her.

"This is what I missed most. Your soft lips." They laughed as they continued to kiss. "I didn't find Raff knew how to pleasure a woman."

Mari pulled back as if she had been slapped. "You promised you wouldn't."

Aveline laughed and kicked her legs up, water sloshing. "I would never," she squeezed Mari's hands, "trust me." Her handmaid couldn't help but smile. Aveline pulled Mari's hand into the water and between her legs. She tried not to splash hot water onto the floor.

***

They lay naked on Aveline's bed. She drew a finger over Mari's breasts. "We've taken too long," Mari said. "Aida will be quite suspicious if we don't unlock the door and get you dressed." She began to move, but Aveline held her close.

"I haven't seen you in months. The world can wait a bit longer." Aveline kissed Mari's sweet lips. "Tell me what the world of Rowan was like while I was away. Meet anyone?"

"Worried about new handmaids?" Mari gave a sly smile. "There is no one but you." She pushed the princess' mahogany hair back. "The king was said to miss his children immensely; I didn't see much of him. Always coughing and sweating, that one. Prince Bertin made it safely to Vaandet, but hasn't been heard from since. 'No reason to worry,' they say. Little Baldewin has written back, and Blis has given reports of his exceptional fishing skills. Apparently he caught a great shark, teeth as large as your leg."

"Baldewin?" Aveline laughed. "My brother has a hard time catching flicker bugs."

"There's a war in Viguran," Mari said, and Aveline stopped laughing. "Believe it or not, it isn't against the Rainvealandians. Each other. King Hurvir died. Your cousins fight one another. The Council wishes for your father to do something; the Chancellors wish for him to stay out of it. Obviously, he has done nothing, and winter is here."

"Devro leads an army?" Aveline sat up. "Just a few months ago he was celebrating with Bertin about fucking every whore in Gereduss."

"It's just what I hear."

Mari had a way about her that got anyone to talk. Rumors could fly all day in the washer rooms, but Mari would be the first to know. She just had to find the right knight or page to spill his secrets. If she weren't a handmaid, she would make an excellent spy. But Aveline didn't need a spy. "And who is winning?"

"Redington fell to Ultiir, and Devro couldn't even take some small town named Riverton. The councilors think Ultiir will win."

"Which would mean Devro's death." Aveline sighed, remembering when he was younger than Baldewin and missing his father. She would muss up his hair. He absolutely hated that. "Well, at least Father has kept us out of it. It's been only a decade since the last of the flames were extinguished."

"Is the king going to be happy about Raff dying?" Mari moved closer, her feet intertwining with Aveline's. "There will be many lords and chancellors happy about this, expect many offers of marriage."

"If they haven't realized by now I'm not interested, then the Four help them."

"If it means they become royalty, I don't think they'll care." Mari shook her head.

Aveline chewed on her cheek as if she were in deep thought. "They'd probably let me fuck you as long as I gave them children. That or murder you."

"And how do you think they'd do that?" Mari giggled.

"Poison. Push you off a cliff. Trample. So many gruesome ways that we shouldn't even talk about them." Aveline wore a smile and slightly tickled Mari, the warm bed shaking. Mari grabbed Aveline's hands and pushed them down.

"But you would protect me. My knightly princess." Mari said as she straddled Aveline, bending to kiss her lips. "You would never let anything happen to me."

"Never." Aveline returned the kiss, forgetting her father and the lords that all wanted to wed and bed her and the handmaid who would be waiting outside the door. Wishing so much for this moment to last forever.

There was a knock on the door. Aida said, "My princess. I need to speak with you."

Aveline pushed a chuckling and blushing Mari off to find her robe made of the finest wool in Rowan. "Can't it wait?"

But there was no answer, only the jangling of keys and the turning of the knob. Mari dashed for her clothes, and Aveline tried to slip the robe on quicker, but a gaggle of knights and guards and servants were outside her room staring at Aveline and Mari's nakedness. The princess felt her cheeks go red. Sir Delmar, one of her father's household guards, closed the door behind him and Aida. If Delmar had an ounce of emotion in his rigid steel body, Aveline would believe he had been crying.

"My princess," the knight bowed, "I bring my most sincere apologies for barging into your room like this." He took a deep breath. "Your father, the King, is dead."